# Thrown into Nature

# Thrown into Nature

by Milen Ruskov

Translated from the Bulgarian
by Angela Rodel

Library of Congress Cataloging-in-Publication Data:

Ruskov, Milen.
[Zakhvurlen v prirodata. English]
Thrown into nature / Milen Ruskov ; translated from the Bulgarian by Angela Rodel. – 1st ed.
p. cm.
ISBN-13: 978-1-934824-56-6 (pbk. : alk. paper)
ISBN-10: 1-934824-56-9 (pbk. : alk. paper)
1. Tobacco–Europe–Fiction. 2. Satire. I. Rodel, Angela. II. Title.
PG1039.28.U75Z3513 2011
891.8'134–dc23
2011020161

This book is published within the Elizabeth Kostova Foundation's program for Support of Contemporary Bulgarian Writers and in collaboration with the America for Bulgaria Foundation.

Printed on acid-free paper in the United States of America.

Text set in Bodoni, a serif typeface first designed by Giambattista Bodoni (1740–1813) in 1798.

*Design by N. J. Furl*

Open Letter is the University of Rochester's nonprofit, literary translation press:
Lattimore Hall 411, Box 270082, Rochester, NY 14627

www.openletterbooks.org

# Contents

# Thrown into Nature

There is hardly anything more natural than hating Nature. Yet people don't realize this due to their crazy ideas. For example, many think that this world is ruled by the Devil. As some of the ancients put it, the Devil saw the Kingdom of God and tried to make something similar. He is a sorry imitator, by their own admission. Yet not entirely inept, they add, and mighty cruel, too. But all of that is stuff and nonsense. Others reckon that the world is God's doing. If this is so, then He is not who they think He is but just some moronic mad scientist. All that is stuff and nonsense, too. But if it's not the one, nor the other, then what is it?—you may ask. That is a stupid question. This is what: the world is simply mad Nature's work. Which is precisely why it looks the way it does, since it is her work. She is absolutely mad, the incarnation of chaos, a game of blind chance. I feel a deep-seated hatred of Nature. Yes, I do! If there is something I deeply and truly hate, it is Nature. Is there anything more endlessly energetic, more lavishly fertile, yet crazier, than she? Of course not! If Nature put on a human face and strolled around the streets of Sevilla, she would have long since been locked up as a dangerous maniac, perhaps even burned at the stake by the Inquisition. She would be of the female sex, of course, giving birth to a child every five minutes, laughing and jumping about at the same time, and impregnated without a visible agent, as if by the wind itself. Yes, Nature is absolutely mad!

Yet she and she alone is the procreator of the world. Not the Devil or God, not some evil genius or some moronic mad scientist, much less the Good Lord, but simply a mad, all-powerful, all-purblind, accidental and chaotic Nature. As a member of the medical profession, it actually becomes me to hold such an opinion. Moreover, it shows that I've found my true calling, since I sincerely and profoundly profess the above-stated opinions.

My name is Guimarães da Silva. The "da Silva" part is made-up, by the way, since an aristocratic title causes people to pay more attention to what you say. And besides, Dr. Monardes wanted me to change my name so he could introduce me as his assistant without embarrassment. "This is my assistant da Silva," Dr. Monardes now says, and it really does sound better that way. Sometimes he even presents me as "Dr. da Silva." Of course, I am not yet a doctor—although I hope to be some day—but rather a mere helpmate and student of Dr. Monardes. Incidentally, he never mentions that I am Portuguese. The Portuguese are thought to smell bad, spread malaria (since they wade through the swamps around the city), and to constantly present themselves as noblemen who just happen to end up in Sevilla and who try to swindle everyone they can out of piddling sums. "I," he says, "am João da So-and-So, and I have come to buy a parcel of land in Peñana at a good price" or "to build a ship in Cadiz." Then he starts playing the fool, so that you'll swallow the act and decide to join the venture, usually for cheap or at a huge profit, at which point he disappears with the ducats. The curious thing here is that the notorious seductive power of money addles the mind of the one forking it over—a relatively rare and interesting phenomenon that lies behind the prosperity of many a crook, for example, the owners of gambling houses—for if he had preserved even a bit of his presence of mind, he would have asked himself why anyone would come to buy land or to build a ship in Spain, given that it is far cheaper to do so in Portugal. Yet clearly people cease thinking in such cases. For this reason, Sevilla is full of fake receipts from Portuguese shysters. Even Dr. Monardes has one.

At the inns, they now ask the Portuguese for their money up-front, since previously they would stop for the night, eat and drink their fill—but never so much as to not be able to get up before the first cock crowed the next morning and sneak away without paying. Rumor has it that they would only pay some servant to wake them up early in the morning. Since most of the servants at the inns are also Portuguese, this made it all the cheaper for them. A Portuguese would kill a man for a ducat and himself for two. The only thing preventing him from doing the latter is the fear that you would swipe them afterwards. A real sly dog.

Of course, all these revolting characteristics do not pertain to me. I consider my fellow countrymen to be complete abominations and if I were in the habit of paying attention to abominations, I would be ashamed of them. But I do not pay attention to such things, nor, in recent days, to practically anything. The side effect of this, however, is that one suffers from insomnia. Yet such disinterestedness is also one of Dr. Monardes' pieces of advice. "Don't pay attention to anything except medicine," he says, "and to a number of very simple and obvious everyday necessities, which are, in fact, so self-evident that you may easily carry them out without paying them any particular attention. You must"–the doctor insists–"always keep your mind focused on important things, and in the absence of such things, on nothing at all. Although in the latter case you ought to think long and hard about why and how you ever reached such a condition in the first place." Yes, Dr. Monardes is a person from whom one can learn much, not just about medicine, but about life in general. He understands the modern world and human nature like no other.

My Portuguese provenance, of course, can easily be discerned from my name. So how did I hit on precisely that name? When Dr. Monardes requested I add an aristocratic title, I recalled the village where I was born. The principle behind such appellations, as everyone knows, is to indicate where you come from. However, the village had a nondescript name. Yet by way of compensation it was ringed by magnificent forests. Thus, I decided to christen myself "da Silva," after the Latin for "forest." Dr. Monardes approved the name, and I like it as well–it was a good choice.

Perhaps my reader might object that this does not fit in well with my hatred of Nature. First of all, I would like to state that it is in no sense obligatory for something to fit with anything else whatsoever, except for in the healing practices of medicine, but even then it is far from necessary in all cases and as one gradually comes to understand, sometimes it is impossible and even harmful. I know of many cases in which the most logical path to healing has turned out to be fatal. In my work with Dr. Monardes, I have been witness to cases in which the most illogical intuition turns out to be life-saving. Incidentally, Dr. Monardes is a person with exceptional intuition. The exercise of reason is something he places in strict boundaries and always keeps reigned in, like a horse trained under a heavy hand. "Every disease can have at least three causes," Dr. Monardes says. "Your knowledge helps you to distinguish them. One of them always pops into your mind first. And it is usually wrong."

I suspect that if this were not the case, every reasonably well-read person could become a medical man. So why do I want to become one? Above all because this profession is no worse than any other, and often more profitable, too. At the same time, it offers me the opportunity to confront Nature. People are the victims of Nature. Not that I have any love lost for people. People . . . What can I say? . . . The craziness of the universal procreator is reflected in them, they are her offspring. But the sick person is a victim of Nature. In her madness she has created within his body one endlessly complex and poorly regulated mechanism, always on the verge of breaking down, yet at the same time unpredictable, chaotic, and random—he might collapse from the tiniest thing, yet he might also withstand the most monstrous experiences. Take, for example, the sailor, Francisco Rodrigues, one of the eighteen survivors from Magellan's expedition (who was also Portuguese, by the way, which is surely one of the reasons he died in so absurd a fashion), who somehow endured a three-month fever in the middle of the Pacific Ocean, far from any source of succor, only to die from the prick of a rusty nail on the vessel *Hyguiene*, anchored in the Port of Sevilla, of all places, as he was looking her over, deciding whether to join her crew—an endeavor that he incidentally was under no financial compulsion to undertake, since Magellan's spices had made him rich. He intended to take to the seas again because he was squandering his wealth so freely that in five or six years' time, as he liked to say, it would be all gone.

This unpredictability of the body—to get back to my original thought—is a consequence of the chaoticness, randomness, and unpredictability of Nature itself. Did I say unpredictability? In fact, this is not always the case. If there is any great marvel whatsoever in this world, it is that Nature can sometimes be controlled. For that, of course, extensive skills and knowledge are necessary, but in principle it is possible. Figuratively speaking, you can drag Nature out of the madhouse and force her to do something. Of course, she continues lurching and grimacing, keeps babbling nonsensically, but she does it. Then next time she won't do it. It depends.

There are certain means through which she can be forced, in particular circumstances, to act as we wish. Such a means, practically omnipotent, was discovered by our seamen in the Indies over the past half-century or so. This well-nigh magical means was completely unknown to Antiquity, whose number includes even Herodotus, Heraclitus, or whatever they called that mighty ancient healer, whose name escapes me for the moment. Of course, we are talking about the almost almighty tobacco. This is precisely the medicine to which Dr. Monardes has dedicated his book about its healing powers. Dr. Monardes is an ideal innovator, a true discoverer. This was the first and, at the time, the only book of its kind in Europe. However, I will let the author speak for himself:

*My assistant and colleague Señor Dr. da Silva asked me to write a few words in his work—a request I responded to joyfully, being flattered by the faith shown in me, for which I wish to thank him sincerely. Henceforth I shall express myself more briefly (due to pressing engagements).*

*My tract about tobacco was published in Sevilla under the title "On Tobacco and Its Great Virtues, by Dr. Nicolas Monardes, M.D. LL.D. I.S.O. M.A. D.J. M.C." The latter is a selection of my titles. It is also known by the same name in France (without the titles, however). The tract in question is part of my book "A Medical History of Remedies Brought from the West Indies," or, in short, "Historia medicinal." In England, due to the singular whim of its translator, it appeared under the title "Joyfull News out of the New Found World." Following my indignant inquiry, I was assured that in England if something does not begin with "Joyfull News" no one buys it or reads it. The English, as I came to understand, look upon all books, including medical writings, primarily as a means of entertainment to pleasantly while away one's spare time, for which reason every other title there now begins with "Joyfull News." For example, if the work in question addresses the massacre in Lancaster, the book will be published as "Joyfull News out of the Massacre in Lancaster." I give this example because I have seen it with my own eyes. In short, I was forced to back down.*

*This was merely a clarification. Now I would like to offer the reader some useful advice:*

*1. Go to bed early. The best time is around eight o' clock in the evening in the winter and nine o' clock during the summer.*

*2. No fewer than eight hours of sleep.*

*The advice above could be paraphrased more simply as follows: Go to bed one hour after sundown, get up one hour before sunrise. The more attentive reader will most likely note that this is precisely a simplified paraphrase. However, with the passage of time I have become convinced that not only in England, where it is absolutely necessary, but also everywhere else, it is best to state things in a simplified manner, as this is the only way they will be understood. With the exception of France, however, where it is preferable to state things as complexly as possible, ideally such that nothing whatsoever can be understood. Then in France they will declare you a philosopher.*

*3. Food–three times a day. Lavish breakfast, fair-to-middling lunch, light supper. The reader may imagine food as a slide: in the morning you find yourself at its highest point, at noon in the middle, and in the evening at its lowest part. Its lowest part is not necessarily a place where one falls on one's arse and subsequently spends the next hour thus in the privy.*

*4. Meat dishes should be alternated with meatless ones, ideally on the same day, but if this proves impossible–then every other day. Overconsumption of meaty foods leads to diseases of the kidneys, while eating only meatless fare weakens the organism.*

*5. Moderate labor. If possible–none at all. Avoid working in the afternoon and especially the evening. Do not forget what the Bible teaches us–labor was something used to punish Adam.*

*6. Warm clothes during the winter. If when you look outside you reckon you will need one woolen jersey, put on two. It is of particular importance to keep your feet warm, thus the same applies to socks as well. Countless people die of colds that could easily be avoided, except in the cases of the most destitute, among whose ranks our reader can scarcely be counted. Furthermore, one's neck should be wrapped in a scarf.*

*3a) It is sufficient for a person to go to any pub whatsoever to see gluttonous animals. Overeating gathers all the bodily fluids in the stomach, leads to a feeling of heaviness, and upsets the activity of the entire organism (from whose extremities the fluids are withdrawn so as to aid digestion within the stomach). In cases of systematic abuse, this leads to corpulence, which thins the bones and encumbers the heart. Stop gorging yourself!*

*3b (7.) It has been said many times, but let us repeat: Do not abuse alcoholic beverages. Two glasses of wine a day maximum, one at noon and one in the evening. Spirits—only in the winter, 75 gr. maximum. Yes, I know it seems like very little. This is not news to me.*

*The above-mentioned advice could be formulated in a more simplified manner (and summarized, which is, in fact, the same thing) as follows: He who eats and drinks a lot dies young. You have certainly heard the so-called blessing "Eat, drink and be merry!" To the same effect they may as well have told you: "Die sooner!"*

*8. Use tobacco habitually, in the form of smoke for inhalation. This protects the organism from infection and strengthens it as a whole. Señor Dr. da Silva has informed me that in the present work he will discuss several illustrative examples of tobacco's healing power, thus I will conclude, remaining*

*Your fervent well-wisher*
*and most humble servant,*
*Dr. Nicolas Monardes,*
*M.D. LL.D. I.S.O. M.A. D.J. M.C.*

*P.S. For other examples of the healing power of tobacco see my above-cited treatise "On Tobacco and Its, etc."*

My intention in the present book is to describe approximately thirty-six examples of the healing power of tobacco (it is I, Guimarães). I do not know whether it will be necessary to cite all of them—this question will be decided in the course of the writing. In any case, I can categorically claim that the unconquerable substance alluded to here can cure between thirty and forty illnesses and bodily indispositions. Now I will begin to cite them, beginning with the most illustrative:

# 1. Against Death

Of course, I realize that death is neither an illness, nor a bodily indisposition. However, it could be considered their most extreme consequence and ultimate goal, thus in this sense it is uncontrovertibly—and inextricably—linked with them. Did I say inextricably? No! And no again! I personally witnessed how Dr. Monardes, with the help of the healing power of tobacco, resurrected a man from the dead, just as in biblical times the ancient Jew Lazarus was resurrected. This took place in the village of Casas Viejas, (the more recent case, that is), where we had been called to save a man suffering from sharp pains in the stomach accompanied by a fever. When we arrived—which, given the roads in Andalusia, took a fair bit of time—he was no longer suffering from anything, but rather lying there stiff, stark, and yellow on a wooden bed. The man was dead.

*Murdered by Nature!* I thought to myself. She is mad—and heavy-handed, just as most madmen are. She had struck this man in the stomach or elsewhere, perhaps in several spots simultaneously, and had killed him. But why did she do it? This would be the logical question. Hadn't she herself given him life? Well, the simple truth is that she didn't do it on purpose. She didn't smack him deliberately, but rather in a fit of frenzied arm-flailing. The man just happened to be somewhere in the range of her numerous arms, in the wrong place, and now he was lying before us prostrate and, by all outward signs, dead.

Dr. Monardes' preliminary examination quickly confirmed my apprehensions.

"This man is dead," said Dr. Monardes. "How long has he been this way?"

Amidst the general wailing, we finally received the answer that he had been that way for only a short while. Then Dr. Monardes took a cigarella out of his inside pocket, bit off the tip, looked around, and, not seeing a more suitable receptacle, spit it onto the floor (this was a typical village home), after which he lit it with much puffing. Here I surely need clarify what precisely a cigarella is. It closely resembles that which is known in the south as a "cigar," and as a "cheroot" in the north, but is slightly thinner and rawer, for which reason it burns with more difficulty and much crackling. Normally the sailors at the port smoke cigarellas, since they are considered lower quality than cigars; however, since the tobacco in them is rawer and not as dried out, their healing power is far greater. So, as I was saying, Dr. Monardes took out a cigarella and after a minute, or at most two, managed to light it. This so impressed those present that the wailing subsided–the only sound was the doctor's puffing and the cigarella's crackling, accompanied by the heavy scent of tobacco, which enveloped us.

"Guimarães," said the doctor, handing me the cigarella. "Breathe smoke into his mouth."

Now, this was something I had no desire whatsoever to do. These country folk are sick with all kinds of diseases, all manner of fevers, and I was afraid of being infected. Noticing my hesitation, the doctor said: "Don't worry, it's the perfect disinfectant."

I knew this was the case, yet sometimes fear just takes hold of you. I took several deep drags off the cigarella, rolling the smoke between my cheeks as if gargling–and speaking of gargling, I asked the villagers for a glass of *pereira*, i.e. pear brandy, and gargled with that, too, took another drag off the cigarella and was now ready for action.

First, I had to open the man's mouth, which turned out to be no easy task, but once I grabbed him by the cheeks with one hand and pulled at his jaw with the other, I finally managed to open his mouth. I exhaled the tobacco into it, making sure not to let my lips touch his. This did not work very well, however. The smoke entered his mouth and then exited again, so I had to blow on it to chase it back inside. I soon sensed that our heads were wrapped in smoke, yet only a small fraction of it was going inside the wretched peasant's mouth.

"That's not going to work," Dr. Monardes said with a certain—absolutely understandable—irritation, as he clapped me on the shoulder from behind. "Give it to me."

I stepped back ashamed, but relieved. Shame or no shame, "fear guards the vineyard," as they say in my homeland, Portugal, where, incidentally, they say all sorts of twaddle. Yet one shouldn't expect such people to say anything but twaddle. A while back Dr. Monardes' publisher, Señor Diaz, was collecting money for advance subscriptions to a publication he called "Folk Wisdom." I told him that such a title was misleading in its very essence and that such a book should be called "Folk Twaddle" and that only in such a case would I pay for it. Moreover, he was confused about the very character and function of such a book—he imagined it as something which you could read to learn life lessons, whereas in fact it could only be a collection of inanities which you could read for entertainment and a good laugh. He replied that this was not the case and quoted several sayings which he clearly considered gems of folk wisdom, upon which I asked him what he would say about the proverbs "You can tell a man by his clothes" and "You can't tell a man by his clothes," which, by the way, could be found one after the other in the book subsequently published by said Señor Diaz. Upon which he replied that at the end of the day he was a publisher and his job was to make money and that no one would buy anything entitled "Folk Twaddle." Now there's a good argument, finally. I told him he should have begun with that and gave him a certain paltry sum. I read the book I later received with great satisfaction as a collection of jokes, then gave it to a beggar in Sevilla. "A gift for you from your brethren," I told him. He couldn't read, but would surely find some other use for it—such people are very imaginative, when they happen to get their hands on something. In the end, their entire life passes in preparation for that.

But to return to our story. In any case, fear got the best of me, and I stepped away from the dead man in relief. But Dr. Monardes! I would say that his very body, his stance, his shoulders, his feet firmly planted on the ground—all this radiated confidence and determination. He inhaled on the cigarella two or three times, blowing the smoke from his nostrils like a fire-breathing rhinoceros, two thick streams of smoke rose from either side of his face and for a moment he reminded me of a mythical bull with horns of smoke, at which point he leaned over, pressed his lips tightly to those of the dead man, and began exhaling tobacco smoke into them.

"Guimarães," the doctor cried shortly in a husky voice, his eyes watering, shouting over the cigarella's crackling. "Come here and pulpate!"

In this situation, "pulpate" means to press on the stomach. And that is what I did. When the doctor blew smoke into the man's mouth, I would wait a moment and pulpate. We only needed to do this a few times, perhaps five at the most. After which the doctor abruptly drew back with impressive agility and raised the man's head with his hand, such that for a moment it was level with mine, facing towards me as I bent over him. The man opened his eyes. What eyes! Although I only saw them for a moment, I will never forget them! Glassy eyes, huge and round as a fish's, with a very strange emotion written in them: some mixture of horror and utter confusion. I suspect that this is how a person coming back from the dead looks. He positively cannot figure out what is going on. But all this lasted only an instant, like I said, because in the following moment Dr. Monardes turned the man's head, deftly tucking it under his elbow. Then I, led by lucky intuition, pulpated him one last time. Lucky intuition is so called, since it shows up in the details, which no one could possibly teach you, so tiny and insignificant are they on the one hand, yet so often decisive on the other. And suddenly the glassy-eyed man took a breath with whistling lungs and proceeded to vomit. He continued to vomit as the doctor held his head to the side with one hand, while handing me the crackling and already half-extinguished cigarella. I took it, inhaled a final drag, and dropped it into the glass of pereira, where it went out with a loud hiss. I thought to myself: "If you are dead, it will raise you from the grave, if you are alive, it will send you there." Of course, that was a completely unfounded outburst of superstition, stimulated by the powerful and exotic qualities of that vigorous substance.

The man was saved! He soon came to his senses, his breathing normalized, and he even answered questions by nodding his head.

The doctor turned to the others, whose stupefaction is impossible to describe. "He'll recover. He needs to keep to bed and recover his strength, and he'll be on his feet in a week."

Tired, but satisfied by a job well done, we climbed into our carriage and set off back to Sevilla. It had grown late, the sun was already setting behind the naked hills of Andalusia.

"Night is falling," the doctor said.

"Yes, night is falling," I nodded. At such a moment, one feels the urge to gaze at and revel in "the beauty of nature," as they say. But what beauty? Sloping hills covered with grass yellowed by autumn, here and there scrawny olive groves, the red sun up above amidst a darkening sky the color of pale indigo, peeking through a grayish veil—if I may put it like this, the dirt road ahead with its brown dust and small half-unearthed colorless stones. What disconsolate grayness, what boredom, what ugliness and what tiresome monotony! . . . It was only then that I realized what had happened!

"Señor," I said. "We just raised a man from the dead! We saved him!"

"Well, he'll die again," Dr. Monardes smiled. "Only some other time."

How modesty adorns a man! You'll never catch Dr. Monardes getting puffed up over his unbelievable achievements, you'll never see him wallowing in self-satisfaction like a pig in the mud. No, he is always disciplined, businesslike, with brisk, energetic movements, careful, on his guard, concentrated yet calm at the same time. An inimitable physician! What luck I had to stumble across such a teacher. And so on.

# 2. Intestinal Worms, Enemas

Is it even necessary to continue after such a strong example? Yes and no. No, because the previous example was extraordinarily and definitively illustrative—such a powerful substance, which can raise someone from the dead, obviously needs no further arguments in its defense. And yes, for two reasons: first, if I do not continue, this composition would become impossible, which I personally would find very upsetting. My career path clearly passes through it. And second, it is advisable to indicate other, more mundane examples, which nevertheless will be of use to the reader so that he may learn how to employ the powerful substance of tobacco in his everyday life, and not only when he dies. After all, a man doesn't die every day, he's not a fly. Rather, he struggles with other, often tiresome and shameful, yet nevertheless vexing, problems and indispositions. And ceaselessly at that, I would say.

In his young years, when he was still trying to build his practice and thus save himself from the terrifying and deadly trap of poverty, from which perhaps even tobacco cannot save you and which usually hangs like the Sword of Damocles over every young person's head, Dr. Monardes specialized in a particularly widespread illness—intestinal worms. A huge number of children in Spain suffer from worms. More even than in Portugal. Here worms afflict both the rich and the poor, absolutely everyone. This, of course, is due to poor hygiene. No one washes his hands except before prayer. Some, by the way, also wash them after prayer, it must be admitted.

My point is that Dr. Monardes was exceptionally specialized in the healing of worms and hence became an exceptional specialist. His name as a master in curing this illness became known far and wide in Sevilla, all of Andalusia, certain regions of Portugal, and even in the north all the way to Asturias and the Basque country, where it spread, albeit in a changed form and was known as Masañas, transforming as it was passed by word of mouth. Rely on what people say and look what happens! But to return to our topic:

And so, Dr. Monardes made his name in worms and established a prospering practice. Actually, prosperity is often founded on some such thing. His wealth dates back to that time, and even to this day it is based on the curing of that illness, and not the doctor's numerous, far more serious medical achievements. It could be said that Dr. Monardes' wealth is shored up by worms, that he has turned worms to gold. And since there are many worms in this country, the doctor's gold is also abundant. "If you want to get rich," the doctor says, "take up something small that everyone uses or which everyone suffers from, but which few produce or cure. Worms, spices, and the like. Only fools throw themselves into grand undertakings and call their foolishness pluck."

Petty things for a petty world, so to speak. But getting back to my original thought.

Many years later, when I was already studying with the doctor, he was called by the king himself, Don Felipe II, whose son, the future Felipe III, had come down with a case of worms. It was then that I saw the Escorial Palace for the first time. Some say it is the ugliest large building in the world, while others argue the opposite, i.e. that it is the largest ugly building in the world. In my opinion, both sides are right. As soon as I saw it from a distance, my soul felt oppressed and cringed like a wet cat. I had never seen anything like it—it resembled a giant prison with a parade entrance. And to complete the absurdity, statues of the Jewish kings had been erected over the entrance, with David and

Solomon in the middle. And this by the same man who so cruelly persecuted the Jews, which only confirms my conviction that we have a madman as king. His appearance strengthened this impression—with the Bible which he supposedly never lets slip from his hand, with a huge gold cross around his neck, and in his royal robes, he looked like the embodiment of un-combinable things, like a cross between fish and fowl. And just as dangerous, in a certain sense.

Although the palace looked quite severe on the outside, inside it was luxuriously furnished and its walls frescoed. The Catholic rulers lived well.

They sent us to the boy. When we entered little Felipe's chambers, we caught him scratching his backside. Many believe that he later went mad, and if this is the case, I suspect it might be due to some extent to our encounter. Dr. Monardes decided to use not the usual, but instead an elite, tobacco treatment on him, one fit for a kingly personage. To this end, we made an infusion from tobacco leaves, as well as tobacco syrup. We smeared Felipe's navel with the syrup and gave him the infusion to drink. He vomited, but Dr. Monardes said this was a good sign, as the tobacco had obviously begun cleansing his organism, and made him drink some more. After that, in order for the treatment to be both maximally effective and quick, he decided to give the boy an enema. For this purpose I had to insert a small glass tube into his backside.

"Ouch!" Felipe groaned.

"That's enough ouching!" I said, rather peeved with a view to the following procedure I had to perform, which I will describe presently. But then a quick thought flashed through my mind, so I continued: "Your majesty, the ruler of the largest empire in the world cannot be moaning and groaning. He must be brave and strong."

The boy looked at me and nodded. "What a fool!" I thought to myself. I am not particularly fond of children. Still less I like the spoiled little monsters from royal courts. And still less if they have worms. And especially if I must insert a glass tube into their backsides and blow tobacco smoke into it, so as to cleanse their bowels from the inside, as was required for the procedure I was faced with. The persistent thought that some worm might crawl through the tube and into my mouth kept running through my head. Yet loyal to my duties, I lit a cigarella and began exhaling tobacco fumes into the tube, blowing as hard as I could so they would not come back out. At the same time, the doctor gave young Felipe a bit more of the infusion, so as to attack the worms from both ends. This raised my misgivings to the level of acute alarm, as I imagined what would happen if he were to get the runs while I was blowing tobacco fumes into the tube. In Sevilla there is a man everyone calls Shit Mouth, thanks to his habit of constantly making gloomy prophecies (which incidentally never come true, except with respect to Shit Mouth himself), but, of course, this expression could also have a literal meaning. I imagined what Francisco Rodrigues would say in the pubs, if such a thing were to occur. He would say: "Hey, there's our friend Guimarães, who ate royal shit."

"But what if he . . ." I said, unable to fully suppress my misgivings.

Dr. Monardes shrugged, as if reading my thoughts. "This is medicine! It is a difficult profession, Señor da Silva," he added, standing by my side and looking down at me.

Difficult, yes, but sometimes you get lucky. The whole procedure went smoothly, we gave him the enema and the doctor left the boy, who looked completely dazed at that point, to sleep. We would wake him after two hours to give him some food and a mild laxative and with that, the doctor reckoned, his treatment would be successfully completed.

As we paced back and forth in the hallway, a priest appeared, sent to help us in case the need arose. I forgot to mention that this outwardly freakish building is also freakish in content, combining as it does a royal palace and a monastery. The priests here are either hypocrites or fanatics, so you cannot hope to have a worldly conversation with them, and indeed, this one soon began prattling on about the soul. Dr. Monardes is in principle a calm man in his fifties, of average height with a well-trimmed, grayish beard, which he strokes with his hand when he portrays pensiveness. He is calm, as I said, yet the word "soul" is something that can infuriate him. I noticed how, as the priest kept talking and talking, Dr. Monardes stroked his beard tensely, trying to restrain himself. But the priest wouldn't shut up. "Why not?" I asked myself. "Is he simply a windbag who, now that he has found an audience, cannot shut up? Or is he a fanatic who has taken it upon himself to preach to us? Or is he a hypocrite who is counting on us to praise his righteousness and zealous faith to high-ranking personages?" Who knows? In any case, at a certain point the doctor could not stand listening to any more of his slimy, somehow sing-song voice and said: "The soul, father? What exactly are you calling the soul? There is no such concept in medicine, señor. In medicine, the soul is a *functio* of your corporality. Your body has four fluids, four humors, warm and cold and two others; it also has organs, between which these fluids move. Your body is eight-tenths water. Water, padre. And while these things interact according to the laws of nature, something else appears, which you call the soul. But it is merely a kind of *functio* of the humors and organs."

"That is not so, señor," the priest objected. "The soul is immortal. How could that which you describe be immortal? The body decays, yet the soul remains."

Fortunately, the doctor got a hold of himself and let the argument drop. The last thing I needed was for some ecclesiastical idiots to clamp my feet in an iron boot. Because their faith and love for their fellow man does not hinder them from torturing him like beasts in God's name. Thus the cruel madness that nature has instilled in all her creation comes out in them. Fortunately, many things are forgiven to the members of the medical profession. For a long time now we haven't heard of a medical man being persecuted by the Inquisition. This is so because our very profession is thought to make us quite absorbed by the body, hence some of our convictions are benevolently ignored as a type of occupational illness or mental injury. Otherwise they would have to burn up more or less all the medical men, yet even priests fall ill now and then and need a doctor, since pain is difficult to cure with prayer, no matter what they might say. Despite this, however, a doctor still may not say everything he thinks without risking a wealth of troubles, and big ones, at that. Dr. Monardes knew that far better than me and prudently fell silent. "To risk making yourself dependent on other people's benevolence is a serious form of madness or idiocy, which every intelligent person should avoid," Dr. Monardes says. Of course, he says that in a different context, referring to medicine itself, having in mind how important it is to lead a healthy life, lest you have to resort to the benevolence and intellect of doctors, who could easily be both malevolent and stupid—such examples abound. However, that statement is admittedly true in a much wider sense as well.

The time finally came to wake up young Felipe. As soon as we entered the room, something in his look unambiguously suggested to me that the boy was not well at all. He had not fallen asleep, but had passed out, as the doctor soon found.

"Complications have arisen," Dr. Monardes said. "Quick, Guimarães, get the citronella."

Citronella is a substance discovered by Dr. Monardes, which is made up of citrus fruits, glycerin, and rose dust, and in the form of a tincture it is used for coming to after a faint. Most of our medications, however, were in a bundle we had left—due to its great weight—in an area near the entrance to the palace. We had taken only the cigarellas, tobacco infusions, and one or two other items. Now here's an opportunity, I thought to myself, for this monk to make himself useful.

"How is our regal lad, señor?" He asked me when I came out.

"Very well," I replied. "He's recovering."

And then I sent him to bring the bundle of medicines.

"You should have gone yourself," Dr. Monardes reproached me, as I came back into young Felipe's chambers.

"I don't know the way, I would get lost in the hallways," I replied, which (in and of itself) was true.

"Listen here, Guimarães," the doctor said, handing me a cigarella. "If something happens to this little fool, I have money stashed in Sierra Morena and more left in trust in Cadiz. We'll go there, get it, and flee to France."

"But how will we get out of here?" I asked. "We don't know the way."

"I remember it," Dr. Monardes assured me. "That's the first thing I notice when I go anywhere."

"But how will we flee to France? They will be looking for us everywhere!"

"Don't worry about that," the doctor replied. "No one who has money and knows how to use it is ever found, as long as he knows they are looking for him. All the Italians know that. And my father was Italian . . . Remember our friend Frampton? We'll sneak out the same way."

Frampton was that Englishman engaged in wholesale trade in Spain who was locked up in Cadiz by the Inquisition, but he escaped and later translated Dr. Monardes' book in England. Of course I remembered him, how could I not! I must admit, as strange as it may seem, at that moment I felt a joyful excitement. The thought of fleeing to France with Dr. Monardes' gold aroused in me an unexpected surge of strength. Not that I meant him any harm, God forbid!, but fate works in mysterious ways: What would happen if, when we went to France, some calamity befell Dr. Monardes? I would be left with all the money. How much was it? Certainly quite a lot—the doctor was a celebrated personage with a huge practice, famous throughout the entirety of Spain, under one name or another. And how nice it is to live without working! I would even say that is the meaning of life. No work, no responsibilities, just your heap of gold and the pleasurable life! Not such a great meaning, I agree. But, then again, it's all you really have in the world of Nature, and you should be real, shouldn't you? You are either real or a fool.

At that moment my thoughts and our tense conversation were interrupted by a weak cough. It came from the young Felipe.

"Cigarella!" Dr. Monardes cried.

At the next moment, both of us huffed and puffed with all our might like a stove in the Pyrenees in January. My lucky intuition again called and I stood close to the patient's bed, so as to administer to him at closer range. Dr. Monardes instantly followed me. The young Felipe, in a half-stupefied state, opened his eyes slightly and, despite his weakened condition, raised himself up on his elbows and continued coughing painfully, as if coughing up his entrails.

"He'll faint from the cigarella!" I said.

"Come on, come on," Dr. Monardes replied. "Strike the iron while it's hot!"

With these words he blew a thick, enormous stream of smoke, which looked impossible for the human mouth to contain, toward young Felipe's face.

Did I say cough out his entrails before? No, I should have said that now. For a moment I thought that the boy would disintegrate before my very eyes.

"I can pulpate!" I suggested, led once again by my intuition.

"Under no circumstances!" Dr. Monardes restrained me with his hand. "His stomach is completely empty."

Clearly, my lucky intuition had led me astray this time.

At that moment we heard panting and the sound of a heavy object being dragged down the hallway—it was our bundle, along with the padre.

"Bring the citronella," the doctor said.

I readied myself, and when I opened the door I exhaled a thick stream of smoke right in the padre's face. He stepped back as if hit by a pear or some such thing.

"Thank you!" I said, but then thought to add: "Drag it inside."

The padre, bent double with coughing as well, pulled the bundle into the room. When I turned towards Felipe, he was already sitting up in bed and trying to look at us through his coughing fit. The doctor handed the padre the cigarellas and told him to carry them out, while he himself took the tincture of citronella, wetted a sponge with it, and held it under the boy's nose. I opened the barred window. A cold autumn breeze wafted over me. What a wonder Nature is, nonetheless! The cigarellas had an effect, of course, but with their help alone I doubt we would have succeeded. No matter what the doctor might say, I think that Nature within this boy had awakened and, led by her indestructible instinct for survival, had urged him to come to. Something in her gears had rattled, some lever was pulled and the whole mechanism began turning, clattering, roaring, inaudible to us, since it was happening somewhere in the depths of his body, in that lower abyss, unlike the heavenly one, in that microcosm, and now there he was, wide awake, with a cleansed stomach, trembling from weakness and the cold autumn wind. Yes, the young Felipe was sitting turned to one side amidst the rumpled silk sheets of his bed, next to which Dr. Monardes was squatting, staring at his backside, and if I did not shut the window the boy would certainly catch a chill in no time in such a state, but in any case he did not have worms anymore, as Dr. Monardes announced with a gleeful ring to his voice. Well, if he does catch cold, most likely someone else will treat him. We were here for the worms. Yet chills seized me so I quickly shut the window. That's the last thing I needed right then, some cold. After that we ate rounds of beef and drank Madeira in the company of Don Felipe II himself, king of this failed empire—the only one in the world that has gone bankrupt, even as galleons loaded with gold from the New World and spices from the Indies arrive in its ports daily. Why is it bankrupt? Because of the armies of thugs defending Catholicism in the Netherlands, in Italy, against the Turks or in the Indies? They do matter, but not much. It's all because of theft, what else? *But how is it possible to steal so much?*, someone might ask. Someone who is poorly acquainted with human nature. Oh, it's possible, I would reply, and how! In principle, if something is bad, it's possible. And there was one person here, in particular, who could explain exactly how it all happens, although he would surely take that secret with him to the grave. There he was, Señor Vazquez de Leca—a Corsican by birth, who grew up a slave of Algerian pirates, and later became a citizen of Sevilla and now first minister. Yes, fate is all-powerful! They say he has made some people richer than the Spanish treasury. Sandoval. Espinosa. Not himself directly, he's not that stupid. They say the whole network starts right from the ports. He has an attentive and intelligent gaze, refined manners, deferential language. They also say that he has an iron fist, but that doesn't show from his folded white fingers, upon which there is only one—but what a one it is!—ruby ring. Spain is bankrupt, because the money has passed into someone's private possession. If the country needs money for something, they turn to Señor de Leca. He usually finds it. That's why he is first minister.

Meanwhile, Don Felipe was saying something about God and the Catholic Church. Señor de Leca was nodding his head gravely. Dr. Monardes was eating a beef round. I was drinking Madeira. The boy was asleep in his chambers, healthy—or at least worm-free. Everything was fine.

Travelling back home in our carriage, I shared some of my thoughts regarding Señor de Leca with Dr. Monardes. "A strange fellow, that Señor de Leca," I said. "If everything I've heard about him is true, he's made some people very rich, but not himself."

"What's so strange about that?" Dr. Monardes replied. "Power is what tempts him, not riches. People are different. Those like him are the most refined examples of the human animal species. He wants to rule, to make decisions and to govern. Through wealth he has made many people dependent on him. He has bound them with a golden chain, which no one breaks, and now they are loyal to him, literally to the grave. In all cases and on every occasion. He can always count on them, as long as he diverts what they want their way. Everyone at court owes something or other to the merchant Espinosa. Espinosa fills his own pockets thanks to de Leca. If someone at court does what de Leca wants, he'll keep his possessions. If he doesn't, Espinosa will call in his debts. A fine system, works flawlessly."

"But why does he bother with all that?" I asked, even though I understood very well. I simply wanted to hear the doctor's opinion. "He could make himself very wealthy and sit back and enjoy the good life."

"He doesn't want to sit back and enjoy the good life, Guimarães," the doctor replied. "Like I just said, people are different. He is not like you. One man wants wealth, the other wants power. There are even some who want yet a third thing, but let's leave them aside. As far as our question is concerned, the difference is clear: Wealth makes you free, while power gives you the opportunity to rule everyone else. Sometimes the two are mutually exclusive and you must choose one at the expense of the other."

"But why are they mutually exclusive?" I objected. "If I have a trading company, then I rule everyone in it."

"Don't be stupid, Guimarães," the doctor replied, slightly irritated. "That's not the same at all. I'm imagining what Señor de Leca must feel about all those who own trading companies and surely even about people like Cristobal de Sandoval and Espinosa as well. He feels a deep contempt for them. And I think he is precisely right. As long as he wields power, he will have everything he needs, in exactly the quantity he requires. Thus, he is *de facto* and in *functio* in the same situation as the rich, but with one serious advantage over them—he can destroy them at any moment. He can make it such that they lose their wealth and even their lives. But they cannot do the same to him."

"Who knows?" I objected, now utterly serious. "If he starts persecuting some of these people, they could still say plenty of things about him."

"But they can't prove them," the doctor replied. "If he has not diverted funds towards himself, then no tracks lead back to him. The worst that could happen to him is that he could lose his post due to suspicions. But the worst that could happen to them is that they could swing from the gallows. By the way, he has surely taken care of himself," the doctor continued after a pause, "and if they really started digging things up, they would find evidence against him. But first, they would really have to start digging things up, and that wouldn't be easy and usually doesn't happen. Besides, who would do the digging? The one assigned the task may have dipped his paws in the honey as well, so guess whose side he'll be on in such a case—Señor de Leca's or the person accusing him? The more you think about, the more difficult the whole business looks."

"Ye-s-s-s, indeed," I drawled and fell silent.

We travelled in silence for some time. Then the doctor took out two cigarellas and gave me one. We kindled them.

"What's going on, señores?" The coachman Jesús yelled from his box. "Did something break?"

"Don't worry," I replied. "It's just the cigarellas crackling."

The doctor blew a few smoke rings and said, "Many try to be like Señor de Leca, but very few succeed. As the Bible says: 'Many are called, but few are chosen.' Most come to ruin for want of sufficient intelligence, discipline, or simply luck."

"Yet isn't it strange," I said, exhaling a stream of smoke towards the ceiling of the carriage, "that all these Spaniards are so loyal to a Corsican? Not that it matters. I'm simply pointing it out as a curiosity, as a bit of folk wisdom."

"Well, whom should they be loyal to? To Don Felipe? What kind of Spaniard is Don Felipe? All of his relatives are in Vienna. No one here is a Spaniard, Guimarães. You are not a Spaniard, de Leca is not a Spaniard, Don Felipe is not a Spaniard, even I am not a Spaniard. Like I've told you, my father was Italian and my mother was a Jewess. In any case, there are no Spaniards in Spain. At one time the Moors lived here, but they've been chased out and no longer do. Now there are Castilians, Andalusians, Catalonians, and so forth who have come from Lord knows where, but there are no Spaniards in Spain. Perhaps only the stablemen are Spaniards."

"The stablemen are usually Portuguese," I said.

"So there's not a single one," Dr. Monardes replied.

"But if that's the case," I said after a short pause, "then there are no Portuguese in Portugal, either, according to the same principles."

"Not surprising," the doctor replied.

"Yes, but I'm Portuguese."

"Or at least that's what you think," Dr. Monardes nodded. "People are constantly thinking all sorts of things, which in most cases make no difference whatsoever, and your case is just such a one."

"Señor," I said, changing the subject. "You are not patriotic in the least."

"Oh, on the contrary! I am very patriotic!" Dr. Monardes exclaimed. "At least in every practical sense that does not contradict sound reason," he added after a short pause.

"But how could the two things possibly fit together?" The question was on the tip of my tongue when I remembered that it was not at all necessary for them to fit together, but since I had already opened my mouth, I changed the subject to the first thing that came to mind: "It's amazing how you managed to build such a career, señor, being the son of a foreigner."

The doctor studied me for a long time with an astonished and reproachful gaze.

"Guimarães," he replied, "I've told you a hundred times. Don't make me think you've lost your mind."

"Yes, I know about the worms, but I still can't believe things happened just like that, that from such a lowly thing such magnificent results could follow. Such a solid practice . . ."

"I've never said that things happened just like that, Guimarães . . . Do you even listen to me at all?"

"Yes, señor, of course. I just feel like chatting," I admitted. "To make the time go faster . . ."

"Ah, so that's it . . . Worms are worms, my friend, and I really did work hard, but if I hadn't married the daughter of Dr. Perez de Morales, I might still be rummaging through the bums of poor little brats for a pittance to this very day. But Dr. Morales left me a fine practice. And three thousand ducats. I was his assistant, just as you are mine now. But unfortunately, all of my daughters are already married . . ."

"Don't worry, señor," I said, raising my hand. "Once I master the trade, everything else will fall into place on its own."

"If you say so," Dr. Monardes replied. "I'm glad you think so. That's for the best in your situation. You know, of course, that my surgery is in the house on Calle da la Sierpes. But you don't know that the house belonged to Dr. Morales."

"Really?" I replied in sincere amazement.

"Yes. I took over his practice and inherited his surgery, and since then things have taken off in a whole new way. I now have a completely different clientele, in most cases."

"Yes," I nodded. "Sandoval. Espinosa. The king himself, obviously."

"Precisely. Yet despite this I would not have achieved any particular financial prosperity if I were not also involved in trade. I inherited this trait from my father, along with my interest in books. My father had a keen flair for business."

"Yes, but you've achieved far more than he ever did."

"That's true," Dr. Monardes concurred. "But he dealt in books, not in slaves. The slave trade is far more lucrative. And I must admit that in this respect, too, I have been lucky. Back in the day, Nuñez de Herrera suggested we form a partnership for slave trading in the New World. You've seen Nuñez de Herrera, right?"

"Once," I said. "He had returned from Panama."

"Ah, yes. May he rest in peace. Although it's hard to believe about a person like him, the truth is that homesickness for the motherland tormented him. He suffered from nostalgia. If you ask me, it shortened his life, since he lived without any joy. He only seemed truly happy when he returned to Spain. Which happened only rarely. But he had no choice. Back then, when the trade was expanding, he had to move to Panama, which made things much easier. It was obvious that I could not go. I had my practice here. He was the one who had to go. Besides, he was the real businessman of the two of us. He started off with slaves, then expanded into gold and other goods. Believe what you will, Guimarães, but I could drop my practice tomorrow and still make enough from trade to feed a hundred beggars in Sevilla. And I owe this in large part to Señor Herrera. To you, I will leave my olive press, to remember me fondly by. It can easily feed four or five people."

"I'm more interested in your real estate business, señor," I replied.

The doctor shook his head.

"That may be the case," he said. "But that business is more risky. Back when Don Felipe declared Sevilla the central customs house for all goods from the New World, the city expanded greatly and one could make lots of quick money in real estate, but now things have quieted down and the market is slower, if there's even a market at all. People have changed. Before, when someone arrived, he looked to buy a house or land where he could build one, whereas now they come and sleep on the streets or wherever they happen to land. Just look at what's happened. Sevilla has filled up with beggars. They roam the streets practically in droves. The ones who came first were civil servants, merchants, those kinds of people. But now they're ne'er-do-wells from the villages and riffraff of every stripe."

"But your friend Cervantes says that Sevilla is a beggar's paradise. Here we have the fattest, best-fed beggars in the world, according to him."

"Ah," Dr. Monardes waved dismissively. "Don't go believing everything he says . . . The things he says surely landed him in prison—where he is now for theft."

"And petty theft, at that," I added.

"And petty theft, at that, precisely," Dr. Monardes nodded in agreement. "Otherwise I wouldn't have mentioned it. It's . . ."

At that moment we heard the voice of Jesús the coachman, who always knew the way.

"Señores, Sevilla." I looked out the window—indeed, the lights of Sevilla were visible in the distance, heaped into several piles in the night, surrounded by gloom like coals in a dark room. Whose room? And for what reason? Nature's room, señor. For no apparent reason. Indeed, it would be strange for anything at all to appear in such a pitch-dark night.

"Hey, Jesús," Dr. Monardes yelled suddenly. "Are you a Spaniard?"

"Of course!" Jesús replied. "Why wouldn't I be?"

"Where are you from originally?"

"Where am I from originally? I guess I've got to be from Sevilla. I don't know. I can't remember."

"And where is your father from?"

"Well, my father is a different story! He came from the Holy Lands, señor. Hence the name. If I'd been a girl, I would've been called Maria Immaculata."

Dr. Monardes turned to me. "See? Not one. Not a single one."

*My sincerest thanks to Señor Dr. da Silva for granting me the opportunity to sincerely express and so forth, etc.*

*What do these various churchmen, these so-called philosophers and other clever windbags, mean when they use the word "soul"? What is the soul, in their view? In response to this question they offer some complex and entirely unfathomable answers, some conundrums and other such mind-bogglers, which depend entirely on their unfathomableness, combined with a profuse stream of words, to convince you of their correctness. The intelligent person, however, quickly notes their vacuity and even their naiveté, as well as their utter lack of familiarity with and understanding of human nature. Dr. da Silva has informed me that earlier in his work he has revealed the true medical opinions on the so-called "soul," how it is a type of interaction and* actio pro functio et junctio *of the four bodily humors with the numerous organs and so forth. Thus, I will not expound on these arguments. I will merely note the utter indefensibility of belief in the soul from the point of view of everyday common sense. Let's take as an example that whole rabble one sees in the streets of Sevilla—all those drunkards, bandits, Portuguese vagrants, streetwalkers, laborers, beggars, crooks, murderers, out-of-work sailors, hayseeds, and so on and so forth. All of them, we are told, have souls. Very well, let us assume that I am willing to accept this. But then they tell us, on top of everything, that these souls of theirs are immortal! That is just too much! Even by the windbags' own logic, this is clearly nonsense. However, I am a Renaissance man, a humanist. Such things cannot fool me. From their words it appears that God is some dustman who collects and preserves everything. What a concept! But no, they say, he does not collect them, but rather sends them to hell, where they burn for eternity. For eternity? First, I would venture to say that this is one and the same thing, i.e. those utterly useless, vacuous, ugly, and sometimes even terrifying souls are still being preserved. If this were the case, the whole Universe would soon be filled with a mob of such souls, it would start to resemble a spiritual junkyard. Second . . . Etc.*

*And another thing. They say, or rather de facto presuppose as* nativum givenum, *that each soul is valuable in and of itself. This is the height of inanity! What value could the soul of a killer have? If you find this example extreme, how much value could there really be in the soul of that whole multitude inhabiting the cities as well as the villages, and even in the so-called "ordinary person"—what value could his soul really have? None, I say. Even if the soul really existed, it would resemble everything else we see in nature and the world, which is either well or poorly made, either precious or worthless, with all the levels between them, as between gold and charcoal. The soul of a fool would be exactly as he is—i.e. a foolish soul, while the soul of a thief would be a thieving soul, the soul of a beggar a beggarly soul, and so on and so forth, etc. Ergo, the world would be full of foolish, mediocre, useless, evil souls, which no one has any need or use for and which are simply trash, things to be thrown away. They would be a huge majority, just like the people who have them. Could those clever windbags possibly imagine that all this rabble was created by the God they speak of? This only goes to show what foolish—or perhaps hypocritical and deceitful—souls they themselves have. And just as nature throws away bodies after they die, assimilating them and turning them to dust, so should God throw away those souls, turning them into nothing, as they have no value whatsoever. So nature will reject their bodies and God reject their souls, and that circle in the middle is what they call their life. The rejected ones are bold enough to claim they are God's creation. It's laughable! They hardly deserve the majesty of Nature, let alone the God they speak of. In Spain you'll often hear it said: "I swear on my immortal soul!" Your immortal soul, did you say? It is most likely not worth a thing, my friend, and is entirely superfluous. The whole mistake begins here—they think that the soul is of value, and from there follows an entire series of mistaken conclusions. Whereas in reality, the soul, if it exists, could not possibly be anything particularly special—it would be something like the leaves on the trees, like drops of rain, the stones on the road or the grass in the field. In other words, it would simply be a part and functio of nature, something right alongside the rest, which in no way occupies any special place within the system of nature—as the churchmen and all philosophers since that madman Plato would have you believe—something of no particular significance at all, simply a part of the great natural cycle of creation and destruction as an end in itself. Incidentally, despite the fact that this cycle is repetitive, nothing ever returns, any such claims are empty gibberish. Once you're gone, that's the end, it's over. There is no second time. Because Nature really does revolve, but not around your so-called "soul." She revolves around her own self.*

*And Plato really is a madman. A reader need only read his description of life in Athens during the Age of Atlantis to realize that he filled his writings with every more or less coherent fable that occurs to him and that taking his absurdities and ravings seriously constitutes a grave and laughable mistake. If all of his works were to disappear in an instant, this would be no loss whatsoever to humanity. Incidentally, I would argue that it would be no loss whatsoever to humanity even if it itself were to disappear. Humanity is unbreakable, in other words, and that's precisely what humanism is. Yet Plato did it great harm. He is the source of that utterly mistaken conception of man and his nature, which is also to blame for these meaningless formulations about the soul. I will not enter into detailed discussion of this, etc., suffice to say that from the medical point of view, man is simply a biological species, one of many, with certain abilities that differentiate him from the other animals, yet in general outlines and in his fundamental principles fully sharing their nature, which, by the way, is far more varied than we tend to realize. Although not every humanist would admit it, the truth is that man is simply a pipe—as are all biological species in their essence, with the exception of plants and minerals. Man is one of these creatures. A pipe, through which nature passes—it goes in through one side and out through the other. This is one of the ways Nature keeps herself in circulation, in eternal motion. (I hasten to add, however, that the tempting opposite suggestion, namely that Nature is a pipe through which man passes—going in through one side and out through the other—is not true! In principle, tempting things are not true. The most pitiful things are usually the closest to the truth, etc.) What soul? What immortality? Do they realize what they are saying? Does the pig that they gobble up on Christmas—as if to show through the connection of these two things what profound nonsense has pierced their minds—does the pig, I say, have a soul, and is it immortal? But no, they consider themselves something far more special, something entirely different. Although they themselves may live like swine, and frequently do far more revolting, terrible, and preposterous things than those good-natured animals. And of course, they are far more gluttonous. And incomparably more vain. This is the most terrifying of all the animals, I say, and it is no accident that it rules.*

# 3. For Having a Good Time

Since I am afraid that the reader may be tired of the medical details with which this work is filled, or at least will be, I intend to cheer him up by telling him the story of my visit with Dr. Monardes to England, whence we went at the invitation of said Señor Frampton. Some time ago, Señor Frampton escaped from Cadiz on one of Dr. Monardes and Nuñez de Herrera's merchant ships, and since then he has felt enormously in his debt.

We left Cadiz with the caravel *Hyguiene* on a beautiful summer day. Oceanus Occidentalis lay in front of us, to our right was Costa de la Luz, lit, as always, by the sun.

"The dunces who read Plato have been searching for Atlantis since time immemorial," Dr. Monardes said, sitting on deck in a wicker chair, his legs crossed on a heap of gaskets, a book in his lap, "while here it is, before their very eyes."

I looked around: Costa de la Luz, Oceanus Occidentalis, the caravel *Hyguiene*, Dr. Monardes.

"In what sense?" I said.

"In the sense that I'm talking about Cadiz. The island used to be called Gadeira. And that's where the name of the town comes from. First, it was Gadir, then Gades, and later it became Cadiz. And now the island is called Isla de Cadiz. This is exactly what is meant. An island beyond the Pillars of Heracles. That is the island of Cadiz." Noticing my incredulous look, Dr. Monardes said, "This land is very old, Guimarães. Andalusia. People have lived here practically since the world was created. In England, where we are now going, there was only the wind whistling through the hills when people were already living here."

"Yes, but what kind of people!" I said dismissively. "What were they good for? Nothing! Monkeys, savages!"

"Better monkeys and savages than the wind whistling through your ass, believe you me," Dr. Monardes objected. "Did you know, my friend, that I've found pottery from time immemorial in the yard of one of my houses near the Guadalquivir? Remind me some day to show them to you."

"Yes, by all means," I said, with the full knowledge that I was lying. There is hardly anything of less interest to me than pottery from time immemorial. Dr. Monardes, though a great physician, has his own peculiarities, just like every man (but not every man is a great physician).

We traveled in silence for a while, whereupon Dr. Monardes grunted, lifted his eyes from the book he was reading, and said with irritation: "Look what a Northern fool has written here: 'To laugh often and much; to win the respect of intelligent people and the affection of children; to earn the appreciation of honest critics and endure the betrayal of false friends; to appreciate beauty; to find the best in others; to leave the world a bit better, whether by a healthy child, a garden patch or a redeemed social condition; to know even one life has breathed easier because you have lived. This is to have succeeded." In the next instant, the doctor abruptly threw the book into the sea with surprising force, shouting after it, "To have succeeded, you fool, means being rich and in perfect health. Rich and healthy! Just that and nothing more. I cannot bear these windbags any longer!" Dr. Monardes turned to me. "They blather pure nonsense to fool themselves and the rest of the world into thinking they are something besides miserable losers, and they call it philosophy." He turned back towards the sea, adding, "These works deserve to be devoured by fish. Then perhaps some fish will begin speaking wisely."

I laughed and said, "Like the goldfish in the tale of the fisherman, señor."

"A goldfish? By no means!" Dr. Monardes objected. "It would have to be a clay one."

"So why do you read these bores, señor? Read Rabelais. The greatest writer."

"Why do you think so?" Dr. Monardes asked. He didn't read such books, feeling a certain unjust contempt for them.

"He is a medical man just like us," I answered. "The printing of his first three books has been halted, and the fourth has even been banned by Parliament."

"No wonder," the doctor nodded. "What is parliament? A place where representatives of the provinces meet. What could be expected of such provincials except the bold combination of stupidity and theft? Thank God there is not such an abomination in Spain!"

"And the greatest of the poets, señor," I added, feeling encouraged, "is Pelletier du Mans. What a book, señor: *L'Amour des amours.* It consists of a cycle of love sonnets followed by verses about meteors, planets, and the heavens. Who else has written such a book? Nobody!"

"Indeed!" the doctor agreed. "But you surprise me, Guimarães. I thought you concentrated on medicine."

"Well, I do concentrate on it, señor. I read these other things in my spare time, if something catches my interest. Why do you torment yourself with those sagacious fools?"

"Because I'm a Renaissance man and a humanist," the doctor replied. "I must read them."

"Renaissance man? Humanist? Who gives a damn about that?" I said. "You are a rich man, señor, very successful in your career. What do you need the Renaissance and humanism for?"

"Such is the fashion, my friend. And fashion is a great power, a mighty eagle in the sky. It is more important than you think, and it is most certainly my duty to impress upon you a correct understanding of such matters, lest you should say some day 'The doctor told me so many other things, but not that.' You must learn to distinguish the two kinds of fashion, Guimarães: one is short-lived, while the other yields results tomorrow. If you want to achieve a better lot in life, you must be able to recognize the latter and follow it. Tomorrow it may not make any difference that you were rich and highly successful in medicine. It may turn out that the only important thing will be whether you were a man of the Renaissance and a humanist."

"What does it matter what matters tomorrow?" I objected. "*Carpe diem*, seize the day. Tomorrow never comes, as the Arabs say."

"Yes, that is what they say, and see how they ended up," the doctor retorted, pointing first at the shores of Andalusia and then at the African coast. "Chased out! Tomorrow will come, fear not. It always does."

I was not particularly convinced, but preferred to stay silent. I was beginning to feel seasick in any case.

"When you vomit, be careful here," Dr. Monardes said, pointing at the deck beside him. "This is the nail Francisco Rodrigues pricked himself on years ago."

"Why, haven't they gotten rid of it?" I exclaimed.

"Nothing ever disappears in Spain, my friend," the doctor replied and headed for his cabin.

The English are nice chaps, although perhaps a bit foolish. They definitely seem more foolish than the Spaniards, perhaps even more so than the Portuguese; why, they even seem more foolish than those sorry potatoes stuck in the ground—meaning the Bulgarians, of course—although I'm not sure I would be willing to swear to this last statement. The English constantly act witty in order to look smart; although their wit is usually rather trivial. They radiate certain white-bread mediocrity. But I prefer them to the Spaniards. Spain is singed by the sun, supposedly suffused with light, but is, in fact, somehow a dark and bitter country, while England, supposedly veiled in mist and rain, looks somehow green and cheerful; more cheerful, in any case, and gentler. You can say many things to an Englishman and he will keep trying to be smart and witty, while a Spaniard will simply jump up to cut your throat. He calls it pride, but I'm a foreigner and I see it for what it really is: a morbid self-respect, enormous self-love, and an unrestrained nature. You can't be too careful with a Spaniard. He's dangerous. And even when he's warmhearted, he is not cheerful.

The Englishman, on the other hand, is cheerful. I like this very much because I'm a fan of burlesque. As Dr. Monardes says, "What passes for a burlesque in Spain is considered a tragedy in England." This is indeed the case! You can see nothing resembling English burlesque in Spain. Theater is flourishing here, and burlesques are onstage everywhere. In Spain, they call Lope a comedian! What kind of comedian is he?! Come here if you want to see what burlesque means, what a true farce is!

Señor Frampton introduced us to a remarkable man called Ben, a great connoisseur of theatre and comedy, who was also devoted to burlesques, and he showed us round the theaters. Yesterday, for example, we went to the Globe Theatre to watch a tragedy, which I didn't mind, since, like I said, English tragedies are like Spanish burlesques. You always have a wonderful time no matter what you're watching.

Being gallants and beaus, we took seats on the stage itself, on the stools to the side of it. According to local notions, the gallant, generally speaking, is a man who (as Señor Jonson, our friend who took us to the Globe, put it) has nice clothes, shapely legs, white hands, Persian locks, a tolerable beard, a sword, and six pence to pay for the stool. We met almost all the requirements, and certainly the most important of them—the last one.

All the local gallants smoked, though they smoked pipes, a vulgar habit imposed on them by those Anabaptist crooks, the

Dutch. Dr. Monardes and I were the only ones smoking cigarellas. The very moment we sat down, the serving-boys gave us a candle each, setting them down on the tables in front of us, and everyone began lighting his pipe; the doctor and I lit our cigarellas. In the meantime, the play had begun. A cloud of tobacco smoke swirled over us and also over the stalls, because many people down there had lit their pipes as well. I heard the actors rather than saw them, because of the aromatic smoke wafting through the air.

*"Our valiant Hamlet did slay this Fortinbras,"* I heard somebody say at one point, so I squinted to see what was going on, but there were just two men talking about something, wrapped in smoke like angels descending from heaven.

Meanwhile, someone tapped me on the back. When I turned around, I saw a serving-boy. "Hazelnuts, sir? Apples? Walnuts?"

Señor Jonson, who was sitting next to me, said, "I want apples and hazelnuts."

"The same for me," I said.

*"Good Hamlet, cast thy nighted colour off, and let thine eye look like a friend on Denmark."*

However, I couldn't see any woman on the stage.[1]

"Who is this Denmark?" I said, turning to Mr. Jonson.

"Well, Denmark is . . . never mind." He waved his hand dismissively as he lit his pipe and, sucking at it with delight, said: "By this light, I wonder that any man is so mad, to come to see these rascally tits play here—they do act like so many wrens—not the fifth part of a good face amongst them all." But he always spoke like that, wherever we went. "At least they don't sing here," he added. "Their music is abominable—able to stretch a man's ears worse than ten pillories, and their ditties—most lamentable things, like the pitiful fellows that make them—poets. By this

1. This is an untranslatable pun, as the name of the country Denmark sounds like a woman's name in Bulgarian.

vapor—an't were not for tobacco—I think—the very smell of them would poison me, I should not dare to come in at their gates." He took the pipe from his mouth and munched a few hazelnuts. "A man were better visit fifteen jails—or a dozen or two hospitals—than once adventure to come near them . . . Hazelnuts, sir?"

"No, thanks. I have my own," I answered.

*"Soft you now! The fair Ophelia! Nymph, in thy orisons be all my sins remember'd,"* a voice from the smoke reached my ear.

I stared and in the mist made out the vague outlines of a female figure hesitantly stepping towards the man who was speaking. At the next moment, I nearly lost my life! I spat and turned to say something to Señor Jonson and was nearly impaled by a sword whose point, fortunately, was topped with a chunk of apple. As far as I could see, some chap had leaned over and was stretching his sword in front of Señor Jonson and another man, trying to pass the apple to some other bloke sitting on the other side of Dr. Monardes.

"Hey, amigo," I cried out, "you almost skewered me!"

"A thousand apologies, sir," he cried out in reply. "That's for Mr. Perky next to you."

I drew back, and Mr. Perky in return extended to his friend his own sword, on whose point there seemed to be a piece of pluck. At the first moment, I thought that my eyes, teary from tobacco vapors, were deceiving me, but as the sword passed just under my nose, I caught a certain unmistakable aroma, and then I saw that Dr. Monardes next to me had taken a cigarella in one hand and his Spanish dagger in the other, with a piece of pluck stuck on top of it, and was eating most happily without saying a word to me.

I turned to Ben and said, "Where is this pluck from?"

"From the servants. Two pence. Would you like some?"

"That wouldn't be half bad," I answered.

"Hey, boy," Señor Jonson called out and raised his hand.

"Who's calling me?" a voice came from behind the vapors.

"Over here, over here," Ben cried.

*"That is the question: Whether 'tis nobler in the mind to suffer the slings and arrows of outrageous fortune, or to take arms against a sea of troubles, and by opposing end them?"*

"Don't suffer! Take arms!" Mr. Perky cried out. Señor Jonson gave a piercing whistle. In a short while, everyone was whistling. I began whistling, too. The chaps in the stalls also began whistling. The man on the stage continued speaking, but nothing could be heard. Then boos were heard from somewhere. We all began booing. Someone with the voice of the Leviathan itself cried out from the stalls, "Boo! Boo!"

A few people from the stalls joined him. Then all the groundlings followed suit. One of us gallants also cried out: "Boo! Boo!"

"Boo! Boo!" I began yelling, too.

"Who called me?" My ears barely caught question. It was as if Fate itself had made me look in that direction because the boy had already turned around to leave.

"Over here, over here!" I cried out and raised my hand. The boy saw me and leaned over the table towards me. "Pluck for me, too," I hollered to him.

"Very well, sir," he hollered out in return, taking three steps into the vapors and suddenly disappearing like the apparition of St. Sancho at Casa de Toros, St. Anselm in Malaga, Saint Nicholas the Wonderworker in Sierra Blanca, and many others. Spain is full of apparitions that disappear.

Meanwhile, the audience had begun stamping their feet. I continued to yell and also began to stamp. Someone shook my shoulder. It was Dr. Monardes.

"Guimarães," he yelled in my ear, "do you have more cigarellas?"

"Boo!" I yelled, shook my head affirmatively, thrust my hand into my inside pocket, brought out a cigarella, and passed it over my shoulder to Dr. Monardes.

"God bless you!" the doctor said.

*"Alas, poor Yorick!"* was heard from the stage when the noise subsided. *"I knew him, Horatio."*

"I knew him, too," Mr. Perky cried out, and everybody laughed.

Meanwhile, the boy had brought the pluck; a pleasant aromatic vapor hung over it. Since I wanted to try the sword trick for myself, I asked for Mr. Jonson's sword, stuck a bit of pluck on the tip, reached past Dr. Monardes and said: "This is for you, Mr. Perky."

Mr. Perky put his hand to his heart and gave a slight bow.

Señor Jonson, whose head was enveloped in vapor from his pipe, was talking about something with his neighbor on his other side and had been spitting on my feet for some time; inadvertently, of course. Pipes make you spit quite a bit, incidentally. After some hesitation (during which time he continued to spit on my feet), I gently tapped him on the shoulder and said: "My friend, you're spitting on my shoes."

"Really?" Señor Jonson said, very surprised. "A thousand apologies, mate."

That's what they say here—"a thousand apologies." Who would apologize to you in Spain? If you asked for an apology, a Spaniard would take that as an insult.

"Now, listen here," Señor Jonson said after a while, taking a drag on his pipe, "that's a great phrase . . . That man Bill . . . he always does that . . . he puts one ingenious phrase . . . in a sea of nonsense." He tossed two hazelnuts into his mouth. "Here is it." Señor Jonson raised a finger. "Now!"

*"What's Hecuba to him,"* the line resounded from the stage, *"or he to Hecuba, that he should weep for her?"*

"Marvelous!" I exclaimed, throwing up my hands.

"Isn't it? Bravo! Bravo!" Señor Jonson cried out and broke into applause.

"Bravo!" I called out as well.

The gallants joined in. However, I suspect that our enthusiasm would soon have subsided unnoticed if that mighty voice from the stalls had not come to our aid.

"Bravo!" the Leviathan thundered and began applauding. His applause was also gargantuan, it echoed like cannon shots.

*Who is that giant, who is that Gargantua*? I wondered and turned to the stalls, but nothing could be seen there, since it was enveloped by smoke.

Soon everybody was crying *Bravo! Bravo!* and applauding. Then someone began whistling. Mr. Perky, Dr. Monardes, and Señor Jonson beat out the others, being the first to begin booing.

Naturally, I joined them immediately. Amidst the general heckling, a thunderous voice could again be heard from the pit: "Boo! Boo!"

"Boo!" we also began shouting.

Soon everybody was booing and stamping their feet.

*That's how things happen in reality*, I suddenly thought, who knows why. All sorts of thoughts cross your mind in such a situation.

*"With sorrow I embrace my fortune,"* a spectacularly dressed man said from the stage. He approached us, grabbed Señor Jonson's pipe, took two drags, and went back to the stage, showered by universal applause.

"That's Fortinbras," Señor Jonson yelled at me. "He's one of a kind!"

"*Take up the bodies,"* the stylish man continued and kicked one of the men lying on the stage. *"Such a sight as this becomes the field, but here shows much amiss. Go, bid the soldiers shoot."*

A moment later, the bodies got up and began bowing to the audience.

"What, it can't be over so soon?" I cried out, extremely disappointed. An excellent play!

The audience got to its feet and began applauding wildly, accompanying that with salutatory cries.

While rising, I inadvertently overturned my plate of pluck. With almost superhuman dexterity, Dr. Monardes speared a chunk of it on his dagger in mid-air and brought it to his lips, without a word.

"Damnation!" I said, staring at the pluck scattered on the ground, clapping my hands all the while.

Well, that was all for tonight.

"What a marvelous play!" I said to Señor Jonson as we walked in the fresh, cool air of the London night.

"Yes. The audience here has good taste and is very hard to please. You can't put on just any old play," Mr. Jonson replied. "But this is nothing! You should see *Every Man out of His Humor*. Now there's a true burlesque! Phenomenal! This was still a tragedy, after all."

"Yes," I said and, absorbed in the conversation, nearly bumped into the legs of some thief hanged on the Tower Bridge. "Why on earth do they have to put them here?" I exclaimed.

"Oh, nobody pays them any attention." Señor Jonson waved dismissively. "Unless they begin to smell bad." He pointed at his pipe and added: "But with the help of this, you almost don't smell anything at all."

# 3b.
# The Title Will Be Thought Up in December

People often seem wretched, and Nature—harsh and indifferent. *Where to in such a world?* you may ask yourself, eyebrows arched, extremely confused.

"Go to the cities," Dr. Monardes says. "You should love cities, unless you are a fool, a rustic." I am coming to love cities more and more. Cities and lights. Especially at night, when a light rain washes the dusty, empty streets, over which floats a transparent mist, while street lamps shed their light on the gutters running with gurgling droplets—it's like a hot spring with steam above it—at such moments, cities are magnificent. Given my preferences—my love of cities and a deep interest in medicine—I wonder whether I'm not a Renaissance man and a humanist, too. In any case, I think it is not entirely out of the question. Not out of the question at all.

Then two phrases began intrusively running through my head: "Urbi et Orbi, the Holy Father, Urbi et Orbi, the Holy Father;" who knows why. I was heading for Ram Alley, near Fleet Street. I was bound for Louse & Barker's tobacco shop, which was open at night. They sold not only tobacco but spirits as well, though the latter unofficially. Dr. Monardes was already there. While I was hopping over the puddles along the road, my cigarella kept going out in the drizzle. Since I was still far from Louse & Barker's, it was quite quiet. Fitful gusts of wind were the only sound. It also seemed to me—although perhaps I was mistaken?—that in the distance I could hear the roar, the splash of the Thames, which, I thought, quite resembled the Guadalquivir. Urbi et Orbi, the Holy Father.

"Oh, there's Guimarães," Dr. Monardes cried when I arrived.

He was sitting at a table with the two proprietors, Timothy Louse and John Barker. Señor Jonson was also there, as well as Señor Frampton and two other men I didn't know. One of them was dressed like something between an Italian and a jester, insofar as those are different things, and was constantly declaring that he was from Italy and that his name was Sogliardo. He lavishly accompanied these claims with Italian words and phrases.

Dr. Monardes has one gesture, which is as unforgettable as it is indescribable—hence this description will not do it justice!—which roughly involves half-closing his right eye and opening only the left half of his mouth. This gesture categorically means "bullshit." That was exactly the gesture he made then in reference to the so-called Sogliardo's chatter. Being of Genoese descent, the doctor can always tell by someone's speech whether he is Italian or not.

The said Sogliardo had come with another gentleman called Shift, who made his living by giving lessons in elegant smoking to young gentlemen, mostly from the countryside, who wished to become gallants. He and Sogliardo, who was his disciple, had just come back from St. Paul's Cathedral on the doors of which, as was the custom here, they had posted Señor Shift's handbills. They even showed us one they had left over. The bill read:

Dr. SHIFT of Oxford
Will teach every young man
In the art of smoking as a perfect
GENTLEMAN & GALLANT,
As well as in the rare skill
Of making corollas of smoke,

The practice of the Cuban ebullition,
Euripus, & whiff
Which he shall take in here in London,
And evaporate at Uxbridge, or farther,
If it pleases him.

"As far as Uxbridge?" I asked, truly amazed.

"If it pleases him," Dr. Shift nodded. "If not, he can do it even farther." And as if to prove his words, at that moment he opened his mouth and let out a large puff of smoke which, frankly, I had failed to notice him inhaling.

Then he and Sogliardo began demonstrating their, in my opinion, rather dull abilities. Sogliardo made large smoke rings, through which Mr. Shift, slightly bent forward, blew thick round puffs. Then Sogliardo demonstrated *euripus*, which means exhaling fumes in perfectly straight lines, equally wide at both ends. He left the Cuban ebullition to Dr. Shift, however, as a particularly difficult number, or so they thought. In this trick, you exhale out your nose and inhale from your pipe very quickly, almost simultaneously, so that puffs of smoke come from your nostrils and the bowl of the pipe, alternating rapidly. I must admit that Mr. Shift had mastered that skill quite well, and soon his head began to resemble a volcano belching out steam. "Just like Vesuvius!" as Señor Louse exclaimed. Everybody was very impressed by Shift and Sogliardo's skills. Except me, of course.

"That's nothing special, señores," I turned to Shift and Sogliardo.

"Nothing special?" Sogliardo exclaimed. "*Madre mia*! This is the art of smoking in its most perfect form, sir. You can hardly do half of these things, I daresay."

Everybody at the table looked at me with a mix of pity and contempt, probably imagining that I was overcome with envy. With the exception of Dr. Monardes, of course, who knew the truth. These two fellows and their pathetic tricks would not make a splash in Sevilla at all. You can see a dozen men like them in every pub. But that's the way it is—Spain is fifty years ahead where tobacco is concerned.

I, for one, have devoted one year, eight months, and three days of my life to the art of smoking, thanks to a small inheritance left to me by my deceased uncle. I made my living with that skill in the last seven months of this period, until Dr. Monardes saw me in a pub and invited me to become his assistant. These English fools never knew—indeed, they could not even imagine—what it means to make your living with this art in a city like Sevilla. They would most likely have been thrashed for showing off tricks such as theirs, because the audience would think their time had been wasted. I myself had been thrown out of the Holy Anchor and two or three other places several times at the beginning of my career. Making those sailors and other vagabonds who puff all day long, from morning till night, pay out of their pockets to see your tricks—well, it was a beastly difficult thing to do, and if you didn't do it well, it could be very dangerous, too. Seven months. I made my living with that skill, and that skill alone, for seven months. Had it not been for Dr. Monardes, I'd probably still be doing it even now. And I made a pretty penny, by the way. Felipe Rojas and I divided the pubs in Sevilla between ourselves so as not to interfere with each other, and I performed in some of them, he in the others. And don't think I just waltzed into the spot. I did not. A certain Pedro de Almeida worked there before me, but I ran him out. I still don't know what happened to him after that. My apologies, but that's how it goes; this craft is ruthless, as they all are.

"Watch my lips," I turned to Sogliardo. "You can read, can't you?"

"Of course," he replied, a little offended.

My question was indeed inappropriate. But old habits die hard: you always need to ask that question in the taverns of Sevilla.

"All right," I said. "Watch carefully."

Then I took a deep drag on the cigarella, held the smoke in my mouth—you must feel that it is under your control, that it obeys to you—rolled it between my cheeks and exhaled: *G.*

I took another drag on the cigarella and exhaled a vertical line, followed quickly by a dot above it: *i.*

The next letter was one of the most difficult. I inhaled deeply and half-closed my eyes in concentration. If you have talent for this job and, I would immodestly add, perfect facial muscles, something will speak up in your head at the right moment and say: "Now!"

"Now!" I heard the thing say and exhaled: *m.*

Then it was easy: *a.* Then: *r.* Then: *a,* followed quickly by a wavelet above it. And that's where things went wrong—the wavelet crossed the *a* in the middle. That's how it goes, if you lose your concentration in this work even for a moment, if you imagine that you are on the homestretch already, the smoke will immediately punish you. Smoke is very fickle.

"Just a moment, señores," I said, raising my hand. "Let me do that one over."

This time I was careful and, of course, there were no difficulties: the *a,* then the wavelet above it: *ã.* Then: *e.* And finally: *s.*

"*Gimarães,*" Sogliardo uttered, looking at me enraptured.

"That's my name," I said.

"Unbelievable!" Señor Jonson exclaimed. "Absolutely unheard of . . . But where is the *u*?" he added a moment later.

"What *u*?" I asked.

"In the beginning. Between *G* and *i.*"

"There is no *u,*" I said, shrugging my shoulders.

"Only hoity-toity snobs in Portugal add the *u,*" Dr. Monardes interjected. "Priests and the like. Señor da Silva is not that sort of a man at all."

"Unbelievable!" Señor Jonson exclaimed again and began clapping his hands.

It is embarrassing for me to describe the following scenes. Let me merely say that I became the center of attention, not only of our table but of the entire pub, whose visitors, it turned out, had fixed their eyes on my performance.

Who knows how long it would have lasted, if at one point, after a series of shouts that no one noticed at first, our attention had not been riveted by the most unsightly man I had ever seen in my life, and whose companion alone could match him in this respect. The ridiculous appearance of these two individuals was really so indescribable that I simply refuse to describe it. On top of that, they were armed, which at first made me think they were actors in a burlesque, coming straight from the stage. It turned out, however, that it was the local sheriff accompanied by one of his deputies.

"Louse," the sheriff said, "how long will you go on giving us trouble? There's been another complaint."

"That can't be!" Señor Louse exclaimed.

"Here's what it says," the sheriff said and opened a scroll, looked at it, knitted his brows, jerked his head back, and fell silent. An awkward pause followed, during which he and his assistant studied the scroll silently. The whole pub had gone quiet, everybody stared at them anxiously. Then the sheriff quickly turned the scroll upside down and said: "Well, here's what it says: 'A complaint against Timothy Louse and John Barker, by . . . I will not mention the name . . . Sir, these two scoundrels keep their tobacco shop open all the night, light a fire there, while not having a chimney, and allow the scum of society to drink spirits that they sell without license, to the great disquietude and annoyance of the whole hardworking neighborhood. Signature: Jack Swift, a licensed dealer in spirits.' Well," the sheriff raised his head, "what do you say, gentlemen?"

"Impertinent slander!" Mr. Louse said. "A lie from the first to the last word!"

"How so?" the sheriff objected. "Is this not a tobacco shop? Are you not open all night?"

"With permission," Mr. Barker said. "We pay the municipality six pounds a month, sir. Loads of orphans can be fed with that money."

"Yes," Mr. Louse intervened, "what happens to this money, sir? Where does it go?"

"It goes where it needs to." The sheriff raised his hand. "And is it true, gentlemen, that you sell spirits in your shop? Without a license?"

"Defamation!" Mr. Louse exclaimed. "These gentlemen carry drinks with them. How can I forbid them to carry whatever they wish? I am a trader, sir, not a bailiff."

A clamor of approval arose from the tables.

"He's not a bailiff, he's not a bailiff," voices called.

*That was a mistake*, I thought. However, as if reading my mind, Señor Barker quickly said: "But everyone is welcome here. Bailiffs are welcome, too."

"Even more welcome than others," Mr. Louse added and nodded.

"Come to our table, sir," Mr. Barker invited the sheriff, "to discuss things calmly."

This was apparently exactly what the sheriff was waiting for, since he headed for our table immediately. I hardly need mention that things were settled after a short while, nor how. In Spain it is done in exactly the same way. As Dr. Monardes once remarked during our journey to England, with respect to certain of my concerns: "There aren't cannibals in England, they will not eat us." Well, he was right. These are civilized people.

But of course, there are some differences. That stupid sheriff somehow turned the conversation to the Great Armada and how they sank it and so forth.

"What nonsense!" I exclaimed. "That's why it was sent in the first place—to sink."

"Whatever do you mean?" the sheriff said with surprise.

"Señor," I said, "they kept that Armada at anchor in a Portuguese port for two years, without supervision. Do you know what it means to keep something in a Portuguese port without supervision? And for two years! Good God!" My emotions were running high. "I doubt you have the slightest idea, señor. Everyone swiped whatever he could. I have a friend who built his house with boards from the Armada. I myself have a shirt made of a mast from the Armada. Even today, the Portuguese in Sevilla sell shirts made from the Armada's sails."

"They're fakes, however," Dr. Monardes intervened, "because now they count as souvenirs and sell for a higher price."

"That's right," I agreed, "but it was true in the beginning. Believe me, señores, if it had been an English fleet, it would never have gotten out of the port after two years in Portugal. While the Spanish Armada got out and even went sailing."

"It was not necessary for your people to pursue it at all," Dr. Monardes broke in again. "It would have sunk on its own."

"Excuse me, but I remain a bit skeptical of your words. How could such a thing be possible?" Mr. Shift wondered.

"It is actually very simple, sir," I replied. "At one point Señor de Leca, the first minister, refused to give more money for the Armada, so they wondered what to do with it. Finally they decided to load whoever they didn't need on it and send them out to drown at sea. They wanted to cleanse Spain a little. So they loaded up as much Castilian scum as they could, they loaded up misbehaving nobles, they loaded up Lope . . . Have you heard of Lope?"

"It rings a bell, but I'm not sure," Señor Jonson replied.

"Lope de Vega. The man who wrote four hundred and twenty plays in one year!"

"That can't be!" Mr. Jonson exclaimed. "That's absolutely impossible!"

"Ha!" Dr. Monardes chimed in. "You don't know Lope. Sometimes I think they built the whole Armada just to get rid of Lope."

"Yes," I said, "and when we heard the Armada was sunk, we all breathed a sigh of relief, saying: 'It's over, Lope is done for at last!' But it was not to be! He survived and came back."

"And does he still write four hundred plays a year?" Señor Jonson asked.

"No," I admitted. "Now he only writes one or two hundred."

"So it still had some effect," the sheriff said, taking a sip from what I believe was his third cup. "Laws should be respected, gentlemen. Superiors should be obeyed. Their orders should be carried out. Even when they seem to be wrong, they usually have something else in mind and are actually right. Isn't it so?" he turned to me.

I hesitated, wondering what to say, but affability got the best of me and I quickly replied: "Yes, it is, of course." And I gave a sweeping gesture of approval.

# 3c.
# The Following Summer

"Look what I just read in a book by a northern philosopher," Dr. Monardes turned to me. "'He who is not ready to die for a cause is not ready to live, either!' Can you imagine?"

"That can't be!" I said.

"See for yourself," the doctor replied and turned the book towards me.

It really did say that.

"What nonsense!" I exclaimed. "He who is ready to die for something is a total idiot!"

"Yes, unless that thing is medicine, but in that case it is usually someone else who dies," Dr. Monardes noted somewhat ambiguously. "If there truly is a Creator, just imagine how furious he must be every time someone dies for the latest bombastic nonsense, or rather, bombastic madness."

"Although some people die for money, inadvertently . . ." I said a bit hesitantly.

"Which is the height of idiocy!" Dr. Monardes snapped. "Do they think their dead arses will shit gold ducats? Take it from me, Guimarães," the doctor continued. "The rich are the same eat-to-shits as everybody else–if not even bigger eat-to-shits." *Eat-to-shit* is a complex concept invented by Dr. Monardes and made up of two words. According to the definition Dr. Monardes offers in one of his treatises, "it describes man from one end to the other as a natural machine and almost fully exhausts his significance as a creature in the wider framework of Nature."

"To tell you the truth," the doctor went on, "when I hear of some fat cat getting killed in a pub or on the street, it always fills me with a certain satisfaction. The son of a bitch, I say to myself. He merely got what he long deserved. Go on back to Nature, your mother! Of course, I myself am rich," the doctor added, "but my case is entirely different."

"These northern people really are crazy, it seems," I said, returning to the previous topic. "They're absolutely fanatical!"

"The Spaniards are even more so." Dr. Monardes shook his head. "You and I are not typical in that respect. You are simply Portuguese. As for me, you mustn't forget that my father was Genoese, while my mother was a Jewess."

"I never forget that for a minute," I thought to myself. However, I said: "But didn't you say the Spaniards don't exist, señor?"

"That doesn't prevent them from having certain qualities," the doctor replied and once again took up his book.

Looking out over the ocean, I thought about everyone who had died for one thing or another. The martyrs, for example. Torn apart by lions, pierced by spears . . . What madmen! Then the heretics burned at the stake. The patriots. A whole ladder of madness. Each one going a step higher than those before him. And what about those who died for some idea? One doesn't know whether to pity or despise them.

"I wonder whether anyone has died for the Renaissance or humanism, señor." I turned to Dr. Monardes.

"Oh yes," he replied. "I've heard of such cases in Italy. Which are most likely due to exceptional stubbornness, rather than anything else."

"But you wouldn't do that, would you?"

"Do what?" Dr. Monardes asked, puzzled.

"Die for the Renaissance and humanism."

"Me? Die for the Renaissance and humanism? Do you even hear what you're saying?" the doctor cried, a bit outraged even. "I wouldn't give my little toe for the Renaissance and humanism.

Look here, Guimarães," he continued, after calming down, "there are two types of fashion. You must learn to tell them apart. The first . . ."

"I know, señor. You already told me that."

"Did I?" the doctor said, taken aback. "Very well then. So you know. But this book is truly insufferable!" he said and threw it into the ocean with a flourish, then rummaged in his bag and took out another one. The doctor has a lot of books.

He began reading once again, and I turned back towards the ocean. I imagined the fish eating those books and going crazy. I imagined all the fish swimming to the surface to sacrifice themselves for something. But there are no fishermen in sight. They flail around helplessly, the water is frothing and foaming with them, everything is teeming with fish unable to do anything. "What is success to you?" one cries out. "Success," replies another, "is filling good people's bellies and winning their respect, having them like you; making them drool when they see you." Afterwards the fish disappear back down into the depths—suddenly sobered up, perhaps—while I remain on deck as before. The ocean is endless, flat, gray, and cold under the cloudy sky. This time I don't think about anything. But when I don't think about anything, that "Urbi et Orbi, the Holy Father, Urbi et Orbi, the Holy Father" starts up in my head again. What a nuisance! How can you get rid of your mind? A tricky task. Has anyone ever died to get rid of his mind? The martyrs, for example. The heretics burned at the stake. Did they die to get rid of their minds? Some of them, perhaps. This is something I'm more inclined to accept. After all, "Urbi et Orbi, the Holy Father" isn't the worst thing to have stuck in your head.

"Guimarães," the doctor said suddenly, raising his head from the book, "do you think I talk too much?"

"On the contrary, señor," I assured him. "I think you don't talk enough."

The doctor nodded and went back to his reading.

Yes, that is what I truly think. The doctor is certainly no chatterbox. Nor am I. This, I feel, makes both of us good company. Although I would perhaps prefer to be with Francisco Rodrigues, who was constantly telling all sorts of cock-and-bull stories. And who pricked himself on that nail, which I, in my carelessness, have placed my hand next to and from which I immediately pull it away. Dear God, one's life is always hanging by a thread. And they think they are risking it . . .

"How is the book, señor?" I asked Dr. Monardes as I passed by him.

"Oh, this one is better," he replied. "By the Roman Epictetus."

"I can't stand anyone who complains. There is always a door open, you can always leave, if you don't like it."

"Those aren't his exact words, but that's the general meaning," the doctor replied, rather surprised. "A door and so on . . . Well, well."

He thinks I am practically illiterate, but he is mistaken. He thinks I am foolish and ignorant like all Portuguese, but that is not true. I am much smarter than most Portuguese. It's true, it's true. Smiles here are unwarranted.

I nodded at the doctor and headed back to our cabin.

# 37. Costa del Sol, Costa del' Luz

As you round Cape San Vicente, Spain begins. The *Hyguiene* sails on the blue waters–onward, onward, *Hyguiene*! The day is sunny, the sky clear. The water splashes cheerfully around our keel. The wind spreads the sails. Beaches, low forests, and cliffs stretch before us. That's how it is along the whole southern coast. Costa del Sol, Costa del' Luz.

Namesakes of our commander-in-chief, Duke de Alba–albatrosses–soar high in the sky. They are heading for Costa del Sol. From Costa del' Luz. Costa del' Luz is on this side–by Cadiz, with Sevilla above–it is facing the ocean. Costa del Sol is on the other side, by.Malaga and Granada, and looks onto *Mare Nostrum*. These are the two bluish-green eyes in Spain's swarthy face. Spain is a bit cross-eyed. Turned to the south through Andalusia, with one eye she gazes to the west, towards the ocean and the Americas–Costa del' Luz; and with the other, to the east, towards the Mediterranean and Europe–Costa del Sol. The sun shines upon both of them. As our caravel "ploughs the waves" as they say, even though there are no waves today, the eye before us constantly changes color–from blue to green and back again. Pelletier du Mans, if only you could see it now!

*L'Amour des amours*, Costa del' Luz. A long strip of coast looks completely white. The birds circle in the sky above it, as if it were the skeleton of a giant fish. Those are low cliffs of white limestone, with strips of sand between them whitened by mussels or the sun. Beyond–low sandy hills sparsely scattered with olive trees, fishing villages here and there, with absolutely identical white, flat-roofed houses, and then the coast once again, low gray cliffs, green forests, beaches white as salt. And in the distance, where the wind is blowing us—Cadiz. In the very center of Costa del' Luz, open before us—listen to this, Pelletier!—open before us like the core of a watermelon, with seeds of ships, people and houses, sweet and juicy, like a drop from the wild heart of Nature.

# 373.
# Clarification?

Imagine my surprise, when a month after our return to Sevilla I go to call our coachman Jesús from the Maria Immaculata Theater, where he earns a little extra cash in his free time—and I go to call him not just because I feel like it, but because the doctor and I have to go see some damnable sick man in Peñana—so I walk into the theater and hear that inimitable thundering voice: "Enrique, Jesús! Bring out the bucket!"

I turn in the direction of the voice, and whom do I see? Rather disconcerting attire, extravagant yet at the same time clearly cheap, a slightly feverish expression, a body anxiously leaning forwards, hands firmly gripping the backrest of a chair—it is Lope. I have never seen him, but I can hardly be mistaken.

"Lope," I say. "Is it you?"

Everyone speaks to Lope like that—using his first name and without introducing himself. He also answers them in the same way and doesn't introduce himself either. But on the other hand, everybody already knows him.

"Who else could it be?" He answers as loudly as ever, throwing me a cursory glance. "What, do I look like St. Agnes to you?" He turns towards our coachman. "Jesús, what would you say in this situation?"

Jesús, as far as I can tell, is playing a villager with a bucket.

He shrugs. "I'd say: 'By all the saints, my wife refuses to do the laundry.'"

"You can do better than that!" Lope bellows.

"By all the saints," Jesús says, raising his arms towards the sky, "my wife is sick, she refuses to do the laundry!"

"Dead!" Lope shouts.

"By all the saints," Jesús repeats, "my wife is dead, she refuses to do the laundry!"

"That's good." Lope turns to the side. "Write that down. We'll smooth it out later."

Off to the side, sitting in the darkness, is his assistant, who writes down the lines.

"Lope," I shout (since everyone here is shouting), "just what were you doing in England?"

"I've never been to England. I've only been around it," he replies. He most likely means his return with the Armada, when they sailed around the entire British Isle.

"Come on, come on, don't give me that hogwash," I say.

A clarification for the reader: I am skeptical and astute, dear reader, it's difficult to foist such hogwash off on me. Very difficult.

Lope seems to sense this, since he doesn't reply, but merely shrugs his shoulders.

"Jesús," he yells toward the stage, "kick the bucket and cry!"

Jesús kicks the bucket and starts howling like a coyote.

Lope shakes off his shirt with one hand and wipes his brow with the other. "Who told you to fill up the bucket, you dunces!" he shouts.

"Enrique!" Jesús replies immediately.

"Lope," I shout, "you have to write something about England."

"Maybe. Tomorrow," he replies. "Tomorrow I'll write a play about England."

"What about the one about Maria de Blanca, señor?" his assistant calls out.

"So the day after tomorrow, then," Lope says, looking at me in earnest for the first time. "I'll write a play about England the day after tomorrow."

"Lope," I say, "I'm going to need Jesús."

"Take him," he replies.

Jesús stumbles on a step coming down from the stage, but keeps his balance. He says something that I will not write down here.

"What . . ." he continues, but I cannot hear him, since his words are drowned out by Lope's voice. I signal to him to go outside. Outside, the warm sun shines on my face. The hubbub of the street sounds like the babbling of a brook. I sigh.

"We're going to Peñana, Jesús," I say.

He again says something that I will not write down. I shrug and the two of us set out for Dr. Monardes' large white house. Or more precisely, the one where he is at the moment. Some clod is walking right in front of me, constantly getting in my way.

"Hey, you clod," I say, "stop bumping into me!"

He opens his mouth to reply, but here Jesús breaks in and again says something that I will not write down. If one decided to write a work in which one describes what the citizens of Sevilla say, half of the book would consist of ellipses.

The fellow steps aside and mutters something under his breath. Jesús and I walk on ahead. The pleasant sunshine continues to warm my blood.

"Jesús," I say, "have you nothing else to say?"

"What else can I say, f . . ."

No, there's no escape.

Dr. Monardes is waiting for us at the door to his yard, on the street. He is surrounded by children and is giving them candies. When he sees us approaching, he chases them off with his cane, shouting, "Shoo, scram, I've got work to do." The doctor carries a cane to add to his elegance and authority, not for any other reason.

"It's about time, Guimarães," he shouts. "I thought you'd left for Portugal."

"What would I do there? There's nothing in Portugal," I say and help Jesús harness the horses. "Lope is here."

"It can't be!" the doctor exclaims.

"He's here, he's here," Jesús cuts in. "We're putting on a tragedy."

"Where?" the doctor asks.

"At Maria Immaculata," I answer.

"Well, come on, then, let's quick go see what these pests want and get back as soon as possible. The early bird . . ."

"Gets the worm," I say, finishing off his phrase.

A minute later we are already on the road. I stretch my arm out through the window of the carriage. I feel the oncoming wind. The sun shines pleasantly and I close my eyes. I feel the sunlight and the shadows from the branches along the road dancing on my eyelids, I sense the gust of movement on my fingers. I hear the clattering of the wheels, of the horses. Next to me, Dr. Monardes lights up a cigarella. I open one eye for a moment and look over at him. He is turned to the side, looking out the other window of the carriage; he is split in two vertically by the light and shadow. I close my eyes again and listen to our journey. Urbi, Urbi et Orbi, the Roman Epictetus.

# 4.
# Female Swelling

In Peñana, it was not a sick man who awaited us, but a sick woman. She was lying swollen in a bed with the curtains pulled aside, groaning. Her enormous white stomach seemed to take up half the bed.

"Relax, woman," the doctor said, putting his hand to her forehead, "we'll set things aright. What month of swelling are you in?"

"The eighth," she replied and kept moaning.

Since I knew what to do in such cases, I asked them to bring kindling, lit a fire, and waited next to it with a large tobacco leaf across my knees.

"What's your name?" I heard the doctor's voice behind me.
"Maria," the woman replied.

"Why do I even bother asking?" the doctor murmured.

When the fire was sufficiently kindled, I pushed aside two coals with a pair of tongs and began turning the leaf above them like a pig on a spit. The leaf must be heated up, it must get hot, but not burn. Since I am quite experienced at this task—"roasting the tobacco," as Dr. Monardes calls it—I was ready very soon. It used to take me two or three leaves to get the desired result. However, with practice one can achieve unbelievable skill in all manner of things.

I took the hot leaf, tossing it from hand to hand, went over to the bed, and carefully placed it on the swollen woman's navel.

"Ouch!" she said.

"This is Señor da Silva," the doctor explained, "my assistant. This leaf will warm you up, it will draw all your humors up and via the umbilical cord it will reach precisely where it needs to go."

But the leaf did not have the desired effect. Typically, it is not sufficient on its own. The woman kept groaning, and after waiting a bit to confirm that the leaf alone would not do the trick, the doctor dug around in his inside pocket and took out a cigarella.

"Woman, this," he said, holding the panacea upright with three fingers before her eyes like a spear, "is a cigarella! I would like you to take a very gentle puff on it, hold the smoke in your mouth without inhaling, and then let it out. Do this two or three times. Then you must swallow the saliva. But puff very gently," the doctor said again, handing her the lit cigarella, "otherwise you could harm the fetus."

"It won't make her miscarry, will it?" The husband, who had been standing with me in the opposite corner of the room, turned to me in alarm.

"Nonsense!" I said, cocking my head to the side, as was my wont in such cases. "Why would she miscarry?! What you see before you is Nature itself, not some basket of eggs! This is strong stuff!"

I thought of that sonnet by Pelletier in *L'Amour des amours*, where he describes how the Earth in its youth collided with some kind of heavenly body in the form of a medusa and miscarried the Moon. "Tossed from the womb unripe," those are his exact words. He's talking about the moon, of course, that it is unripe. Otherwise, Pelletier says, the Earth would have given birth to another planet. Mars, who had caused the Earth to swell, was extremely disappointed, he turned his back and grew completely cold to her. From then on, the couple, at one time fused by the hot flame of love, parted ways. The Moon, born prematurely, circled stillborn in space. But nowhere does he say what happened to that Medusa. The first time I read the book, I impatiently leafed through the whole thing to the very end to see whether it mentioned what had happened to Medusa, but I didn't find anything. I was so fired up that after that I carefully reread the whole thing line by line, but again didn't find anything. I did, however, discover a great poet. Every cloud has a silver lining, as they say.

The cigarella did the trick. The woman calmed down, her pains subsided. She was lying on the bed with a sweaty brow and her big white belly, swollen like . . . like I don't know what–like Achilles' shield, like a round hill above a river, like a marble cask, like a stack of hay. Nature had filled her up and stretched her seams to bursting. How awful–I thought to myself–to be so close to Nature, to be so completely under her power. Nature does what she likes and won't spare you for a second. Unless mighty tobacco is firmly squeezing her throat with his sturdy fingers!

"It's quieted down," the woman said, placing her hand on her belly, slightly below the tobacco leaf.

"I'll say! How could it not . . ." The doctor said, shaking his head.

Then he turned to the husband and said, "I'll leave this cigarella here, in case you need it. But don't you smoke it up prematurely!" He raised an admonishing finger at the man.

"No! Of course not!" the chap replied, releasing a torrent of words and empty twaddle. The doctor listened to him with an air of boredom, pursing his lips. I, however, lost patience and lashed out at him.

"Shut up!" I said. "We're not here to listen to your drivel."

And he shut up. The last thing we needed was to miss crazy old Lope thanks to this windbag.

When we got outside, the doctor said to me: "Guimarães, I must reprimand you. You should not have lashed out at the man like that. The woman is sick, but he is the one paying. Never forget who is paying. When all is said and done, he is the important one for us."

"Of course he'll pay, to hell with him, what else can he do?" I replied.

"That's true, but still," the doctor insisted. "This will be very important for you in the future, in principle."

Then we got into the carriage, set out for Sevilla, and willy-nilly we began talking about Woman.

"The human female," the doctor said, "is Nature's favorite weapon. I am sure that in her eyes, woman ranks highest in the hierarchy of all creatures, far higher than you or me. There is no creature higher than she. You will object that females of all species reproduce, some of them far more profusely than the human female. For example, bees, caterpillars, and so forth. That might be true—but then again it might not—but that is not the point. Woman not only reproduces Nature, but besides she can sing, speak, play music, deck herself out in front of the mirror . . . and think," the doctor continued after a short pause. "She can laugh, leap, talk, sing. That verges on the impossible."

"Yet Nature does not spare her, either, she torments her as well," I said. "She is that reckless."

"Oh, she doesn't do it out of recklessness," the doctor replied. "You must have a proper understanding of such things if you wish to become a good physician." He raised his index finger. "Nature acts through abundance. She gives birth to such an abundance of creatures that she can afford to be indifferent to every one of them individually. Human females, for example, are so numerous, that even if half of them were to disappear in the next second, this would not have any particular consequences, except that it might become a bit quieter."

I thought of Jesús at the theater and how he exclaimed: "By all the saints! My wife is dead, she refuses to do the laundry!"

"Certain inconveniences would result, too" I said.

"Minor ones," the doctor replied. "In any case, there would be enough women left for Nature to continue reproducing. Like the leaves on the trees, Guimarães. Who pays attention to a single leaf? Even if they all were to fall at once, they would come back again next year."

"Yes, but certain things are very rare, unique," I objected.

"That odious old man Plato says the same thing," Dr. Monardes nodded. "By the way, nearly all old men are odious, for easily discernable reasons. But I'll expand on that thought some other time. As for the things you were talking about—well, Nature will fritter them away in any case. As she cannot multiply them to abundance, she doesn't know what to do with them. So there's no sense in talking about that. That's the whole point, that's the secret and the key—the abundance. Everything tends toward abundance. Life tends towards abundance and death tends toward abundance. Absolutely everything. Because of this, nothing makes much sense. With the exception of medicine, of course."

"Your wisdom tends toward abundance as well, señor, yet it is still very meaningful," I said. I had assumed the stance I assume when I am deeply impressed. I learned it from Francisco Rodrigues. He claimed that it was very ancient, that it came from antiquity itself and was thought up by some Rodin character, if I'm not mistaken. This Rodin character himself was supposedly Greek. I don't know where Francisco Rodrigues learned all these things. I assume he learned them on Magellan's ship. Three years at sea is a long time. Everyone would have talked about everything he'd ever seen, heard, read or that had ever crossed his mind. When you think about how something that took you a year can then be retold in five minutes, or a half an hour at most, it's even a bit frightening. Once you start telling your story, you can easily reach the conclusion that you've wasted your life and your time.

"Abundance, Guimarães," the doctor went on, rather encouraged by my reaction, it seems to me, "that is the secret of all things and their inherent goal. If they were made in a slightly different way, that would have been their only goal, but since they are so abundantly made, they . . ."

"Señores," at that moment we heard Jesús' voice as he stopped the carriage, "I've got to make a quick stop . . . I can't hold it any longer."

He passed by us with rather stiff movements, crossed the road, and squatted in the tall green grass.

Does even that tend toward abundance? I wondered.

"Jesús," Dr. Monardes called to him. "What are you doing in that grass? You'll pick up some tick."

"I can't s . . . on the road, señor," he replied. His backside gleamed a faint white amidst the grass in the dusky air, like an old, time-worn silver coin on a hunk of dung, as Pelletier would say (perhaps).

"Why not?" the doctor replied. "The road is already covered with crap."

"I can't," Jesús said again. "It'll scare the horses."

"I see . . . what?" the doctor exclaimed.

"The horses, it'll scare the horses, señor."

"Ah, I understand," the doctor said, but from the look he gave me it was clear that he didn't understand much. I didn't understand either, but the absolute last thing in the world, really the very last, that I would sit down to think about is what Jesús the coachman is trying to say.

"Come on, Jesús," the doctor shouted after a while. "We'll miss Lope."

"Oh no, by no means, señor," Jesús shouted back. "I'm coming, I'll be right there."

After a minute or two he really did appear, hastily hitching up his pants.

"It's only human, señores!" he said as he passed by us.

"Yes," the doctor replied. "Where there's one, there's also the other."

I quickly grasped his meaning and laughed. Leaving modesty aside for the moment, I must share with the reader—so he will not be wondering in the future—that I grasp things quite quickly; I discover that which was left unsaid and master new knowledge at an impressive speed and, as people who know me say, with astonishing insightfulness. I am not proud of this, nor do I boast about it; rather, I have humbly come to accept these qualities of mine as a fact of life. After all, I could not be anything other than what I am. Fortunately, and unlike many others, I do not have to be something else. This thought fills me with deep satisfaction, despite the fact that for now I am rather poor. However, this usually does not last long for people like me. Take Dr. Monardes, for example . . .

"Sevilla, señores."

Yes, indeed.

At the Maria Immaculata Theater, Jesús is standing on stage with his arm raised toward the sky, yelling: "By all the saints! My wife is dead, she refuses to do the laundry!"

He lets out a sob and starts tearing his shirt, which was probably sewn especially for the occasion from some yellow and red checkered tavern tablecloth. Next, he kicks the bucket, which is once again full of water, and splashes several people in the front rows, who begin grumbling in dissatisfaction, but at that moment Lope's people on the left side of the stalls drown them out by hollering ecstatically and clapping their hands as they jump to their feet. Gradually, everyone stands up and begins clapping. I do, too, willy-nilly. Jesús, grinning from ear to ear, runs to the side and leaves the stage. Don Garcia de Blanco chides his beautiful daughter for not wanting to marry the wily Moor Alfonso, who pretends to be a nobleman from Aragon, but who is really a merchant from Granada, a Morisco. Standing next to the don is the local priest, Father Rodriguez, his hands meekly clasped across his chest; he also urges the beautiful maiden Maria to marry the "nobleman" Alfonso. The wily Moor has promised him one hundred ducats for his help. Afterwards the pair intends to swindle Don Garcia and divide his properties between them. The beautiful maiden sobs. She runs off stage, followed by the priest and a brooding Don Garcia, who walks slowly, his hand on his brow.

Then, amidst showers of applause, her true love appears on stage—the Caballero Morales, riding a horse, his unsheathed sword in one hand and the banner of Hernàn Cortes in the other.

The horse is covered in a yellow cloak that's embossed with the red lions of the Habsburgs, while Enrique's dirty, decrepit boots are visible beneath it, along with two other feet. No, they are not Jesús's. He got lucky this time.

Caballero Morales gives a speech about love. He has fought in the name of love in America, against the Turks, against the Berbers, in Italy, and in the Low Countries. He has killed many an enemy. After wild applause, he waves his sword and the banner of Hernàn Cortes. The horse romps from one end of the stage to the other. From my seat in the balcony I can see very well who is whinnying beneath the footlights to the left—it is Jesús, of course. Good choice.

Lope's people down below have been on their feet since the caballero's appearance and have not stopped clapping and shouting the whole time. I am also on my feet. Finally, Caballero Morales swears upon the Holy Blood that he will win the heart and hand of the beautiful maiden Maria or die, and exits the stage, so I can sit down again. Relieved, I light a cigarella. The surrounding darkness carries me off, the stage seems to drift away from me, and I hear the lines floating from it like a faraway hum, like the babbling of a brook, wrapped in the vapors of the cigarella.

People are like this small, darkened theater—I think to myself—they put on their plays inside. And when you step outside, Nature begins. There everything is bathed in a completely different light. No matter whether it's day or night—a completely different light begins. The streets begin, and the buildings, the Guadalquivir, the bridges in the distance, people scurrying to and fro, the hills begin, the roads, the clouds, the olive groves, the vineyards, the rivers, the wind . . . And it has no end. It stretches forth infinitely, in all directions. Nature.

I notice with a start that everyone around me is on their feet and quickly get up. The cigarella hinders me, so I toss it down into the stalls. I don't know what happens to it afterwards. But I do know what is happening on stage.

Caballero Morales is embracing the maiden Maria, his sword still in his hand. Next to them, run through, lies the perfidious Moor. Don Garcia de Blanco, raising his palm, solemnly blesses them. Off to the side, Jesús, followed by a few more representatives of the peasantry, gives the treacherous priest a boot to the backside, kicking him off the stage step by step while waving the banner of Hernàn Cortes. At that moment Jesús' wife appears. Come on now, Lope, that's really too much—I think to myself—now you've even got people rising from the dead. But no, she hadn't died, but rather had gotten lost in the forest. The two of them embrace; then she starts bawling him out about something. The caballero and Maria, locked in an embrace, approach them. Smiling, the caballero takes Cortes' banner from Jesús and gives him two small coins as a sign of gratitude. While Jesús and his wife bow before him, the horse once again appears on stage, this time with six legs beneath it. Caballero Morales and Maria get on, the caballero says a few lines to the audience about their happy future, and the pair exits stage right, waving. Jesús had said that morning that it would be a tragedy, but Lope clearly changed his mind at the last minute.

Then Don Garcia begins reciting his closing monologue. However, the audience in the stalls has started to leave—nobody feels like listening to closing monologues. Lope's people vainly try to stop them by blocking their way—but there are too few of them. They've got to get rid of that old-fashioned practice of closing monologues. People don't want to listen to monologues anymore—they want action, they want something to happen. It's not like it used to be. This actor, however, is good—he quickly finishes his monologue and shouts "Long live the king!" Everyone stops in their tracks. Lope jumps up on stage and starts bowing, his hand on his heart. Soon all the actors have joined him, holding hands. Jesús is there, too. That's our Jesús—I'd say he did a very fine job. The others were very good as well. When all is said and done, Lope isn't so bad. Although he's far from perfect, he really does have a knack for certain things. If I think about it, I could even say what things precisely. The audience around me is applauding enthusiastically. Well, well, Dr. Monardes is climbing up on stage to shake hands with Jesús. I would go up there myself, but I'm too far away. I wave to them to get their attention. Jesús finally sees me and points me out to the doctor. They both lift their hands in greeting; I do the same. I wonder where Dr. Monardes' daughters are. Some imbecile kicks me in the shin. Yes, I need to make my way towards the exit.

This mob could trample you like nothing. I sweep along with the crowd, my hand on my purse, and just when I think it will never end—here I am outside, on the street. I take a breath, relieved. The night is a warm June night, a barely perceptible breeze creeps gently across my face, the light of the torches glows all around and long shadows stretch from the people like swaying X's. Up ahead, beyond the stretch of houses, several stars shine meekly in the distance, the sky looks cool, it looks lighter tonight. The night of Andalusia, Pelletier, the sky of Andalusia. What a pity you've never seen them. Or perhaps you have seen them?

What about my purse? My purse is right where it should be. The mosquitoes of the Guadalquivir buzz around my ears. I light a cigarella and they disappear. Perhaps they are already dead. I search the hubbub and the people surrounding me, trying to spot Dr. Monardes and Jesús. Then suddenly I remember those little islands down the Guadalquivir, the ones the water yieldingly skirts. I've passed by there and sometimes I've wondered what is on them, what would I see, if at the same moment I were there, looking towards the road I am travelling along? Dr. Monardes and Jesús, as I see them now, coming out of an exit on the ground floor, advancing with small steps in the tangle of people, which gradually scatters and dissolves into the street, as if someone is untangling it strand by strand. I call out, raise my hand to get their attention, and head over to them.

# 5.
# Driving away So-Called "Spirits"

Once, when we were in Utrera where we cured a man of aching joints, on the way back in the evening we passed by the church of St. Getafe there. A group of people had gathered in front of it, speaking over one another excitedly. They claimed that there was a spirit inside the church. And not a good spirit, but a bad one, who was making mischief and frightening people. They even said that it was inside at that moment.

This gave me a cold chill between my shoulder blades. I didn't like this business one bit and suggested to the doctor that we get out of there as quickly as possible.

"Under no circumstances!" Dr. Monardes replied. I could, it seemed, even sense a certain gleeful excitement in his voice. "That's just the peasants' prejudices, Guimarães," he said. "There are no spirits. You and I will go inside now to see what is really going on."

This idea did not please me in the least. There are certain things I positively do not wish to have anything to do with. However, the doctor's energetic, exhilarated look clearly told me that there was no way I could get out of going into the church. I sighed inwardly at the inescapable side effects of the scientific worldview and took the staff the doctor handed me—one of the three we carried in our carriage to defend ourselves against robbers or wild animals. The doctor twirled his staff in the air a few times, tapped it against his palm, and, visibly satisfied, strode forward. I followed after him, with Jesús behind me.

The church's large wooden door creaked shrilly as we entered. We were met with darkness, scattered here and there by the candles burning in the candelabra and by a space in front of the altar lit up as bright as day, where a priest was kneeling. He turned his head towards us. Even from the entrance I could see how frightened he was. And almost at the same instant I understood why—the communion dishes, on a long table to the side, began rattling as if there were an earthquake. The doctor set off at a brisk pace down the aisle between the pews, heading toward the table. When he got there, he swung his staff with all his might over the dishes, lowering it abruptly to the sides from time to time, as if thrashing some unseen enemy in the air. His staff whistled through the air, but the dishes beneath it continued rattling. This only seemed to put the doctor on his mettle and he ceased to stand on ceremony. His staff rained blows in all directions, on the table, on the dishes, everywhere.

"Come on, Guimarães, go around to the other side," the doctor shouted. I quickly grasped his meaning, and since it was impossible to pass by the doctor without—literally—risking my life, I jumped along the seats of the pews to the other side of the room and headed for the table with the dishes, swinging my staff above my head. The noise was indescribable—the doctor's staff was crashing down on the table and the dishes, which went flying and fell to the floor with a crash, the padre was praying in a loud voice, and Jesús was lighting all the candelabra with a huge, hissing candle. I felt a rush of courage and absolute confidence in the success of our undertaking and brought my staff down on the right side of the table with all my might, while the doctor swung his on the left. A moment later our staffs crashed together and it was a true wonder they did not break. But ash is a hard wood. At that instant the candles on a candelabrum about a dozen yards from us went out, as if snuffed out by a gust of wind. Whatever had been rattling the dishes had now moved towards the right wall of the church.

"Over there, Guimarães," the doctor yelled and ran towards that place.

We both rushed that way, our staffs swinging. But the thing reappeared on the other side of the church, close to a candelabrum near Jesús—several candles went out, while the flames of the others swayed to one side. Jesús, who, as I said, was nearby, leapt in that direction, swinging his staff, and knocked over a candelabrum, which fell noisily to the ground. The doctor quickly squeezed his way between the pews, while I rushed towards Jesús, leaping along the seats. The padre kept praying in a loud voice.

"Stop crossing yourself and grab a staff!" the doctor cried at him.

I had already reached Jesús and was swinging my staff between the candelabra, but the thing, it seemed, had gone into hiding.

"Wait!" the doctor cried, lifting his hand. "Stop!"

We began looking around. There was not a living soul in sight, so to speak, with the exception of the padre, who was standing a few paces in front of the altar, clutching a crosier.

"Let's call an exorcist, señor," the padre called out.

"We don't need any exorcist." The doctor shook his head and, upon brief reflection, added: "Here's what we'll do: the padre will go down the aisle between the pews; Guimarães, you go along the candelabra on the right side; Jesús, you walk along those there; and I'll pass in front of the altar."

And so we did. I again ran along the right wall of the church, swinging my staff over my head. Since I was being careful not to knock over some candelabrum, I didn't see what was going on elsewhere, but I heard staffs whistling through the air, the clicking of the doctor's heels on the stone slabs before the altar, the padre's loud prayers, and, at one point, the crash of a toppled candelabrum as well—clearly, Jesús must have knocked one over. There was no trace of the thing, however—it either had left or was hiding. So that's what I told the doctor: "Señor!" I shouted. "The thing has either disappeared or is hiding."

"It hasn't disappeared," the doctor replied. "But this isn't going to work."

The four of us stopped in our tracks and began looking around in hopes of catching a glimpse of some movement somewhere. I thought I saw a candle flicker and took a swing in that direction, but no, it was the candle's own doing.

"What is it?" cried the doctor.

"Nothing, señor," I replied. "I was just seeing things."

"Listen here," the doctor said in a moment, stroking his beard. "Guimarães and I will light a cigarella each at either end of the aisle and will walk towards each other. Come on, Guimarães."

I hopped over the pews to the far end of the aisle, took out a cigarella, and waited for the doctor to give the signal.

"Ready?" Dr. Monardes cried from the other end, a cigarella in his mouth and a candle in one hand. "Now!"

I lit the cigarella and slowly started walking towards the doctor.

"Here's some for you as well," he called out and tossed one cigarella each to Jesús and the padre.

"That's more like it!" Jesús cried, while the padre reached for the cigarella with both hands, dropping the crosier, which fell to the floor with a clatter.

"Jesu Christe!" he exclaimed.

The tobacco smoke began wafting through the air between us and over our heads.

"Light another one, Guimarães," Dr. Monardes cried from the other end of the aisle, his head swathed in smoke as if he were walking in his very own tiny cloud of fog. I lit another cigarella. I felt like I would take flight. I even had the feeling that my feet were leaving the ground and that if I looked down I would see that I had started levitating like Simon Magus. At that moment we heard something squeaking against one of the church's stained glass windows, as if a wad of paper were being rubbed against it. The sound lasted only an instant, and when we looked over to where it was coming from, we heard it again, only this time from the other side.

"Jesús," the doctor cried, "open the door!"

"Right away, señor," he shouted in a raspy voice, and I turned around, wiping my watering eyes, to see what would happen.

Jesús opened the door, it once again creaked shrilly, and a rush of cold evening air burst into the church and made the candles' flames flutter. But no, they fluttered in the other direction, towards the outside—as I realized shortly, seeing how some gust of wind raced through the candelabra on the other side, moving from the very back near the altar and along the left wall of the church toward the door. Then it disappeared. The candles' flames straightened up, becoming almost still.

"Praise be to God!" the padre said, pressing his palms together.

The doctor snorted and came towards me, his heels clicking, two cigarellas in his mouth, a staff in one hand, a candle in the other and that cloud of fog above his head, which looked as if it were hurrying to catch up with him.

"Señores," the doctor said after taking the cigarellas from his mouth, "our work here is finished. I don't think this type of illusion will happen again in this church. But if it happens again," he turned towards the padre, "you know what to do." He took Jesús' staff and gave it to the priest. "Don't cross yourself, but take a staff." Then the doctor extinguished the cigarellas with spittle and also gave them to the padre. "Here are two cigarellas for you as well," he added, then turned around, passed by us with brisk steps, and went outside. "Come on, Jesús," he called from outside without turning around, walking towards the carriage. "We're not staying here for ages."

"I'm coming, señor," Jesús replied, holding the door to let me pass.

It was already completely dark outside. The group of people was still there, it had even grown, and they stared at us speechlessly.

"Thank God they didn't steal anything!" the doctor cried, already inside the carriage, leaning out through the door as he propped it open with his hand.

"What happened, what happened?" the people started asking.

"Inside there was something which . . ." I began to answer.

"Science triumphed, fools, that's what happened," the doctor cut me off. "Science triumphed."

I got into the carriage, the doctor shut the door on his side, I did the same on mine, then we felt the carriage sway slightly—Jesús had jumped up onto the coachbox. "Gee! Gee!" he cried and in a moment we set out.

The road from Utrera to Sevilla is long, and for lack of anything better to do, the doctor and I began discussing what had happened.

"That thing was unbelievably quick, señor," I said. "It went from one end of the church to the other like the wind."

"That's true," the doctor replied. "Spirits are like that."

"But didn't you say that there are no spirits?"

"In principle, that's true. But misunderstandings always occur. There are no spirits," Dr. Monardes nodded in assent. "But there are misunderstandings. Just as in science, Guimarães: There's a rule, but there are also exceptions."

"So it turns out that there are spirits after all," I said, after a certain amount of reflection.

"How's that?" the doctor replied. "There are no spirits! There are some confused, not-quite-fully-dead idiots, the result of a misunderstanding in the functioning of Nature, and even these are exceptionally rare. Have you seen flies that disappear?"

"No," I admitted.

"From time to time, especially in Spain, since it is in the south," the doctor raised his finger admonishingly, "some fly, as it is buzzing around your room, disappears. If you are in the habit, as I am, of immediately killing every fly which enters your room, sooner or later you will notice this. It's not that it has hidden or landed somewhere out of sight. That happens, too, but that's a different case altogether. Instead, it simply disappears. It's flying along and it disappears. Sometimes it reappears again afterwards, other times not. This is simply a mistake in the functioning of Nature, *functia erronea.* It's the same thing with these so-called spirits." The doctor fell silent and we travelled in silence for some time, our bodies swaying from the juddering of the carriage along the rocky road. Forward and backward, left and right; forward and backward, left and right. "In principle, five is more than three," the doctor began again. "If you don't believe me, give me five ducats, and I'll give you three. However, three watermelons are bigger than five apples, and sometimes even three apples can be bigger than five other apples."

"That's true," I nodded, somewhat surprised. "Three apples from Pedestra are usually bigger than five apples from Roquelme. Those are places in Portugal," I explained.

"See! But you wouldn't say, I hope, that three is more than five. It is simply a misunderstanding. Misunderstandings are resolved when you add certain clarifications to your rule. Sometimes lots of clarifications. There are no spirits, but sometimes clarifications are necessary. This need for clarifications is what we call a 'misunderstanding.'"

"I see," I said.

"In any case, it is not, as the ignorant peasants think, some immortal soul which flies hither and thither through the air and which can think and perhaps even feel, which has a memory and could communicate something to you. It is simply some incorporeal animal mass, some not quite fully dead thing, which can rattle the dishes or some such nonsense, but hardly anything more. It is an exceptionally rare error on the part of Nature, something like a freak with three arms, which is best destroyed immediately, otherwise it will only cause needless problems."

"But we don't know how to destroy it," I noted.

"We don't know," the doctor agreed, "but we can guess. With a staff. With fire. Like any other animal. I'm willing to bet that they can't stand fire."

"You hate spirits, señor," I said. "You hate misunderstandings," I quickly corrected myself.

"I hate them," the doctor confirmed. "I hate everything that does not exist."

I was about to say something, misled by my tongue, but managed to stop myself at the last moment, thank God. The tongue can lead you terribly astray. You have to be very careful with it.

"The non-existent is truly revolting, Guimarães," the doctor continued. "It constantly presses towards life. It wants to come here, to this planet, which is dirty enough as it is, and to foul it with its body, to buzz about with its trifling soul, to multiply and impose itself on other existing things such as you and me. The world would be clean, simple and clear, it would be shining and sterile like a surgical knife, just like on the other planets as far as we know, if only Nature here were a little more sensible, a little more restrained. But she is not. She constantly makes mistakes. And she must constantly be watched over and assisted, which is precisely the job of medicine. Nature is female in spirit, she has feminine urges. She always wants to give birth, to multiply, to give life. To preserve all living things. She wants to preserve both the lion and the antelope; both the pig and the acorn. This is a huge misunderstanding and it gives rise to many problems, my friend. Many more than we realize," the doctor raised his finger. "If it were up to her, she would even preserve the freaks. Because she does not differentiate between good and evil, beautiful and ugly, useful and useless. All of that means nothing to her. If it were up to her, she would give life to everything non-existent. The non-existent is enormous, Guimarães," the doctor turned to me. "It would inundate us like an ocean, like a flood. Remember this one thing: Never give the non-existent any chance whatsoever."

"But if we were guided by that principle, señor," I objected, "we would never have discovered the Indies, we would never have discovered tobacco, that great medicine."

The doctor shook his head, but merely said: "Remember what I told you."

"All right," I nodded.

We rode in silence for some time. And then who knows what came over my tongue—boredom probably—and I said: "Perhaps things are not that simple, señor."

I could hardly have picked a worse thing to say. Telling the doctor that what he is saying is simple is practically a mortal insult to him.

"So you think that I speak about rather simple things, is that it?" the doctor replied, keeping his face deceptively calm. I've learned to recognize that expression. "You think that I talk about superficial things?"

I had expected something like that and had even come up with what to say. I meant to say, "What I mean is that perhaps science has not yet understood certain things completely. What's more, they go beyond the sphere of medicine and in that sense do not concern us greatly." But instead I said: "No, señor. I only wanted to say that we cannot close our eyes to the obvious. There was something in that church that was rattling the dishes. Isn't that so? To call it a misunderstanding means to pretend that we didn't see it. It may not be a spirit, like the ignorant peasants think, but it is hardly just a misunderstanding. It could be something else, something more complicated. What's more, I know that when a cat crosses my path, I really do have bad luck. By God, señor, that's the truth. And old Agrippa was right, too, when he said that if a bird flies overhead from your left, from behind your back when you step outside, it's a bad sign. But if it passes to your right side, from front to back, then it's good. I've noticed that, too, señor, and if I see a bird to the left, I always go back inside."

"Guimarães, do you hear what you're saying?" the doctor exclaimed. "I can't believe my ears! Is this why I've been teaching you all these years? What is this nonsense? And by the way, Agrippa didn't say that, but Pliny the Elder in his *Natural History*, the said Pliny being the biggest fool in the world and his books a load of cock-and-bull. What have I come to—you citing Pliny to me! It appears I have been wasting my time with you."

"But how should we call such things?" I insisted.

"I told you: misunderstandings," the doctor replied categorically. "You don't understand the meaning of the word, since you only see as far as your nose, like all ignoramuses."

"I understand it, señor," I objected. "Three apples, five apples . . . But it seems too simple to me."

The doctor smacked himself hard on the forehead, then rapped twice on the ceiling of the carriage with his cane—a sign to Jesús to stop—reached past me, opened the door, and said: "Get out! Get out, get out!" he repeated, seeing my disbelieving stare.

"But señor, that's absurd!" I exclaimed.

"Which means it's just like nearly everything else," the doctor replied. "Now you'll have something to think over as you walk back to Sevilla. Get out! Your head needs a little airing out as it is."

I toyed with the idea of taking slightly tougher measures. But at that moment I heard the voice of Jesús, who was standing near the door: "Come on, amigo, you heard what the señor doctor said."

The two of them would have been too much for me. So I simply got out and stood motionless, watching the carriage drive away from me. I will not describe here the thoughts that were running through my head. They cannot even be called "thoughts" exactly.

The carriage stopped unexpectedly, perhaps fifty yards from me. Jesús climbed down and came towards me with a staff in his hand.

Has it really come to this? I looked around and saw a serviceable rock by my right foot. It would do the trick nicely if need be. But there was still time. Jesús stretched the staff out in front of him, shook it, and yelled: "This is for you."

In what sense? I waited for Jesús to get closer. He stopped two or three yards away, held the staff out to me, and said: "The doctor sent me to give this to you. You might need it."

Then he turned around and went back to the carriage with quick steps. It took off again shortly and sank into the night, only the clattering of the wheels and the horses on the road could be heard.

I could hear it getting farther away from me for a long time. At night these roads are completely deserted and the sound carried long and far in the silence. The dark mass of the trees rustled along the road. The moon was in its second quarter and lit up the road in front of me well enough, but the woods on either side sank into the darkness. I again fell to thinking about that misunderstanding, that so-called "spirit." I imagined it floating over the trees, watching me from behind. It seemed that I could feel some presence behind me with absolute certainty. The carriage could still be heard in the distance, very faintly, very far away. Yes, I could've sworn there was someone behind me. I grasped the staff firmly, counted to ten, and suddenly turned around by enormous effort of will. My heart seemed to leap to my throat. Nothing. Of course, there was nothing there, no one. Some sort of apprehension had wormed its way deep into my mind, however. If I can only reach the bend above Borsetto, where the forests end and bare hills begin. I lit a cigarella. The crackling thundered in the night like a musket—which the Spaniards discovered some time ago and which is now very much the fashion—sparks flew from the far end. I felt my tranquility starting to return. I felt certainty taking hold of me with every subsequent step. What a silly thing superstition is! You are a fool, Guimarães, I thought to myself. Here you are, supposedly a doctor, supposedly a man of medicine, yet deep in your mind lurks the most rustic, ignorant superstition. The cigarella crackled again, as if to confirm my thoughts. I felt my so-called "soul" growing light, my bodily fluids settling in their proper places, steadily taking up their preordained paths. You must be fearless—that is the most important thing in life, I said to myself. Nothing and no one notices you, it is only your fears which frighten you. Everything calmly follows its path, and as long as you don't get in the way too much or you don't accidentally end up crossing it at the wrong time, nothing will happen to you. It happens only very rarely, very rarely, but you are constantly consumed by apprehensions and fears, since your fears envelop you like a cocoon. "You scatter their wrapping/ and before the shimmering *l'Amour*/ fear flies away *toujours*." Eh, Pelletier? I wonder whether anything like this ever happened to him? I doubt it. Such things only happen to fools who don't have the good sense to hold their tongues.

I lifted my gaze. During the day it's not so, but at night the sky looks huge, strangely deep, high and remote, filled with huge voids, with vast distances. This is the true sky—the day lies. It's because of the stars, scattered on its black background at night. How many times would the road to Sevilla fit into the distance to the closest of them? I imagined someone who had to travel to, say, Andromeda. This thought filled me with a certain amount of courage. Compared to him, I was in a far better situation. Far better. What would I do in his place? What would I do if they told me: "Guimarães, here's food, water, everything you need, you have to go to Andromeda," for example? What if there were no way to get out of it? I think I would fall into despair. Perhaps I would simply lie down by the road and wait to die. Or else I would set out and endlessly trudge along the roads like the Wandering Jew. What a terrible fate the Wandering Jew had!

Only now do I realize that. And these people, these pilgrims, who shuffle along the roads for years to get to Jerusalem or somewhere—what kind of people are they? Or else in the opposite direction, like Jesús' father . . . But they know how long the way is—from Spain it will take them about two years. Besides, they seem to find it interesting to go from city to city, from country to country, to see the world. They walk for two years and afterwards talk about it their whole lives. But that wouldn't be interesting for me. Compared to them as well, I am in a much better situation. And what about Francisco Rodrigues? What to say about Francisco Rodrigues? He travelled for not two but three years, surrounded by water most of the time, no less—the monotonous blue ocean, where you can't see much of anything except water from one end to the other and some waves, say, which could swallow you up at any moment. Boring and terrifying. And when he got back, he pricked himself on a nail and died. Compared to him, I am in a much better, infinitely better situation, without any doubt whatsoever. Francisco Rodrigues had just made up his mind to get married when he died. He strung a lass along for two or three years, but kept putting off marrying her. I would often tell him: "Francisco, you've strung the girl along long enough. Marry her." But he would say: "Nothing of the kind! She'd only gobble up all my money. Womenfolk, brats, now there's the expense of a lifetime!" But in the end he'd made up his mind and kept saying: "When I get back from this voyage and bring home a little money, then I'll get married." I told him that the girl wasn't so wild as to wait for him another two years while he sailed, and we argued about that quite a bit—would she wait for him or not? And afterwards he pricked himself on that nail and suddenly died.

The girl married someone else and now she's got a wife and kids. That is, a husband and kids . . . That dark and winding wide line down there must be the Guadalquivir.

I took a rock and chucked it over there. I was starting to think I'd missed when I heard it plunk into the water. Deep water, there's something that always gives it away immediately. You can't ever mistake it. Guadalquivir.

This stupid staff has done nothing but tripped me up. I just about killed myself. It made me so mad that I felt like chucking it down into the river after the rock. I refrained, however.

Urbi et Orbi.

Hey, that girl wasn't named Maria, by the way. An unusual girl, her name was Juana. I pondered the human female. How different Nature has made the male and the female! (Here I must make a clarification for the reader. Despite not being as long as the road to Jerusalem, of course, the road to Sevilla was still by no means short. Hence I had time to think, or rather to run through my mind various things for which I otherwise wouldn't have given a brass farthing.) The female is smaller, different in every possible way. Would she be able to build the Escorial Palace, for example? I highly doubt it. I try to image a group of women carrying the enormous stones necessary for its construction, but I cannot. Not that I think much of the Escorial. On the contrary, like I said, it is the biggest ugly building in the world. Or the ugliest big building. But anyway–I don't see how the human female could build the biggest ugly building in the world. If Nature consisted solely of females, such a building would simply not exist. What does that mean? That means Urbi et Orbi, the Holy Father. The Roman Epictetus, *L'Amour des amours.* I wonder whether Magellan could have been a woman? Would the human female have discovered America at all? What does the woman have in common with seafaring, with crossing the oceans? She will tell you that it is utter nonsense. How would you get her to board some reeking, rolling deck and to set out "onward toward the horizon," as Francisco Rodrigues used to say? There's no way you can get her on board! Francisco Rodrigues even tried to write a poem on that topic (seafaring), inspired by a poem of Lope's. This took place in the Pedro's Three Horses Pub on San Francisco Square. But he only managed to come up with two lines, or rather, a line and a half:

*We'll chase the sun a-racing, onward o'er the wilding sea,*
*It's gold we are a-chasing . . .*

That was it. I told him, "Francisco, you're not cut out for this, give it up!" But he kept struggling and straining, and in the end got mad and yelled: "What more do you want? To hell with these poets, they're complete idiots!" And I, driven from my right mind by the Jerez, started arguing with him and telling him about Pelletier du Mans. This was the second time I got thrown out of a pub. And not by Francisco Rodrigues or some such thing, but by Don Pedro himself. Pedro is built like a rock, by the way. He could lift those three horses, so to speak, with one hand. "I," he said, "don't want any French dogs in here." "What does that have to do with me?" I said. "I am Guimarães the Portuguese from Portugal, the most beautiful country in the world" (like I said, I was not in my right mind). "I," he said, "don't want any Portuguese dogs in here either." And so it was. No, I don't think that females would have discovered America. "Woman," says Pelletier du Mans, "loves the home hearth." That Pelletier du Mans is awesome. But then they wouldn't have discovered tobacco, either. This thought startled me so much that I stopped in my tracks. I lit a cigarella. Then I continued on my way. How cleverly Nature has done things, I thought to myself. She made both the male and the female. If she had made only one, the world would be different . . . Ah, Sevilla. Sevilla is so far. Infinitely far. If I were a female, I surely would have shat myself from fear. Alone on the road at night, darkness all around, the trees rustling, and who knows what out there. But if I were a woman, I wouldn't have found myself in this situation in the first place. If I were a woman, I would never have set foot anywhere near Dr. Monardes, that much is certain.

It can't be! It can't be, yet it is: that is the Maria Immaculata hill. As soon as I come out around it, I will see Sevilla. I ran up ahead. There it is. The lights, the river, the bridges, the cathedral

. . . With leaps, I rushed down the road. Soon I entered the city. A drunk or a tramp was lying on the road, and since the streets are narrow in this part of town, he was blocking it completely. I nudged him with my staff: "Hey, morisco," I said, "great spot you picked to sleep, perfect for tripping people!"

He mumbled something and turned over. I jumped over him, very carefully, however, since some tramps just pretend to be drunk, and when you go to jump over them they suddenly reach out and grab you you-know-where and start squeezing and twisting until you give them your purse. This latter happens very quickly, incidentally. After that, they give you one hard, final squeeze and as you're doubled over, they jump up and run away. I've also heard of one such scoundrel, who had really bad luck and was killed on the spot by a eunuch. But I'll tell that story some other time. What I want to say is that I jumped over that good-for-nothing's feet, very carefully, and then yelled over my shoulder: "It's truly a miracle that Jesús didn't run you over."

This incident, however, reminded me, that I was in perhaps the most dangerous part of the entire journey. At night, Sevilla is a terribly dangerous city. That's all I need, I thought, to have walked all this way through field and forest in the middle of the night, unmolested, only to have something happen to me at the end in Sevilla. But it could happen as easy as anything. At night, Sevilla is far more dangerous than Nature. This is the case because Nature is frequently deserted, while Sevilla is full of people. It began to drizzle. I ran ahead through the streets. Luckily, nothing happened to me. When I reached Dr. Monardes' house, I saw Jesús walking a mare in front of the barn.

"It's about time, señor," he called, "we thought that you'd gotten lost somewhere."

"I'll give you what for . . . What's wrong with her?" I nodded at the mare.

"She's sad," Jesús replied and stroked her on the neck.

Jesús is crazy.

I walked past him and went into the barn. Clearly, I would have to sleep here tonight. Pablito snorted when he heard me come in.

"Hey, Pablito," I said and tapped him lightly on the forehead with my staff. He was here even before me, for five or six years now, and he's as good as gold.

I found a dry, level place at the far end of the barn and blissfully relaxed onto the straw. The straw is old, it's been rained on, it's slightly rotted and has a peculiar smell. I lit a cigarella, inhaled the smoke with pleasure, and listened to the raindrops murmuring softly on the roof beams. I felt the exhaustion draining out of my limbs along with the soft murmur of the rain, with the smoke of the cigarella. In Sevilla, it almost never really rains, it merely sprinkles like now. "La lluvia en Sevilla es una pura maravilla," as they say. Yes, a pure marvel! Some hazy female face emerged in my consciousness, leaned over me, and said "Good night, good night" several times. Who was she? I didn't recognize her. I tried to discern her features more clearly, but could not. I went over to the window and drew the curtain so as to see her more clearly. At that moment the door opened and Francisco Rodrigues entered the room, bathed in light. "Womenfolk, brats . . ." he said and shook his head. I turned toward the window and looked outside. But it was not Sevilla. There were fields, low hills scattered with olive groves and a dirt road which wound between them off into the distance, lit up by the bright sun. "How hot it is," I said and wiped the sweat from my brow.

# 6. On the Connection That Some Representatives of the Common Folk See Between Tobacco and the So-Called "Devil." A Concrete Example of the Driving Out of the Latter and How He Flees from Tobacco As from Incense

After the barn burned down, I did not go out with the doctor for some time. I stayed at the house to help Jesús build a new one. Many details surrounding the fire remain obscure, but let me first state that which is known: thanks to Pablito's squealing and the fact that Jesús was outside, the fire was noticed right away. Jesús came into the barn and woke me up—it is a true miracle that I escaped unscathed, since the fire was raging all around me, and its poisonous smoke could have killed me in my sleep. When I woke up, my first thought was that I'd ended up in hell—flames curled all around me and a suffocating black smoke was drifting about. My second thought was that Jesús, whose sweaty and somehow enormous-looking face was bending over me, had ended up there, too, but this surprised me far less. Fortunately,

I managed to come to my senses quickly and got out of the barn after helping Jesús free the frantic Pablito. It's no accident that they say something "burns like straw." The fire was crackling and swallowing up the barn with unbelievable swiftness, almost like the wind, and if it hadn't been for the rain, which, as luck would have it, had begun in earnest, and if Jesús hadn't been awake, thus allowing us to take measures quickly, not only would the barn have burned down, but the house next to it, too, and perhaps the neighboring ones, as well. To say nothing of me. I got extremely lucky, indeed–I must admit that the rain, Pablito, and most of all Jesús saved my life.

Other troubles awaited me, however. I hardly need describe how Dr. Monardes looked when he saw his barn burning and what kind of mood he was in thereafter. As we put out the fire in the barn, he was occupied with that thought alone, but on the following morning he began to ask himself–and to ask us, as well–how the fire had come about. I had expected something of the sort. I was also not surprised by Jesús' ugly insinuation that I was to blame for the fire. He suggested that I had lit a cigarella, fallen asleep, and that the cigarella had set fire to the straw. Of course, I categorically denied this. To be perfectly honest, I remembered that I had lit a cigarella, but I also remembered clearly that I extinguished it. If I were to admit this, however, the doctor would never believe me and I would pay very, very dearly. Farewell, studies! Farewell, medicine! Back out on the streets and into the pubs to earn my keep doing tricks with smoke . . . No, I couldn't let that happen.

The doctor, however, was very inclined to believe Jesús. I raised one eyebrow skeptically, cocked my head to the side, made a face which is very difficult for me to describe, but which I intuitively felt was very convincing, and said (all of that simultaneously): "Señor, a bit of logic, please! If I had really fallen asleep with a lit cigarella, it would have first set fire to the straw around me and I would've been the first to burn. But as Jesús himself said, the fire did indeed start at the far end of the barn where I was, but from the other side."

"It could've rolled over there or something," Jesús objected.

"Bah!" I said, waving my hand dismissively. "What is this, a hill by the river? That's not the way things work."

I will risk digressing here for a moment with the suggestion, which may come as a surprise to the reader, that my highly developed facial musculature, perfected via my masterful smoking in pubs, played an exceptionally important role in this case. Naturally, given the situation, I pushed its possibilities to the limit and tried to accompany my words with such convincing expressions so that no one would be able to resist them. Happily, I must say that this appeared to have had an effect.

The doctor lowered his eyes from me, slowly turned towards Jesús, and fixed him with his heavy, icy gaze. I felt the rage growing within him.

"Oh no, no, señor," Jesús said in a frightened voice, waving his hand in front of his face.

"That was a big mistake," I thought to myself.

"I'll kill you, you lout!" the doctor cried. "Just what were you doing awake at that hour?"

Jesús took off running and the doctor chased him with his cane in hand. As I have noted on a previous occasion, the doctor carried that cane only for elegance and, in fact, ran quite quickly.

But Jesús also runs quickly, and he is quite a bit younger, besides. The two of them crossed the lawn in front of the house and disappeared around the other side. I leaned against the pear tree I was standing near and lit up a cigarella, relieved. I had a slight headache. I wondered whether Jesús really had started the fire. But no, to be frank, that seemed rather farfetched to me.

In any case, the doctor finally got us together and said: "I don't know which of you good-for-nothings caused that fire and what exactly happened. If one of you is guilty, he can consider himself very lucky. Very lucky! The two of you will get to work immediately, this instant! I want that barn rebuilt within a month. In the meantime I'll hire a new coachman to make my calls, since you won't be available, idiot," the doctor cried, and he took a swing at Jesús with his cane, but the latter quickly jumped back. "And you both," the doctor continued, a bit more calmly, "will work day and night if need be, but in one month I don't want to see any sign that there was a fire here. No fire at all! Not a trace! Like an ice rink! Like Denmark!"

Denmark—ah yes, that was a country to the north. How could I have forgotten?

And that's indeed what happened, although it took not one month, but two. Since in any case I could not accompany the doctor during that time, I will take this opportunity to go back and recount why the two of us went to England in the first place—a not insignificant detail, I dare say. Señor Frampton had long been inviting Dr. Monardes to England, but the latter certainly would never have gone if Frampton had not sent him an intriguing letter, whose text I will cite here verbatim, since I found it one day while rummaging through the doctor's drawers (I was looking for something else, which I could not find, with the exception of some ducats, which I found along with a note saying how many there were in total and the count was exact; the doctor incidentally had gone on a house call all the way in Frontera, while that numskull Jesús was pounding away downstairs with a hammer and calling to me ceaselessly, as if I were his wet nurse). But getting back to the letter. Here is that part which particularly interested Dr. Monardes:

"I have been told about a layman," wrote Señor Frampton, "who lives in Haslingdon (a quite poor man) and who supposedly smoked all day long and squandered the money he could have used to ease his impoverished family's suffering on tobacco—as the local ignoramuses there constantly reproached him. I will refrain from commenting on their foolishness and move directly to the more interesting part of the story. This man dreamed that he was smoking tobacco, and that the devil was standing next to him and filling the pipes for him one after the other. Despite everything, in the morning he again took up his old habit, telling himself that it was just a dream. But when he lit his pipe, he was overcome with such a strong feeling that the devil was really standing next to him and doing the deed he had dreamed of him doing, that the man was struck dumb with shock for several minutes, and when he came to his senses, he got up and opened the Bible that was on the table and came across Isaiah 55:2. Upon which he hurled the tobacco into the fire and smashed his pipes against the wall."

"What does Isaiah 55:2 say?" the doctor asked.

I opened up the Vulgate and read aloud: "Why do you spend money for that which is not bread? And your labor for that which satisfies not? Listen diligently to me, and eat you that which is good, and let your soul delight itself in fatness."

"What a loathsome passage!" the doctor exclaimed. "From that, it follows that man is some king of pathetic animal who must think only about how to fill his belly."

"It seems like a metaphor to me, señor," I said. "For the Heavenly Kingdom and so forth."

"Of course it's a metaphor," the doctor replied, looking at me coldly. "Do you honestly think I can't recognize a metaphor?! But it is a bad, tasteless metaphor. As if only bread is important, and fatness."

I preferred not to argue with him.

"We must meet this man," the doctor said and stroked his beard. "Señor Frampton has long been inviting me to England. We'll go."

And that's how we ended up on the *Hyguiene*.

That man was named Thomas Jollie and we visited him, accompanied by Mr. Frampton. We saw him one very frosty morning in the yard of his house, standing stripped to the waist, splashing himself with water from a pail, snorting and bending this way and that, which in the first instant made me ask myself what on earth he was doing, but then I realized he was doing exercises.

"This chap is crazier than a German soldier," Dr. Monardes said as soon as he saw him. "That's how they toughen them up there. Whoever doesn't die from that kind of toughening up really does become very dangerous."

I regretfully tossed my cigarella into the snow. It was unthinkable to smoke before such a man. Besides, you never know what to expect from such types.

In fact, the man turned out to be good-natured, while the conversation was far more humble than we had expected. The said Thomas described his dream and how he had opened the Bible and come across Isaiah, and other things which we already knew from Señor Frampton's letter. The doctor seemed interested in what the devil looked like exactly and asked him to describe him in the greatest possible detail.

"I don't know, sir, I didn't see him too clearly," the man replied. "I'd say: a tall goatman with graying hair and a thin, longish face."

The doctor asked him what "goatman" meant exactly, and after some time we arrived at Señor Frampton's suggestion that this was something like a centaur with two feet.

"How was he dressed?" Dr. Monardes asked.

"As normally as can be, sir," Thomas replied, "except that he had hooves instead of shoes. And above that he was dressed in trousers, a workman's jacket like the ones the tradesmen wear, and a loose shirt with a low collar, all dark in color, but which color exactly I couldn't say. Don't forget that I saw him in a dream and my attention was focused mostly on his hands as he filled my pipes and kept giving them to me one after another."

"So that means he had fingers," Mr. Frampton broke in, "and not pincers or eagle's talons or hooves or something like that?"

"The hooves were on his feet, sir," Thomas said, and—who knows why—he pointed at Mr. Frampton's feet.

Dr. Monardes and I both looked in that direction, and Mr. Frampton crossed his legs.

"No, sir," Thomas continued, "he had your most average, ordinary human fingers. Perhaps a bit longer and bonier."

The doctor asked him what exactly this so-called "devil" had done in his dream to incite him to make such a "fateful decision," as the doctor put it, to give up tobacco. Mr. Jollie merely repeated that he had filled the pipes—"very skillfully," Mr. Jollie noted—and handed them to him one after the other. He didn't remember him doing something else or saying anything. He just filled the pipes and gave them to him.

"And he didn't make any kind of a sign or a face at you, he didn't wink?" Dr. Monardes asked.

"I don't remember him winking at me," Mr. Jollie replied. "No, no sign at all," he added categorically after a short pause. "He just filled the pipes and gave them to me."

It's astonishing how when they hear trivialities, all of them utterly unsurprising, people assume a thoughtful expression. At that moment, Dr. Monardes, Mr. Frampton, and I all wore thoughtful expressions. I suspect this is due to the boredom trivialities inspire. Somewhere deep inside you sleep begins to take over. Add to that the exhaustion of disappointment as well, when you've been waiting to hear something particularly interesting, and you get a thoughtful expression. That's the alchemy at work here, if you ask me. Moreover, people with thoughtful expressions usually aren't thinking about anything. They're actually falling asleep. Well, that was the case with me, at least. I looked thoughtfully ahead with an utterly empty head. There was a workbench in front of me covered in sawdust and strewn with a few tools. "How depressing"—this thought flashed through my mind. No wonder that the devil himself went gray here, or perhaps he had left all the grayness in his wake.

We finally left Mr. Jollie's—in fact, we had spent only a short time there, as the clock in the carriage showed us, even though it had seemed very long to me indeed–and we continued on towards Eton College, where Dr. Monardes was to give a lecture about tobacco and other new medicines brought from the Indies. The dean of the college, Mr. Whittaker, was a great admirer of Dr. Monardes' work, an inquisitive man open to knowledge who wanted to be in step with the latest developments in science and particularly medicine. He was the same person who, several years earlier during the most recent plague epidemic in the region, had arranged for all the boys at Eton to smoke a pipe every morning as a disinfectant, and it comes as no surprise that not a single one of them suffered from that terrible disease. The same was true of all the owners of tobacco shops in the vicinity, Mr. Frampton assured us. The evil contagion did not dare cross any tobacconist's doorstep. The doctor listened to this, his face glowing, and nodded in satisfaction. Yes, he had perhaps discovered the greatest medicine in the history of mankind and he had every reason to be proud of that. But his satisfaction exceeded all bounds when we entered the courtyard of the college and saw all the boys officially dressed in their black students' togas, lined up in formation along the parade alley, each one with a lit pipe in his hand. They all took a drag at a sign from the dean, as he walked towards us with a smile, his arms outstretched, accompanied by the teachers' thunderous applause. An indescribable moment! The doctor's eyes teared up with emotion. My eyes also teared up, but for other reasons.

After that the doctor gave an inspired and stirring speech in the ceremonial hall. I just met, he said in a joking voice, a man who claimed to have seen the devil in a dream and that the devil drove him to give up tobacco. The public reacted to this with condescending laughter, which Mr. Frampton and I joined in as well. "Look," the doctor noted, "what superstition leads to!" Then he spoke of modern times, of the fact that we need to leave medieval superstitions behind and to embrace science's new discoveries, to rush towards those limitless horizons which science opens before us. We live in a new time, the doctor said, in which science has triumphantly stepped over the prejudices of the past (I thought of that bum lying on the streets of Sevilla), an exciting and volatile time, in which new foundations are being laid, whose golden fruits will be harvested by future generations; a time—the doctor continued—of rebirth, of Renaissance, of the triumphant might of knowledge and of science, that sun that rends the darkness, which you—he turned towards the audience—my young friends, have been nobly called to dedicate yourselves to, under the deft guidance of your wise teachers and especially Mr. Whittaker, one of the age's brightest minds. Wild, long-lasting applause ensued, as the public got to its feet. Smiling, with hand on heart, Dr. Monardes took a slight bow from time to time in various directions. Then he spoke of new medicines that had come to us from the Indies, and particularly about tobacco and the huge number of illnesses this newly discovered substance could cure. He predicted a long and distinguished life for this new medicine. Some day, the doctor said, even the lowliest peasant in the Old World will know what tobacco is and perhaps will even use it himself, tobacco will be everywhere—on the streets, in the alehouses, in the inns, in the homes of the rich and the poor, in the houses of the nobility, of merchants, tradesmen, villagers—everywhere. It will become the most celebrated plant in the world, more famous even than tomatoes and peppers, mark my words. It will triumph as very few things in the world ever have, the doctor said, and this will come about far sooner than most think. We are already seeing the first harbingers of this eminent epoch, he said. The spirit of the new knowledge will spread gradually, little by little and invisibly at first—it will spring up here, it will spring up there, in this college, in that city, on that street. And so on until that day when suddenly and seemingly out of the blue the world will change completely. The self-satisfied ignoramuses of the past will see how it comes crashing down on their heads, how the habitual routine of the life they know flows away like water running through their fingers, they will look on bewildered and ask themselves: How so? What's going on? And they will have to trace the answer far back into the past. But we know. "The world will change completely some day," the doctor concluded. "And thanks to us in no small part."

A magnificent, superb, stirring speech by Dr. Monardes! I was proud to be the student of such a man. With the power of an ancient orator, he stood before an unfamiliar audience and conquered them with his mighty speech, his extraordinary knowledge, and his sharp insight. Mr. Frampton was beside himself with ecstasy. I was, too, in a certain sense. Bravo, Dr. Monardes!

"Dr. Monardes is my teacher!" I turned to a tutor standing near me, involuntarily pointing a finger at my own chest. "I am a student of Dr. Monardes!"

"An enviable fate!" he replied. "I truly envy you, sir!" the man added, applauding all the while.

That night, perhaps as a result of the excitement and impressions of the day, I also dreamed of the so-called "devil." But I dreamed of him in the gardens of Alhambra, standing where two pathways met under a right angle; they were lined with green hedges like a high curbstone, leveled off at knee height. Behind him I could see rose bushes with dark red roses, as well as lighter ones, whose color I cannot see how to define other than as rosy-pink roses. Above them, scattered about a dozen yards apart, towered tall palm trees, and along the length of the pathway the "devil" had come up, just in front of the hedge, red poppies and some purple flowers whose name I don't know were growing in long stone flowerpots. To the right, perhaps a hundred yards from me, rose the high walls of the labyrinth covered in greenery. A magnificent place, indeed, very picturesque.

But the so-called "devil" was no less picturesque. He bore no resemblance whatsoever to the one Thomas Jollie saw in his dream. On the contrary, this one was dressed in the latest fashions popular with Spanish aristocrats—in green and white striped "pumpkins," as those greatly puffed-up pants reaching to mid-thigh were sneeringly called, with silk stockings beneath them reaching just to his hooves; on top he wore a black jacket with gold embroidery, cinched at the waist and cropped at the shoulders; from beneath it flowed the sleeves of a loose shirt in the same green and white stripes, with a high pleated collar that reached to his chin; he also wore a short mantel that hung to his waist, gloves, a sword, a cap with a pheasant feather, and a large gold cross on his chest. No, he did not look anything like Señor Jollie's devil, and if it weren't for the hooves, I would have taken him for some Spanish courtier. In my dream, everything was bathed in bright colors, as if sparkling in the light of the noonday sun. But there was not a living soul in sight, it was just me and that picturesque figure before me. To my credit, I must stress that I was not frightened in the least.

"You must be an apparition," I said to him. "The devil does not exist."

"That's true," he replied. "I do not exist."

And as he said this, he leapt up and spun around in a circle.

"How absurd!" I said. "And what is that cross on your chest?"

"What, don't you like it?" he replied, lifting it with his fingers. "If so, then you have no taste. This is an exquisite work of goldsmithing."

I snorted derisively. This was some kind of clown!

Believing in the devil was as absurd as believing in anything whatsoever.

"I can read your thoughts," he said and pointed his finger at me before continuing: "I'll test out my new sword on you. Try to defend yourself. This is no joke!" And with that, he hopped twice like a fencer, bringing first his left leg forward and then his right, with the sword in one hand and the other hand clapped on his waist behind him.

"Don't go looking for trouble!" I said and reached under my jacket to the left where my Spanish dagger was.

"Can you imagine how strange it sounds to be run through by someone who does not exist? In the morning they'll find you dead in bed, but with no trace of a wound."

My head was bowed, but I had fixed him with the corners of my eyes. From this distance, he wouldn't even have time to move. I hurled the dagger at him with a lightning-quick movement, I could hardly tell myself when I'd done it. But there was no one there. It sliced through the air and disappeared into the palms in front of me.

"That won't work"–I heard a voice behind me, turned around, and saw him about a dozen yards away from me.

"Best to wake up," I thought to myself and tried to do so, but I couldn't. "This arrogant Spanish self-confidence is starting to make me go mad," I said to myself, and for the first time I felt not exactly frightened, but rather confused. At that moment he landed with a giant leap in the rose bushes to my left.

"You ought to join the travelling actors," I told him. "With that get-up and those leaps you'd enjoy a fine career with them."

I reached into the right side of my jacket to see whether I happened to have my second dagger, but I knew that I didn't–I only carry it in very special cases. But my hand did run across my cigarellas and I took one out to try to pull my thoughts together.

"A travelling actor is something far grander than you think," he replied. "I should invite you to one of my performances so you can see what real fireworks are all about . . . What is that reeking thing?"

"This?" I replied, taking the cigarella from my mouth. "This is a cigarella. It's made of . . ."

"I know what it is," he interrupted me. "But that one smells terrible."

"Because it is made of rawer tobacco," I said. "It's healthier that way."

"If I run you through," he said, "you'll surely stink up my whole sword. It will probably reek for a week after that."

"Best to give it up then," I replied, for lack of anything else to say. I didn't know what to say or what to do. To be frank, absolutely nothing came to mind. I thought about running away, of course, but immediately rejected this idea—first, because with those leaps he used to get around, he would've caught up with me immediately, and second, because this was only a dream. Confusion is extremely paralyzing. I've noticed this other times as well.

At that moment he landed in the path in front of me with a huge leap.

"Stench or no, I'll run you through anyway!" he said and minced towards me with tiny quick steps as in a dance, stopping abruptly from time to time.

"In England they tell about a guy like you who could jump over walls and hedges," I told him. "They call him Spring Heeled Jack."

"I know," he replied. And he started running, if that's the word, towards me with his tiny steps.

Without knowing myself what I was doing, somehow by instinct, I hurled the cigarella at him. Or rather, to be more precise, I established that that was what I had done in the following moment. He was already only five or six steps from me when I saw the cigarella smack him in the forehead . . . and he vanished. He simply vanished, disappeared. I whirled around to see whether he hadn't leapt over me again, and when I turned, I felt a sharp pain in my hip and realized that I had fallen out of bed, that I was in one of the rooms at Mr. Frampton's house, and that I'd obviously woken up. I reached out and lit a cigarella to make sure of this. The cigarella blazed up with a merry crackle and began glowing in the darkness. Clearly, I had woken up. Yet some doubt still gnawed at me. I got up, opened the door, and stopped for a moment, hesitant, telling myself, "This is very foolish, Guimarães," but I decided that since I'd already begun I may as well see this business through to its end, so I kept going and went into the neighboring room where Dr. Monardes was sleeping. He was there, in bed, with his white nightcap on his head. I went over and shook him by the shoulders.

"Is that you, señor?" I whispered.

"What?" the doctor replied half-asleep, but opened his eyes.

"Is that you, señor?" I said again.

He looked at me in silence, his eyes open. This continued for some time.

"No," he yelled finally, "I'm St. Nicholas the Mariner!" And as he said this, he threw a small wooden box that had been on the nightstand next to him at me.

Fortunately, I quickly ducked, the box hit me in the shoulder and two cuff links tumbled out of it onto the floor.

"What do you want, you silly fool?" the doctor yelled angrily.

"Nothing, nothing, señor," I replied, quickly slipping towards the door. "I just wanted to make sure that it was you."

"And you woke me up for that?" the doctor yelled—this was most probably a rhetorical question—and felt around on his nightstand, but there was nothing else there, and in any case I had already left the room.

The doctor continued shouting various things from inside. Señor Frampton also appeared. I was forced to give an explanation, so I told them what had happened. Then I went back to my room. I could hear the two of them talking in Dr. Monardes' room.

"You need to get rid of that fool, señor," I heard Frampton say. The son-of-a-bitch!

"I know, I know," the doctor replied, and he said something else I didn't hear.

And then he began to list my virtues, he stressed my resourcefulness, my studiousness, my quick wit, my increasing and ever-deepening medical knowledge, and proclaimed his certainty that I would be a very worthy successor to him, and foretold a great career for me in the medical profession on the basis of my—as he put it—exceptional qualities. I blush as I recall this! But here are the words of Dr. Monardes, written in his own hand:

> Dr. Monardes: Señor Dr. da Silva is my most remarkable and in essence my only student. All the others who declare themselves such are despicable impostors and scoundrels. No one else knows (with the exception of myself) like Dr. da Silva how to cure dozens of illnesses with the healing power of tobacco, and instead of throwing your money down the drain, if you truly would like to be cured of your ills, whatever they may be, or to hear an edifying lecture about tobacco at your college or university (for a modest fee), by all means please apply to Dr. da Silva. By all means to him.
>
> Greetings,<br>
> Dr. N. Monardes

# 7.
# Curing Lovesickness

On July 15, 157 . . . , a clear sunny day, at around two o' clock in the afternoon, I tripped over one of the beams we had brought for the new barn and very nearly hit my head on the side door of Dr. Monardes' house. Very nearly. This dangerous incident brought back memories. The door was neglected, its paint peeling, no one used it anymore. Before, when Dr. Monardes' daughters lived with him, they would go in and out of it. Or more precisely, only the second daughter, Magdalena, would go in and out of it. The older one, Maria, was already married and living with her husband Rodrigo de Brizuela, a merchant.

But I was talking about the younger one. What a lively girl! Thin and pretty, you really felt like snapping her in two, but at the same time you inwardly felt somehow sure that even if you folded her up in a figure eight (8), she would keep murmuring something with her sweet little mouth. I watched her scampering about, jumping around Dr. Monardes' neck when he returned from his house calls in the evening, like a little fawn, I heard her ringing laughter. Always cheerful, always ready to laugh—at anything and everything. Even if you only lifted your finger, she would laugh (as long as it wasn't the middle one, of course). Being, especially at that time, a young man, I was captivated by her—with her black hair, her dark eyes, her thin, perky figure, and her ringing laugh, she was one of the prettiest girls I had ever seen. Besides, she was also heiress to thirty thousand ducats, or more precisely fifteen thousand, if we subtract those which would go to her sister (who was already married, like I said). And now I see the arbor in which I declared my love to her. I had been on her scent for some time—as folks have put it ever since the distant past when everybody had dogs—looking at her amorously and so on, hence she was fully aware of my feelings. One evening, when the doctor and Jesús were out, I was pacing back and forth on the lawn under her window, hoping she would notice me. I remember I passed the time by dividing fifteen thousand by various numbers. She came out, ostensibly to get water from the well in the garden. I said to myself "Now or never!" and strode decisively—but with a love-struck look—towards her. One way or another, we finally ended up in that arbor I was talking about. I threw myself to my knees before her, banging up my knee terribly in the process, incidentally. I did not let this on in any way, of course, yet I know what I was going through. I remember very well what I said, since I had rehearsed the words many times. I said: "Señorita, I am in love with you. I love you passionately. Love is burning me up like a fire. I have tried in vain to suppress my feelings for you, dearest girl. Only you can ease my suffering, only you can extinguish this raging fire with your small white hand. Give me your hand, señorita, become my wife!"

As I said this, I took her little hand and pressed it to my lips, my head bowed, as I had seen it done in a certain place.

She laughed, tapped me lightly on the head with her other hand, and said: "Silly fool, that's from Lope!"

Here, I will admit, I made a mistake. I don't think the cause was yet lost. However, instead of thinking up something more fitting, I said: "Lope? Lope who? Is this some rival of mine, señorita?"

"Ugh!" she said, wrested her hand away, and ran towards that side door, saying only: "These Portuguese!"—and shutting the door behind her.

I have never come that close to success again. Damned books! The truth is that women have been reading more and more lately. This is likely the reason for many misfortunes, not only my own. Reading is a completely useless habit for women. A learned woman is an utter absurdity! Women should not read, they should only get married, have children, and bring them up, take care of their appearance, which is their most important part—which they know very well, by the way—look after their husbands, cook, keep the house in order, and if they are poor, do the washing and so on. As it has been since time immemorial, and as it should be. Yes, indeed, that's how it should be. Reading is utter foolishness for them, they merely waste their time with books and fill their heads with needless fabrications. Actually, reading is utter foolishness for men as well, books are totally useless for them, too, and a pure waste of time. Men should not read, but rather should be merchants, earn money, be soldiers and conquer lands, be sailors, discoverers, cross the seas, build cities and bridges, ships, roads, stride boldly, briskly, and quickly through the world—now that's how men should be. As Dr. Monardes says: "There's no need for any more thinkers. First, there are enough of them already, and second, thinkers are foolish. A pack of smalltime tricksters, who struggle to make a little money with ranting." He's right. They are a pack of smalltime tricksters, who try to pass off their ranting as some kind of substance on par with meat, fruit, and wood, so that you'll give them some money, not for any other reason. And afterwards they take the money and buy themselves meat, fruit, and wood. Because meat and fruit can be eaten, and wood can be burned—they are real. That's the whole point.

Upon my word, sometimes I think that if someday people quit buying all the things that they don't actually need, the only people left on earth would be farmers, a handful of craftsmen, and huge crowds of completely useless tramps. The physicians would also be left, always. And the soldiers would stay on—to chase away the tramps. The king's people would also remain—there's no getting around them. And then everything would again start becoming as it is now, little by little. A vicious circle.

By the way, Nature would also be there the whole time. And

if she happened to change her intentions, in the end she would be the only one left.

And afterwards perhaps everything would again start becoming as it is now, little by little. Or perhaps not.

Of course, as far as books are concerned, physicians are the exception. I mean that unfortunately there is no way to become a physician without reading books. But for all other undertakings, and perhaps even for medicine, it is far more important to know how to reckon than to read. Isn't that so? In the future, reading will most likely become useless for medicine as well. Some even think that this future is already upon us. I personally think, however, that it would be good, at least in this case, to wait just a bit longer. One way or another, tobacco will cure all illnesses—the only thing left is to figure out exactly how—and then all sorts of books will become utterly useless for anything at all. No one will read any longer, this useless habit will disappear, books will be forgotten, except as an absurd curiosity from the past, and then things in the world will start to fall into place. Nature will rise up in her full power. Man, too. Together with the wind and the elements, he will stride through the world mighty and invulnerable, cured of absolutely everything by tobacco. When this comes to pass, he will once again embrace Nature as his very own—now harmless—mother.

Urbi et Orbi. Farewell, Roman Epictetus! Even though this same Epictetus was a wise man, he never wrote a line in his life—the books in his name were written by his foolish, mediocre students. He himself understood splendidly that this had no point. Look at Socrates! And then look at that monstrous fool Plato, who squandered his life in ceaseless copycat scribbling, day and night, tirelessly, like a true maniac. Just take one, then take the other! And finally Christ, too. Did Christ ever write anything? Not a word! He came, saved whom he could, they say, and then left. Afterwards the fools start jabbering, jabbering on endlessly, they confuse everything and use his name to justify who knows what. And yes, thus folly triumphs in this world—it triumphs by means of books.

Of course, that is a rule, every rule has its exceptions, and this very book you are now holding in your hands, dear reader, is one of them. One of the last.

Anyway. What I was trying to say is that my love remained unrequited, and I cured myself of it not by reading something or other, but with the help of tobacco. I can claim with complete confidence that a cigarella every morning, another after a hearty lunch and a third before bed, followed by a good night's sleep and moderate labor during the day to distract your thoughts from the object of your amorous desires, completely and totally cures lovesickness in two, or at most three, weeks. One cigarella in the morning, one after a hearty lunch, one before bed. In two weeks you'll have completely forgotten what the fuss was even about. That's the way it is, man is actually built quite simply. I would even say that he is built very simply, at least on the spiritual level. In fact, this is to be expected. Whoever heard of one animal being lovesick over another in Nature? Books have thought up all that, books and various absurd individuals such as Lope and so on. For a thousand years now books have been beating it into mankind's head that he is not an animal, but something else, and he has begun to believe this fable to such an extent that he has even begun to suffer from lovesickness, which would surely drive the heavenly spheres—if they were really alive as the ancients believed—to burst out in thunderous laughter. I can also imagine what Dr. Monardes would say on this question! But this is precisely the correct, medical, and scientific view of things, in accordance with the laws of nature. Look at the bees, the ants, the birds in the sky, dogs, cats, and even Jesús—do any of them suffer from lovesickness? Absolutely not! But if you've let books get under your skin—as it seems I have—you will need tobacco to cure you. But it will cure you. It will cure you, and how! It cures everything.

# 8. Against Bad Breath

The doctor was called to a lass who was to be married in two days' time, but who suffered from bad breath in the mouth. What a bad luck! Indeed, such things do happen. I personally feel great sympathy towards the victims in such cases. It is as if Nature is mocking them. They not only suffer from the illnesses or indispositions themselves, but they are also ashamed to admit it. These illnesses and indispositions, however, are quite real, and even though they may appear at times trifling and insignificant, one mustn't forget that sometimes a pebble can overturn the cart.

The doctor for his part is rather dismissive of such cases. I would even say extremely dismissive. He listens with half an ear and treats them somehow mechanically, distractedly, as if his mind were elsewhere. And his mind really is elsewhere, this is not only an outward impression.

In this case, he even refused to make the call. Not that he refused the commission–he almost never did that, as long as you paid the fee–rather, he sent me instead. The treatment of bad breath is easy and the doctor trusted me to handle it on my own.

The lass lived on Imagen Street, so I went on foot. She was a pretty girl, black-haired, dark-eyed, by the name of Maria, around twenty years old, a thin little thing. But with bad breath. When I spoke to her from a distance of two or three feet, I immediately caught a whiff of the foul odor coming from her mouth. I could not help myself and jerked my head back. I almost stepped back. How she could get married in such a condition, I can't imagine.

The groom would have to be some Byzantine prisoner with a hacked-off nose. But I would set things aright.

First, I smeared the girl's belly with gas. Then I requested they bring me a brazier and I charred two tobacco leaves in it. I smeared their ashes on her belly, too, on top of the gas. It isn't a pretty sight, but it'll do the trick. The girl had to go to the privy. Then again. Then yet again. Etc., as the doctor says. This puzzled me a bit, although I didn't let on. Her family began getting nervous and questioning me.

"It's nothing to worry about," I said. "That's how the organism cleanses itself, it's casting all the poisons out of the body. Afterwards her bad breath will be gone, too."

As far as I could recall, however, the treatment was not supposed to go quite like this. I decided to repeat the procedure. This time I hardly managed to smear her belly with gas before she again rushed out to the privy. I wondered whether we couldn't move the whole operation out there, somewhere closer, but the privy, of course, was located in the yard, there were no conveniences at hand, and it would be somehow inappropriate . . . In short, it was impossible. When the girl returned, I smeared her belly with the ashes from the tobacco as well. She dashed outside again. There was no longer any doubt but that the girl had diarrhea, and a rather serious case at that. I also wouldn't say that her bad breath had disappeared, although now it was more difficult to perceive, given the combination of various odors. As if this wasn't enough, the girl also began to weep. Her father started flying at me, the family barely managed to hold him back. But for how long? He was completely red in the face, foaming at me with rage—typical Spanish madness. I could almost see myself from the outside, standing there with one open palm raised and with a tobacco leaf in the other hand, saying: "Calm down, calm down." While in front of me the beet-red Spaniard was foaming at the mouth, the girl was weeping or rushing outside again, and two women were holding back the Spaniard, but shooting daggers at me. "At least the groom isn't here, too," I thought to myself. The other thing I was thinking was that we needed to call Dr. Monardes. And that's exactly what we did; we sent one of the servants to call him over.

When the doctor arrived, he calmly entered the room and began questioning the girl—whose diarrhea had meanwhile begun to subside. The two of them managed to conduct a relatively lengthy conversation, after which he nodded at me calmly to go outside to discuss what had happened. The presence of the doctor and his confident manner suddenly inspired calm in all of us, but especially in me. I somehow felt certain that he would solve the problem. The doctor radiated such assurance, such confidence about his person—that was one of the great secrets of his success in the medical profession. This confidence, of course, was due in large part to his enormous wealth of knowledge, but not entirely. It was also a mysterious gift, which some people possessed, others not.

When we went outside we ran into the girl, who was going back inside. The doctor smiled, while she hung her head and ran into the house. She had stopped crying.

"What happened, Guimarães?" Dr. Monardes asked, staring at his shoes as he lightly tapped around them with his cane. This was a very, very bad sign.

"The young lady got the shits, señor," I replied, throwing up my hands.

"And no wonder, eh? No wonder!" the doctor said, this time bringing his cane down close to my shoes. He knew they were watching him from inside, and this made him restrain himself somewhat. "Listen, you idiot," he went on in a hushed, but very clear voice. I heard him very well, in any case. "You have to put tobacco ashes on the stomach *AND* on the shoulders. And on the shoulders! So that the tobacco pulls the hot humors upward. Otherwise it gathers all the hot humors in the belly, turning it into a veritable volcano. And on top of everything this is a young girl,

Nature has made her stomach boil and churn with hot humors as it is, who knows what horrors are brewing there without your meddling. Then you come along and put tobacco on her stomach to pull in even more hot humors." The doctor smacked himself on the forehead. "Now her stomach is like molten lava, Guimarães. Are you crazy or what? I wouldn't be very surprised if she burns the boards of the outhouse and if instead of bad breath, steam and the stench of sulfur start coming out of her mouth."

"Well . . . I'm still learning, señor," I replied.

"Yes! And I am the one to blame for that!" the doctor said, having turned his back on me to return to the house.

As soon as we entered to the girl's room, he turned to those present and said: "My student has acted rightly and with a little more patience the girl's illness would have been cured in that way, too. However, there is an easier and quicker method of healing, which I will now employ."

When I again began to burn the tobacco leaf in the brazier, the girl and her parents looked horrified, but the doctor assured them that he would not smear her belly and gently asked Maria to pull down the sleeves of her undershirt, and he proceeded to smear her shoulders with gas and then began to rub the tobacco ash into them, giving me a discrete sign to leave the room. I went out into the yard and lit a cigarella. Soon the girl once again passed by me, first in one, then in the other direction. On her way back, I smiled kindly and nodded politely. She, however, fixed her gaze on her feet and quickly ran into the house. "Hello, señorita" was on the tip of my tongue, but I restrained myself. Afterwards I gazed up at a bird in the sky. Its movements struck me as somehow strange. It swooped about on the air currents with its wings spread wide for some time, then it dove, plunging suddenly downward like a stone, its wings gathered to its body, after which it flapped them again and began climbing, once again floating upon the air, turning with wings outstretched, diving down, again flapping and rising upwards, circling above one part of the city. One doesn't usually stop to think that flying is not only pleasant, but surely difficult as well. You have to constantly keep track of the air currents, which are always changing, and to go from one to another, then at some point you hit a hole and suddenly plunge downward, so you've got to flap your wings and rise with another current, and if it's not going the direction you want, you've got to switch again. You have to be always on the alert, concentrated on your movements. Like a swimmer. Except, of course, that swimming in air is surely easier. But if I were a bird, for example, my entire attention would be fixed on my movements, I wouldn't be able to think about anything else. Certainly with the passing of time birds get used to it and begin to do it almost unconsciously, yet despite this, walking over land could easily turn out to be the simplest way to move. You can stop somewhere, lean against some wall, light a cigarella, and stare up at the sky at great length, for example. Birds can't do that. If they stop, they'll immediately plunge downward or the air current will simply carry them off somewhere. There's no wall to lean against. Of course, there aren't any cigarellas, either. They're constantly on guard, constantly vibrating as one with the air. This is surely the reason people seem more intelligent than birds, they've thought up so many things—they've built cities, written books, tended vineyards and gardens—because their minds are much freer to think about other things, rather than being focused on their movements. Besides, nothing grows in the air and a city couldn't just hang there. Birds could never do any such things, Nature herself has preordained this. And yet, I would prefer to be in their place. To dart from one place to another, to ramble about in the air, soaring on its currents. It must be a wonderful feeling. Oh, how fine it is to be a bird! And how stupid it is to be a human, how pathetic it is to be a human, to struggle your whole life for bread, to plow and sow to get by, to survive with trickery and force amidst the other beasts of the earth. What a slavish fate! Nature herself has made men slaves, she has created them as pathetic servants, to lead a pathetic existence upon the harsh face of the earth. All men are slaves by birth, slaves of Nature, slaves of scarcity. Even if you are Don Felipe II, emperor of Spain and the Indies, you are still a slave by birth. Pathetic creatures, pathetic captives. But like all pathetic creatures, they don't realize it either. And what to say about those madmen who hope to be resurrected in their bodies, or else hope to be reborn in new ones—so as to continue their pathetic existence, if possible, forever? What madmen, indeed! But what can you expect from servants, from the obedient brainless creations of Nature? She has simply made them so. To earn their daily bread through labor and the sweat of their brow, as it says in that book, and even to thirst for more of the same. How much better it would be to rise high above it, above that slavish earth, to soar through the air like the birds, who neither plow nor sow, in the air, where nothing grows, since they have no need of it. What happy creatures! They are Nature's privileged children, not man, I daresay. She has made them with love, while him she has made with cold reason, insofar as she possesses the latter at all. What unhappy, self-absorbed animals, creeping painfully across the earth, constantly threatened by hunger and disease and by their own kind, even a bit of bad breath in the mouth can ruin their lives, but despite everything they fancy themselves the pinnacle of Nature, her highest creation, even "the image and likeness of God." Good God! I am imagining how laughable this must look from the outside. And from above. If birds had more time to think, and if their minds weren't as consumed with movement as I suspect they are, they would surely think the same about people. But it seems that Nature has to a great extent deprived them of the ability to think. And who knows if thinking is even a blessing at all. Thinking might be the greatest foolishness, a pure waste of time, milling the wind and chasing words. Look, just now the cigarella burned my fingers and I threw it on the ground without thinking at all. And I acted rightly. If you can simply act rightly, what's the point of thinking? There is no point. No, none at all. A man does the most thinking precisely when he doesn't know how to act rightly. As long as he's not some gaper—one of those whose "thoughts wander", as they say—he becomes thoughtful for that purpose alone.

Incidentally, the bird, which continues to circle above the La Macarena Quarter in my opinion—but who knows, it could be much farther away, this is not obvious in the sky—is not a pigeon. It's bigger than a pigeon, but it could hardly be a bird of prey—first, because there aren't such birds here anymore, and second, because it looks smaller than they are.

After an hour or so, as the doctor and I were leaving, I told him what I had seen.

"That was a falcon," the doctor replied. "They're left over from the Arabs. Way back then, the Arabs bred them, and when our people chased out the Arabs, the falcons left the cities, too. Now they are multiplying in the Sierra Morena."

"Gee! I didn't know that," I said.

"You don't know anything, Guimarães," the doctor replied.

Ah, that Dr. Monardes! He always cuts you down like that. But then again, he was the one who cured the girl. "Her breath smells like violets," was what he said. He had forbidden her from eating meat and had left a cigarella just in case—if her bad breath came back before the wedding, she needed only to take a few puffs and it would disappear.

"You owe me a ducat," the doctor said. That was the fee. "I couldn't take anything after your bungling."

Yes, back down to earth. Here I am, striding firmly down Imagen Street as the doctor's carriage drives off. I don't mind. The weather is fine, dusk is falling, and I'm heading towards San Francisco Square, straight for Don Pedro's pub. Well, we killed off this day, too.

I found Rincon and Cortado inside, in particularly high spirits. I suspect that has something to do with the plunder of carts carrying the royal taxes on ships from the Indies—these carts had recently been robbed on the road to Madrid, in the Sierra Morena. They found the guards a full two days later, tied to trees, half dead from hunger and thirst, reeking of piss and shit, since when you're tied up, you do such things in your pants, like it or not. I don't exclude the possibility that they were found precisely thanks to the stench. And yes, I very strongly suspect that Rincon and Cortado had something to do with it. But in any case, I'm not the royal treasury, so I'm absolutely safe in their company. They even offered to buy me a round, since I started patting my pockets nervously, assumed a surprised expression, and said that I'd forgotten my money. Then my tongue loosened up and somehow or other I told them my thoughts about birds, what an easy life they lead.

"Come on, now," Rincon objected, "what's so easy about it? Would you like having to fly all the way from the Hansa down to Egypt and back every year?"

"That could never happen to me," I shook my head. "I would never set foot in the Hansa. It's cold, there's the Baltic Sea, the people are rather strange . . . it's out of the question."

"Fine," Rincon nodded, "I just said the Hansa as an example. It doesn't have to be the Hansa. It could be from somewhere else in Germany or Holland, or from England or France. There are lots of birds in France, too."

"The prettiest ones are there," I agreed.

"And every year they fly south. Some stay here in Andalusia, but others keep going all the way down to Egypt."

"I've been there," Cortado cut in. "Alexandria is a really nice city. But you've got to be careful and keep your eyes peeled."

"And then from there they go back to France. Twice a year," Rincon said, lifting two fingers in front of my face. "Would you like that?"

I thought of the night that I walked back to Sevilla, but despite this I said: "What's the big deal? They just fly through the air. It's not like walking over land. I can't imagine it's particularly tiring."

"That's what you think," Rincon objected. "But if you were in their place, you'd be singing a different tune. The ones that get tired and lag behind the flock fall into the sea and die."

"That's right," Cortado nodded. "I've seen them in the sea near the Greek islands. They land on the mast, take a rest and fly off again. But if there's no mast, then where do you land? I've even seen how they fall into the sea. They fall in and drown."

"Drowning is a really painful way to die," Rincon said. "It's not like getting stabbed and that's that. I've seen a drowning man. That's painful business."

I was about to ask him whether he hadn't been holding the man's head under at the same time, but luckily the wine had not scrambled my wits to such an extent, so I was able to stop myself in time. Such jokes can suddenly make your life miserable. Instead, I told them about the girl with the bad breath who was going to get married. It turns out (Cortado knew this) that she was supposed to marry one of the soldiers from the royal guard whom they had found tied up in the Sierra Morena.

"Well, no harm done. She'll stink of garlic, he of shit, a perfect match," I said. Just look at how fate brings like things together, or else Nature makes more alike those which have come together, I thought to myself and the vivid picture of the girl running back and forth across the courtyard sprang into my mind. "Well, what do you know! It's a small world!"

"It is a small world," Cortado nodded, laughing.

"Come on, now," Rincon shook his head. "The world is enormous. Sevilla is small."

"Exactly. That's what I meant to say," Cortado agreed.

When I thought about it, that, in fact, was what I meant to say, too. We made a toast to Sevilla. Say what you will and despite everything, Sevilla is a beautiful city.

How nice, I thought to myself, that I came to Sevilla. And that I'll become a doctor. I'll heal people, I'll make money.

My whole life was before me. Well, almost my whole life.

Rincon lifted his hand and signaled to Don Pedro to bring us more wine and tapas.

# 9. Against Aching Joints

Before, Don Pedro was nowhere near as strong as he is now. He has always been as fat and maybe even a little fatter, but not as strong. He suffered from bad aching of the joints, which seized him periodically. Don Pedro had not taken a cure for many years, then underwent treatment, to no effect, with Dr. Bartholo, until one rainy autumn he turned to Dr. Monardes for help. The case was one of Dr. Monardes' greatest medical successes and became legendary. In general, one of the best ways to become famous and to summon a great wind in the sails of your career, so to speak, is to cure the owner of a pub. This is one of the most important conclusions I came to from this story. I suppose that the same is true, in descending order, for the owner of a barber shop, for vendors at the market, for curates, especially in village churches, and possibly even for the sisters from the convents who sell sweetmeats in the morning. I will keep this in mind in the future and perhaps will work half-price in such cases, unlike Dr. Monardes, who was unyielding in this respect, and, incidentally, in all other respects as well.

But getting back to this unprecedented, unbelievable, and legendary case. I had the good fortune to accompany Dr. Monardes at the time and to see everything with my own eyes.

When we arrived at Don Pedro's large house on San Francisco Square, behind the pub, we found him in bed. His joints were aching all over his body, especially his knees, fingers, and also his waist.

"Don Pedro," Dr. Monardes told him frankly, "you are too fat. Take a look at me," the doctor continued, gesturing towards himself, "you and I are more or less the same age, but see how I look and how you look."

He was right. The difference was staggering.

"Ah, well . . ." Don Pedro replied from his bed.

"I will help you," the doctor said, "but if you go on eating this way, if you continue to be so fat, the results won't be very impressive or long-lasting. The weight of your flesh is straining your bones, Don Pedro, and the pressure is starting to wear on your joints. It's like a coat on a hook—the heavier the coat, the more the hook sags. Remember that. I will help you and you will start feeling better, and when one starts feeling better, one is all too likely to forget such things. That's why I want you to promise me that you will try to lose weight. And try seriously. You'll simply eat less, Pedro. There are more complicated ways to do it, but that is not only the simplest, but also the best way."

"I promise," replied Don Pedro. At that moment, I suspect he would've promised anything.

"Good," the doctor replied, and we started the procedure.

The procedure is complicated, even though to the untrained eye it may not seem so. First, a large leaf of tobacco is ground up in a mortar and then boiled. After that, the tobacco juice is strained and left to cool slightly—but only slightly! In the meantime, another tobacco leaf is heated up amidst the coals, but you must be very careful about exactly how much you heat it—this determines precisely which components remain within it and in what quantities. If the leaf catches on fire, you may as well toss it out—it won't do you any good in such a case. As soon as it starts smoking lightly—and I mean lightly!—you must pull it out of the coals immediately. The reader would not believe how many leaves one must burn up all for nothing while mastering this skill. What's more, the coals are always different and you somehow have to learn to judge by sight how hot they might be, and act accordingly. Moreover, the large tobacco leaves, although they are called by one and the same name, are always different sizes, and for this reason you must also develop a very flexible intuition. De facto, it turns out that in every case you are holding leaves of different sizes over coals of different temperatures and pulling them out at different moments—no two cases are identical. Thus, you must somehow learn to sense the tobacco intuitively, to cultivate a special mastery, which I, fortunately, already possess—after countless hours in Dr. Monardes' laboratory, under his angry shouts that you are an idiot, that you'll burn up his entire supply (absolutely impossible!) before you learn the simplest things, that he brought himself a world of troubles with you, that if you don't get it this time he'll boot you back out onto the street (but he doesn't boot you out), and other such things, all of this in the hot and heavy air of the laboratory where you're sweating like a negro and can hardly breathe, and your head is spinning from the tobacco fumes. And the worst part is that you yourself begin to feel like a total idiot and seriously begin to wonder whether you aren't by chance some sort of imbecile from birth, and until now you simply never noticed it—you begin to ask yourself this in all seriousness as you see how Dr. Monardes simply waves and does with the greatest of ease that which you've been slaving over for an hour, that which in his hands looks so simple, while you have a devil of a time—sweaty, wrapped in vapors, flushed, dizzy, and exhausted. And all of this is repeated for each of the various diseases, for which the leaves must be burned differently. The same goes for the juices as well, by the way—which leaves, how finely ground, how long they must be boiled, and so on. But in the end you learn. And even you, despite supposedly being trained for this, are surprised at how much more complex things actually are than they seem from the outside. But that's what a profession is all about. That's what it means to have a profession, especially if you are good at it.

After that, we daubed Don Pedro's sore spots with the tobacco juice, then placed the heated leaves on top of them, binding them in place with strips of cloth soaked in the tobacco juice. This turned out to be a long and difficult job, since Don Pedro had to keep turning over from his back to his stomach and vice-versa, yet he couldn't manage this on his own and we had to help him, meanwhile the leaves on his back would fall off and I had to keep them in place, worrying all the while about what would happen if Don Pedro didn't manage to turn over and accidentally rolled back the other way–I did not discount the possibility of him breaking my arms, to tell you the truth–in short, the whole business dragged on much longer than usual, and at one point I even had to reheat the tobacco juice, as it had cooled off. After we had finally bound him up, with tobacco leaves under his bandages, we went back to Dr. Monardes' house. We would return two hours later to repeat the procedure. It would be done three whole times the first day.

When we returned for the second round of bandaging, we found Don Pedro in a slightly better state, as he was able to roll about in bed far more easily. We repeated everything–the daubing, the leaves, the hot bandages on top.

When we returned the third time, we found Don Pedro already sitting up in bed.

"I'm hot," he said and tugged at the collars of his undershirt, which had a slit down to the chest. "I'm really hot. But I feel a lot better, doctor. I can barely feel the pain anymore."

"Now we'll get rid of it entirely!" the doctor replied decisively, visibly enheartened by this turn of events. Dr. Monardes' face always glows when a treatment is going well, he starts to look downright happy. And knowing how much he loves people, my only explanation for this is that he experiences deep professional satisfaction in such cases. Surely he says to himself something like: "Look, I was right again. Once again, I did exactly what needed to be done." In any case, his satisfaction is enormous and his face takes on a kinder, somehow even cheerful expression. It is pleasant to work with Dr. Monardes at such moments. He starts to seem even more decisive, even more confident, his mind grows sharper than ever, his movements become lighter and more exact, his compact, agile figure itself begins to exude some lightness, even gracefulness, I daresay.

This time the procedure went much more easily, incomparably so. As we were placing the hot leaves on his knees, Don Pedro even stood up to make it easier for us.

"How are you?" Dr. Monardes asked him.

"Much better," Don Pedro replied. "Except that I'm really hot."

As we tied on his bandages, he kept panting and tugging aside the collar of his shirt, which was already completely open. "Really hot, really hot," he said over and over. Finally, he simply grasped the bottom of his shirt with his bandaged hands, with the tobacco leaves sticking out over his fingers, and slipped it off over his head.

"He mustn't catch cold," I turned to the doctor, since the day was a cool, autumn day. The doctor himself looked shaken.

"You mustn't catch cold, Don Pedro," he turned to the tavern keeper.

"Then you'll cure my cold, doctor," Don Pedro laughed. "I can't take it anymore. I'm really hot."

Without a doubt, he looked far better.

The doctor decided to complement the procedure with something we had not done until then—or, at least, something I had not seen him do since I had been his student.

"We'll strike the iron while it's hot," he said and patted Don Pedro on the shoulder, making his flesh jiggle like jelly.

Don Pedro laughed in response. The doctor asked the servant Maria to bring a tin dish and did the following: he reached into his bag of tobacco leaves, pulled one out, which, however, did not please him, so he dropped it back in and pulled out another medium-sized leaf, which was not remarkable in any way at first glance, then he went over to the half-extinguished fire, took out two glowing coals with a pair of tongs, put them in the brazier, brought it over to the table, lit the leaf, dropped it into the dish, bent down, waved his hand over it twice, directing the smoke towards his nose, and, looking visibly satisfied, turned to me and said: "Guimarães, come here and help move this table over to the bed."

"Step back, boy," Don Pedro said to me. "I'll grab it from this end."

"Don't, Pedro," the doctor tried to stop him. "You mustn't strain yourself."

"Don't worry," Don Pedro replied.

The doctor did not object, but rather stepped back from his end of the table and gave me a telling look. Yes, of course. I went over and grabbed that end. Then Don Pedro and I moved the table several feet, next to the bed. The table was not heavy.

"Now sit on the bed, Don Pedro, and inhale the tobacco vapors."

Don Pedro sat on the bed, pulled the plate with the slightly burning leaf towards himself, bent over it, and began inhaling the vapors. Here I must clarify, so as not to leave the reader with an incorrect impression, that, of course, the leaf was not burning with a flame, but was simply smoldering in the dish. The vapor it exuded was thick and strong.

While Don Pedro inhaled the tobacco vapors and nodded his head, Dr. Monardes explained to him how the treatment would proceed henceforth. For a week, we would come to change Don Pedro's bandages twice a day, and after that once every three days as long as was necessary–but it would hardly last longer than a month, the doctor said–and we would no longer apply the tobacco leaves, but would just bind him in the bandages soaked in tobacco juice.

But man proposes, God disposes, as the superstitious peasants say. In fact, all of our plans got muddled up, although "muddled" is hardly the right word for it.

For just as he was leaning over the dish with the tobacco

leaf, inhaling and nodding his head, his two huge palms planted on the table to either side of the dish, at a certain point Don Pedro stood up abruptly, with a simultaneously glowing, hazy, and somehow dazed look—an unforgettable look, which seemed to pass right over our heads—and strode decisively to the door, clomped down the stairs, and went out into the yard, naked to the waist, in the cold evening air.

"Oh ho hoooo, some cool air!" he said and flung open his arms, his hands squeezed into fists which he swung left and right, as if they had been cramped up, while the flesh on his elbows and shoulders shook mightily. "It's hot. Hot!"

Afterwards, under our astonished gaze, he went over to the grindstone he used to sharpen knives for the tavern, grabbed it with both hands and simply tore it out of the ground. Yes, he literally tore it out, as if pulling a cork from a bottle. Then he tossed it aside and shouted: "I feel reborn!"

The doctor and I exchanged glances, but only for the briefest of moments, since our attention was once again drawn to Don Pedro, who went over to two grindstones that were stacked one on top of the other off to the right and first lifted the one and threw it aside, then the other.

"Ughhhh!" Don Pedro said.

He set off for the other end of the yard, which was strewn with old tables and other smashed up things from the tavern, passing by a large jug on his way, which he lifted and hurled off to the side, where it fell and shattered on the ground with a crash, water spilling from it. Don Pedro laughed and continued on his way. He reached the end of the yard and began tossing the smashed up tables and chairs into a pile in the very corner near the fence.

"This place hasn't been cleaned up in years, doctor," he yelled and hurled a broken three-legged stool onto the pile.

"Don Pedro," the doctor called in response, "that's enough now, don't strain yourself, you need to take care."

"This is no strain whatsoever, don't you worry," he replied, continuing to fling the tables and chairs into the corner.

Don Pedro's family had come out into the yard and were shouting at him to stop, to go back inside where it was warm and so forth, but he merely shook his head, without answering them at all. At one point, however, he turned to us, and I was stunned by his appearance—he was standing there before us smiling, flushed, huge. I turned to the doctor.

"I know what you're going to ask," he nodded. "I know what this is, but I don't know the word for it. It is the opposite of a complication. Rather, the opposite of a 'severe complication.' We don't have a word for that in our profession."

"Improvement," I suggested.

"Let's say," the doctor shook his head hesitantly. "A severe improvement."

Don Pedro continued piling up the odds and ends from the tavern. They had been accumulating there for years, tossed into a heap, their quantity was enormous. There was no longer any doubt in my mind that he would clean up that whole jumble that had accumulated over the years in one afternoon or even less—in an hour or two, just like that, before our very eyes.

"Wow, this fellow just doesn't quit, huh, señor? He's not of German descent or something, is he?" I asked.

"Well no, of course not, I've known him since childhood!" Dr. Monardes snapped. "I shouldn't think so," he added a short while later. And then he said: "Go get him, Guimarães."

"Go get him, señor?" I repeated.

"Yes," the doctor replied. Short and to the point.

Now this was something I had no desire whatsoever to do. I imagined how Don Pedro would grab me and toss me on top of those tables and chairs. I slowly headed towards him. But no matter how slowly you walk, sooner or later you cover one hundred yards. It goes without saying that contrary to my hopes, no miracle occurred and Don Pedro continued, puffing and snorting, to work away at his task. When he noticed me, he said: "So you've come to help out, eh?"

Yes, you're telling me, I thought to myself. I shan't be a minute.

Then I waited a short while for him to turn towards me, but he seemed to have forgotten me. I stepped closer and tapped him on the shoulder as he bent down to pick up an old vise.

"What is it, boy?" He turned his head towards me, still bent over.

"Señor," I answered, "the doctor says you need to come back inside. He sent me to get you."

"Is that so?" he replied, straightening up. Then he looked around at the objects scattered on the ground and said: "Very well then."

I set off and several steps later I snuck a glance over my shoulder. And indeed, Don Pedro was following me. This time I covered the distance to the house's entrance much more quickly. When we got inside, Don Pedro agreed to put on his shirt and lie down in bed. He even let us tuck him under the covers.

"Good, Pedro," the doctor turned to him. "The treatment is producing results."

"Amazing results," Don Pedro nodded animatedly. "If only I'd known to turn to you years ago, my friend!"

"Since things are going better than I had expected," Dr. Monardes went on, "we will change the plan. I will come to see you tomorrow and change your bandages. After that, we will repeat the procedure only if you start experiencing aches and pains again."

"Fine. Whatever you say, doctor," Don Pedro replied.

The doctor stroked his beard pensively and asked, after what seemed to me some hesitation: "Pedro, is there some German in your family tree?"

"No. Why?" Don Pedro asked, surprised.

"Oh, I was just asking," the doctor replied. Let me say here, by the way, since I'll hardly have the opportunity later on, that this answer has always seemed like something big to me: they ask you "Why?" and you answer "I was just asking."

We left after that. The next day we changed his bandages, but only once, and without having him inhale tobacco vapors, and that was the last time, and I mean the absolute last time, we ever needed to treat Don Pedro's joints. He didn't feel bad at all anymore, not because of his joints in any case, they got better once and for all. It goes without saying that Don Pedro was exceptionally grateful to Dr. Monardes and always spoke of him with nothing but praise. I also think that he harbored good feelings towards me, too. It's true that he later threw me out of the Three Horses on several occasions, but he threw me out somehow carefully, with a certain concern, I would say. I don't even think "thrown out" is the precise term for it. He more took me from one side of the door and dropped me on the other. I've seen him throw other people out–take Rincon, for example–and that is another thing altogether. Incidentally, Don Pedro might find himself in hot water with Rincon in particular–Rincon is very handy with a knife, and even though Don Pedro could strangle him with three fingers, he might come to grief, as they say, with Rincon. But on the other hand, Rincon knows when to watch his step and is very sly. You could live with him your whole life and never even know he had a knife. When it comes to money, however, everything suddenly changes. It changes drastically. If you happen to cross his path at such a moment, you are in dire straits, literally in mortal danger.

Crazy José crosses my path this evening. Crazy José is completely harmless, however. He is bent over some beams by the side of the road and is speaking to the cats that are hiding under them. He is trying to lure them out, clapping his hands. One might imagine that the cats love him and play with him, but this is not the case at all. In fact, they don't pay him any attention whatsoever, they don't come out from under the beams. If you want them to come out, you need to toss them something to eat.

Then they'll pay attention to you, they'll start playing with you, fawning all over you, rubbing against your legs with their tails in the air, they'll stand still and let you pet them and they'll purr. Cats. Nature has made them that way. Crazy José stands bent over the beam in vain, trying to lure them with a cajoling, child-like voice, clapping his hands. He lifts his head and looks at me with a foolish grin as I pass by him.

"You have to give them something, José," I tell him.

He keeps looking at me with that same foolish grin. I doubt he understands what I'm telling him at all.

# 10.
# For Long Life

While we were in England, Mr. Frampton had planned to take us to a 110-year-old granny who had smoked tobacco for decades and who had not given up her pipe even to that very day, according to Mr. Frampton. What better proof of the wondrous longevity resulting from tobacco use? Of course, Dr. Monardes, and myself as well, were extremely intrigued by this. The granny was called Goody Jane, and she lived in North Witch. As the name of the hamlet in question implies, it lay quite far to the north, and we had the opportunity to go there only after our visit to Eton, which I mentioned a bit earlier in this medical work.

Mr. Frampton recounted to us veritable miracles about this Goody Jane. He claimed that although she was bent double by the years, practically like a ring-shaped bun, she was fully in her right mind, all of her mental abilities if not entirely, then to a great extent preserved, and that she smoked a pipe every morning upon rising. As she had done, like I said, for decades on end.

"She's been smoking longer than you've been alive, Guimarães," Mr. Frampton said to me on the way, and those words, like Urbi et Orbi and other such things, imprinted themselves deeply upon my memory. Perhaps forever.

Indeed, what a granny she was! We travelled all night so as to catch her in the morning as she smoked her first pipe—and so it was. Her family led us to a small one-room shack next to the house—she lived in said shack (since her family had taken over the house)—and we found there an unbelievable creature, with a recognizably human appearance, despite everything, truly bent double nearly to the ground, almost like a small ring, dressed in something difficult for me to define, but undoubtedly with a wool sweater-vest on top, sitting on a bed next to a metal stove, which pleasantly warmed the entire space, which incidentally was not larger than two by three yards and which included, besides the stove, a small low table and yet another bed on the opposite side, covered in woolen blankets. The floor, just like the entire structure itself, was made of the most ordinary dirt. In other words, if someone reckons that the good granny's longevity was due to an especially wholesome quality of life, he is sorely mistaken.

Goody Jane received us very graciously, due surely in large part to the two pounds of first-class tobacco which Mr. Frampton brought her as a gift. She had not yet lit up her morning pipe—in fact, we had gotten her out of bed—and the three of us bore witness to this, I daresay, majestic, in light of the circumstances, ritual. Goody Jane lifted the lid off the stove, reached into the fire with her tobacco tongs, took out a coal, touched it to the pipe, inhaled audibly on it, then touched the coal to the pipe several more times and lit her pipe. She complained that in the past instead of a stove she had had a fireplace with a chimney, but after setting her skirts on fire several times, her grandchildren had brought her this stove. I watched dumbfounded as she puffed as quick as can be on her pipe—her face was wrinkled like earth cracked by drought, grayish-black like soil, with small eyes sunk deeply into their sockets and white hair pulled back from the tiny, wrinkle-riven face. She looked like a skull come to life, with skin on top and little flesh stuck on here and there.

"How long have you smoked, grandmother?" Dr. Monardes asked. It must be noted, by the way, that she could hear very well, as long as you just spoke up a bit, of course.

"I can't remember, my child," Goody Jane replied. "Many years. Since the time of King Henry."

"Seventy years," Mr. Frampton nodded approvingly. "At least."

"What did you say?" Goody Jane asked.

"I said that it's been seventy years," Mr. Frampton repeated.

"Ah, it's been more than that," the old woman replied and puffed on her pipe. It was a battered clay pipe, blackened from the heat.

"It couldn't be that long, but never mind," Dr. Monardes said. "And how do you feel, grandmother?" he asked. "How is your health?"

"I'm not well, my child," Goody Jane replied. "I don't know if I'm in this world or the next."

Then she began to list off, in a lilting voice, all the illnesses and aches she suffered from.

"But you're still alive," Dr. Monardes interrupted her at a certain point, "and from the looks of it, fully in your right mind."

"Ah yes, I'm alive, my child, alive," Goody Jane replied. "God bless you with a long life, too! And I do everything myself. Because otherwise, if you just lie in bed, what kind of life is that?"

"And what do you eat, Goody Jane, what do you live on?" Mr. Frampton broke in, opening a notebook across his knees, with a quill in one hand and an inkpot on the little table next to him, visibly determined to take notes.

"A crust of bread, a little soup, a bit of fruit," the granny replied. "Whatever the children cook. Just enough for one such as myself, my child. But they keep bringing me food, they do. They take good care of me. I'm very satisfied, God bless them!"

"So, a crust of bread, some soup," Mr. Frampton repeated, writing in his notebook.

"And a bit of meat now and then, my child," the old woman said and giggled, or at least I would use that word for lack of another, more suitable one. "But at my age a person's got to be careful with meat so as not to go running straight to the privy, or, worse yet, filling your pants. My stomach doesn't digest anymore, not like it used to. The curse of old age, my child."

"And what kind of tobacco do you smoke, grandmother?" Dr. Monardes asked.

"Well, whatever I can get my hands on, my child," Goody Jane replied. "Any kind of tobacco. It's the one joy left in my life."

"And how many pipes do you smoke, and when?" Mr. Frampton asked, slightly bent over his notebook.

"I smoke one in the morning, then another, then another, and sometimes one more."

"But at what times of the day?" Mr. Frampton asked.

"Well, how should I know? During the day," the granny replied. "As the case may be. When I eat something, I smoke afterwards."

"And what time do you eat?" Mr. Frampton pressed on.

"During the day, sonny. At noon," the old woman replied. "When they bring me something, and if I feel like eating. But I don't really feel like eating much anymore."

"Goody Jane," Dr. Monardes said somehow solemnly, yet also affectionately, as he got up, bent down (because of the low ceiling), went over to her, and grabbed her hand with a warm gesture, "you are living proof of the awesome power of tobacco to grant longevity!"

"Am I?" Goody Jane replied, lifting her face to him.

"Most certainly!" Dr. Monardes nodded. "Tobacco, due to its extensive healing properties, has lengthened your life by decades. It keeps you alive."

"So if I stop smoking, will I die?" the old woman asked, but this question was posed in such a way that the doctor hesitated as to how to answer. To me it seemed there was a certain hopefulness in her voice.

"It is highly possible," Dr. Monardes agreed. "But you go on living. There will always be time to die."

"I hope so, I hope so," the granny replied.

The doctor patted her gently on the shoulder, straightened up (as much as was possible), turned towards us, and said: "Let us be going, señores. Let's leave this good woman in peace."

"Thank you and Godspeed," the old woman said.

"I almost forgot," Mr. Frampton said, as he reached into his inside pocket, pulled out his pipe box, an impressive work of ivory, took one pipe, and placed it on the table next to the bag of tobacco. "We've brought you a new pipe, Goody Jane."

In fact, this was his own pipe. A beautiful, expensive pipe made of briar.

"Thank you and Godspeed," Goody Jane began repeating.

I hung back a bit, and as I was going out, I turned towards the old woman and said, "Grandmother, my name is Guimarães and I am from Spain. Actually, I am from Portugal, but I went to Spain and from there I came to England."

The old woman looked at me in silence.

"Grandmother, I just wanted to tell you that you are the most remarkable señora I have ever seen," I finished. "I have seen many human females, they clearly can be found everywhere on earth"—I waved my hand—"but . . ." No, words were not coming to me easily this day.

"Thank you and Godspeed," the good granny replied and I left, with a certain sense of relief.

With that, our visit ended. A memorable visit, indeed. "She has been smoking longer than you've been alive, Guimarães." I asked myself whether I would really like to attain such longevity with the help of tobacco. And if I don't, does that mean I should give up smoking? That would be unpleasant. But you can't have it both ways. Similar thoughts, or rather semblances of thoughts, occupied my mind as the carriage carried us through the snowy, bare, somehow disconsolate fields. Dr. Monardes and Mr. Frampton, incidentally, were very enthusiastic about the visit, but I couldn't say the same for myself. Life is a strange thing, isn't it, Pelletier? You want it and you don't. It lures you and repulses you. Like a bitter medicine or like a sweet drink that makes your head hurt afterwards. But how can you stop? You can't ever stop. Nor do you want to. So you keep drifting along through the fields, through the snow, like some Pelletier, like some Medusa, your mind flutters here and there, like a dropped kerchief, and where you are off to, by the way, where exactly you're going, goodness only knows. Urbi et Orbi, amigo.

# 11. On the Debate by the Honorable, Learned Scholars Dr. Cheynell, an Englishman, and Dr. Monardes, a Spaniard, with the Foolish and Ignorant English King and His Sycophantic Servants Who Present Themselves before the Civilized World As Physicians—to Their and Their Chieftain's Great Shame

I have always thought that the English king is a fool. The present one, as well as all those before him.

Our Spanish king, on the contrary, is an intelligent man. But he is crazy. That, I presume, is the main reason why we have not yet conquered their small, forested island. The other reason is most likely that Señor de Leca has no financial interest in that.

Because—let's not deceive ourselves—conquering their useless island would take a big army and a huge amount of money—and for what? A few fields, meadows, sheep, forests, some rocky peaks up in the north, and a slate mine here and there. Duke de Alba would get the best of them in the end, as he does with everyone, but it would be quite difficult, would take a long time, and would cost an enormous sum. It is much better to invest those funds in conquering the Indies, which will repay you richly—with ten thousand or so thugs you can conquer boundless lands; rivers of gold and silver, tobacco, and all sorts of exotic goods will flow your way. Who needs that small rain-soaked island up north? Yes, Señor de Leca is right, as usual.

But I have strayed from the topic, or rather I would have strayed if I had begun it in the first place. And the topic is as follows: the debate, which the English King James I organized at Oxford on the topic "Whether the frequent use of tobacco is good for healthy men?" The question mark here is pure hypocrisy and is intended solely to satisfy the formal requirements of debate. Because the truth is—and everyone knows it—that James is a great opponent of tobacco and—in the words of Mr. Frampton, who received this information from inside sources—the king intended to use this forum to introduce his latest essay, entitled "A Counterblast to Tobacco," and to stigmatize that good plant with the help of several stooges. The ultimate goal of this operation, according to Mr. Frampton, was to raise the duty on tobacco two- or three-fold. And when you take into account how in demand that commodity is, Mr. Frampton said, that would significantly increase the royal treasury's income.

In any case, we decided to attend the debate, especially because there were many lovers of that transatlantic panacea at Oxford, so the king's argument could hardly slip by without meeting some kind of resistance. Thus, from Goody Jane's we headed south to Oxford and arrived there shortly before the debate.

We went into the packed ceremonial hall at Christ College, where the event in question would take place, and at that foolish Frampton's insistence, and alas, Dr. Monardes' as well, I was saddled with the task of recording the statements made at the debate. For this purpose and with the aid of Mr. Frampton, who had acquaintances here, I was seated at a long table at the end of the platform designated for all those taking notes. Thanks to Mr. Frampton, I was seated next to Isaac Wake himself, the public orator of the university, who was recording the event for Oxford. There were several bearded ninnies to my other side, whose names I didn't bother to remember or even to learn. Mr. Wake, however, was a very pleasant man with wonderful manners and a murmuring voice, whose speech flowed like silver—as the saying goes, who knows why—and with whom I conducted a pleasant conversation, at least until the moment at which I told him—as a joke, of course—that with a name like his, he was very lucky he didn't live in Spain, and even though he laughed kindly, after that he refused to utter a single word, and responded to my questions by nodding and shaking his head—for the affirmative or the negative, respectively, as it were—and when that was impossible, he put his finger to his lips, which were pursed as if to say "sh-h-h," even thought he didn't say it. A sly Jew, no doubt about it. I wondered whether his family wasn't one of those whom the Spanish king had chased out many years ago, and perhaps I had inadvertently touched on a sore topic. But how could I have known?

In the meantime, the debate had begun with a speech by the English king, who was met by applause and standing ovations from the public—we were also forced to stand up, and I clapped along with everyone else, unlike, as I noticed, Dr. Monardes, who was blowing his nose at that moment. But I was even more stunned by Mr. Frampton, who was indeed clapping, but not like the others, but with the backs of his hands. I'll be damned! I would've done it, too, if we scribes hadn't been on the platform itself, so close to the king. An empty formality wasn't worth creating Lord knows what kinds of trouble for oneself.

The king was dressed in a black jacket, cinched at the waist and covered in gold embroidery; from beneath it flowed the sleeves of a loose shirt in the same green and white stripes, with a high pleated collar. Below the jacket the king wore green and white striped pumpkin pants reaching to mid-thigh, with grey silk stockings beneath them reaching down to his long pointed shoes, which were white. He had a waist-length red mantle draped over his shoulders, from beneath which the gilded handle of his sword peeked out. He also wore a cap with a pheasant feather, gloves, and a chain with a large gold cross on his chest.

After the applause died down and the audience once again sat down, he took the podium and paused for a long moment, probably to intensify the dramatic effect, before saying: "Learned gentlemen, our fortunate and oft proved valor in wars abroad, our hearty and reverent obedience to our Princes at home, hath bred us a long, and a thrice happy peace: Our Peace hath bred wealth: And Peace and wealth hath brought forth a general sluggishness, which makes us wallow in all sorts of idle delights, and soft delicacies, the first seeds of the subversion of all great monarchies."

Aha, I thought to myself, so that's the bone sticking in your throat, is it? The subversion of the monarchy. You're afraid they'll pull the rug out from under you. Then no more pumpkin pants, no more pointy shoes, no more gilded sword—back to Nature, an animal among animals. Or, as is far more likely in this case, straight to the chopping block.

"And surely in my opinion," he continued, "there cannot be a more base, and yet hurtful, corruption in a Country, then is the vile use—or rather abuse—of taking Tobacco, which hath moved me shortly to unmask this vile custom. And now, good countrymen," he gestured to the public with a broad sweep of his arm, "let us, I pray you, consider, what honor or policy can move us to imitate the barbarous and beastly manners of the wild, godless, and slavish Indians, especially in so vile and stinking a custom? Shall we that disdain to imitate the manners of our neighbor France (having the title of the first Christian Kingdom) and that cannot endure the spirit of the Spaniards (their King being now comparable in largeness of dominions to the great Emperor of Turkey)—Shall we, I say, without blushing, abase ourselves so far, as to imitate these beastly Indians, slaves to the Spaniards, refuse to the world, and as yet aliens from the holy Covenant of God? Why do we not as well imitate them in walking naked as they do? In preferring glass, feathers, and such toys to gold and precious stones, as they do? Yea," he raised his voice, "why do we not deny God and adore the Devil, as they do?"

These last words were met with wild applause from the audience. But not from Dr. Monardes and Mr. Frampton, whom I glanced at—Dr. Monardes was once again blowing his nose, while Mr. Frampton was clapping in his extremely unusual manner. I scribbled down various things on my paper, pretending to take notes, at least until the moment I noticed that Isaac Wake was looking askance at me. I then drew a Star of David on my sheet. Wake quickly averted his gaze. The ninny on my other side, however, stared bug-eyed at the star on my sheet. I quickly crossed it out and grabbed my quill such that I—ostensibly accidentally—showed him my middle finger. After that, they both left me alone.

"What is the smoking of tobacco," the king continued, "or as some say lately, combining the two words into one in an absurd fashion, tobacco-smoking? As if we could say nose-blowing"—had he noticed Dr. Monardes? My gaze quickly met Dr. Monardes' for a moment—"privy-going or book-reading, just like those unintelligible Germanic peoples, who combine so many words into one that I've heard an entire pilgrimage to Jerusalem can be described by a single word in their language."

"Yes," I thought to myself. "Will-o'-the-wisp-chasing."

"What, *ipso facto*, shall we say, then, about this custom?" James continued. "Learned gentlemen, I would say this is a custom loathsome to the eye, hateful to the nose, harmful to the brain, dangerous to the lungs, and in the black stinking fume thereof, nearest resembling the horrible Stygian smoke of the pit that is bottomless."

Applause burst out once again. Dr. Monardes was also applauding. Mr. Frampton, however, kept on as before. "You can always tell an experienced man"—I thought to myself. That's what experience is—you do one and the same thing, since it works. When and if it stops working, all of a sudden it turns out that you know nothing.

"And what effect does this vile custom of tobacco-smoking have on our subjects? It has a categorically and unambiguously bad effect on our subjects. Because tobacco-smoke is very pernicious unto their bodies, too profluvious for many of their purses, and most pestiferous to the public State. It gives our proud nation a bad name. But are these statements of mine simply being made *ipse dixit*, unproven by facts? Gentlemen, I was aghast to read in a book by the French traveler Sorbière, who recently visited our beautiful capital city of London—primarily to spy, which we pretended not to know and good-humoredly turned a blind eye to, so as not to sour our relations with our French "cousins"—I was aghast to read that in his opinion the English were naturally lazy and spent half their time in taking tobacco. And if you object that we could expect nothing more from a French spy and from a Frenchman in general—that is, a representative of a nation famed for its superficiality and frivolity—then I will respond that our fellow countryman and friend Sir Grey Palmes makes the same and even more frightening claims when he states absolutely categorically that if tobacco be not banished, it will overthrow one hundred thousand men in England, for now it is so common that he, Sir Grey, has seen ploughmen take it as they are at plough."

A muted "oooh" swept through the hall like grumbling, but I

couldn't discern whether it was because of the ploughmen who smoked at plough, or because of the implicit threat of tobacco being banished. Probably both, since it seemed to me that everyone looked shocked.

"Yes, yes, gentlemen," the king went on. "Tobacco is far from being the innocent peccadillo of our learned class. On the contrary, it has penetrated deeply, and perhaps even more deeply, within our common people and has turned into a mass contagion. I now have the honor," he turned to the side, "to introduce to you the learned man Joshua Sylvester, who can recount for you even more shocking examples and whose name is perhaps familiar to our learned audience because of his work"—here, the king looked down at the notes in front of him and made a long pause—"his work 'Tobacco Battered and the Pipes Shattered' and so on. I am certain that he himself will state the full title of his work, which I enthusiastically recommend. Please, gentlemen, a round of applause for the scholar Joshua Sylvester."

The following moment, a little twerp dressed all in black took the podium, a man simply impossible to describe, since he was so nondescript—it was as if he were disappearing or melting away like a spot before your eyes, with the exception, however, of his exceptionally malevolent, angry, glittering eyes. He bowed to the king, who had retired to his place behind a long table on the platform, and then turned to the audience—Joshua, that is—with the words: "Most honorable gentlemen, the work, which his Majesty condescended to mention, is called 'Tobacco Battered and the Pipes Shattered about their Eares, that idely Idolize so base and barbarous a Weed, or at least overlove so loathsome a Vanity, by a Volley of Holy Shot Thundered from Mount Helicon.'"

Did I really write that down correctly?

"In what sense?" A voice from the audience called.

"In the sense that tobacco is battered and pipes shattered by a volley of holy shot thundered from Mount Helicon," Joshua replied. "Meant for the ears of those that idly idolize so base and barbarous a weed, and so forth. This latter is a parenthetical remark."

"Aha," I heard the voice of my neighbor Isaac Wake, who was nodding his head as he wrote something on the sheets in front of him.

"Learned gentlemen, I have personally witnessed," Joshua continued, "an even more shocking example than a ploughman with a pipe in his mouth. Once I was clerk to a curate in Lincolnshire, who was accustomed to retiring to the vestry before the sermon and there smoke a pipe while the congregation sang a psalm—usually the twenty-first. One Sunday, he could not resist the diabolical temptation of his vile habit and smoked a second pipe. Since the congregation in the meantime was confused and grumbling, I went in to him and warned him that the people were getting impatient, but he replied: 'Let them sing another psalm.' 'They have, sir,' I replied. Only then, with a sigh and great dissatisfaction did he extinguish his pipe and go out before the congregation, to whom, incidentally, he preached a sermon on the subject 'How important it is to do things quickly and not to put them off until tomorrow,' and to provide a personal example of this, his sermon was quite short, after which he dismissed the congregation and went back into his vestry to finish smoking his pipe."

The mixed sound of murmurs of discontent and suppressed laughter swept through the audience following Joshua's words. Even my neighbor Isaac gave a faint smile.

"A striking example," the king called at that moment, "of the sluggishness that has recently seized some representatives of our clergy and how they are in a position to neglect their holy duties because of a barbarous plant."

"Precisely," Joshua nodded. "And all for a stinking, fuming and not only useless, but clearly harmful weed. Yes, harmful. Because our learned physicians, who praise its healing properties to the skies, are frankly and undoubtedly mistaken. Actually, how frank this really is, I couldn't say," Joshua noted almost as an aside. "But I have no doubts whatsoever that it is undoubted. Gentlemen," he began again, "contrary to their claims, tobacco has harmful and poisonous qualities! Because when it is taken into the body, tobacco vexes and unsettles it, inducing the powerful purging of distillations in both directions, above and below, it induces spiritual confusion, as well as torpor and dullness of the senses and limbs. Its torpid and dulling qualities are most noticeable when the fumes are taken through the mouth, since then it induces drunken dizziness in the head, and if a great quantity is consumed, it leads to a dull clumsiness of the senses and limbs."

What kind of nonsense was this? I looked at Isaac's paper to see if I had understood correctly–but yes, he, too, had written down the same thing. How absurd! I personally never experience any dulling of the limbs and senses at all after a cigarella. On the contrary, even!

"I must pause to address an objection by our vulgar tobacconists," Joshua continued, as if reading my mind, "which I frequently hear them make against the harmful qualities I claim are inherent in tobacco. They say that after using it, they do not experience any ills or strong purging of distillations, nor any dulling of the limbs and senses. To those, I would reply that abuse of tobacco has made them insensitive, people without senses. How else could we explain the fact that our licentious smokers squander and expend not only their time, but also their health, money, and mind, in taking these loathsome and harmful fumes? Despite the fact that for now they might look fine, be it thanks to their youth or their strong constitutions, this senseless smoking will suddenly ruin their bodies, poison their stomachs, spoil their digestion, and fill their organisms with harsh and harmful crudities. Besides erroneously redirecting Nature's activities, they also irritate the lungs, perturb and harm the energies of the soul, spoil the breathing, and destroy the circulatory function of the liver. I am truly astounded at the madness of these people. What is so special about these fumes that could provide such great satisfaction? It's obviously not the smell, as it is unpleasant, and certainly not the taste, which is acrid and revolting."

Oh, how Dr. Monardes was looking at him at that moment! His head tilted slightly to the side, he was gazing at him with scathing contempt, half-smiling. His entire expression, his stance unambiguously sent the message: "You are ignorant! You need to educate yourself!" I needed to master that expression, it would certainly come in handy in the future. So I began at that very moment–I tilted my head to the side, smiled slightly, and kept writing down this monstrous nonsense.

"Being overly hot," Joshua was saying, "tobacco smoke overheats and dries out the liver, interferes with the digestion of meat in the stomach, and casts it out of the stomach undigested when smoked before said meats are absorbed by the body. For similar reasons, some people use tobacco to purge phlegm. But this is a very dangerous and unjustified practice, which causes violent vomiting, chronic illnesses, and feeblemindedness. My experience shows, gentlemen, that a mere drop or two of pure tobacco juice applied to the tongue of a cat induces strong convulsions and even death in less than a minute. It is true that this very same juice, sprinkled on gauze and applied to the teeth, is useful in curing a toothache. However, it should be used only on those who are accustomed to smoking, otherwise strong nausea, vomiting, swooning and so forth will ensue. When droplets of this same juice are sprinkled on a crust of bread and swallowed immediately into the body and the stomach, a quick and agonizing death also ensues, as my experiments with the poor in London have demonstrated."

"The poor have distressed organisms," a voice from the audience called. "They suffer from malnutrition, poor digestion, suppressed vital humors, and dullness. That doesn't prove anything."

"On the contrary, sir," Joshua objected. Laughter from the audience followed. "What I mean to say"–he lifted his hand–"is that yes, they suffer from all those things you mentioned, but the cause of their deaths is tobacco and nothing else. If you don't believe me, I would not object to you subjecting your own self to this experiment, sir." Silence in the hall. What nerve!— "Among our vulgar tobacconists," Joshua continued, "there is also another extremely dangerous practice which is founded upon a completely erroneous belief. They believe that the warm tobacco vapors will protect them from the damp and rainy weather. For this reason they frequently, before going out into the damp and windy streets, use tobacco. This is a mistake! You should not go outside immediately after smoking, but should refrain from that for at least half an hour, especially if the season is cold and damp, because as a result of the strong effect of tobacco, the pores of the body are opened, even in its most external and superficial parts, which can lead to unspeakable ills from the sudden entrance of air into them."

Well, he was right about that. If damp, dirty, and cold air gets into the body, it can cause swelling, mix with the cardinal humors and corrupt them. But after all, isn't that why people wear clothes, instead of walking the streets naked like Adam and Eve? Yes, for Adam and Eve, tobacco surely would have been harmful for the above-mentioned reason. But not for modern man. Here Joshua's statement was a typical example of the speculations that contemporary opponents of tobacco make use of to defame it.

In the meantime, Joshua said a few words in closing and retired from the podium. The king got up, probably to give the floor to someone else, but at that moment a striking man with a pipe in his hand stood up in the audience—yes, he held it in front of himself in his left hand, so that all could see it; of course, the pipe was not lit, that would have been an extreme act of impudence, but even this gesture was sufficiently ambiguous and acted as a brave provocation to those slanderers of tobacco.

"Who is that man?" I whispered to Isaac Wake. He, however,

clearly due to rancor, did not answer me, but put a finger to his lips in a sign to keep quiet.

"That's Dr. Cheynell," the ninny to my other side said, to my surprise. "Second to no doctor on earth in his qualities and knowledge."

You see, one never knows who's going to turn out to be useful to him. I nodded in a sign of thanks to the ninny and, quill in hand, once again discretely raised my middle finger, this time aimed at Isaac the Jew. I am sure he noticed it, although he didn't let on.

"Gentlemen," Dr. Cheynell began in a loud voice from where he was standing in the audience, "I intend to speak in defense of tobacco's healing properties by respectfully objecting"—here he bowed—"to our enlightened king, whose duty, after all, is political, rather than medical: he must protect our bodies not from illnesses and contagions, but from our external enemies, to fight not against *bacillusae* and *bacteriae*, but rather against hostile armies, who, sword in hand, attack our good nation, and in the fulfillment of this duty our present king is better than any other in the world, he is irreproachable and his deeds serve as a model, may God grant him health and long life, so that he may wisely rule our proud monarchy for many years to come."

Dr. Cheynell once again bowed, while the public got to its feet and gave a long round of applause. Dr. Monardes was also applauding. We scribes were on our feet and clapping, too. The king stood up and began giving small bows to the audience in various directions, his hand to his breast. When that finally ended, Dr. Cheynell went on: "I also intend to dispute the irresponsible and at times foolish claims of the previous speaker Joshua, whose surname I have forgotten . . ."

"Sylvester," someone called out.

"Perhaps," replied Dr. Cheynell. "Whose claims, I say, completely contradict the truth and the scientific facts of medicine. It is a mistake and a very dangerous, depraved practice when clergymen take up medicine and make pronouncements about the healing properties of some substance or other. Just as a physician, through his ignorance of complicated theological matters, could in certain circumstances harm and even ruin a believer's soul if he thoughtlessly undertakes to fulfill the functions of a curate, so, too, could a curate, if he tries to act as a doctor, cause harm and even ruin that body of that same believer or of someone else. For this reason, I would like to begin from a bit farther away," the learned physician continued. "It seems to me, gentlemen, that we have strayed from that original sacred source of truth, just as Adam and Eve strayed from the Garden of Eden. When tobacco was first introduced to Europe, its discoverer, Dr. Nicolas Monardes, as well as other highly learned physicians, considered it a medicine with almost magical powers and not coincidentally have called it the 'herba panacea' and 'herba santa' in their works. Because this medicine does indeed possess many of the qualities considered by some as characteristic of the mythical panacea. For this reason, one of our countrymen has called it 'Divine Tobacco,' while another of our countrymen has christened it 'our holy herb nicotine,' named after the Frenchman Nicot, one of its first discoverers. But how, one might ask, did this 'herba panacea,' this magical herb appear in our England? As far as I am aware, this came about thanks to three proud captains from our glorious navy, namely Captain William Middleton, Captain Price, and Captain Koet. They are precisely the ones who, nearly thirty years ago, first smoked tobacco publically in London, and people from all over the city flocked to see them in the small Cheapside Square, where they were standing. We can only guess what their conversation was. Perhaps they spoke of their seafaring exploits? Or of the exotic, faraway lands that unfolded before their eyes? Or perhaps they discussed the quality of the tobacco they were smoking? This we will never know, gentlemen. Which is a great pity, I would add."

"They talked about the price of eggs, sir, I was there," a puny, grizzled man called from the audience.

Dr. Cheynell did not pay him any attention.

"Unfortunately, I was unable to join the London citizenry, learned gentlemen, for at that time I was here, here in this same Oxford, where, being only a youth, I was studying the medical sciences." These words were met with polite applause. After waiting for it to end, the doctor continued: "At that time, gentlemen, pipes had not yet been invented, so the captains smoked rolled-up tobacco leaves, or cigars, in the matter in which the Spaniards smoke them to this very day, calling them 'cigaras' or 'cigarellas.'"

Well, now this was a slightly inaccurate statement on Dr. Cheynell's part, and for that reason Dr. Monardes, as I noticed, shook his head at that moment. Indeed, cigars and cigarellas are far from one and the same thing, and if in Sevilla someone asks you for a cigar and you sell him a cigarella, he'll give you a sound thrashing, or at least will try to. Let me clarify: the cigar is a luxury item, while the cigarella is an everyday healing remedy. But we couldn't expect Dr. Cheynell to know such details, just as we do not know the difference between their various kinds of pipes, do we?

"However, the true credit for introducing tobacco into England," Dr. Cheynell continued, "must go not to the aforementioned captains, who, heeding the inexorable laws of the seafaring life, likely soon set sail again after this short stay in their homeland, but rather to Sir Walter Raleigh. Everyone knows the story of how Sir Walter's servant Ridley doused his lordship with the tankard of ale he had been called to bring when he saw Sir Walter smoking for the first time and thought his master was on fire. Sir Walter, let us recall, patiently wiped his face with the tablecloth and turned to his devoted servant with the words: 'Master Ridley, we are today lighting a candle in England which by God's blessing will never be put out.' Whereupon he again lit his pipe. By the way, gentlemen, those were Sir Walter's exact words, which I know from the man himself. Let me also add that today Master Ridley himself is an avid smoker and spends most of his meager spare time in Sir Walter's garden with a pipe in his hand."

Some of the audience—albeit a minority—responded to these words with spontaneous applause. Of course, Dr. Monardes and Mr. Frampton were among them. It became clear that Mr. Frampton could also clap in the more usual manner. For a moment—only for a moment—the thought had crossed my mind that he actually did not know how to do it. But of course, this was not the case.

"For that reason our bard and my friend, the Dean Hole," Dr. Cheynell continued, "exclaims in a wonderful poem:

*Before the wine of sunny Rhine, or even Madam Clicquot's,*
*Let all men praise, with loud hurras, this panacea of Nicot's.*
*The debt confess, though none the less they love the grape and barley,*
*Which Frenchmen owe to good Nicot, and Englishmen to Raleigh."*

The hall burst into laughter. Without a doubt, the learned doctor had managed to lift the oppressive atmosphere that had reigned until that moment. I would say that with the abilities that he had demonstrated so far, he could easily don a barrister's toga. A most remarkable señor!

"To be absolutely faithful to the historical truth," he went on, "which in time will be commemorated, since it marks the beginning of a new era for our country, or at least for English medicine—something which most people today may not realize—let us clarify, gentlemen, that Sir Walter himself was initiated into the art of smoking by his assistant Thomas Hariot, whom he, paraphrasing our Holy Book in jest, called his 'Faithful Thomas.' Thomas Hariot was sent by Sir Walter to study which plants grow in the newly discovered pristine lands of Virginia and after he returned from there, he published his findings in a slim quarto from 1588, which some of you have likely seen, under that title 'A briefe and true report of the new found land of Virginia' and so on—I cannot cite the entire title for you, gentlemen, since it consists of precisely 150 words. It was namely from this work that we understood for the first time—at least we here in England, I mean—that when tobacco leaves are dried and ground into powder, the Indians take in the smoke or fumes, by sucking them in through a pipe made of clay into their stomach and head: from whence it purges superfluous phlegm and other gross humors, opens all the pores and passages of the body: by which means the use thereof, not only preserves the body from obstructions: but if also any be, so that they have not been of too long continuance, in short time breaks them: whereby their bodies are notably preserved in health, and know not many grievous diseases wherewithal we in England are oftentimes afflicted. Here with us, gentlemen," the learned doctor continued, "is a prominent Scottish physician, whose name is perhaps unknown to most of you, namely Dr. William Barclay." Dr. Cheynell gestured towards one place in the hall where an intelligent-looking, middle-aged man with a very white face, reddish beard, and straw-colored hair stood up, with his hand on his heart. Some of the audience applauded as he stood up, and even the king waved to him in greeting. "Mr. Barclay, who, by the way, is a fellow countryman of our enlightened king, recently published a book in Edinburgh, which I heartily recommend to you, under the title, 'Nepenthes or the Vertues of Tobacco.' What a wonderful title, gentlemen! Because yes, just like the magical nepenthes of the ancient Greeks, tobacco drives sorrow and the painful spirit of taedium vitae far from us. But more interesting for us physicians are its physical properties. And although they are praiseworthy, just as with every strong medicine, we must not abuse them, as Dr. Barclay clearly shows. Our Scottish colleague, who, like most of his fellow countrymen, is highly observant of our weaknesses, which we Englishmen often do not notice, writes in his work"—the doctor bent down, picked up a book and read from it: "'Tobacco smoke may be taken for the said medicinal effects, but always fasting, and with empty stomach, not as the English abusers do, which make a smoke-box of their skull, more fit to be carried under his arm that selleth at Paris *dunoir a noircir* to black men's shoes than to carry the braine of him that can not walke, can not ride except the Tabacco Pype be in his mouth.' Mr. Barclay goes on to say that he was once in company with an English merchant in Normandy–between Rouen and Calais –who was a merry fellow, but was constantly wanting a coal to kindle his tobacco."

Everyone in the hall laughed. It is really tiresome. I know that feeling all too well. It happens with cigarellas, too, if you don't have a light at hand. Even though cigarellas are much easier to light, much easier. The Spaniards thought these things through a long time ago. We're already returning from where the English are going, as they say. Normandy? Was Pelletier from Normandy, perhaps? Where are you from, Pelletier? From Mans. But where is Mans?

"I would say, gentlemen," Dr. Cheynell continued–who, incidentally, was making me feel proud of the profession I had chosen–"that if tobacco is used wisely and in accordance with Nature, there is no medicament in the world that can compare with it. In tobacco there is nothing which is not medicine, the root, the stalk, the leaves, the seeds, the smoke, even the ashes. But especially the juice, which is terribly fatal according to one of my opponents, and who stooped so low as to use the common folk of London as an example. May I ask then why did he not use ants, crocodiles, sheep, or dung-beetles as examples? What an idea, most honorable gentlemen!"

"Then why do you use the Indians as examples?" a voice called from the audience. "They aren't even Christian, unlike the common folk."

"Oh, that's completely different," Dr. Cheynell replied. "We use the Indians as an example because they are still the innocent children of Nature, among whom we do not find the distinctions that exist within our old nations. They are still in a state of nature, very close to man's primordial state, like the first generation after Adam and Eve. That is completely different," Dr. Cheynell repeated. "But getting back to tobacco juice. The juice of that plant possesses wondrous digestive, cleansing, and coagulating abilities, thanks to which it has an incomparable power to heal all wounds or cuts to the body, ulcers, scabs, and so forth, for which tobacco deserves very high marks. But now I arrive at the properties of the smoke, which is taken through a pipe first into the mouth, from whence some thrust it towards the nostrils, while others suck it directly into the stomach and chest as a remedy against all diseases, especially those brought about by cold, that is, which come from cold and wet causes. I approve of and recommend tobacco smoke as necessary and useful to people with an elevated content of cold and wet elements in their bodily composition, as well as throughout the cold and wet season, as long as the tobacco is used appropriately, i.e. in a temperate and timely fashion, because then, thanks to its warming and drying properties, it helps the brain, which is overly cold and wet, reduce that state to the normal temperature. It casts out rheums and coldness of the head and is useful for all illnesses of the body and brain being of a cold and wet cause, by drying and absorbing the superfluous air and crudities in the head. Indeed it does, at least at first, chase away melancholy and awaken dozing vital energies, helps against toothaches, swelling of the gums and aching joints. It guards against the decay of the four cardinal bodily humors, by drying up the crude materials within the body and is very useful not only against colds, but also against all ills of the stomach, chest, and lungs due to cold and wet causes. It is, finally, a very good remedy against overeating, since, as our opponent pointed out, it induces quick expulsion—evacuation in our medical language—expulsion, as I said, both above and below, of things contained in the stomach, and for the same reason quickly relieves those suffering from windiness by instantly driving the latter from stomach and bowels. Let me conclude, gentlemen, by saying that tobacco can be used as a general means for strengthening the organism, as well as perhaps for some of its more exotic effects. Because the Indians, from whom we learned this method of taking tobacco, first smoked it to fall asleep when their bodies were weary from labor and such efforts, or else when they wished to foretell future events, since the smoke produced, at least in them, a lightness in the head, followed by a dream with various visions and revelations. For this reason, when they awoke, they felt, as a result of said dream, very rested and refreshed and able, thanks to the visions, which the smoke, to a great extent, induced, to foretell, as they think, all important things they wish to know."

"And you, sir, as a smoker, could you not foretell a few important future events concerning England?" the king said, provoking laughter all around. "Because if that is the case, I could dissolve my council and appoint you in its place. But if you cannot, I think in that case I would be satisfied with some Indian."

Indeed, Dr. Cheynell could have spared those final words. He, however, took the king's rebuke with a smile and replied confidently once the laughter had died down: "That, Your Majesty, I cannot foretell. But my soothsaying does lead me to believe that Dr. Monardes himself, the discoverer of tobacco, is here in our midst. And if you think that it stands close to reason, then I would object that it's not closer than Spain. And yet he is here among us, in this hall."

"Really, sir?" the king raised his eyebrows.

"I believe so, Your Majesty, even though I have never seen that illustrious man, whom I have always fervently wished to meet since the beginning of my career, when I studied his works with such delight."

At that moment, my teacher stood up and said: "It is so, Your Majesty. I really am here. My name is Nicolas Monardes, doctor from Sevilla."

His words had an indescribable, staggering effect. All those present were so shocked that they didn't even think to applaud as politeness required. Isaac Wake had stopped writing and was staring open-mouthed at the doctor. It seemed to me that even Dr. Cheynell was surprised, although he shouldn't have been. How had he known? Surely thanks to Mr. Frampton, since Dr. Monardes also looked very surprised.

The king was the first to recover from the shock, saying: "We all know your name, sir. Both those who agree and disagree with you."

A burst of applause followed. Part of the public got to its feet, clapping enthusiastically. The doctor nodded his head and turned in various directions, raising his hand in greeting. A few of those seated near him shook his hand.

"Please take the podium, sir," the king invited him.

"That won't be necessary, Your Majesty. I will speak from the floor like my most learned colleague Dr. Cheynell, whom it is an honor for me to meet"—our señor nodded at Dr. Cheynell. "Besides, my speech will be very short. Because everyone who would like to know more can learn it from my works, which Mr. Frampton, who is seated next to me now, was so kind as to translate into the wonderful English language. For certain imperfections in the use of which I do hope you will forgive me. I could, of course, speak Latin, but that might pose a difficulty to some members of the audience."

"Yes, yes," agreed the king, "as learned men we all know Latin, but there's no need."

"Precisely," Dr. Monardes nodded.

Now is the moment to offer some clarification (this is me, Guimarães). The reader might be wondering how I learned English so quickly as to be able to act as stenographer. I learned it on the ship, the *Hyguiene*, on our way here. The truth is that I have an exceptional gift for languages. One might even say that I am a born grammarian. Of course, I have a gift for many other things as well—I myself am surprised by that, dear reader, believe me—but in this case we are talking about this particular gift. Of course, we can't discount the lessons which Mr. Frampton gave me over a year while he was a prisoner of the Inquisition, before he escaped. Incidentally, Mr. Frampton did not wish to give me those lessons and agreed to do so only after I promised him a reward of seven cigarellas a week, which I was later forced to raise to ten. But, of course, at the end of the day, it cannot be attributed to the cigarellas. Cigarellas can do many things, but they cannot teach you a language and give you the ability to make use of it. For that, you need a gift, señores.

But getting back to Dr. Monardes.

"Sometimes it is permissible," he said, "for everyone to smoke tobacco fumes as a preventative measure. For example, if someone, even if he does not suffer from mucousy phlegm, or rheum, as we call it, has to travel in foggy, windy, or rainy weather, especially during the winter, it could be expedient for him, even if he does not suffer from rheumatism or cold temperature, to inhale four to five puffs of tobacco smoke immediately upon arriving at home or at the inn, so as to prevent the discharge of mucousy phlegm or other harmful agents, which could befall him due to the bad and unclean air. Ergo, the smoking of tobacco must be practiced primarily after travelling in foggy and rainy weather, since it hinders the inflammation of the mucus membranes and hence rheum, and generally removes all harmful agents, which the moist and foul air normally induce within the head and other parts of the body. The smoking of tobacco at such a moment is beneficial for every bodily state, except for when the brain has a very dry composition. This was the fully indisputable example for the advantages of its use, which I can give and which will be difficult even for skeptics to dispute. We must also remember that there are two ways of using tobacco: the first is to hold the smoke in the mouth and from there to pass it through the nostrils to warm and dry the brain and to dissolve and disperse the cold humors and unnecessary air found therein."

"Wherein?" A voice from the audience called.

"In the brain," Dr. Monardes replied. "The other way to take it is into the lungs and stomach to disperse and destroy impurities and flatulent winds, which irritate these organs. Consequently, if you wish to know whether tobacco smoke is useful or harmful for your body, first you need to consider whether it will be proper for your head: because if your brain is too cold and wet or filled with unnecessary matter, then the holding of smoke in the mouth and passing it through the nostrils will be of use to you. My experience has shown, señores, that the brains of almost all people are filled with unnecessary matter. This is very strange, since their brains are clearly short of certain extremely important things, while at the same time they are filled with a load of unnecessary matter. How this happens is at first glance a great mystery, but in fact, like most great mysteries, it is no mystery at all, but simply and purely an inexplicable fact of Nature. You might ask yourselves why that fact is as it is, what the explanation for it is, but the answer very frequently is that there is no explanation and that the fact is as it is simply because it is so. We frequently reason assuming that Nature is obliged to give us some explanation. But in fact, she owes us nothing, let alone an explanation. And one of the most striking characteristics of tobacco, señores, is that also without giving any explanations–neither to Nature, nor to ourselves–it simply regulates the activity of Nature in a particular way. You can easily recognize truly powerful things by the fact that they neither give explanations, nor allow them, rather they simply act in a particular way, whose characteristics we can merely register and nothing more. It is in this registering, namely, that our life-saving science expresses itself."

The more insightful segment of the audience applauded this profound claim. Indeed, Dr. Monardes' ability to see the grand scheme of things is downright amazing and immediately sets him apart from other representatives of the medical profession, who are often highly learned, but spend their whole lives sunk in details due to their narrow view of things. Thus, they are capable of spending years debating some or other niggling property of tobacco, reaching absurdly complicated extremes in their pettiness, without being able to see the place that wondrous plant occupies in the grand scheme of things. But not Dr. Monardes.

"Ergo our medical science, like every other science," Dr. Monardes continued, "must express itself primarily in that: in the registration of facts, without too much speculation over their causes. Too much speculation is usually the source of errors. And it most probably is due to unnecessary matter in the brain. Here, for example, even though I cannot explain it convincingly, I can register the fact that tobacco is an effective diuretic in cases of dropsy and difficulty in urination. I can also establish that a strong infusion made from the stem, with dock and alum added to it, gives good results when applied externally for skin diseases and especially scabies—to this end, some boil tobacco stems in urine. It is also, by the way, a flawless treatment for scabies in dogs."

"And for that end, what urine should it be boiled in? Dog's urine?" A voice from the hall called, followed by laughter by one half of the audience.

"No," replied Dr. Monardes with an icy calm, after waiting for the laughter to die down. "You find the wittiest fellow nearby and boil it in his urine. Sometimes"—the doctor's voice rose above the laughter bursting from the other half of the audience—"along with him, too. But I've heard that this only ruins the mixture. However, I do not know this first hand, so I cannot claim this with certainty. I do know, however, several absolutely indisputable facts relating to the use of tobacco amongst the Indians, and I can simply keep these facts in mind, without speculating overly much and trying to explain them at any cost. Through these facts I have come to know several indisputable effects that this plant has, and if I would like to achieve the same effects, I simply need to apply the same or a similar procedure. Too much speculation in this case can only hurt us. Following the path of logic, it is entirely possible for us to reach the convincing conclusion that it is impossible for a given substance to have certain effects, yet contrary to our convincing conclusion, it *de facto* has them. It is also possible for us to give an incorrect explanation for its actually existing properties, and when afterwards someone refutes our explanation, he could reach the conclusion that the very properties described by us *de facto* do not exist, which, however, would not be true. For example, I can claim that it is an absolute fact that the Indians smoke tobacco to banish exhaustion, as mentioned by my most learned colleague, Dr. Chey- . . . Chou . . ."

"Cheynell," Mr. Frampton prompted.

"Yes, Dr. Cheynell. Señores, it is an indisputable fact that the Indians of our Occidental Indies, do use the tobacco to take away weariness, and to take lightsomeness of their labor. As a result of their evening dances they become so much wearied, they remain so weary, that they can scarcely stir; and so that they may labor the next day, and return to do that foolish exercise, they do take the smoke of the tobacco at the mouth and nose, and they remain as dead people, and being so, they are eased in such sort that when they are awakened of their sleep, they remain without weariness, and may return to their labor again. And so they do always, when they have need of it: for with that sleep they do receive their strength and are much the lustier. Despite that they sleep only three or four hours, at least since the Spaniards are there."

Not a word about so-called "visions" and foretelling the future. The doctor is no fool, no sir!

"And they also use it against hunger and thirst. This is a fact. When they shall travel a long way through any dis-peopled Country, where they shall find neither water, nor meat, the Indians put a little ball of tobacco between the lower lip and the teeth, and they chew it, or rather, ruminate, swallowing the spittle. In this way they do journey, three or four days, without water or weariness. How is this done? Very simply: The balls of tobacco bring phlegm into the mouth, which they then swallow into the stomach, which does retain the natural heat, which does go consuming, and maintaining them—which we do see happen in many beasts, for that much time of the winter, they are shut up into their caves, and hollow places of the earth, and do pass there without any meat. Here I could risk offering an explanation and say that for that, they have to consume the natural heat of the fatness which they had gotten in the summer. The Bear, for example, being a great and fierce beast, much time of the winter is in his cave, and does live without meat, or drink, with only chewing his paws, which perhaps he does for the same reason as the Indians. This is a fact. This is why, most learned señores, I summon all scholars, and especially physicians, to simply take into account the facts, which unambiguously show that tobacco has exceptional healing properties and qualities strengthening to the organism, which strongly resemble the panacea of the ancients, for precisely which reason I took the liberty of calling it the 'herba panacea' in my works. It is not necessary for a panacea to have a nice smell, nor a pleasant taste. The important thing is for it to be a panacea. For those other things, you need Indian aromatic sticks, which come from the East Indies, by the way, not from the West, or figs from the Barbary Coast or Lebanon. But for good health, you need tobacco."

After that, the doctor thanked the audience for their attention and concluded his speech by sitting down in his seat. His statement had a strongly encouraging effect upon the supporters of tobacco. I had the feeling that things were gradually slipping out of the king's hands and going in an entirely different direction than that which he had intended. Despite his smile, it seemed that I could read certain signs of irritation and even alarm on his face. And these only grew when a man by the name of Tobias Venner stood up in the audience and said the following: "Gentlemen, we shall earn the scorn of future generations, if we do not recognize one very important and life-saving property of tobacco, which neither Dr. Cheynell nor Dr. Monardes preferred to emphasize. But I would like to stress it. Because among tobacco's numerous medical properties we can also count its effect as a prophylactic measure against the plague. I have personally witnessed how in the city of Birmingham, where, due to the exceptionally unhygienic customs of its inhabitants, the plague recurs more often than anywhere on this earthly 'sphere,' as is said lately, I personally have witnessed how during the last plague the market-people there brought their provisions, having their mouths primed with tobacco as a preservative. One could see them chewing tobacco anytime one passed through the market place. Some of them stuffed their mouths so full of tobacco that, when you add to that their abominable dialect, a man from central London such as myself could not understand what they were saying at all. I would like to note, however, that contrary to uninformed expectation, nearly all of them survived. Furthermore, it has also been noted that that cruel affliction never dared pass the doorstep of a tobacconist. For example, Mr. Howell in one of his 'Familiar Letters' dated January 1—I can't remember the year—says that the smoke of tobacco is one of the wholesomest scents that is against all contagious airs, for it overmasters all other smells. And I've heard that even our most learned King James found it true, when being once a hunting, a shower of rain drave him into a pigsty for shelter, where he smoked a pipe full to overmaster the repulsive scent."

A surprised "aaaah" ran through the crowd.

"Your information is to some extent true, sir," the king admitted. "Indeed, some such thing did occur once and we sought shelter in the pigsty of the Venerable Preston, the bishop there. However, I did not smoke the pipe, rather Lord Lonsdale did, on my orders."

"Now that you mention the Venerable Preston's pigsty, Your Majesty, this reminds me to add that in many places tobacco is used in churches as a disinfectant, as anyone who finds sufficient courage and patience to undertake a journey through the English countryside will discover."

"That's true," the king nodded. "I can only confirm this unfortunate fact."

"And allow me to note in closing, Your Majesty," Venner continued, "that many of the unfortunate characteristics of tobacco emphasized here are not actually due to the plant itself, but to the substances it is mixed with. It is widely known that so-called 'Birmingham tobacco' is heavily mixed with coltsfoot. Hardly anyone will be surprised when I say that in Birmingham, a city known for its counterfeiters, some of whom recently swung from a rope thanks to their counterfeit coins, in Birmingham, I maintain, it is absolutely impossible for a man to supply himself with pure tobacco. For such simply does not exist there, gentlemen, anywhere in the city. My friend from London, Ridgecole, had the misfortune to spend a whole week in that city without taking tobacco with him from London, and he told me how one evening he nearly died from smoking only a half-pipe of tobacco, which he unwisely bought in the city of Birmingham. When we later examined this tobacco in my laboratory on Fenchurch Street—I am an apothecary, gentlemen—we were astounded to find that this tobacco contained huge quantities of salt. This caused me to think that in Birmingham they wet the tobacco and salt it, which is not visible to the naked eye, but which undoubtedly makes the tobacco considerably heavier, and allows the unscrupulous shopkeepers there to fill their pockets at your expense. Of course, if you smoke salt, a whole host of unpleasant things might happen to you and your health might suffer seriously. But not because of the tobacco, gentlemen, but because of the salt. Thus, I will take the liberty of giving our smokers a piece of advice. Most of you have heard tobacconists, especially those who have long been in the business, saying that 'the Man in the Moon could enjoy his pipe.' Hence, the Man in the Moon is represented on some of the tobacconists' papers with a huge cloud of smoke billowing from his pipe and covering the entire sky, and underneath the words, 'Who'll smoake with ye Man in ye Moone?' My advice, gentlemen, is to look for this sign. That tobacco is pure and real. Not that the Birmingham counterfeiters could not counterfeit these papers—of course, they could—but at least they have not begun to do so as of yet."

A useful speech, indeed. How nice, I thought, that the debate about tobacco has shifted from a theoretical to a more practical vein. And even nicer still is the fact that in Spain such a problem does not exist. Where tobacco is sold in rolled-up leaves as cigars and cigarellas, such things are harder to do. Here they sell tobacco ground for pipes, and really anything could be mixed in there. It's no coincidence that the Dutch thought up this business. Those hucksters are constantly lying. That's why they came up with tobacco for pipes. They claim that they supposedly do it because that's the way the Indians themselves smoke it, but in fact they do it to cut the tobacco. Ask anyone in Spain about the Dutch and you'll get an earful. If they weren't such terrible liars, Duke de Alba would've gotten the best of them long ago. But no. They show up somewhere, our people go to engage them in battle, and they strike you somewhere else entirely. They are always up to tricks, constantly lying about something. Revolting people.

"Yes," the king called. "A Tobacco-seller is the only man that finds good in it which others brag of, but do not; for it is meat, drink, and clothes to him. I would call his shop the Rendezvous of spitting, where men dialogue with their noses, and their communication is smoke. It is the only place, by the way, where Spain is commended in this country, and preferred before England itself. Well, gentlemen, does anyone wish to take the floor before I make my concluding remarks?"

Dr. Cheynell raised his hand and once again took the floor. He stood up, still holding the pipe in his left hand, and said: "My intention, Your Majesty, honorable gentlemen, is to conclude this debate on a brighter note with the help of art. As they say, what else is art for, if not for that? Because our men of letters have discovered several charming properties of tobacco, which the heavy medical works do not mention. For example, one writer comes to mind, who in the part of his book dedicated to the Drunkard, wittily remarks that 'Tobacco serves to air him after a washing' [*i.e.* a drinking-bout]. Our poet Marston also described—in what seems to me chronological order—a whole series of actions, which make our lives pleasant and happy, when he says:

*Musicke, tobacco, sacke and sleepe,*
*The tide of sorrow backward keep.*

"I think, most honorable gentlemen, that he has every chance of being right. And please note that here also tobacco and wine go hand in hand. Thank you, thank you"—Dr. Cheynell bowed amidst the good-natured applause that had broken out. "Gentlemen," he continued afterwards, "sitting here next me is a little-known bard, whose name, I am certain, will live on in the future, even though you may be hearing it today for the first time. This is Mr. Barten Holiday. He wrote a poem of eight stanzas with a chorus to each in praise of tobacco, up to the exemplary requirements of the spirit of burlesque, and filled with inimitable wit—so inimitable, that one would say it had been boiled in dog's urine . . . thank you, thank you . . . in which poem, as I was saying, he shows the herb, which he calls 'Mr. Tobacco,' as a musician, a lawyer, a physician, a traveler, a tramp, and a braggart. Did I leave anything out, Mr. Holiday?"

"Yes," the latter replied. "Tobacco is also a critic."

"Ah, yes," Dr. Cheynell nodded. "I propose, gentlemen, that we hear this wonderful poem from Mr. Holiday himself."

With these words, Dr. Cheynell sat down, while Mr. Holiday, standing up next to him, cleared his throat, bowed, and said: "This poem, gentlemen, was written for accompaniment by harp and choir. Unfortunately, I do not have either one or the other of these at my disposal at the moment, for which reason I beg you to be satisfied by the words alone.

"Mr. Tobacco . . .

"Oh yes, let me just say as well that I will skip the choral section, which otherwise follows each stanza.

*Mr. Tobacco*

*Tobacco's a musician,*
*And in a pipe delighteth,*
*It descends in a close*
*Through the organ of the nose*
*With a relish that inviteth.*

*Tobacco is a Lawyer,*
*His pipes do love long cases;*
*When our braines it enters*
*Our feet do make indentures,*
*While we seal with stamping paces."*

I did not record any more of it, since it seemed to me unimportant. The poem, however, really was witty and was met with laughter and heartfelt applause. This poet indeed can look forward to a great future. Hardly as great as Pelletier du Mans, but still, he is nothing to sneeze at.

After that, the king took the floor and gave a short concluding speech, namely the following (after at least two minutes of addresses): "If there are men whose bodies are benefited by tobacco-smoke, this does not so much redound to the credit of tobacco, as it does reflect upon the depraved condition of such men, that their bodies should have sunk to the level of those of Barbarians so as to be affected by remedies such as are effective on the bodies of Barbarians and Indians! This is why I kindly suggest that both these people and the doctors who believe in the healing power of tobacco should take their medicine of pollution and join the Indians."

With that, the debate ended, in good spirits, and, it seems to me, satisfaction on both sides. In any case, our party had every reason to be satisfied. I along with Mr. Frampton, Dr. Monardes, Dr. Cheynell, Dr. Barclay, the bard Holiday, and the apothecary Venner stayed until late in the pub of the Toga and Rabbit Inn, where we spent an exceptionally pleasant evening. I was put up for the evening in the most luxurious room I've ever been in at an inn. It even had a terrace made of pure stone. Since I was still feeling highly excited from the debate and didn't feel like sleeping, I went out on the terrace and gazed at the stars in the sky. There's Venus, the brightest star on the horizon. Up there, above the moon, is Mars, twinkling slightly. In the other direction, down and to the right—Jupiter. I wonder what it is like to be a planet? Pelletier talks a lot about that. To drift through endless space, amidst the black horizons of the cosmos, alongside the stars and other planets, yet always following your own path, in your own unwavering orbit. Having the sun circle around you. To be Mars, Venus. Big and round, hanging in the sky like a giant fruit, swept through it like an enormous bird. If you're the Earth, you'll stand in the very center of the universe, and various people will jump all over you like lice. In what sense are they alive, and the planets are dead? This is some kind of misunderstanding. The planets, now that's real life. Just imagine living, or more precisely, existing, without experiencing hunger or thirst, without being hot or cold, without getting old? Not needing anything. To have countless things all over you. Take the Earth, for example, how many things it has . . . They all have countless things, yet at the same time are so different. Worlds. Each one of them—a different world. That's the Big Thing—being a planet. But yes, that's Nature for you. They are her big, majestic children. They are Nature herself. Or perhaps it is actually the other way around and they are the parents of Nature. While man is most likely just some jabbering, jumping nothing. But how to reach for that, how to reach that golden fruit hanging high in the sky? It's impossible. You were not meant to, by nature. Adam would be leaping endlessly towards that golden apple, and he'd still be in Paradise. No, it is not for his mouth.

And that idiot with his kingdom, with his social customs, with his pompous self-satisfaction. What bullshit! So the Indians are barbarians? Fine, so they're barbarians. But he himself is exactly the same, a most ordinary animal.

I took out a cigarella, took a drag off it, and felt a powerful rush of energy wash over me. Like Old Testament might, if I may express myself that way. Tobacco, Pelletier. What to do now?

*Musicke, tobacco, sacke and sleepe,*
*The tide of sorrow backward keep.*

I'll go to sleep. At least I'll try to.

# 12.
# For the Treatment of Domestic Animals and the Quick Accumulation of Wealth

One day, back in Sevilla again, Jesús came up to me with a puzzled look and said that a very strange dog had gotten into the garden.

"How could it have gotten in?" I wondered, since the garden had a high fence.

Jesús gave me a long and, as was to be expected, very confused explanation, which I will not torment the reader with here; rather, I will retell it coherently and in its essence: when Jesús passed by the Hospital of the Resurrection with the carriage, a dog started following him. But it wasn't one of those usual dogs you see wandering about the city, but obviously a well-kept, large dog, a shepherding breed, and, according to Jesús, it had a gold collar, or rather a hoop, around its neck. This caused me to raise my eyebrows skeptically, and I asked Jesús why, if the dog really had a gold hoop around its neck, he hadn't gotten down from the carriage to take off the hoop, even if that meant taking the head off with it—in case there was no other way of doing it; something which Jesús, as far as I know him, would do without batting an eye. But he replied that this was impossible and that I only needed to see the dog to understand why.

"Fine," I said. "Bring the dog over and let's have a look at it."

"I can't, señor," he replied, and so on, in the sense that the dog had followed him to Dr. Monardes' house, entered the yard when he had opened the gate to put the carriage inside, and was now rolling around in the doctor's tobacco plants.

"What?!" I exclaimed. "The doctor will kill us, you idiot! Or what, after building a barn, now you want us to plant a garden, too?!"

I ran towards the part of the garden where the tobacco plants were, with a visibly worried Jesús at my heels. We didn't have to search for long. The dog greeted us with a growl, its big canine teeth gleamed threateningly in the sun, along with the golden hoop around its neck. I immediately understood what Jesús was talking about. This was a big, strong dog, a shepherding breed, and it was visibly filled with animosity.

"Good boy, good boy," I said and quickly jumped back, running into Jesús, who was hiding behind my back, and almost fell. I would've fixed him good any other time, but now I didn't dare take my eyes off the dog. "Easy there, easy," I said. "Nice doggie, nice doggie."

The dog, however, didn't look too impressed by my words and kept growling at us menacingly. We stood there looking at each other for some time, not moving. Of course, the thought flashed through my mind that we could simply run away, but then the dog might chase us—and how could I be sure that it would chase Jesús, and not me? I tried to solve this problem by telling Jesús: "Run, Jesús, my friend!"

"Oh no, señor!" he replied.

So we stayed there, nailed to the spot. Fiendish cur! After growling for some time, it clearly decided that we were completely harmless and began rolling on its back amidst the doctor's tobacco plants. It had flattened a perimeter several feet wide with its powerful body and was now rolling around there. It looked harmless, obviously very satisfied, its paws were lifted in the air as if it wanted to play. Not that I had any intention of playing with it, but still, this calmed me a bit. My heart, which had been beating wildly, gradually returned to something like its normal rhythm. I was at a loss for what to do. For starters, I lit a cigarella. And then, oh wonder of wonders: the dog jumped at me, lightning fast, and before I knew it its front paws were on my chest, and its muzzle was more or less right in my face. It really was a big dog—standing up, it was almost as tall as I am. A long, curving tongue hung out of its open mouth and seemed to vibrate in the air. I got the impression that the dog was sniffing hard at me.

At the first moment, of course, everything swam before my eyes, and I noticed all these things only when the picture cleared up. I am inclined to think that someone else would have shat himself in such a situation. But not me, of course.

The dog, however, looked friendly enough. It crossed my mind that this was somehow connected to the cigarella. I took a long puff on it and the dog stretched its neck towards me and stirred, its heavy front paws shifting on my chest. Yes, there was undoubtedly some connection. The scent seemed to entice it.

I took advantage of the situation in the best possible way and very shortly the dog was again rolling around in the tobacco beds, while I was kneeling beside him, cigarella in hand, examining him closely. BERGANZA was written on its golden hoop in large letters, and a little to the side, in smaller letters: el Bávaro. The hoop was indeed very beautiful, thick and expensive—an exquisite piece of work. A scar from a wound was peeking out from beneath it. When I raised the hoop to get a better look at it, the dog growled menacingly and I quickly dropped the hoop.

"What does it say, señor?" asked Jesús, who was standing next to me.

"It says Berganza," I replied. "Berganza the Bavarian."

"How's that for a name!" Jesús said.

"There's nothing that strange about it," I objected. "His name is Berganza and he's from Bavaria. A Bavarian shepherd."

"He couldn't possibly have come here all the way from Bavaria, could he?" Jesús wondered aloud.

"I doubt it," I replied. "The dog is Spanish. Berganza isn't a German name."

"What will we do, señor?" Jesús asked.

Yes, good question. It had been running through my head for some time now.

"First, we need to inform Dr. Monardes," I answered. Of course we had to do this. Jesús, however, did not look very convinced.

"Can't we just make him leave?" he suggested.

"Look how he's rolling around in the tobacco plants. That dog isn't going to leave here voluntarily."

"But can't we somehow trick him into leaving?" Jesús asked, staring at my smoking cigarella.

"Here's the cigarella," I said, holding it out to him, "you trick him."

He, of course, did not express any desire to do this. So we headed for the doctor's house. The dog, however, set off after us. Somehow I didn't want us to arrive at the doctor's together, so I threw the almost burned-out cigarella onto the dirt of the walkway. The dog bent over it, started sniffing it and barking, while jumping back and forth.

"That dog is crazy," Jesús noted, with that rustic penchant of his for stating the obvious.

I went into the house (Jesús remained outside) and called to Dr. Monardes, who came down into the vestibule. The doctor hated being disturbed in his study, so our conversations often took place here.

"Señor," I said, "a big dog came into the yard, a Bavarian shepherd. His name is Berganza."

"What are you jabbering about?" the doctor replied with his back to me as he the poured himself rosemary syrup, which he drank for refreshment,

"I'm completely serious, señor. A very big dog. He's wallowing in the tobacco beds. His name is Berganza. He has a hoop around his neck and his name is written there."

"Get him out of there immediately! Get him out of the tobacco!"

"We can't, señor. The dog is very big and does not seem amicably disposed."

"So how did you find out it's a Bavarian shepherd?" the doctor asked.

"That's written on the collar, too, señor," I replied. "It says 'Berganza the Bavarian.'"

"So you're trying to tell me that there is a big German dog in my yard?"

"Yes, señor," I was forced to admit.

The doctor looked at me in silence for some time.

"That's all I need right now," he said suddenly, taking a swipe at me with his cane (not that he caught me unawares, of course), "to meet my end devoured by a dog! And how is it that you, idiot, allowed a German dog into my yard?"

"It wasn't me, señor. Jesús let him in."

"Jesús!" Dr. Monardes cried. "Come here this instant, you blockhead!"

Jesús, who had been listening outside the door, came in at that very moment, waving his hand in front of his face and saying: "No, no, señor! I didn't let him in. He came in on his own! Against my will. How could I stop him?"

I took a chance here and intervened, coherently recounting in Jesús' place how the dog had ended up in our yard. After all, we had to do something as quickly as possible. I really didn't feel like planting a garden. And I sure didn't want that dog hanging around here.

The doctor lit a cigarella, sunk in thought.

"Argh!" Dr. Monardes sighed deeply. "New headaches every day! . . . Fine, let's go see this dog."

"Why not wait, señor?" Jesús suggested. "It might leave. It might disappear on its own."

"Such things never disappear on their own," Dr. Monardes replied. "Money disappears on its own, but such things never do."

We went outside and set off along the sunlit walkway—Dr. Monardes and I next to each other and Jesús slightly behind us. We walked in silence, all three of us with cigarellas in hand, the only sound was our shoes crunching on the sandy ground. "How hot it is," I thought to myself.

"Berganza. That name sounds familiar to me from somewhere," the doctor broke the silence.

"I don't think there is anybody around here with that name," I said, mentally going over all the dog owners I knew, and all the dogs I'd ever seen as well.

"No, there isn't," Dr. Monardes agreed.

When we saw the dog, which was once again rolling around in the tobacco, the doctor froze in his tracks. I thought his heart had sunk at the sight of all that trampled tobacco and the ferocious dog in his garden, but that wasn't it. It was something else entirely.

"That's the king's dog!" Dr. Monardes exclaimed. "Berganza. Good God! What is the king's dog doing in my garden?" he turned his astonished face towards me.

I merely shrugged in reply. I myself was very surprised. The doctor went over to him, puffing on his cigarella, which was clenched in his mouth, grasping his cane firmly with both hands and holding it horizontally in front of him. The dog greeted him amicably, rolled towards him, and lay on its back, lifting its strong paws bent in the air. The doctor leaned over him and stroked his stomach. The dog rolled over onto its other side, then back again. He was playing. Jesús and I came a few steps closer.

"He seems to like the tobacco," the doctor noted, smoke billowing over the dog's head. "Easy, easy now," he said as he picked up the hoop around its neck. "This dog is injured. He has a scar on his neck," he noted. Then he drew up the dog's obedient head with his hand and said: "On the other side of the hoop it will say 'Felipe.' Here, come take a look."

I got closer to the dog. It really did say "Felipe."

"This is the king's dog," Dr. Monardes repeated, getting up and exhaling a long stream of smoke from his mouth, which slowly wafted through the air over our heads. "Since the dog is here, the king surely must be here, too. You need to find him and tell his people that his dog is here with us, and that they should come and get it. No, wait!" the doctor said after a brief pause. "Better yet, don't do anything at all. Leave things as they are. They will come looking for it themselves. Jesús, go out and find out whether the king is in the city. And let the dog stay here just as it is."

"Señor," I said in jest as we walked away, "what if we could sic the dog on the competition, say Dr. Bartholo . . . can you imagine?"

"Ha ha!" Dr. Monardes laughed heartily. "And afterwards no one could accuse us of anything!"

With these words, he went back into the house and I sat down on the steps in front of it, relieved.

It's no accident that the doctor had achieved such unparalleled success in his career. What is the secret of success in the medical profession? Knowledge, of course, as in every profession. But there is something else as well, which is also valid for every profession and which I must call, for lack of a better term, the ability to predict the future. Dr. Monardes was a genius in that respect. He was able to predict the future as well as those witches whom they burn at the stake, but unlike them, not only was he not burned up, he also earned thousands of ducats and fame throughout Europe. Long before he took up medicine, sailors with cigarellas were as common as blackberries in the port of Sevilla. But the doctor foresaw that tobacco had a great future, and he became grand and rich. He also foresaw that the New World would need slaves and got into that trade, together with Nuñez de Herrera, and became if not grand, then at least richer. Nobody could predict the future like he could. And it's not that tobacco is so very curative–it is, of course, and this is important, but if you go down to the chemist del Valle's, he can tell you dozens of substances, which, although they don't have the healing power of tobacco, nevertheless they have many merits, but no one has ever heard of them and almost no one uses them. While almost everyone now uses tobacco, especially in the medical profession, and it is celebrated around the world. Why is it celebrated and used, while these other things are not? Lord only knows. And Dr. Monardes, as well. Thanks to his ability to predict the future.

Although in this case his conjecture was not completely true. It was, however, confirmed in its essence. Because that very evening the royal physician, Dr. Bernard, turned up at our door. Dr. Bernard was a man with kind manners and expression, whom you see and instantly remember, without quite knowing why. He had an oval visage, chestnut hair, smooth open forehead, lively eyes, a hooked but well-proportioned nose, a coppery beard, and fair complexion. His figure was midway between the two extremes, neither tall nor short, somewhat stooped in the shoulders, with a pot belly and plump legs. Despite his youthful appearance, I would bet he was around fifty. No, the king wasn't in Sevilla. But yes, Dr. Bernard had arrived looking for the dog, Berganza.

While he was still explaining the purpose of his visit, I interrupted him, announcing with the satisfaction of a bearer of good news: "Señor, your dog is here."

Dr. Bernard was visibly delighted, but Dr. Monardes shot me a short, withering glance. Later, as we walked over to the dog—in his impatience, Dr. Bernard had gotten a few yards ahead of us—I turned to my teacher and quietly asked: "What's wrong, señor?"

"Idiot!" Dr. Monardes hissed. "We could've gotten at least one hundred ducats for searching for and finding the dog. At least one hundred."

"But perhaps the king will reward you in any case," I said.

"Oh yes," the doctor replied contemptuously, "he'll give me something that costs twenty."

Well, that's how you learn. Especially when you're young. At least with Dr. Monardes you really can learn lots of things from various fields.

While walking down the pathway, Dr. Bernard informed us that his assistants had told him that passersby had seen the dog near the Hospital of the Resurrection and that someone had further told them that he had seen it take off after Dr. Monardes' carriage. Dr. Bernard had been following the dog all the way from Toledo. Luckily, he said, it rarely went unnoticed—people usually noticed it wherever it went—so Dr. Bernard was able to follow it from town to town and from village to village all that way.

"Unbelievable!" Dr. Monardes exclaimed.

"Indeed it is, señor," Dr. Bernard agreed. "To tell you the truth, I didn't think we'd be able to find it despite all our efforts. Yet fate has smiled upon us! Unless Berganza has left your garden in the meantime. But I have reason to believe, especially given what you've said, that he will stay wherever there is tobacco."

Yes, so it was. We found Berganza in the tobacco. Not in exactly the same place, but again in the tobacco beds. He had trampled down a new section and was now rolling around there. The dog greeted Dr. Bernard rather hostilely, but with kind words—and most of all, with the help of a cigarella—the physician managed to win Berganza's good will.

The story which Dr. Bernard told us, his face glowing with joy as he stroked the dog sitting next to him, was almost unbelievable.

"Señores," he said. "Berganza was chosen for an experiment. Some people at the court—Duke de Sartoza, Duke de Molina, Cardinal Gonzalez, and others, all passionate hunters—claimed that nothing could counteract the crossbow shooter's herb. Here it must be noted as justification of their ignorance that with the help of this herb they have indeed killed many a savage beast in the Sierra Morena and elsewhere. They claimed that you need only smear the tip of your arrow or spear with the crossbow shooter's herb and it will kill absolutely any beast it hits, even if it strikes an otherwise nonfatal place."

"What is this crossbow shooter's herb?" I asked.

"The crossbow shooter's herb is . . ." Dr. Bernard began kindly.

"Long story," Dr. Monardes interrupted him with an impatient wave. "Now's not the time to explain the pharmacopeia. My disciple will learn that later. Please, go on, señor."

"He could've explained it to me in that time," I thought to myself, but didn't say anything.

"Of course, señores," Dr. Bernard replied. "Most willingly. It is indeed a pleasant and edifying story. Led by your excellent works about tobacco, señor"—Dr. Bernard nodded to Dr. Monardes—"as well as by my own inferences, I reached the conclusion that tobacco would be a wonderful antidote to the herb in question. After all, since it can act as an antidote to so many things and can heal almost every kind of wound by draining the pus out as if with a surgical scalpel or like a superb disinfectant, it makes sense that it could also neutralize the crossbow shooter's herb. This little debate of ours turned into a major topic of conversation at court for more than a month. All sorts of things can become a major topic of conversation at court. Finally, the king also took an interest in the matter and decided that the dispute should be resolved purely and simply with an experiment. We had planned on just taking some dog—or for greater certainty, two—from the streets of Madrid and conducting the experiment on them, when something happened that changed our plans. I hate to admit it, but Don Felipe has been having troubles with some of his relatives in Vienna lately. Troubles whose essence I cannot go into, but suffice to say that they are with Margaret of Austria."

"Ugh!" Dr. Monardes wrinkled his nose and waved dismissively.

"Yes, precisely," Dr. Bernard nodded. "This has distressed the good Don Felipe so much that he decided that we should experiment on the dog given to him as a puppy by Margaret. Namely, Berganza."

"What bad luck!" I exclaimed.

"Well, it's not so bad," replied Dr. Bernard, seeming a bit offended. "Besides, it turns out that Don Felipe had something else in mind, which we did not know then. We conducted the experiment about a month ago, on the morning of May 3rd, in this year of our Lord. In order for it to be completely convincing, and also at the insistence of Duke de Leon, who had taken my side and had wagered his estate in Padritos against Duke de Molina, I could not conduct the procedure on the paws or any other safer place on the body. Duke de Molina had explicitly requested that the incision be made in the throat–only in that case would he bet his hunting park in Extremadura that the dog would die. By the way, it later turned out that due to unpaid debts he had already long owed that park to Señor Espinosa, the trade magnate and your fellow Sevillian. Anyway. After all, almost everyone at court owes something to Señor Espinosa. I made a thin cut in Berganza's throat–actually much thinner and shorter than the unpleasant scar you see at the moment–but Duke de Molina insisted it be widened for the experiment to be completely convincing and threatened to withdraw from the bet otherwise. Since many of the others in the hunters' party had also wagered something or other on this experiment, he found strong support. In the end, the party of my adherents also joined them, since otherwise the bet threatened to fall through. So I was forced to make the rather large cut that you now see."

"Interesting people we've got at our court," said Dr. Monardes.

"Oh, without a doubt," Dr. Bernard nodded. "After I made the incision, I squeezed a few drops of the crossbow shooter's herb inside, whereupon Berganza almost immediately began to lose consciousness and stagger, his entire body began to tremble, his legs gave way beneath him. Every second mattered, señores, as you can surely imagine. I quickly continued with the experiment, urged on by the cries of Duke de Leon and members of his party, smearing the wound with tobacco juice and then covering it with finely ground tobacco leaves. This also had a quick effect. At first, Berganza's condition merely ceased to worsen, but around an hour or so later he began to visibly improve. In the meantime, a heated argument had arisen amongst our courtiers, since Duke de Leon wished to help the dog by lighting a cigar and so filling the air around him with rehabilitating tobacco fumes. Naturally, this would not have been easy, since we were outside, but when you take into account that Duke de Leon's party was quite numerous and if they all lit cigars simultaneously–which, by the way, they all were categorically ready to do–it could very well have had the desired effect. Of course, Duke de Molina and the hunters objected, Cardinal Gonzalez even gave a long and eloquent speech about why this should not be done, going so far as to cite, to my surprise, two of St. Thomas Aquinas's theological postulates, which I could also try to recall, if you wish," Dr. Bernard said, appearing to rub his forehead unconsciously.

"No, no, that doesn't interest me in the least," Dr. Monardes replied.

"Very well," Dr. Bernard continued. "To make a long story short, such a heated argument broke out that some suggested consulting the king. That, however, was impossible, since during those hours of the day Don Felipe is engaged in his long morning prayers, so those present decided to turn to the first minister, Duke de Leca, who in principle did not show any interest in what was going on and who at that moment was working on something in his office. Duke de Leca came in person and said that it was shameful to deny someone's right to smoke tobacco in Spain whenever and wherever he wished because–now these arguments I remember very well–Spain is tobacco's discoverer, many who live here owe their prosperity to it, and with an eye to the country's trade interest, it should even be mandatory, to say nothing of the 'absurdity'–as he put it–of forbidding anyone from smoking. And to set an example, he personally lit a cigar, followed immediately by Duke de Leon's party, as well as by myself."

"Señor de Leca is a smart man. I have always maintained that," Dr. Monardes nodded.

"Without a doubt, without a doubt," agreed the royal physician. "I am happy to inform you, señores, that after an hour and a half our Berganza had fully regained consciousness and stood up, albeit with a rather dazed look, and was surrounded by the exultant party of Duke de Leon, whom, incidentally, I was hardly able to restrain, as they all wanted to stroke and pat him and, despite my vigorous objections that now was not the moment for it, to toss him chunks of meat and sweets in their desire to fortify him. Good thing Berganza was tied up and unable to reach these treats; besides, he was still rather weak and did not show any particular interest in food. I assure you, señores, that a whole heap of meat and sweets piled up there."

"The latter especially could be very harmful to his vision," Dr. Monardes noted seriously.

"A most pertinent observation," agreed Dr. Bernard. "In any case, two hours and fifteen minutes after the beginning of the experiment, Berganza looked fully recovered. Before untying him, I insisted that all the food piled up nearby be removed and said that the experiment could not be considered finished until Berganza was untied–an opinion which Duke de Molina heartily seconded. This suggestion of mine, made with a view to the expediency of the moment, later turned out not to be such a good idea, but I mustn't get ahead of myself. Duke de Leon himself set an example by first beginning to carry away full handfuls of meat and sweets, followed quickly by all of his supporters, hence the pile of food was quickly cleared away. It was obvious that Berganza was already completely fine, he strained mightily at his leash and I didn't see any reason not to untie him and let him go free to play in the royal gardens. So that's what I did, and then, señores, he ran away. But something in the way in which he ran away told me that he wouldn't simply be found somewhere in the royal park. I think Duke de Molina noticed this, too. In any case, he insisted that before the experiment be considered finished, we find the dog and wait until the next morning to be sure that his recovery was not only temporary and that he continued to be alive and well the following day, too. Yet another heated debate arose around this, and since no one dared disturb Duke de Leca again, we decided to wait for Don Felipe to finish with his morning prayers and to consult with him. In the meantime, Duke de Leon's people swarmed the park searching for Berganza, and Don Felipe unexpectedly appeared of his own accord prematurely, rather peeved, since his prayers had been disturbed by the cries of those searching for the dog. Don Felipe ruled that Duke de Molina was right and that the experiment could be considered finished only after the dog was found and we could make sure that it was alive and well the next morning, too. It goes without saying that the dog was not found. As I came to know later, Duke de Leon's party secretly gathered in one of his chambers in Escorial that very afternoon, and those present decided to send people out to look for Berganza, especially since they feared that Duke de Molina's hunters would also send people out to kill Berganza and so prove that they had won the bet, or at the very least nullify it."

"So that means when the dog comes back now, Duke de Leon will win the estate in Extremadura, and everyone in his party will win the things they bet on with those from Molina's party?" Dr. Monardes asked.

"That's the way it turns out," replied Dr. Bernard.

Dr. Monardes once again shot me a withering, scathing glance, but merely said, "Gee."

But how could I have known? Oh, if I'd only known . . .

"Of course, someone informed Don Felipe about the gathering at Duke de Leon's, so he knew about it that very same evening, even before receiving a letter with the same information from First Minister de Leca. Incidentally, Duke de Molina's party had not organized the fiendish plot which Duke de Leon had suspected them of. Molina's people hadn't gotten together at all to discuss what had happened. But in any case, there was clearly a problem, and it could, at least potentially, grow to absurd proportions. For this reason, Don Felipe decided to take action and called me in. He also had another reason for trying to find the dog. I, of course, am telling you this, señores, in the strictest confidence, as fellow physicians, and also because its consequences will soon become known to all."

"Of course, señor, you can count on us," Dr. Monardes assured him. "Nothing will leave this company."

"I'm silent as the grave, señor," I, too, hastened to assure Dr. Bernard.

"Very well," he replied. "The point is, señores, that Margaret of Austria wants to somehow acquire our territories in the Low Countries, or at least the part of them that remained at our disposal after the Dutch Revolt. This would be very difficult to arrange if she hadn't found unexpected support at our court in the person of Señor de Leca himself—whose support, of course, she could hardly have any inkling of. Señor de Leca thinks we must give up the Low Countries because—put in his own pragmatic terms, señores—we have already stolen everything valuable there. Since our troops have plundered Antwerp, Brussels, and other cities, we no longer have anything to gain from those territories, yet we continue to waste lots of money on wars with those crazy Dutchmen, which have dragged on for so many years now. Señor de Leca has calculated that it will take at least twenty to thirty years—and years of peace and benevolence on the part of nature, at that—for the Low Countries to be rehabilitated after our operations there, before they will really begin to turn a profit as they did back in the days before the Dutch rebelled. For this reason he figures it would be good to transfer our possessions there to the Austrians, let them rehabilitate the place. Besides, until now they've only watched from the sidelines, even though they're our allies; let them rebuild the Low Countries now, that's what he says. And then, he says, we'll see. But that will take so much time that it will surely be the job of the next king, so let him decide what to do, if the Austrians even succeed at rebuilding those countries in the first place. As a rule, Señor de Leca thinks we should give up everything unnecessary in Europe that only creates trouble for us—'little lands, lots of expenses' is what he says—and focus all of our efforts and resources on the New World, which is a true source of inexhaustible wealth, still pristine and unmatched by anything here, in his opinion. Don Felipe, however, is not totally in agreement and doesn't feel like giving up the Low Countries. He was kind enough to confide in me that he has long since wondered what to do, and since it is very hard for him to make a decision, he has decided to leave everything in God's hands, and if I find Berganza, he will give the Low Countries to Margaret of Austria, and if not, that means it is God's will and he won't give them up, despite all of Duke de Leca's arguments."

"So that means that when Berganza returns now, Margaret of Austria will acquire the Low Countries?" Dr. Monardes asked.

"That's the way it is," replied Dr. Bernard.

This time Dr. Monardes did not look at me. Instead he looked up, towards the sky.

"What would happen," I thought to myself, "if right now, at this very moment, somebody killed Dr. Bernard? Jesús, for example." But I quickly dismissed this thought.

And rightly so:

"Several of Duke de Leon's commodores are waiting for me outside the door to your wonderful garden," he said, glancing around approvingly, "and when we put Berganza in my carriage, Margaret of Austria can consider the Low Countries her own. Of course, she will find this out only a month or so from now, when the letters reach her. Unless Don Felipe reverses his decision. But I've known him for many years, and as of yet he has never reversed a decision after saying that he has left it in God's hands."

"Most commendable." Dr. Monardes nodded, lit a cigarella, and cleared his throat. I lit a cigarella as well. Then Dr. Bernard did, too.

"To tell you the truth, señores," he continued, "when Don Felipe entrusted me with this task, almost no one believed that we would be able to find Berganza. And it truly would have been difficult, had I not received the unconditional support of Duke de Leon's party, which, by the way, includes several noblemen from your Andalusia. I doubt we would have succeeded had the good duke's supporters not roused their subjects to action and organized scouts in various places and so on. You can't imagine how many places they are searching for Berganza now. They are looking for him from Cadiz to Santander."

"Oh, I can imagine it very well," Dr. Monardes replied and exhaled a powerful stream of smoke. "But what happens to Duke de Molina's people?"

"Nothing," Dr. Bernard shook his head, smiling. "Nothing happens to them." He took a gold chain out of his inside pocket, hooked it to the dozing Berganza's collar, gave him a friendly pat, and said: "Come on, Berganza, come on, my friend. It's time for us to go."

Berganza got up clumsily, yawning with his enormous mouth. At that same moment, we heard stomping along the path, the clang of iron or some such thing, accompanied by—so it seemed to me, at least—the vague, yet worrisome sense of a human presence, and soon we saw several commodores, five in all, with Jesús, who was white as a sheet, leading them. "Leading" is not exactly the right word—one of the commodores, a very tall man, who looked even bigger thanks to the armor covering his entire body, had grabbed him by the back of the collar such that Jesús was not so much walking as mincing along ahead of him on his tiptoes. They had surely forced him to bring them to us. Without going into unnecessary detail, let me just say that the commodores looked very, very impressive with their shining armor covering them from head to toe and with halberds in their hands. A large *L* for Duke de Leon was engraved on the left side of their breastplates.

"Ah, there you are, señor," one of them said to Dr. Bernard. "We were beginning to worry that something had happened to you, since you were taking so long. But wait, that's Berganza!" he suddenly exclaimed, realizing who the dog before him was.

"Indeed it is. I am happy to inform you, señores, that our search has been crowned with success and that in the home of my friend Dr. Monardes, I am completely safe. Your concerns were unfounded. But all's well that ends well. And you can let that poor man go, by the way."

The tall commodore, who was standing at the far end of the group, let go of Jesús and gave him a friendly—in a certain sense—pat on the head with his metal glove. Perhaps I was hearing things, but I could've sworn his head clanged at that moment. Poor Jesús looked pretty bad. I had never seen him like that.

"Jesús, why didn't you call for us? We would've answered from here."

"Uh . . ." he replied in a choked voice, "I couldn't."

"Señores, I sincerely thank you for your invaluable assistance," said Dr. Bernard as he shook our hands. "We wouldn't have succeeded without your help. I am certain that His Majesty will not forget your incomparable service."

After that, we walked back to the garden gate, chatting with Dr. Bernard about the Andalusian heat. We, along with the commodores, helped him somehow load the struggling Berganza into his carriage and answered his final goodbyes with a wave as his carriage drove off down the road. The commodores were riding in a separate carriage. One of them—the one who had spoken in the garden—came up to us and said, "Señor Monardes, it is an honor for me to make the acquaintance of a great physician such as yourself. You cured my sister. I am Captain Alvarez of the royal guard. At one time, we lived in Formentera de Leon," he said, taking off his metal glove and holding his hand out to the doctor.

"Ah yes, now I recall," replied the doctor, shaking his hand. I know Dr. Monardes quite well by now, and from the confident and warm way he responded I would be willing to bet that he didn't recall a thing. "How is your dear sister?" the doctor asked.

"Very well, señor, thank you," Captain Alvarez replied with a cheerful laugh. "She married Duke de Leon."

"Well, what do you know," said the doctor. He's had quite a few surprises in one day, I would say.

"Señor," the captain continued, "I, too, would like to thank you in the king's name for your help today."

"I am honored to be at our king's service," replied Dr. Monardes. "Please give my personal greetings to Duke de Leon as well."

"By all means, señor," the captain replied, and he saluted and got into the commodores' elongated wagon, which took off after the royal physician's carriage.

The doctor and I remained on the street until the carriages disappeared from view, then we went back into the garden. The doctor was walking a step ahead of me in silence, his gaze fixed on the ground. I didn't know what to expect. The doctor shook his head and laughed. Then he shook his head and laughed again. I smiled. The doctor looked back to see if I was coming, met my gaze, laughed again, and kept walking, shaking his head from time to time.

Jesús was standing by the well splashing water on his face.

"Filled your pants, eh, Jesús?" Dr. Monardes called to him jokingly.

"Are they gone?" Jesús asked, stepping away from the well and glancing over our shoulders.

"They're not going to stay here for ages," replied the doctor. But then he stopped and turned around. I turned around, too. They had left, of course.

"Sons of bitches!" Jesús yelled. "Sponges! They don't plow, don't sow, don't work, yet they eat like pigs! Who feeds them? The people feed them! I feed them!" he cried, dramatically pounding his fist on the shabby, ragged undershirt covering his chest.

The doctor started laughing. "You better feed them voluntarily, otherwise they'll come to your house on their own and devour everything," he said. "Maybe even you. They might even devour the walls . . . And buy yourself some new clothes," he added as he passed Jesús. "Dr. Monardes' coachman can't be walking around in rags like a gypsy. Come tomorrow and I'll give you money for new clothes."

"Tomorrow, señor?" Jesús called, with that unexpected surge of quick-wittedness that was sometimes characteristic of him.

"Fine, here it is now." The doctor stopped, took out his purse, counted out a few coins, and dropped them into Jesús's palm. "All right, all right," he waved at Jesús, who had opened his mouth to thank him. "Guimarães"–he turned to me–"I'm going to lie down. I can't imagine anyone will come now, but if someone does turn up, send him away and tell him to come back tomorrow. No matter what the problem is. Even if the sky is falling."

"Very well, señor, you can count on me," I replied.

The doctor went up the steps to the house and disappeared inside.

I went over to Jesús, put my arm around his shoulders, and said: "Jesús, you're a fool, but I'm an even bigger fool than you."

"Oh, I can't believe it, señor," Jesús replied politely.

"It's true, it's true," I said. "Damn Portugal! Everyone in Portugal is really stupid."

"Hmm," said Jesús.

"It's something in the air there, you know. If you grow up there like I did, there's no way to avoid catching it."

"Hmm," said Jesús.

"Yes. Big mouth, big trouble," I said. "Listen, Jesús," I continued after a short pause, glancing at Dr. Monardes' dark house, "I was thinking of going down to Don Pedro's Three Horses to wet my whistle. If someone comes, send him away, all right?"

"Well, I don't know, señor . . . I was thinking of stepping out for a bit, too."

"Don't," I told him. "I know you and you know yourself. You'll go to some tavern, spend that money, and tomorrow the doctor will ask you where your new clothes are . . . Can't you just picture it?"

"That wouldn't be good," Jesús said.

"That wouldn't be good," I confirmed. "Best you stay here tonight, and if someone comes, send him away."

"Well . . . I don't feel like staying here alone, señor," he replied. For a moment I wondered whether I really shouldn't stay and let him go home to his wife and so on, or even take him with me to the Three Horses, but he added shortly: "Very well. Very well, señor."

"Good," I said and headed down the darkened walkway slowly at first, then faster and faster. Night had already fallen. When I got out onto Calle de la Sierpes, the city lamplighters were lighting the street lamps.

I needed to draw some conclusion from everything that had happened. Even though I wasn't too sure there would be any point to it—such things only happen once in a lifetime. The golden bird alights on your shoulder. You say something stupid. The bird flies away. Farewell, Guimarães da Silva, farewell, fool, you shan't be seeing me again. I had to come up with some conclusion. But what? Something very important should appear in my mind at this moment. But where? No matter how long I turned it inside out, I couldn't find anything too important in there. And that's when the thought struck me. Well, not exactly then, but later that night, as I staggered dizzily back through the streets of Sevilla. But that's how it is, such things dawn on you when you least expect it. It dawned on me that I could become a veterinary physician. I could cure animals with the help of tobacco. The competition in that department was very scarce. There was only one Dr. Duvar, also known as Pablo the Loser. And lots and lots of animals in the villages. No one treated animals with tobacco, even though it was known in principle to be able to cure them of certain things. Why, perhaps it could cure them of all the things it cured people of! Why not? It seemed like a brilliant idea to me at that moment. When I woke up the next morning, it didn't seem so brilliant. I said to myself: "I had to draw some conclusion, and just look at what I came up with!" And indeed, it didn't seem like much in view of the circumstances. Alas, the harsh light of day somehow makes everything fade drastically. But when I thought it over, I started to change my opinion little by little. In fact, the idea wasn't bad at all. I could try it, and if it turns out I've guessed right, I'll became rich and grand. It wouldn't even be necessary to treat animals for all sorts of illnesses. I did a little investigation into how things stood—via Dr. Monardes and others. It turned out that in almost all cases in which a veterinary physician was called involved some kind of wound—broken bones, cuts, bites, punctures, and so forth. Yes, that area of medicine was very backwards. And in such cases, veterinary physicians always used one and the same thing—sublimatum, or ratsbane, in the vernacular. Because of this, sublimatum had become so expensive that it was now more costly than the animals themselves, thus the villagers called a doctor only if they highly prized an animal, otherwise they tried to treat it themselves and it usually died or ended up lame. I shared my plans with Dr. Monardes and asked him whether tobacco really could heal animals' wounds. He said this was almost certainly true and that in the few cases it had been tested to this end, tobacco had done the trick very nicely. The doctor approved of my idea and promised to help me by announcing that I treated animals in the villages we passed through. He even agreed to give out the address of his house, in case someone decided to call for me. He finally even agreed to let me have the carriage and Jesús (who had bought himself new clothes, red from head to toe, such that the people in the villages took him for a gypsy flamenco dancer) when necessary, and in cases where it was unavailable, he promised to lend me the twenty or so ducats (interest free) that I would need to rent another carriage and make my rounds. His only condition was that I not expect help from him which would require his physical presence, since for a person such as himself that would be rather shameful and would give rise to rumors that he had fallen on hard times or some such thing, which, by the way, couldn't be further from the truth.

My first client was the peasant José from Dos Hermanas. The doctor and I had stopped there to make a call, after which we planned to continue on to see another sick man in Alcalá de Guadaira. As we announced on the square in Hermanas that I treated animals, the aforementioned José appeared and said that his cow had cut itself badly on a fence while trying, who knows why, to jump over it. The doctor let me go, giving me some final instructions on the healing of wounds with tobacco and wishing me luck. He would continue on with Jesús towards Alcalá de Guadaira, and they would pass by on their way back in the evening to pick me up from the square in Hermanas. I took a pouch of tobacco and some instruments and went to José's house. His cow had cut itself on the underside of its belly. They had covered the wound with walnut leaves to stop the bleeding, without much success—the leaves were red with blood, a very strange sight indeed. The cow was lying on the hay in the barn, exhausted and surrounded by José's noisy children, and even though it looked weak, I knew that as soon as I began to treat the wound she would go wild, so we called in two more men and even tied her back legs to a beam so she couldn't run away or kick anybody. In the meantime, I boiled the tobacco infusion, and when everything was ready I began working on the wound. I will not recount in detail how everything went—suffice to say that everything went successfully. Of course, the healing effect of the tobacco would become apparent the next day at the earliest and the treatment needed to continue for a week or so, nevertheless, certain signs of improvement were immediately apparent. The bleeding stopped. The tobacco leaves began sucking the impurities from the wound, as we could clearly see when we changed them. The cow calmed down. Overall, things had gotten off to a good start.

"I'm beginning a new life," I said to myself, as I smoked a cigarella in the yard in front of the barn. "Today, July 5, 1586, I am beginning a new life."

I charged José half of what the sublimatum would've cost him and still came out with a tenfold profit, even though I left him tobacco juice and quite a few leaves to apply to the wound over the coming week. He was so impressed that he also brought me a lame donkey with badly festering wounds on its legs, as well as a dog with mange on its neck. I fixed them up, too. José merely clicked his tongue and swore, but with those curses the peasants use to express satisfaction and which they usually only say halfway, finishing them off by spitting through their teeth. He was, as I said, very impressed.

"And so this stuff, señor, this tobacco, it can really cure all these diseases? Well, f . . ."

"Absolutely, José," I assured him. "What do you think this is, after all? This is a great new medicine. From the Indies. These wounds are nothing for it. It is even an antidote for the crossbow shooter's herb."

"Yes, yes, señor. What was that herb?" asked José.

"Long story." I waved dismissively. "We needn't bother with the fine points of the pharmacopeia. Why the devil should you need to know that?"

"Yes, yes, señor," José replied.

They always say that: "Yes, yes, señor." For all their vulgar language, the peasants are in fact meek, obedient people. I suspect this is why everyone does whatever they want with them. However, as meek and obedient as they may be, if you snatch one of their calves or move the fence even a yard, they'll slice you to ribbons without batting an eye. Strange people, a bit crazy. If I didn't know from medicine that all people are of one and the same animal species—that, say, the townspeople of Sevilla or Madrid and these peasants are of one and the same race—I would definitely have my doubts. It is true that they appear outwardly similar, but that isn't definitive proof. The horse and the mule also look alike, but they are different species. "Who knows?" I would say. And then I would give that example with the horse and the mule. But thanks to medicine, I know with certainty that we really are talking about the very same creatures. Say what you will, education has its advantages. Yes, small ones, that's true. But if you don't have any other advantages, as is usually the case, what else is there?

When I was done at José's, some of his neighbors called me over to their places, because they had sick animals as well and because the price of my tobacco treatments was such a bargain compared to sublimatum that, even though peasants are in principle tightfisted, they couldn't resist. I promised to drop by at the end of the week and hurried towards the square, since it was already dark. I found the doctor and Jesús waiting for me there. The doctor did not scold me for being late, but instead asked me how things had gone and seemed pleased by my story. He made things even easier for me by allowing me to go around to the villages by myself with Jesús on certain days, Saturday and Sunday, when he did not travel in principle—incidentally, the doctor was travelling less and less frequently, since it was simply no longer necessary and it bored him; instead, he preferred to treat the well-to-do townspeople of Sevilla, who now made up the greater part of his clientele. In the end, he even agreed that when we only had one call on a given day, after Jesús had driven him to that address, Jesús and I could go around to the villages, while the doctor himself would return home on foot. In the evening, Jesús and I would stop by the house he had visited to pick up his bag of instruments and medicine.

"But what would happen, señor, if another call came up during the day or there was some emergency?" I asked him.

"Well, if a second call comes up, I'll go on foot," said the doctor. "As for emergencies, as you've noticed, the clients usually come to me by coach."

"And your bag of tools?" I said. "It would remain at the first address."

"I have many bags of tools," the doctor smiled.

That was true, of course. Besides that, in his laboratory he had shelves upon shelves lined with ready-made packets of medicine for various common illnesses. He simply passed through there and grabbed two or three, depending on the symptoms they had reported. Dr. Monardes had been a physician for many years.

I think that lately he had begun to enjoy going on foot through the streets. Several times I happened to see him at such moments—he walked along calmly, with a cheerful expression, nodding at the passersby, who greeted him. He looked content. I think, in the spirit of Pelletier, that he found it pleasant to stroll around outdoors, feeling the sun's rays or a puff of wind on his face, he even seemed to find the human hubbub on the street pleasant. The doctor visited pubs very rarely and I personally only saw him in a pub once—at Don Pedro's Three Horses, when he, Dr. Monardes, half-jokingly suggested I become his student after he saw my performance with tobacco smoke. During the years I was his student, I don't think he ever once set foot in a pub. It is indecent for physicians, and even when they do go, they behave a little as though they were at an official reception. Oh yes, one time we did stop into a pub in Carmona, while we were waiting for a dressing to take effect before we had to go back and change it. But that was it.

Once I followed the doctor through the streets to see what he would do, where he would go. In my opinion, he was wandering about aimlessly, tracing out a large square through the streets of the city. I saw him late in the afternoon on San Francisco

Square as I was coming out of the Three Horses (I didn't find anyone there) and took off after him. He went to the cathedral, stopped on the Plaza de los Cantos, lit a cigarella, stared up at the weathervane on Giralda, stood there for a short while, then passed through the Puerta de Jerez into the Alcazar Gardens and came out on San Fernando Street, passed by the Convent of Santa Maria de Jesús, went to the market on Calle de la Feria, bought himself some oranges, continued on along Calatrava and went to the banks of the Guadalquivir, stopped there, peeled an orange and ate it, throwing the others into the river one by one. Afterwards he backtracked a bit on Calatrava, headed down Alameda de Hercules, crossed Imagen, continued along Sierpes, and arrived back home.

Another time I saw him go into his son-in-law Rodrigo de Brizuela's house to see his daughter. Yes, I think he simply likes strolling through the streets—always empty-handed, incidentally.

I also think that he has gotten a bit tired of Jesús and me, so he takes advantage of opportunities to get away from us. Now that his daughters are married and no longer live with him, we are the only ones underfoot around the house, or rather around the garden, since we rarely go inside the house. Yes, he is surely tired of seeing us every day, month after month, year after year. And in my new, brave, worldly undertaking in the veterinary sphere, which smacks of the boldness of youth, yet is still not lacking in insightfulness and a certain inventiveness, he sees a good opportunity to get rid of us, it seems, at least from time to time. I can't blame him, of course. On the contrary, I am grateful to him.

Jesús likes travelling with me. I am a more liberal master than Dr. Monardes. Sometimes I even sit on the coachbox with Jesús as we travel, to feel the wind with my whole body. It's very hot and stuffy inside the carriage. Of course, before we arrive in some village, we stop and I climb back inside. It can't be helped—authority obliges, as they say.

Since he bought himself new clothes, Jesús has become a new man. At least in a certain sense. Ever since the peasants, judging from his red attire, took him for a gypsy flamenco dancer, he really has learned to dance it. Yes, really. And quite well, even. While I go about my business, he stomps out flamenco on the square. I've seen him on my way back—one hand behind his back, the other lifted in the air with fingers spread, his body taut, dancing flamenco. He found a hat somewhere and collects money in it. He never wants for an audience and no matter how small the coins he gathers may be, they obviously add up to something, since he has bought himself a black sash and now, before we arrive somewhere, he ties it around his waist and dances with it on. He also pounded tacks into the soles of his shoes. Besides that, he has taught the horses to whinny when he gives them a sign—something like musical accompaniment. He lifts his hand towards them with fingers stretched wide, flutters his palms and they whinny and shake their heads. Well, they don't always whinny. Sometimes they only snort. Other times they only shake their heads. And sometimes they whinny when he hasn't given them the sign. But on the whole, things do work out once every two tries. I must admit that it looks quite impressive. I have no idea how he does it. I asked him, but he won't say.

"Oh no, I won't say, señor"—that was his answer.

Of course, he dances flamenco only when he is with me. He doesn't dare do it with the doctor since the latter saw him once and gave him a sharp tongue-lashing, saying that if he caught him banging around like a "crooked shutter"—that was the doctor's expression—on the squares while we were working, he would fire him on the spot (his exact phrase was "give him the boot").

"I don't want people to think I am accompanied by idiots," the doctor said. "I may know that's the case, but I don't want other people to know it, too. And get rid of those shoes, you raise more racket than the horses."

For that reason, when he is with Dr. Monardes, Jesús doesn't dare dance. He didn't get rid of the shoes, though. "I don't have any others," he says. I don't mind his dances—it's not all that important for a veterinary physician, so to speak—and Jesús is very pleased.

"Not only do you enjoy yourself and make a bit of money, but the girls also give you the eye"—that's what he says.

My business was going very well. Thanks to José, I gained quite a few clients in Dos Hermanas and the vicinity. I also had clients in Alcalá de Guadaira, Carmona, Espartinas, and a number of other places. I specialized in healing wounds. I refused to do anything else whatsoever. Deliveries, for example. In any case, the peasants are quite specialized in that department, they usually perform deliveries themselves and only rarely call a veterinarian for that sort of thing. You've got to be passing by somewhere by chance and some animal's got to be giving birth at that very moment for them to call you. And that's only if your services come cheap. But they'll call you for wounds, especially if your rates are good and the wounds are bad. I must say that tobacco works wonderfully in such cases. And it's a lot cheaper than sublimatum. As I mentioned above, I sold it at half the price of sublimatum and still turned a nice profit. Despite this, the peasants only called me when the things were getting complicated. Even my prices were often beyond their means. Peasants are tight-fisted. And they're poor, besides. This is a very bad combination, yet a common one. The good thing is that they are very attached to their animals. Very often, if a peasant's wife and cow are sick with one and the same thing, he won't call a doctor for his wife, but he will call a doctor for his cow. Yes, that's how it is. And the poorer the peasant, the truer that is. I suspect that the learned reader will be astonished by this absolutely indisputable fact and will say to himself: "How is that possible? Why would peasants hold their animals dearer than their wives?" he will ask. "Doesn't Dr. Monardes say that woman is Nature's highest creation in the entire animal kingdom, from beginning to end and with no exception? And that within the human biological species the human female is more valuable to Nature than the human male and perhaps Nature herself has arranged things such that lo and behold, the male is killed off in wars, he suffers in building accidents, falls from scaffolding, foolishly dies at sea, and so on, while Nature has safeguarded the human female from such things—why, then, would these damned peasants act in such an unbelievable manner?"

My answer, set forth in the spirit of scholasticism, is as follows:

If a peasant's wife dies, he can still eat his cows. But if his cows die, he cannot eat his wife. Not in Spain, in any case. And then he will slip into starvation, menaced by the gravest poverty. Poverty does monstrous things to a man. It turns him into a werewolf, a vampire, he loses his human appearance and falls back into Nature's slavery, which he had struggled with all his might to wrench himself free from. But you can't wrench yourself free if you're poor. And nobody wants to be a werewolf or a vampire. And not just because of eternal life and that you'll lose your soul and so on. That's the least of your worries. Rather because such things make life much harder. It is extremely hard to be poor. I even doubt that life is worth living if you're poor. Those sly dogs were right to think up so many things to make the world look complicated. Otherwise the poor would've slit their throats and taken their money. The poor are werewolves, vampires—they can kill you just like that. For this reason you have to constantly bamboozle them with thousands of things. But I, Guimarães da Silva, as a student of Dr. Monardes, of course know that which the sly dogs also know. Namely that there are only two things in the world, two states: having money and not having money. Nothing else exists, or if it does exist, it doesn't matter. Having money, not having money—that's everything in this world, the root of all wisdom and the entirety of wisdom itself from beginning to end. Everything else is blah-blah-blah and empty fabrications. The world is very simple, it is an idiot and as simple as a moron. Either you have money or you don't have money. That's it. If you don't, you've got to get some. Somehow.

Just look—I, for example, was on my way to becoming Doctor Veterinaris. For the first time in my life the ducats were flowing to me much faster than I could spend them. This somehow makes you optimistic. I decided to expand my activity with a radical, decisive step. I had managed to convince the peasants to put tobacco in their animals' fodder. That, I told them, would serve as a preventive measure and would protect their animals from more or less all kinds of illnesses. But of course, this couldn't be done with ordinary tobacco, which they could simply go and buy from the port in Sevilla, but with a specially prepared nourishing tobacco, which I sold to them. Nourishing tobacco differs from ordinary tobacco in that someone says it is nourishing and also finds someone else who believes him and is even willing to pay him for it. Only then does nourishing tobacco become nourishing. In a certain sense it really is nourishing, but only for some.

It crossed my mind to wet the tobacco, bake it or process it in some other way such that it would slightly change color and thus be visibly distinguishable from ordinary tobacco, but I decided against it. If I did that, I would start to resemble someone from that despicable tribe of Birmingham counterfeiters. No, doing such things didn't suit me. I sold them tobacco just as it was when it arrived in Sevilla on Nuñez de Herrera's ships. I could have taken it from Señor Espinosa's ships as well, but since Dr. Monardes was a partner of the Herrera family, I, of course, got it from them a bit cheaper. Here, however, I ran into a major difficulty. For my purposes I needed to rent a warehouse in the port. And not some big warehouse, which I couldn't afford and had no use for anyway, but a small warehouse, of the kind which was now getting harder and harder to find, or else just part of a big one—some corner to rent. This turned out to be a devil of a job. Not because it was in principle impossible, but because the merchants, and especially those with warehouses, have a completely different concept of money. In the first instant you might think that they must have made some kind of mistake and can only make out numerals with the greatest effort. Their concept of numerals is completely different. What am I trying to say? I will clarify with an example. For example, if you are a citizen of Sevilla and are walking down the street with ten ducats in your pocket, this makes you quite a wealthy citizen of Sevilla, or at least you seem to be by all outward appearances—you can buy whatever you want and you'll still have something left in your pocket. But if that same you goes with those same ten ducats in your pocket to the merchants at the port, they'll run right over you as if you were thin air, and not because they mean you any harm or some such thing, but because they truly do not notice you. No, this job was definitely beyond my powers. My good idea would purely and simply have fallen apart, if it hadn't been for Dr. Monardes' invaluable help once again. He agreed to sell me, at a friendly mark-up, tobacco from his personal supplies, which he stored in a large structure in his garden, and if my business really took off, he was prepared to give me some space in a warehouse in the port, which he owned together with Nuñez de Herrera's heirs. But for that he would have to speak with his son-in-law Rodrigo de Brizuela, who represented the Herrera family here in Sevilla. Not that it wouldn't have worked out, but Dr. Monardes did not like speaking with his son-in-law de Brizuela.

After this difficulty was resolved, my new initiative got off to quite a promising start. I rented another cart (so as not to soil Dr. Monardes' carriage), and Jesús and I went around to the villages, selling the peasants nourishing tobacco.

"How should I mix it?" asked José from Dos Hermanas, whom I went to first.

"One handful per bucket," I said. "Two for ideal results. You'd best use a handful and a half."

He decided on one handful per bucket and bought quite a bit

of tobacco, since he had lots of animals. Then the other villagers in Dos Hermanas bought some as well. And so on. My business was taking off. I didn't feel like healing wounds and so forth at all anymore, but it couldn't be helped, I kept doing it because of the nourishing tobacco. If I could've just dealt with the latter, I definitely would have preferred it, of course. Medicine, which until then I had always considered an enormous privilege, began looking to me a bit like a thankless profession. Especially veterinary medicine. You go around, stepping in animal shit, manure and mud, you struggle with these big unreasonable animals, they are in pain, you have to constantly watch to make sure they don't kick you, because then you'll have to heal yourself, you constantly have to deal with various peasants who are completely devoid of any artistic flair whatsoever—work-worn, stingy types, rooted in the ground, one would say they were talking trees . . . How different Jesús is from them—I now realized this for the first time. Yes, if I didn't know it from medicine, I would never have believed that people in the cities and those in the villages are one and the same animal species. Jesús dances flamenco, collects tips in a hat; he may be foolish, but he's crafty. Actually, I'm not so sure he's all that foolish. And if he had to work like those crazy peasants, he would surely get sick and die. Nobody can work like them. Well, perhaps Dr. Monardes. But definitely not Jesús. Despite this, I would far prefer his company to theirs. The problem is, however, that you can't sell him nourishing tobacco. There's no way.

For a few months, I sold nourishing tobacco with unbelievable success. What is this pleasant fairytale, I asked myself, what is this legend? Everything was going very well until that idiot, that scoundrel Duvar, Pablo the Loser, started meddling. Like that fly or whatever it was in the Bible, which spoils all the flour. I can't imagine it was a fly—how could a fly spoil flour? Maybe it wasn't flour. Or maybe it wasn't from the Bible. But what I mean is this: Duvar, from whom I'd taken the better part of his business and whom I'd magnanimously left only to perform deliveries—just enough so as not to starve to death, and most of all because I didn't feel like bothering with that—Duvar told the peasants that this wasn't any kind of nourishing tobacco at all, but the most average, ordinary tobacco, which they could buy for themselves five times cheaper at the port of Sevilla. Such things get around very quickly amongst the peasants and they soon began looking askance at me and I began losing clients. Things continued going well more or less, although nothing like before, for about a month, until Señor Espinosa's people showed up. Espinosa had somehow gotten wind that the peasants in the vicinity of Sevilla and even further away in Andalusia were buying tobacco in droves, and he sent his people there to sell it to them—far cheaper than I could sell it to them—thus saving them the trip to Sevilla. Espinosa's people poured out like a waves, like water—uncontainable, getting in everywhere, flooding everything. Wherever I went, they'd already been there. They travelled the roads in carts, taking orders and delivering tobacco. Sometimes Jesús and I would come across them. Lots of people, well organized. As far as I could gather, Duvar, unlike before, had begun saying that ordinary tobacco—even though it is ordinary and not nourishing—was very good for animals. I can guess why he changed his opinion.

My business completely dried up. I continued driving around the environs of Sevilla with Jesús for some time, going farther and farther afield, but in vain. Nourishing tobacco was sunk, at least for me. I had to give up.

"Jesús, I thought it all up," I told him once, one afternoon as we were returning to Sevilla. "It was my discovery."

"Bravo, señor," Jesús replied. "It sure was a good idea. A big thing."

"Yes, I thought up nourishing tobacco. And what did I get for that? Nothing!"

"Well, not absolutely nothing, señor."

"It's nothing," I waved dismissively. "Espinosa will reap all the rewards. Espinosa owes me!"

"You should tell him that, señor," replied Jesús.

I studied him for a long time. Was this good-for-nothing making fun of me? Jesús was staring straight ahead at the road, expressionless. Had he perhaps gotten too sly?

"Yes, definitely," I said in a moment and leaned back.

But I didn't plan on just leaving things as they were. That scoundrel Duvar would have to pay! I would talk to Rincon about fixing him good! Rincon could knock some sense into his head, arrange for him to spend some time at Dr. Bartholo's hospital thinking over what had happened to him and why, the stupid fool. One afternoon I was already on my way to the Three Horses to look for Rincon when I started having second thoughts. The problem was that after they took care of Duvar, he could pay to have them take care of me. Rincon would never turn anybody down as long as they could pay. And if not him, then he'd find someone else. You can find plenty of people for that sort of thing in Sevilla. And what would happen, I thought, if I paid Rincon to make him disappear? That way Duvar couldn't take revenge. Because he would have disappeared. I had earned a little something from nourishing tobacco, after all—yes, Jesús was right—and I could easily pay Rincon to make Dr. Duvar disappear. Reason suggested that this would be the most correct, least dangerous move with an eye to the future. Yet some murky force within me, some superstition desperately opposed this thought. I started wandering through the streets near the Three Horses, wondering what to do. But I couldn't decide. So I decided to ask Dr. Monardes instead.

"Such things are not done," Dr. Monardes answered sharply, looking at me seriously. "Otherwise someone, let's say Dr. Bartholo, could pay for us to disappear. If you pay to make Duvar disappear now, later someone might pay to make you disappear. For some reason, that's almost always how it turns out. The devil does not exist, of course, he is simply a foolish superstition, but don't bank too much on that. Certain things are not worth verifying. If you verify it and it turns out you were wrong, what then? And there are two more problems, which you certainly would have seen, if irritation hadn't clouded your mind. First, Dr. Duvar's disappearance at the present moment would not change anything. That trade has already been taken over by Espinosa, and it will continue, with or without Duvar. In the practical sense, you have nothing to gain from Duvar's disappearance. And you can't make Señor Espinosa disappear, too," the doctor laughed.

"Yes, of course," I quickly agreed. "There was never any question of that at all."

"So that means that besides satisfying your thirst for revenge, you don't stand to gain anything. And second," Dr. Monardes continued, "even Rincon wouldn't be able to work on Duvar's disappearance without first letting that boss of theirs in on it, what's his name, Ma . . . Mo . . ."

"Monipodio," I said.

"Yes, Monipodio. And what problem does the thieves' guild have with stupid old Pablo? Most likely none at all. Otherwise he would've disappeared long ago without your help," Dr. Monardes waved his hand. "So it is highly likely that Monipodio wouldn't agree to it. And if he does agree to it, then it's no longer between you and Duvar, but between Duvar and the thieves' guild. So then you'll have to pay not only Rincon, but the whole guild. That will turn out to be much more expensive than you think. Much, much more expensive," Dr. Monardes repeated. "You should have talked to Dr. Duvar from the very beginning," he continued after a bit, seeing my despairing look, I suppose. "As soon as you decided to sell that nourishing tobacco."

"I didn't think of it then," I said.

"No, you didn't think of it," Dr. Monardes nodded.

"I just thought to kick him out," I said after a short pause.

"That could have been arranged, too," the doctor shook his head, "but in a different way. You shouldn't have just pretended Duvar didn't exist, instead you needed to convince the peasants that he couldn't be trusted about anything. About anything whatsoever. That way when he told them that nourishing tobacco is not nourishing tobacco, but rather the most ordinary tobacco from Trinidad, which everyone can buy from the port of Sevilla, they simply would not have believed him. But then you would've had to take up deliveries, too, and all those other things you had left to Duvar. You needed to supplant him completely, to not give him any chance at all, not a single inch of space. I, for example, would do exactly that with Dr. Bartholo, if it were at all possible. Unfortunately, it is not. What, do you think I have any need to give lectures at the university or to do rounds three times a week at Charity Hospital? Those things hardly make you any money. I make more off my clients in three or four days. Yet the minute I'm somewhere, it means that Dr. Bartholo is not there. That's how these things are done."

I shook my head in silence.

"Thank you, señor," I said in a moment and got up. "Your advice has been useful, as always."

"I wish I could say the same," the doctor laughed, also getting up. "Come on, come with me to visit Doña Maria Hermencia. That lass with the bad breath, remember? She is with child."

"You don't say!" I exclaimed. "It seems like only yesterday."

"Time flies," replied the doctor. Later, as we were leaving his study, he said: "Ditch those animals, Guimarães. Shit, manure, unreasonable peasants . . . There's no point. What's the point of treating the lower species when you can treat the supreme species in the animal kingdom?"

"One could make some profit on it, señor," I answered.

"Well, probably so," said Dr. Monardes, adjusting his hat in front of the mirror. "But if you had wanted to become a merchant, you should've gone to study with Espinosa, not with me. But he would never have taken you."

That was true.

However, over the next several days I continued wondering what to do. No, not about Duvar—Dr. Monardes had banished that thought from my head—but about veterinary medicine as a whole. Nourishing tobacco had fallen through, or rather, had gone to work for Señor Espinosa, but still, all was not lost for me . . . In the end, however, I decided to give up on it. Of course, I could have continued to treat animals. There's a place for everyone under the sun, as they say. The question is which place exactly. A painful feeling seized me. The world began to look narrow to me, somehow clogged up—like a spring covered by a huge stone slab. It could hardly trickle beneath it. You are surrounded by thousands of invisible walls. Some paths are permitted, while others are forbidden. The best ones are forbidden. A big stone slab is blocking them. You've got to be really sharp-witted, to be very strong, decisive, downright reckless to move that slab. And even then it's far from sure. You are more likely to crack your head on it. Because it isn't just sitting there on the path. They're guarding it. Espinosa's people are there, that Captain Alvarez is there, Duke de Leon and his friends, even Rincon is there, in fact, and he's guarding it, too. You don't stand a chance. No chance at all. You can pass by only if they let you. And why would they let you? There would have to be some very special reason.

At the beginning of the next week, the doctor and I were on our way to Utrera and passed through Dos Hermanas. It was a warm, sunny day and animals could be seen on the hills along the road—mostly pigs, but also cows, some shaggy white sheep here and there, donkeys, dogs, horses, buffalo. Animals. Sorrow suddenly gripped me. I stuck my head out the carriage window, my eyes teared up. Animals are good, especially when you are looking at them from a distance. I would say that after the tricks with smoke in the taverns, they were my first serious commercial undertaking. And a far more serious one, at that. I was a hair's breadth from success. Animals could have made me rich. Just as they give food and provide a livelihood to so many people. Heartless humanity, which only torments them, uses them ruthlessly, and only feeds them so as to be able to eat them later, fattened up. Like a thousand-headed, thousand-armed predator. While animals are good. They graze gently in the fields. They wobble slightly, look around with their big, uncomprehending, good-natured eyes. I wonder what Pelletier would say about them? What would he say, if one warm sunny day he were travelling under the southern sky of Andalusia amidst the green fields, dotted with gentle (in most cases) animals, while his carriage drove even farther down, farther south, and they gradually disappeared from view? Farewell, animals! he would say. Good, gentle animals. Farewell! May God bless you and keep you! He alone can save you.

# 13. For the Healing of Scabs

Luisa, a sixteen- or seventeen-year-old lass from Sevilla, had scabs on the back of her neck. Her parents called us to treat her. The girl wore her hair long, so the scabs couldn't be seen, and they were not painful unless pressed, thus they had gone untreated for many years. Her parents said that she had had them since childhood. Recently, however, a new one had appeared, and the girl had asked to be treated. This, of course, was not a problem for us—tobacco heals scabs wonderfully. I stayed at the house on Santa Cruz while the doctor rubbed the scabs with tobacco, after which I parted with him and went to check on the health of a man whom the doctor had been treating for pain in the lower back. Around an hour later I returned to Luisa's house, and what I saw downright astonished me. The girl was acting crazy. Moreover, shortly after I came in, she burst into such violent sobs that you'd think she were being sent to the gallows, and by all appearances it was somehow connected with me.

"Let's go outside," the doctor grabbed me by the elbow and nodded to the girl's mother, who stayed in the room along with her little brother (her father had meanwhile gone out on business). "You seem to be upsetting the young lady somehow," the doctor said once we were out in the yard, as he lit a cigarella with satisfaction.

"I didn't do anything, señor. I don't even know her at all. I saw her for the first time in my life today," I said. And that was the truth.

"I know," replied the doctor. "The girl isn't in her right mind. She's acting crazy."

"Perhaps the lass has fallen in love with someone? That happens to them constantly at this age."

"I don't think so," answered the doctor. "Her parents don't know of her having fallen in love with anybody."

"But would they really know if she had fallen in love with someone?"

"Oh yes, and how!" the doctor exclaimed. "Don't forget, I have two daughters."

"So why is she acting so crazy, then?" I wondered aloud.

"From the tobacco," the doctor replied.

"But what all did you do to her, señor? Did you give her too much or what? . . ."

"No, it was nothing out of the ordinary," the doctor replied. "Tobacco simply has a bad effect on young girls. That's not due to tobacco, but to Nature herself. Nature exerts terrible pressure on young girls for her own ends. It thrashes around inside them like an eel. A terrible business, I know that from my daughters. Young girls constantly look half-crazed, not quite in their right minds, somehow. This is Nature's doing. Just add a little tobacco to that jumble as well and it turns into a complete mess. Once they marry and have children they start to pull themselves together little by little. Nature starts leaving them in peace."

"Yes, she's done her job," I suggested.

"Something like that," the doctor nodded and was seized with a fit of that prolonged, dry cough that had been bothering him lately.

"You haven't caught cold, have you, señor?" I asked politely.

"No," he replied. "I think it's from tobacco."

"From tobacco, señor?"

The doctor nodded, his cheek bulging, threw down his dying cigarella, and started coughing again.

"But I don't cough, señor."

"I've been sustaining myself with tobacco for twenty years longer than you have," replied the doctor. "There seems to be something in tobacco which causes such a cough. After many, many years."

Today is a bad day for tobacco, I thought to myself.

"Let's go inside to see what the girl is doing," said the doctor. "If she starts bawling again when she sees you, go outside and wait for me in the carriage with Jesús. Where is he, by the way?"

"He moved around the corner, señor."

"And what is he doing there?" the doctor wondered.

"Nothing. Just sitting there." I didn't dare tell him. In fact, Jesús was stomping out flamenco and collecting money in a hat. He had now started doing it in the city, too, whenever possible. I was amazed that the doctor didn't notice the horses whinnying from time to time. He surely thought some carriages were just passing by on the street.

This time the girl did not burst into tears when we entered the room. On the contrary, as soon as she saw us, she smiled happily, then rolled over to the other side of the bed and covered her face with the pillow. Her mother scolded her, wrested the pillow from her hands, and forced it under her head. The girl started sniffling.

"Stay like that, my dear, stay just like that," the doctor said, moving her hair and looking at the scabs. "Everything is fine,"—he turned to the mother shortly—"she'll get better."

"I am free to go now?" asked the girl, who had stopped sniffling.

Then in ten minutes she did so many things that if I were to describe them in detail, it would fill several pages. For example, she got up, started singing "Dark-eyed Chiquita" softly to herself—a popular song in Sevilla, mainly among the women—and went, with something I would call smooth leaps, over to the window. Her fragile body seemed to float through the air. She looked out the window, mercilessly crumpling her skirts with her hands, stopped singing and began humming instead, then laughed and said: "Some clown is dancing flamenco and collecting money in a hat."

Fortunately, no one paid her any attention. The doctor at that moment was speaking with her mother and surely thought that the girl was just talking nonsense. Shortly thereafter the whinnying of horses could be heard from outside, but the lass had already turned her back on the window, run to the bed, snatched up her brother, and begun hugging him in a frenzy. Her little brother, a seven- or eight-year-old boy by the name of Pedro, began snorting, his cheeks bulging.

"Let him go, you little hussy!" cried her mother, bounding over to the bed and forcefully tearing the boy out of her arms.

The girl began to cry again, threw herself down on the bed, covered her head with the pillow, and continued sobbing beneath it. In the meantime, her father had appeared. He opened the door, peeked inside, surveyed the above-described scene, then pulled his head back out and shut the door from the outside. The little boy also wanted to leave, but his mother wouldn't let him. The girl suddenly sat up on the bed with a sad face and eyes red from crying and starting taking off her stockings.

"What are you doing?" her mother asked.

"I want to be barefoot," the girl replied curtly and hurled the sock onto the floor.

How nice, I thought to myself, that unlike that little boy, we can always leave. The doctor seemed to be thinking along the same lines as well, since he said goodbye to the mother and the girl, promised to come to see how things were going the next day, and opened the door. We almost ran into the father, who was standing right outside, looking at us with a tortured expression.

"Goodbye, señor," said the doctor.

"Goodbye, señores," the man replied.

I nodded as I passed him. It was on the tip of my tongue to wish him a pleasant day, but somehow I decided against it.

"Jesús," I called loudly, as soon as we stepped out into the yard, "where are you, Jesús?"

Jesús was around the corner, quietly waiting for us on the coachbox.

On the following day, the doctor sent me to check on the girl, Luisa. I didn't feel like going at all, let alone by myself, but it couldn't be helped. My apprehensions, however, were unjustified. This time the girl behaved very demurely, looking down bashfully most of the time and giving one-syllable answers to my questions. Perhaps the effect of the tobacco had worn off, I don't know. Fortunately, it was not necessary to treat her with tobacco again and the doctor's prognosis was that the scabs would disappear within a week.

Returning from there with a light heart, I came across a truly impressive sight. I saw that crazy Dr. Vallejo from Madrid—a one in a million chance. At first I wasn't sure it was really him, but when I asked around at the Three Horses, it turned out that I was right. This Vallejo was a strange doctor, more likely a charlatan, who went around from city to city and nobleman to nobleman with the hope of finding someone who would give him the money to develop his so-called "vaccine." This "vaccine," so he says, is something like a disease, which, if taken in small doses, makes you resistant to the cause. According to him, you could cure almost every infectious disease this way. This would be, he claims, the greatest, most revolutionary idea in medicine from our era. But for every disease the quantity of the "vaccine" was supposedly different and so forth, thus he needed money to research this business. Sly dog. From what I understood, he had gone to Count Azuaga, who had a summer villa near Sevilla, in the hopes of squeezing some cash out of him. The count was a polite man, with a sense for the humorous in life and a certain taste for madmen, as well as for sly dogs, thus instead of throwing him out on his ear, he received him politely, even arranged a reception in his honor, to which he invited the powerful landholders in the vicinity, so they could see such a specimen with their own eyes and hear his cock-and-bull stories from his own lips, after which the count assured him that since he would probably die far earlier than the doctor due to his failure to use the "vaccine," he would will him the estate, so that he could develop his great medicine in peace, and then sent him politely on his way. From there, I came to understand, the said Vallejo had gone to Señor Espinosa, but Espinosa is a very busy man and sent him away without such ceremonies. Incidentally, I asked Dr. Monardes what he thought of Vallejo's so-called "vaccine."

"Ha ha," laughed Dr. Monardes. "He wants to convince us that something which at one of its extremes causes sickness and death, but which at its other extreme is entirely ineffective, and consequently again causes death, becomes curative somewhere in the middle. Now, don't misunderstand me," the doctor clarified. "Taken by itself, that is a completely trivial idea and applies to all medicines. But with the huge and decisive difference that no medicine is created from that which it heals, but on the contrary, it is a different substance, with opposite properties. It has a nature inimical to the nature of the illness. This Vallejo essentially wants to convince us that plague can be cured with plague, cholera with cholera, and so on. Are you even listening to what you're saying, Guimarães?"

"Please, please, señor." I raised my hand, protesting vigorously. "I was just asking."

"Impossible!" the doctor snapped. "Complete and dangerous nonsense. One should have an open mind, receptive to new knowledge, but not so open that his brain falls out"—here the doctor quoted a famous English proverb—"and if the Inquisition were to busy itself with something sensible, instead of persecuting so-called heretics, it would have locked up that charlatan long ago."

The lass Luisa really did recover, at least in the sense that her scabs disappeared after a few days. This came about by rubbing them with an infusion of ground-up, three-year-old tobacco leaves from Trinidad. The results were astounding. On his visit to the girl's house at the end of the week, the doctor took advantage of the opportunity to speak with her father. This business is a bit complicated, thus I will attempt to explain it with a preface of sorts. The doctor had a house in "The Skulls," as the region of Sevilla around the Puerta de Jerez was known; he rented out the house in question. But he had long since gotten it into his head and had been trying—although not very energetically—to buy up a relatively large piece of land next to it and to include it in his yard. The land was empty and belonged to the municipality, because it was an ancient Roman burial ground—hence the name, and indeed, you really could find some bone or other there if you dug a meter or so into the ground. I've even heard that during floods sometimes bones come floating to the surface. For this reason, the municipality had put a ban on building anything whatsoever there, as it considered the space a cemetery. The doctor, as well as many others, had built houses there before the municipality made this decision, which, in a rapidly growing city like Sevilla, became the object of endless disputes, and the municipality perhaps would have given permission to build there if the church, which objected to such building, hadn't gotten involved. To confuse matters completely, the king's people also got involved in the dispute, as they wanted to build a station there to tax the wine and foodstuffs that entered Sevilla through the Puerta de Jerez. The merchants, who until then had pressured the municipality to get rid of the ban, were now divided and began arguing amongst themselves—which side they were on, of course, depended on whether they imported goods through the port, where they were taxed in any case, or whether they transported them via Puerta de Jerez, where they were not taxed.

Of course, not everyone could bring their goods in through the Puerta de Jerez—those who traded in transoceanic goods had to stop at the port, like it or not. Even if they were sneaky enough to stop at the Port of Cadiz and from there to continue overland, they would still get taxed at the Port of Cadiz. Thus, the merchants who traded in goods from outside the country were for repealing the ban, while those who traded in local goods were against it. So this is the situation the doctor was trying to pick his way through and somehow acquire that bit of land next to his house in the Skulls.

Luisa's father, Don Pablo, was the royal chief deputy for taxes in Sevilla. He was precisely the one responsible for collecting royal duty in the port. Señor de Leca had personally appointed him to this post. Don Pablo, of course, knew the royal deputy for buildings in Sevilla, who represented the king on the municipal commission for public works and who was responsible for the royal buildings—the prison, Torre del Oro, where the customs duties were collected, the cavalry barracks, and the royal warehouses at the port. He was precisely the one who would also be responsible for the taxation station that would eventually be built near Puerta de Jerez. But this would come about not at his insistence, but at the insistence of Don Pablo, who was responsible for the royal taxes. The curious thing is that the king's people had chosen exactly the same spot which Dr. Monardes also hoped to acquire—the road simply passed by it. Dr. Monardes spoke with Don Pablo about whether the royal officials wouldn't agree to move their station elsewhere or simply to make it smaller, such that they could split the parcel, say, in two with Dr. Monardes. Of course, to this end, which seemed the most realistic in both señores' opinions, the royal officials would first have to receive the land from the municipality, and then to decide that they didn't need such a large station and to sell part of it to the doctor. That could come about quite cheaply, since they themselves would receive the land free of charge—for the needs of the kingdom. Don Pablo promised to speak seriously with the royal deputy for buildings. That, however, did not solve the problem at all, since, as was said, the land belonged to the municipality and the royal deputy for building had only one vote on the municipal commission for public works, and in the end the decision had to be made by the municipality. But it was still something. Depending on how matters developed, Dr. Monardes and Don Pablo would meet again to discuss what further steps to take. Dr. Monardes also treated the bishop of Sevilla and could speak to him as well, if necessary. Unfortunately, the doctor did not have significant connections in the municipality—the municipal councilors were primarily Dr. Bartholo's clients. Dr. Monardes had strong ties to royal officials, church leaders, and noblemen, but not to the municipal councilors. Of course, he also treated the powerful merchants such as Espinosa, and Espinosa could have helped, but within the municipality he had exactly as many sworn enemies as he did faithful friends, thus this business couldn't be resolved with his help alone. Besides, Espinosa wasn't the kind of person who would help you out just like that, unless he had some personal interest in it, and this business was far too trifling for him to have a personal interest in it.

"Our social system is very complicated, señor," I said conciliatorily, as the doctor and I walked down the street.

"It's not the least bit complicated," Dr. Monardes replied. "Our social system is completely simple. They are all simple. I know history well," Dr. Monardes continued, "and I'm telling you that only two systems have ever existed in the world, in Aristotle's sense . . . Have you read Aristotle?"

"Yes," I replied. "To a point."

"I see," the doctor said, somehow ambiguously. "Aristotle says that four systems of government exist. Democracy, where the people govern . . ."

"What do you mean, the people govern?" I didn't understand. "Who do they govern?"

"Listen to me now." The doctor waved his hand, slightly irritated. "One system, he says, is democracy. Another is aristocracy. There, the most worthy govern. It would've been better if he'd called it meritocracy, but never mind. He had no way of making use of Latin terms. The third is monarchy, in which the king rules. And the fourth is plutocracy, when the richest rule. I argue," continued the doctor, who, truth be told, had been developing a certain inclination towards dabbling in politics for years now, "that nothing has ever existed in the world besides monarchy and plutocracy."

"Here we have a monarchy," I took the opportunity to note. "Don Felipe is a monarch."

"Yes. But besides a monarch, he is also a plutocrat," said the doctor. "Because Don Felipe is a very rich man. That's precisely the interesting thing. The monarchy exists in a mixed form."

"But, señor, I wasn't talking about that at all," I took the liberty of noting. "I had something entirely different in mind."

"I know what you had in mind. But that's not interesting," the doctor replied. "The monarchy, I would say, is simultaneously a monarchy and a plutocracy. And just look at the aristocrats. They are far from being the worthiest men, yet they really are some of the richest. That, consequently, is the first possibility: a monarchy, a mixed system. But if the monarchy or dictatorship falls, then a pure plutocracy begins. No other system exists in the real world. This, by the way, makes a lot of sense. In the first case, power is obtained through force, through the force of weapons at first. Take Caesar, the first emperor. Some scribblers might tell you that Octavian was the first, but don't you believe them. Caesar was the first. How did he become emperor? Through force. He obtained it through the force of weapons. That's how he obtained power, and that's how he maintained it. After all, who owns the armies? Whom do they belong to? While in the other case," the doctor continued, placing a fig in his mouth, "power is obtained by the force of money. Where the power of weapons ends, the force of money begins. Marcus Licinius Crassus. Toss this pit. Sometimes you can even buy a whole empire with money. Didius Julianus. And other times with the force of weapons you can steal the richest people's money and put it in your own pocket. Emperor Maxentius. It is telling, by the way, that both Julianus and Maxentius met bad ends. But that's it, those two systems. There's no place for a third under the sun. And whoever combines these two shall stay in power forever and last throughout the ages."

"Aristotle is a windbag," I noted confidently. "He loves to think up various things. He'll take two things and turn them into four, and make himself look very clever that way."

"That's more or less how it is," the doctor agreed.

He continued walking along in silence, handing me the pits from the figs. I hurled them into the gardens along the street.

"But what about the pope, señor . . ." I said after a moment. "He doesn't have weapons. Fine, so he does have money, that's true, but . . . that's not the point. You understand what I'm trying to say, señor."

"Yes, I understand," the doctor nodded. "But that is a very long story. And at the end we'll still arrive back at those two things, but after lots of chatter."

"That's what I thought, too," I said. "But if our system is simple, señor"—I added after a pause—"why is it so hard from someone to get a hold of a plot of land in the Skulls? Perhaps it isn't as simple as it looks, after all?"

"It's completely simple," the doctor shook his head vigorously. "The system is simple, but very confused."

"Simple, but very confused?" I repeated.

"Simple, but very confused!" the doctor nodded categorically.

We continued walking down the street. And where is Jesús, the reader might ask. Had Dr. Monardes caught him dancing flamenco and fired him? No, Jesús hadn't been fired. The doctor had let him go home, since his wife was due to give birth. Dr.

Monardes was to perform the delivery personally. That's precisely where we were headed now—we were walking down the streets of the Triana slum towards Jesús' house to see how his wife was.

"What a repulsive place!" the doctor said and started coughing violently. "The smells make your head spin and irritate your lungs."

I personally didn't find the smells unpleasant. To me, it smelled like oranges, horses, fried meat, river mud, and tobacco. Nothing was irritating my lungs. And my head? My head was perfectly fine. My mind was clearer, sharper, more focused, profound, and insightful than ever, I would say. I missed the animals. Not that I would return to them, of course. And in fact, it wasn't the animals. I am missing something, Pelletier says, but what it is, I don't know. More precisely, those aren't Pelletier's words, but the Earth's, right after she collides with the Medusa, miscarries, and loses the Moon. I am missing something, but what it is, I don't know. Exactly at that moment, Mars turns his back and begins to move away, finally reaching as far away as he is today.

# 14. Against Toothaches

Urbi et Orbi, *L'Amour des amours.* Jesús' wife gave birth to a pair of twins. Not exactly on the day the doctor and I went to their house, but two days later, and shortly before the doctor arrived, so in the end the delivery was performed by an old woman. "She was so blind," Jesús said, "that I was astonished she didn't miss one of the twins." Jesús is very proud. Proud and saddened at the same time. Why he is saddened is completely clear, in my opinion, when you take into account the fact that even before this he had four mouths to feed, but why he is proud perhaps requires clarification. He is proud because he fathered twins. He doesn't know anyone else with twins, I only know one person, while the doctor, after considerable reflection, was able to think of two. Thus, it really is a rare thing.

Jesús wanted to name the twins Pedro and Pablo, after the saints. But he already has a son named Pablo. The local priest suggested naming him Pablo-Hiero, as two names with a hyphen, but Jesús' wife categorically refused to give the boy that name and was stubborn in her refusal. "I would've given her a good beating any other time," Jesús said, "which would have cleared the problem right up, but now isn't quite the moment for that." In the end, the news got around and even reached Cardinal Rodrigo de Castro himself, the archbishop of Sevilla, who personally wanted to baptize the twins as part of the consecration of a new church in the Santa Cruz neighborhood. He suggested calling the child Pablo Junior, but the mother again refused. She didn't want him to be called Pablo at all like her other son. They finally decided to name him Rodrigo, after the cardinal. But since Pedro and Rodrigo somehow didn't go together, the other twin was christened Alvaro, after the cardinal's nephew. So in the end they named them Alvaro and Rodrigo.

In the meantime, the doctor was called to the prison to examine the Cervantes. The fact of the matter was that the higher-ups had decided to release him, thus the prison authorities wanted to let him go in good shape, so he couldn't complain about them afterwards. They did this from time to time with someone they considered more important or who could create problems for them in some way. Cervantes could stick it to you good in some play, and besides, he was a royal servant, after all. In principle, the prison doctor was Hernando Alemán. He did a slapdash job, and if you are a Sevillian prisoner and expect him to take care of you, you are sorely deceiving yourself. And why should he care, when his salary was thirty ducats a year, two and a half per month? I earned more as a student of Dr. Monardes. Dr. Alemán would've starved to death on that salary if he didn't have a private practice as well. My point is that he usually didn't take care of the prisoners at all, unless somebody well nigh went and died, but in cases when the authorities wanted to cover their asses and free someone healthy, he would examine him and treat him insofar as he could, and afterwards the poor fellow would sign a document saying he had no complaints. Only then would they let him go. Cervantes's case was far better than most, in the sense that he actually was healthy except for a toothache. The prison authorities were prepared to solve the problem immediately by simply having Dr. Alemán pull the tooth, but Cervantes (who indeed had only a few teeth left in his mouth, as I was subsequently able to confirm) asked to keep it. He even suggested to the authorities that he sign the document saying he was healthy and then get the tooth treated once he was out, but the authorities refused.

Why? Why is a good question. Who knows why? They simply refused. Perhaps inexplicably, yet very categorically. You'll never understand the Spanish authorities if you ask why this, why that. The Spanish authorities are a very complicated thing. In order to understand them, you must ask: "What is in the way?" If there is some large obstacle, that means something won't happen. In any other case—it might. Anyway, Cervantes then requested that Dr. Monardes be called in to treat his tooth. Dr. Alemán would not normally have paid him any attention and would have just yanked his tooth in the end, but his son was also a novelist, so he, it seems, felt a certain sympathy for Cervantes. For this reason, he promised to call Dr. Monardes and actually did it. Cervantes, however, did not have the money to pay the doctor's high fee. Instead, he promised to praise him in one of his works. "My very next one"—was what he said.

It goes without saying that Dr. Monardes was not the least bit impressed by this suggestion. Yet he decided to show some good will, and besides, he didn't want to refuse Dr. Alemán and the royal authorities in principle.

"Do we have any appointments today?" he asked me in the morning.

I opened the notebook and said: "Not today. Tomorrow you have a visit to Father Luis del Alcazar, the Jesuit, to check on his fever."

"And nothing else until then?" the doctor asked.

"Nothing else," I replied.

"Good, then let's go see Cervantes," the doctor said. "This one will be on me, since I knew his father . . ."

After all, the prison was spitting distance from us, also on Sierpes Street, near the Duke of Medina Sidonia's palace. It was an enormous prison, or rather, an overcrowded one. Eighteen thousand people passed through it a year.

"If you believe the figure published by the municipal authorities, señor," I said as we walked there, "there could be eighteen thousand people in that prison at the moment. That would mean that every sixth person in Sevilla was a prisoner!"

"That's the spirit of this city," the doctor replied. "Everyone has come here to get rich quickly. Even the beggars came here for that once upon a time. There are typically lots of prisoners in such places."

This was surely true as well, but I would add that the prison in Sevilla was not a municipal prison, but rather a royal one, so it held people from all over Spain. Señor Frampton had also spent some time there. It was a true Tower of Babel inside. I wondered where all those people slept at night. I wouldn't be too surprised if they slept stacked up on top of one another.

No, it was not like Arcadia, as Cervantes would say. Instead of green fields and clear streams—jagged stone walls and bars; instead of pretty young shepherds and shepherdesses, called "pastors" in Arcadia, by the way—angry guards on the one side and cut-throats on the other.

We entered a clean room with whitewashed walls. This was where they examined the prisoners who were to be released. Cervantes was waiting for us inside. I was seeing him for the first time. He was of average height, with an oval visage, chestnut hair, a smooth open forehead, lively eyes, a hooked but well-proportioned nose, a coppery beard and fair complexion, somewhat stooped in the shoulders, with a pot belly and plump legs.

The doctor greeted him and shook hands with him (as did I), looked at his tooth, and started in on the treatment. First, he cleaned the tooth of impurities with a piece of cloth soaked in tobacco juice, then used tweezers to place a small ball of tobacco in the hole in the tooth.

"That," said the doctor, "will prevent any further decay of the tooth and will leech out the puss. Spit, but be careful not to spit out the tobacco. I'll come back tomorrow to change the tobacco. In two or three days your toothache will be gone."

"Thank you, doctor," Cervantes replied.

"Tell me, just between friends, did you really steal that money?" the doctor asked.

"Not a cent of it!" Cervantes replied emphatically. "If I had stolen it, they would know that by now. All the walls have ears here."

The doctor involuntarily glanced at the wall. I did, too. Yes, of course. We should have thought of that. It makes perfect sense.

"You take after your father." Dr. Monardes shook his head. "Back in the day, in order to practice medicine, Rodrigo claimed left and right that he was licensed, but it turned out he was only a bachelor of sciences."

"But he wasn't any worse than any licensed physician," Cervantes replied.

"That's true," the doctor agreed. "Actually, who knows whether he was even a bachelor. But that's neither here nor there. He really was good. In our trade, that's the only thing that counts. And in your trade, as well."

"That is surely the case in all trades, señor," Cervantes said.

"Yes," agreed the doctor.

"Absolutely!" I chimed in. Incidentally, I am not even a bachelor of sciences. It's not necessary. It had crossed my mind to while away a year or two at the university, why not, but they want money on top of everything, which was just going too far.

The doctor continued talking to Cervantes and making little ambiguous jokes with him, which made it clear that he didn't believe him all too much—not him, nor the so-called "honest men"—but then Cervantes said something which I have committed to memory: "That is the philosophy of the ancient cynics, señor," he said. "As old as the world itself and with many merits. But the bad thing about it is that even if Christ himself were to descend to earth once again, you would never believe it. You would think he was simply some charlatan, who says and does those things for his own benefit, led by hidden goals and intentions. You would suspect him of hypocrisy. The cynics say that the world is bad, and that people are hypocritical, vain, and deceitful, and that everyone is only out for his own gain. When everyone believes that, the world remains just as bad as it was, if not worse. It will never get any better that way."

"It will never get any better that way." Dr. Monardes nodded seriously. "It will change through cold common sense. Through medicine, knowledge, and science. That's the only way it will happen."

"That change will hardly be very significant, señor," Cervantes said.

"Who knows? We'll see," replied Dr. Monardes. "In any case, if some people had not discovered the healing power of tobacco, that little ball would not be in your mouth right now and your tooth would not be saved."

"Well, I guess that is something," Cervantes laughed. "Today the tooth, tomorrow the whole jaw."

"I was just giving you a concrete example," the doctor replied. "From now on, you can exercise your own reason and try to imagine just how far it could go. Even though that would be pointless. No one knows how far it could go, nor could anyone possibly know. The moralists keep chattering away . . ."

"I'm not a moralist," Cervantes said.

"The moralists keep chattering away," the doctor continued, while putting his things back into his bag, "about how we can change people, rather than how we can change the circumstances. People cannot be changed, but circumstances can. By the way, our friend Ficino in Italy claims that people can be changed, too. Through education, he says. Who knows? Perhaps. In any case, circumstances certainly can be. Forget the people and change the circumstances. That will actually work. Until tomorrow, Cervantes. And be careful not to spit out the ball of tobacco."

"Thank you, doctor," Cervantes said and got up from the bed he had been sitting on. "I'll be careful."

Thus our first visit to him ended.

On our way out, I spotted Rincon among the people in the corridors and turned to him.

"What are you doing here?" I asked in surprise. At first, I thought they had thrown him in prison.

"I've got friends here," he replied. "I come to visit them now and again."

"Aha," I said, lifted my hand in farewell, and hurried on after the doctor, who hadn't noticed that I had made this detour and who had now stopped and was looking around for me.

"Where did you disappear to?" he asked. "I thought something had happened to you."

"I saw Rincon," I said.

"What? Rincon here?" the doctor said in surprise.

"He's here for visiting hours," I explained.

"I see," the doctor nodded.

The next day we came back to replace Cervantes' ball of tobacco. And on the third day, they released him. His toothache had disappeared and he no longer felt any pain. He still felt some slight tingling when he chewed on that side, but with time that would disappear as well, the doctor said. Cervantes stopped by the doctor's house after being released, and the three of us went to drink a glass of jerez to his health at the Three Horses. Cervantes's family had scattered, nobody lived here anymore. Most of them had gone to Madrid. He only had some distant relatives on Feria Street, and afterwards he was thinking of stopping by there as well. And after that he was going to leave the city and go to Madrid or perhaps Barcelona–he hadn't yet decided. "I'll decide on the way," he said. We chatted a bit at the Three Horses and then went our separate ways–he set off towards Feria, while we went back to Sierpes. Cervantes was in a good mood, happy, as was to be expected. "Free again," he kept saying. "Freedom is quite something." I love seeing people in good moods, happy people. They radiate such vitality, such hope. They radiate freedom. The doctor is almost never like that. For some reason, he always looks slightly annoyed. He also radiates vitality, but his is of a different sort, a different sort entirely.

"I'll put you in my very next work, señor. Without fail!" Cervantes cried, already a dozen feet from us, his hand raised in a parting wave. "I've thought up something about two dogs. It'll be good. Keep an eye out for it."

"Fine. Thank you very much," the doctor replied rather oddly.

Then Cervantes turned his back on us and continued on down the street at a brisk pace, a large sack swaying on his back.

"Perhaps you are the second dog," the doctor turned to me.

"That's fine with me," I said, nevertheless somewhat offended by his remark. "I love dogs. I grew up with them. My father had two dogs in his yard, and in our garden at Rojas . . ."

"Yes, yes, fine," the doctor waved dismissively. "You walk on ahead, you keep bumping into my legs."

We continued on our way.

# 15. Against Fevers from Colds and for Creative Energy

When we went to see Father Luis del Alcazar the Jesuit, an astounding vision unfolded before us. His fever had decidedly taken a turn for the worse, but as the reader will see, for very puzzling reasons. We found him trembling all over—like an autumn leaf, as they say—with chattering teeth, yet dressed only in an undershirt, sitting in his bed, with sheets of paper spread across his lap and on the blankets, with a quill in hand, an open Bible and an inkpot on the nightstand next to him, with the tobacco leaf from yesterday still tied to his head—and spattered with ink from head to toe. Everything on him and around him was spattered with ink—his shirt, the blankets, his beard, his neck, the papers, even the pages of the Bible. His hand was shaking furiously, which perhaps explained the large, crooked letters on the pages.

In the first instant, Dr. Monardes and I froze in our tracks, speechless. The priest nodded at us and greeted us, trembling intensely all the while.

"What's happened to you, padre?" Dr. Monardes found his tongue. "Your fever seems to be getting worse."

This was obviously true. But the padre's answer was rather unexpected: "This fever is a gift from God, señores," he said, and I would note that his voice sounded enthusiastic. "Because thanks to it, I received extraordinary visions last night."

"Yes, yes," Dr. Monardes replied and nodded at me to begin preparing the leaves.

"No, really," the priest went on. "I saw scenes from the Apocalypse, as clearly as I'm seeing you right now."

"We need to treat you, padre," the doctor said.

"Which scenes exactly, padre?" I asked.

"I saw the twenty-four thrones," Luis del Alcazar replied, "with the elders upon them."

"Who?" the doctor raised his head from the brazier which was heating the leaves. It seems that he hadn't quite heard.

"The elders," the priest repeated. "From the first to the last. Twenty-four elders."

"How strange," I said.

"Yes. And light and voices and peals of thunder were coming from the stones."

The doctor placed his hand anxiously on the priest's forehead and nodded. "It's hot. This is a stubborn fever, padre."

"I also saw the seven burning lamps of fire," the priest continued, not paying him any attention. He was speaking to me, as he clearly sensed that I was more interested. "And also the book sealed with seven seals."

"What book was it?" I asked.

"I don't know," the priest replied. "Nothing was written on the outside. But I saw the seals. Strange, red seals."

"Made of wax?" I asked.

"So it seemed to me," Father del Alcazar nodded. "I also saw the seals breaking open. When the first broke open, a rider on a white horse appeared, with a bow in his hand."

"Interesting vision, padre," Dr. Monardes said. "Now sit still and we'll change the leaf on your forehead."

I unwound the white strip of cloth that was tied under the priest's chin keeping yesterday's leaf on his head, and the doctor, holding a new, warmed tobacco leaf in his hand, carefully placed it on his bald pate, after which I retied the cloth.

"Now lay down, father, so we can put leaves on your chest."

"Later I also saw Death, the rider on a pale horse," the priest said, as he lay on his back. "The horse was dappled, gray with white spots. That makes it a pale horse."

"What did Death look like, señor?" I asked as I placed the leaves on his chest.

"Like an ordinary horseman. He didn't look any different from the first."

"But in human form?" I asked.

"In human form, yes," the priest replied. "He appeared after the opening of the fourth seal."

"But father, all of that is already written in the Apocalypse," Dr. Monardes broke in, and I, at least, clearly managed to catch the skeptical ring to his voice.

"That's true," the priest replied, "but it's another thing entirely to see it with your own eyes. With your inner vision," he corrected himself.

"And what else did you see, padre?" I asked with curiosity. "I haven't read the Apocalypse. Or rather, I have read it, but let's not go into that now."

"After the opening of the fifth seal, I saw under the altar the souls of those slain for their faith in God, crying out for vengeance."

"For vengeance?" the doctor asked. The padre nodded vigorously. He was still trembling all over, by the way. "How typical!" Dr. Monardes noted.

"That's all I saw," the priest turned to me. "But the most important thing is that some secrets of the Apocalypse seem to have been revealed to me. In fact, I have no doubts about it whatsoever. I am completely convinced that the first through the eleventh chapters speak of the rejection of Judaism, the punishment of the Jews, and the destruction of Jerusalem. That's just what I'm trying to write out now. With God's help, the hidden sense of the Apocalypse will become clear to me."

"Padre," said Dr. Monardes. "I'll come again tomorrow. But if your fever worsens during the night, send someone to call for me. Don't hesitate and don't wait!"

The priest agreed, and the doctor and I left shortly thereafter. The doctor looked concerned.

"That fever is not progressing well," he said. "It should have shown signs of improvement by now, but it hasn't."

His apprehensions vanished the following day, however. It was, incidentally, the same day that Cervantes was released. In the afternoon after we parted with him, we again went to see Father Luis del Alcazar.

"I received new visions!" he said when we entered the room. "And I think that everything is now clear to me."

The scene which unfolded before us was not much different from the previous day's, with the exception that his fever had subsided, while the ink stains and papers had increased.

"What is it like to be such a person?" I thought to myself. I would say that for a moment a certain fear gripped me.

The doctor placed his hand on the father's forehead, and this time he was satisfied.

"His body temperature seems to be normalizing," he noted. "But obviously you are still trembling, father."

"Yes," replied the priest. "But this illness has repaid me richly. Such visions! The four angels from the four corners of the earth"–he turned to me–"I also saw the fifth, rising from the east, holding the seal of the living God."

"What did the seal look like?" I inquired.

"A regular red seal," the priest replied. "But a lot bigger, of course."

"How big? Like this?" I asked, making a circle with my hands about the size of a fairly large loaf of bread. That's what I had in mind, in any case.

"Bigger, I think," the priest replied.

"Like this?" I spread my hands wider.

"Yes. Something like that," the priest replied hesitantly.

"What exactly is making you tremble, señor? The fever or the visions?" asked Dr. Monardes.

"Surely the fever, although it's hard for me to say," replied the priest. "They both came on at the same time."

"You mustn't strengthen the illness, padre!" Dr. Monardes said sternly. "By trying to hold on to the visions, perhaps you are also trying to hold on to the fever as well."

"No, no, not at all," the priest shook his head. "I assure you."

"Did you see anything else, father?" I asked.

"Oh, amazing things! The star called Wormwood, how it fell to the earth. It says in the Apocalypse that it turned the waters bitter and many people perished from that. I also saw a mighty angel robed in a cloud, with a rainbow above his head, his face shining like the sun. This angel had one foot on land, the other in the sea, and was holding an open book. No, I didn't see what it was"—he quickly clarified to me—"but the visions themselves are not the most important thing, señores. I think I have understood the meaning of the prophecy. Everything must be understood in *praeteritus*."

"In *praeteritus*?" I repeated.

"In the past," the doctor explained, while changing the leaves.

"Yes, precisely," the priest nodded. "It has already taken place. The prophecy is true and has already come about. The Antichrist has passed over the earth. Chapters 12 through 19 describe the Roman Empire's rejection of paganism and acceptance of Christianity. Chapter 20 is about the persecutions of Christians by the Antichrist, who is Emperor Nero. Write out 'Nero Caesar' in Hebrew letters, add them up and you get 666."

"Really?" I said.

"It's true." Dr. Monardes nodded after a brief pause. Yes, he surely knew. His mother was a Jewess, after all.

"My son," the priest turned to me, "Nero ruled from the year 54 to the year 68. Two times seven. This also follows from the Apocalypse. And the final two chapters are about the triumph of the Catholic Church, the New Jerusalem."

"You need to write this down, padre," I said.

"That's precisely what I'm doing," he replied. "I will entitle my treatise *Investigation of the Hidden Sense of the Apocalypse.*"

"I really like your relative Baltasar," I said, meaning it as a little joke. "Especially that poem 'Tres Cosas':

*Three things have caught my heart:*
*The pretty Inés, cured ham*
*and aubergines with cheese.*"

The doctor laughed, but the priest's face assumed a serious and saddened expression.

"Baltasar is a wretch," he said.

"Why call him a wretch, señor?" I objected. "He's a soldier, a sailor. He's travelled the world. And he's a fine poet. He has talent."

The priest shook his head, but said nothing.

The doctor was seized by a long and violent coughing fit.

"What's wrong, señor?" the priest asked, slightly alarmed. "You haven't caught my cold, have you?"

"No," the doctor replied after clearing his throat. "I think it's from the tobacco. From time to time it irritates the lungs, after long use. But this is nothing when compared with its benefits, of course. And this only applies to cases in which the smoke has been inhaled. It does not apply to cases of external application, such as yours. You needn't be afraid."

"I'm not afraid of anything, señor," Father Alcazar replied. "I have complete faith in you."

"Thank you," replied the doctor. "As you should. I'll come back tomorrow to see how the illness is progressing."

After that we said goodbye to the priest and left.

"So that's how it goes, eh?" the doctor said when we got out onto Sierpes. "Three things have caught my heart: the pretty Inés . . ."

"Cured ham and aubergines with cheese," I finished, and we both laughed.

"How strange that I do not know him," said the doctor. "Where is he living now?"

"He's here," I replied. "He came back and is living in La Macarena."

"Well, what do you know," said the doctor.

The following day, the priest was much better, and after a week his fever had passed completely.

# 16. For the Elimination of All Indecision, the Resolution of All Doubts, and So On

I memorized those lines by Baltasar del Alcazar not so much because they are particularly good—frankly, they are not—but primarily because they relate to my personal experience. My heart, too, has been caught by, or is at least strongly attached to, both a lass named Anna, as well as cured ham. I have found myself torn by indecision about which of the two to go to. One evening, after a long day with Dr. Monardes, I felt like seeing pretty Anna, yet at the same time I was also very hungry and felt like going to the Three Horses to eat cured ham. Unfortunately, the two things could not be combined. It's either one or the other. That's how it is in Sevilla with the pretty lasses, or at least with the honorable lasses, as they say, when you are not yet married. And once you're married, they are no longer pretty lasses, but your wife. So in any case, it was pointless to take her to the Three Horses.

I found myself torn by great indecision. I froze in my tracks and simply did not know which way to go. Because pretty Anna and the Three Horses lie in different directions. And not just symbolically, but very literally. If it had been symbolic, I would have easily figured out some way around it. But in this case, it was literal. For this reason, I lit a cigarella, wondering what to do. Both things strongly attracted me. I would say, in the spirit of philosophy, that I resembled Buridan's ass, who starved to death while wondering which stack of hay to head towards. On the one hand, Anna; on the other, cured ham. Given the circumstances described above, such a dilemma is in fact something completely natural. Nature herself has made it such that in man, especially in his younger years, both drives are very strong. Without realizing it, I have once again fallen back on tobacco as a means for correcting Nature—as I now see. Everyone knows what cured ham is. But certainly not everyone could possibly know Anna. She is a pretty girl, tall, healthy. As the doctor once said when he saw her: "She will produce a healthy line." The doctor approved of her highly.

When I finished smoking my cigarella, I felt firmly resolved, beyond any shadow of a doubt, to go see Anna. I even wondered how such a question could ever have entered my mind. There was no trace of my former indecision. And of course, I acted rightly. The human female must be honored! Dr. Monardes is right that she is Nature's highest creation. In any case, she is something far from, and incomparably more than, the animal from which ham is made. It is even indecent to note this fact. Even though, on the other hand, it is simply a fact. The question is—how could such a thought possibly cross one's mind?! I don't know either. It just did. I suspect that this is connected to my longtime study of medicine and the science of biology. As far as I know, people have recently begun calling this a "professional deformation." A nice, useful concept, which, like many other such useful concepts, was probably thought up by some French philosopher, and I accept it readily and with enthusiasm. I hate to digress, yet I would nevertheless like to note that had it been thought up by some German philosopher, it certainly would have been called by at least two or three different names, since nobody would be able to understand which pronoun below refers to which concept above and this would become the subject of endless debates and misunderstandings.

I will give yet another example, also connected, albeit indirectly this time, with pretty Anna. I have already said that Dr.

Monardes lives on Sierpes Street, which, by the way, in typically Spanish fashion, means nothing more and nothing less than "Snake Street." Only in this insane country would they name the city's main street in such a way. And only there would they place the Duke of Medina Sidonia's palace right across from the royal prison. But that's as may be. Getting back to Anna. Anna lives on Feria Street, near the Monastery of the Holy Spirit. Many times, upon leaving the doctor's house, I have wondered whether to take Imagen and to turn at Incarnation Square, or whether to go down Amor de Dios and then to turn onto Morgado. It is extremely difficult to say which route is shorter. Finally, one day I stopped on the corner of Imagen and Amor de Dios and lit a cigarella, trying to settle this question once and for all. I pondered it intently for almost ten minutes, pacing back and forth. I mentally reviewed almost every house, every cross street, every building that I would pass by on one or the other route. I didn't manage to solve the problem, but when I finished smoking the cigarella, I continued straight down Amor de Dios, somehow freed of all indecision. Since then I have always taken that route, with a completely light heart. Of course, the reader may inquire why I did not simply measure both routes in steps. I attempted to do so twice, without success. The problem is that for this purpose, one must be fully concentrated on counting one's steps and must not think about anything else whatsoever. If your mind wanders even for a second, everything comes to naught. "Where was I again?" you say to yourself. "335? 435? Or perhaps 353?" This, in fact, is very difficult to do. Especially since I was going to see pretty Anna, and not, for example, the Franciscan brothers. My mind would often wander along the way, imagining various things. What kinds of things? Things primarily connected with lasses. And for a man with medical interests, fully given over to science, knowledge, and so forth, it is extremely difficult to keep such things completely out of mind. In a certain sense, he falls victim to his professional interests. And this applies, incidentally, not just to a man dedicated to science, medicine, etc., but to everyone else as well. People are inquisitive in principle, especially in certain spheres, and if I were a French philosopher, I would call this "sexual interest–sexual inquisitiveness–sexual knowledge," where said inquisitive drive is also predetermined by Nature. Being fully nonverbal in comparison to the aforementioned virtuosos, she has issued this as a vague, unconscious, unformulatable, yet nevertheless absolutely categorical and effective command. As a rule, Nature somehow gets by without language, that great human creation, fearsome *logos*. Yet she is too wild and primitive, as I have noted more than once.

This is why in the end I cannot measure the two routes in steps. But after the incident in which I lit a cigarella, I have always taken Amor de Dios and all of my doubts and indecisions have vanished, which is by far the most important thing in this case.

And in closing, a third and final example. Let the reader treat this as the Holy Trinity of the wisdom tobacco inspires—a wisdom that expresses itself in decisiveness, the elimination of indecision, and the ability to make decisions quickly. I have the feeling that an insightfulness of sorts lies hidden behind all this, which tobacco provides or unleashes.

I have a friend in the army who invited me to recruit men for a new campaign against the Dutch. This work is temporary—lasting around a month, sometimes two—and is very well-paid. Your job is to stand at the recruiting posts for soldiers in Sevilla or to travel around the nearby countryside and to enlist volunteers. One needs a certain gift of gab for this, whereas the people in the army, especially among the lower ranks, are dumb as stumps. To them, I, as a student of Dr. Monardes and a learned man in general, was practically a gift from God. None of them, of course, had ever heard of Pelletier du Mans. The interesting thing is that you can't gather people together on the square in Dos Hermanas and convince them to join the army simply by telling them they'll make money from it. Those who would find this argument convincing have already gone and joined the army on their own. No, it doesn't work like that. You, of course, have to mention this as well, but you also have to say that with the army they will see foreign countries they would likely never set foot in otherwise, that a life of adventure and conquest awaits them, you must also somehow hint that the job is actually far less dangerous than it may seem, you must impress upon them what a grand thing brotherly friendship between soldiers is, you must convince them that as soldiers in the army they will enjoy great respect, that the army will never abandon them and other such hogwash. Yet even this is not sufficient and is far and away not the most important thing. The most important thing, as a person such as myself established with surprise, is to fire up their patriotism. You must speak to them—and convincingly, too, of course—about how great our nation is, how good, just, and holy its aims are, how noble our nation is, how we are all part of one indivisible whole, which the good king carefully watches over. How great Spain is, our homeland. (I no longer have any accent whatsoever, incidentally.) This produces striking, unbelievable results, especially if repeated long and emphatically enough. So that's what I did. The doctor gave me two months off, and I went around to the nearby villages and towns and spoke on the squares while we recruited soldiers. I was hugely successful. Yet inwardly, all of this troubled me greatly. As a man of medicine, I, of course, do not believe such patriotic nonsense at all. I found myself extremely torn as to whether to continue. I had the feeling that while I spoke, a person inside of me was listening to and laughing at me, he was downright convulsed with laughter. I, of course, suppressed this person, and did not give voice to him even for a second, but this is quite difficult to do all day long for an extended period of time. The reader, who has not had such an experience, will be surprised at how difficult this is. I kept telling myself: "It'll just take me some time to get used to it," but I had trouble getting used to it and felt somehow extremely strained and exhausted, more than I would be just from the travelling itself or if I had been talking about something else. How lucky, I thought to myself, that I live and work with Dr. Monardes, whom I can tell exactly what I'm thinking. With rare exceptions, of course, where at most he might take a swipe at you with his cane or toss some biting (sometimes very biting) criticism your way. But those people from the army wouldn't let you get away merely with biting criticism or even just a cane. Oh no, not a chance! Once you've joined their game, you've got to say what needs to be said, otherwise you're thrown to the dogs. If I were crazy enough to say what I actually thought, I would be lucky only to end up in the Sevilla prison like Cervantes, but unlike him I wouldn't get out after a year, but would rot away there.

This, then, was the reason for my hesitation, for my intense indecision. On the one hand, the ducats; on the other, I had the feeling that it was impossible for me to continue constantly saying things that I didn't believe at all, especially since on top of everything you have to do it enthusiastically and convincingly, as if you believe it with your whole heart, in order to get results. Because if you don't get results, they start looking askance at you, and they could even get rid of you. So either you do it or you don't do it.

One evening, on the way back from Carmona, when I was already thoroughly sick of the whole business, I lit a cigarella with the firm intention of making a final decision about whether to continue or to quit the campaign. I was leaning towards quitting. What nation, I said to myself, what nonsense! Your biggest enemies are here in your own country. There, where you live, where you work, where you take part in dividing up the money. There, where the money is divvied up—that's where you'll find your biggest enemies. Someone gets in your way, and you get in someone's way. There you'll find your most terrifying enemies, and it's usually in your own country, perhaps even in your own city, and not in faraway Holland. What stuff these crooks have cooked up, I thought to myself furiously. The nation, the

Christian world . . . Whereas you are simply an animal, living all alone on the earth. Perhaps you have a family and loved ones, and they are the only real things that tie you to anyone. They are created by Nature. The rest is pure chance, without meaning. You could belong to one nation or another. You could speak one language or another. It's a pure accident. Nothing connects you to those others who call themselves your countrymen or who speak the same language. Absolutely nothing. The world is very, very simple, as Dr. Monardes says. They, however, can't stand this simplicity and constantly think up various things so as to pull the wool over their own eyes. And of course, there are also shysters who have an interest in that. They think such things up—even though in most cases they have already long since been thought up—and trumpet them left and right, as if they were the indisputable truth. But they're not. And no nation exists anywhere except in people's imaginations. There is no nation. There isn't anything at all. Except you, Nature, and money. This is the true scientific view of the world. The medical view.

After smoking my cigarella while thinking about these things, I could suddenly sense a weight being lifted from my shoulders. What a fool you are, I said to myself, to turn down the ducats they're giving you just to blather nonsense loudly on the squares. Well now, I suddenly clearly realized that this was easy money! Much easier, for example, than what I earned with Dr. Monardes. God had been so good as to give me the gift of gab and I could make use of it! What is this mania for truth? I thought to myself, suddenly alarmed. The mania for truth is like every other mania from a medical point of view—it is an illness, a foolish illness. I personally have always been sufficiently levelheaded so as not to give myself over to it.

From that moment on, I did not feel any indecision whatsoever. I continued on with the campaign and stayed with it until the end. That person inside me kept laughing at me, but I laughed right back at him. In the end I had the feeling that we were starting to get along, that we were patting each other on the back. Just like that, as we laughed.

I now no longer have any doubts that I acted rightly. I saved the ducats. I soon forgot my so-called torments, yet the ducats remained. I acted rightly, as a man of medicine, a man of science. I am completely sure that Dr. Monardes, if I were ever to take the liberty of bothering him with my foolish indecisions, would definitely approve of my actions. This is somehow so clear to me that I didn't even consider it necessary to ask him. I also think–if we must delve a little deeper into things–that this hesitation, this "voice of conscience," as it's called, is also something that comes from Nature. It is some manifestation of inertia, of spiritual indolence, of a lack of desire to use one's will in order to force oneself to speak and act in a certain way. It is precisely this necessity to exercise one's will that Nature seeks to avoid. Nature is spontaneous and lazy, not organized and strong-willed. But tobacco overcomes that. With the help of tobacco, we break Nature. We push her in the direction she ought to go. Just as during a medical procedure, dear reader. You may say: "Leave Nature alone!" Yes, but afterwards you will come to us for treatment.

# 17. Against Headaches

The Countess Béjar had suffered from headaches for twenty whole years. As she told us herself, she had gotten used to and resigned herself to them; what's more, she had tried in vain to cure them with several doctors, including the royal physician Dr. Bernard, but lately, after she had entered her fortieth year, when women, on the whole, go mad—this is me talking now—as a result of Nature's bad influence, her headaches became worse than before, almost unbearable—she woke up with one every morning, and it had poisoned all the joy in her life. Migraines—as we physicians call this ailment—can indeed be a great torment. In a certain sense, if a person has a migraine, he doesn't have anything else—he has no husband (or wife), no children, no profession, no post, no money, no satisfaction, no joy, no life. He is, one could say, completely busy with his head.

Countess Béjar finally turned to Dr. Monardes for help.

"Why did you not call me earlier, señora?" Dr. Monardes asked after we had arrived at her estate and listened to her complaints, for which, by the way, it became clear, she had not sought medical help for several years.

"Oh, señor, I had resigned myself to them and given up," she replied. "I had gotten used to my headaches. They would come back once every few days, usually in the evening. Only recently have they begun to appear every morning."

The countess looked terrible. Her figure was relatively well-preserved—as far as that could be discerned beneath her wide dresses and tightened corsets—a woman of around forty-five years of age, of average height, with black hair and very well-kept, delicate, soft white hands with long fingers. But her face was a waxy white, her eyes had a dulled expression, they seemed to me to be constantly narrowed, just like her pursed lips; perhaps the headache was the reason that long fans of wrinkles stretched from the corners of her eyes and mouth. No, she didn't look good.

"I heard," she said, "that you cure many sicknesses with the help of new medicines brought from the Indies. Miraculous things are said about you, señor. That's why I decided to seek your help."

"You've done the right thing, señora," the doctor assured her. "The new things brought from the Indies are above all tobacco and bezoars. You can read about them here," the doctor said and took a copy of his book *Historia medicinal* (the complete edition) out of his bag.

"Thank you, señor," replied the countess. "Unfortunately, I haven't been able to read anything lately because of the headaches."

"We'll fix that, dearest señora, or at least we'll do everything in our power," the doctor assured her, and we set to work.

The doctor took out a leaf of tobacco and began to warm it on a brazier which the servants had brought in.

"Ugh, it smells awful!" the countess wrinkled her nose. There is something in human females which instinctively predisposes them against tobacco. It is as if Nature, which speaks more strongly within them, senses the danger and reacts hostilely.

"It may smell bad, but it works miracles," replied the doctor. "Now please don't move, señora."

He placed the hot leaf on her head, and I bound it in place with a white strip of cloth tied under her chin.

"You can't possibly expect me to wear this?" the countess asked.

"I'm afraid so," the doctor answered.

She looked at herself in the mirror, gave a nervous laugh, and exclaimed, "Oh no, it's absurd!"

Whereupon she called in the maid and ordered her to bring a blue ribbon for a bow, one that matched her dress, with which I then bound the leaf again, removing our white bandage. The maid also brought incense sticks, which she lit at the ends of the countess' large room to dispel the unpleasant–in her opinion–smell of tobacco.

"Señores, I would love to show you around the palace, but how could I do so looking so absurd?!" the countess exclaimed.

The doctor assured her that this wasn't necessary and recommended that she lie down and rest without moving. We would come back in two hours to change the leaf.

And so we did. That day, and the following two as well. The first day we changed the leaf every two hours. The second day we changed it three times, and on the third day twice–in the morning and the evening, before the countess went to sleep. In the meantime, something happened which bears noting: Once, as we were arriving to change the leaves, we met a maid at the garden gate, who was carrying in her hand nothing but the *Historia medicinal* itself, Dr. Monardes' book. I was so surprised that I surely would have let the girl walk right past us before managing to ask her what was going on, but the doctor reacted more quickly than me.

"Girl, what are you carrying there?" he asked.

"A libel, señor," replied the girl, giving a quick curtsy.

I smiled inwardly, but tried not to let it show outwardly. The doctor also maintained an impassive expression, although I'd be willing to bet that he wasn't the least bit pleased–a libel is a small booklet, usually unsigned and filled with slanderous accusations against someone, told in the most ridiculous manner possible. The printer Señor Diaz regularly prints libels in Sevilla–although he, of course, categorically denies this–which mock various members of the city council (or sometimes the whole council) or

Señor Espinosa, the merchant. There is also a slanderous rumor going around that Juan Amarillo and I are the authors of a libel against the father of his former fiancée, with an appendix attacking Lope de Vega, which came out shortly after Lope's visit to Sevilla—a perfectly timed release. This, of course, is not true, but in any case I know very well what libels are. Dr. Monardes may be many things, but he is not an author of libels. But this girl surely thought that every book was called that.

"And where are you taking this book?" asked the doctor.

"To the caballero Señor Fuente," the girl replied. "As a present from the countess."

"Wonderful, my girl," the doctor said with a wide smile, and he even took two small coins out of his pocket and dropped them into the girl's palm, at which she curtsied, her face beaming. "Wonderful!" the doctor repeated. "And why are you taking him the book? Did the countess read it?"

"Oh, señor, she can't read," the girl replied quickly.

I knew that the doctor was up to something. Whereas girls are so foolish. All girls are very foolish. The clever ones, too.

"Why was she taking it to Caballero Fuente?" I turned to the doctor a bit later, as we walked along the path.

"Why do you think?" the doctor replied with a sour expression.

"Perhaps she meant that the countess cannot read because of the migraines. Perhaps things are a bit more complicated," I suggested.

"There are complicated things in my book. And in some others as well. Here"—the doctor made a sweeping gesture with his hand—"there is nothing complicated!"

Yet when we went in to see the countess, the doctor's face lit up in a wide smile. She, incidentally, was feeling slightly better.

Count Béjar was absent, by the way. He was in the army, one of those duffers who occupied a post in Duke de Alba's staff by virtue of his provenance alone and mainly in order to be able to puff himself up like a peacock. The true wonder is that all these fools still do not manage to screw up Duke de Alba's campaigns. Duke de Alba is a great commander. Despite the fact that those idiots are constantly getting in his way, he always manages to bring things to a victorious conclusion. I suspect he does not listen to them about anything. This is surely the reason he reaps victory upon victory and yet has simultaneously earned almost everyone's hatred. They hate him, but they are afraid of him. And since he reaps victory upon victory, they can't get rid of him.

When we went to see the countess on the morning of the fourth day, she met us with a happy expression. She looked almost unrecognizable.

"Oh, Señor Monardes," she said, grasping his hand in both of hers, "for the first time in months I've woken up without a headache. How nice! I feel like a girl."

She really did look rejuvenated. Good health and especially happiness rejuvenate people. This is a fact of life!

Her good mood was not contagious, however, at least not for Dr. Monardes, and, alongside him, not for me, either. Not since we met that maid, I mean. But of course, we did not show this in any way whatsoever.

The countess was very happy, indeed. She played the harp for us, singing some song I hadn't heard before. Yet she didn't seem very content with it.

"The harp is not suitable for happy melodies, which are surely what this young man would like to hear," she said, meaning me. Then she called in the maid and had her bring a lute. It turned out that she could play that instrument as well. And after that she requested they bring a lyra, and she played that, too. She played very well. The lyra especially, being a bowed instrument, is very difficult in my opinion, and I was truly impressed. The doctor, too, it seemed to me.

"Señora, I am astonished," he said, getting up from the armchair he had been sitting in and bowing with his hand to his breast after her performance. "You play wonderfully on all these instruments."

"Oh, thank you, señor," the countess replied. "Although my parents deserve the credit, not me. They strove to give me a very good education. Well, not like yours in the sciences, which are very, very difficult"—she waved her hand coquettishly—"but in the arts and literature."

The doctor and I quickly exchanged glances.

"I can also play the cornicher, the erpsicher, the rancocher and the regalia-violus," said the countess.

"Bravo!" the doctor exclaimed.

He made a few more compliments, after which the countess showed us around the palace. She walked in front of us in her wide, rustling skirts and led us from salon to salon. We entered them through wide openings in the walls, without doors, with various arches above them. Indeed, I thought to myself, in such a wide gown she simply could not pass through a normal door. At the risk of exaggerating, I would say that her gown was as wide as Jesús' whole house.

"What is an erpsicher, señor?" I asked the doctor quietly as we walked a dozen yards behind the countess.

"What is an erpsicher, you ask?" he replied. "You truly are a fool, Guimarães! What a question! Who cares what it is. Just say 'bravo' and don't ask!"

We toured the palace. A palace like any other—big and beautiful. From there we went out into the garden which occupied part of the Béjar estate. Not that it would impress anyone who had been to the Alcazar Gardens, but still it was a very beautiful garden, covered with different colored flowers arranged into geometric figures—red, yellow, blue, and white, with palms and orange trees, as well as all manner of bushes, one of which looked familiar to me.

"What was that plant, señor?" I asked the doctor.

"Coca, a medicine from Peru," he replied. "I have it in my garden. You should plant some tobacco, señora," he turned to the countess. "Many now grow it as a decorative plant. I can give you seeds, if you wish."

"Oh, most definitely, señor," replied the countess. "I would love to repay that miraculous, healing plant. Let the young Señor da Silva bring me the seedlings," she said and smiled at me.

The countess was clearly flirting with me. At first I could not believe it, but she did it quite obviously, and the examples multiplied, such that in the end I was left with no doubts whatsoever—the countess was flirting with me. The human female! Whichever way you look at her, she is what she is.

The doctor looked worried. He was surely afraid that I would get up to some mischief.

"Don't worry, señor," I told him. "I'm not that wet behind the ears."

As we walked through the garden, the doctor was seized with a long and violent coughing fit, so bad that the countess grew concerned. He pressed his thick gray kerchief to his lips. Much matter and rottenness had been coming up from his lungs recently.

"Are you all right, señor?" the countess asked.

"There's no need to worry. It's from the cigarellas," he said and lit a cigarella. "Oh, excuse me, señora," the doctor added and quickly put it out. "You don't like the smell . . ."

"And can't that illness also be cured with your wondrous tobacco?" the countess asked, without realizing what she was saying, I'm sure.

"Of course it can," Dr, Monardes replied. "But it takes a long time."

We left shortly thereafter. Our carriage was waiting in front of the gate to the estate. Jesús was sleeping, stretched out on the coachbox in the bright sun, his face covered by his wide-brimmed hat.

The doctor lifted the hat and waved his hand an inch from Jesús' face. Jesús opened his mouth to curse, but caught himself in time and stopped. The doctor looked at him for a long time in silence, his index finger lifted in warning.

"Nice weather, eh, señor?" Jesús said, righting himself on the coachbox.

"Drive home," the doctor replied and climbed into the carriage.

We set off. As we drove down the road, I turned around to look at the estate. It was hidden behind the park's high hedge, only the wide entrance portal with a bronze coat of arms on its double doors was visible.

"And to think, señor, that that pack rules Spain," I said practically to myself, almost unwittingly.

"That pack rules the world!" replied the doctor. "Not just Spain alone."

And yet they get sick, too, they suffer physically, one migraine can darken their lives, I thought to myself. But not with sympathy. Oh not, not at all. That only makes them more pathetic, all the more irritating. They are slaves to Nature, just the same as everyone else. Examples of the human species. I've read that once upon a time, the Egyptian kings claimed to be immortal. That is to say—that's why they were kings. You are mortal, but they are immortal. Immortal some other time. The Romans understood this best of all. I, he says, am the Divine Augustus. Oh really?, one of the praetorians says. Let's just slit your throat, and then we'll see whether you are immortal or not. And so they slit your throat, and it turns out that you're not immortal at all. They knock down your statues in the squares. And you're no longer worth a straw, you're nothing. It's no wonder if later the praetorians also kill your wife, your children, and your whole immortal family. The praetorians are the people with the weapons. They quickly dispel any immortality and the fog of all sorts of ideas and ideals. There's no fog, no clouds. The world is laid bare in the bright light. Yes, the Romans were clear on this. Nobody has ever been clearer on things than they were. But Nature . . . Could she have made you immortal? I mean really immortal. Oh, of course she could've! At the very least she could have made it so you'd live a thousand years. Why didn't she do this? Well, just because. She didn't feel like it. She is your all-powerful master. Just look around: you'll see that master everywhere around you. Featureless, hushed, the Master of Species. Endless and enormous, from horizon to horizon, it fills everything. And when you look inside, into your own body, you see it there, too. Your master has gotten inside as well, it owns the machine which works without stopping, which you look at from the outside and wonder what could be going on inside. It owns the humors, the organs, the bones, and the tendons, the blood and the veins through which it flows. Your master is all around, outside and inside, everywhere. There is no escape, no getting away, you belong to it entirely. A slave of Nature. This is why they've come up with the soul, books, religion, philosophy—to make it look like there's another path as well, that there is a way around the fence, through the narrow gate of the chosen, through which you can escape, wrench yourself away, be free. But you can't. No, you can't. Nature is your master and possesses you entirely. Only here and there, like small islands in the ocean, are there perhaps things which are truly yours and not hers. Perhaps there are, but perhaps not. Man is too small to measure himself against her. Too small to call her to account. Why did she do things that way, and not otherwise? Well, just because. She doesn't even hear what you're saying. She doesn't notice you at all. She moves somewhere like a vast flood, roaring, thundering, rushing onward. And someone perhaps might even say: How nice that I'm not in her path, she would sweep me away. Oh, don't worry. You are drifting along with her, you are part of the wave, you are a droplet, a fleck of the foam. To find yourself in her path, you'd first have to wrench yourself free of her somehow. So there's nothing to be afraid of.

You, too, are somehow spinning inside that wide and slow whirlwind. Thrown into nature, Pelletier would say. She could have made you differently. As well as all the pathetic, self-loving creatures around you—she could have made them differently, too. But she didn't feel like it. She is the root of all things, the beginning and the end, the secret course of things, their secret meaning, and everything that truly has meaning. Or perhaps not, after all? Could there possibly be something else? Hardly. But still, on the other hand, who really understands Nature? Who can truly say what exists within her? What torments her, what delights her, what goes on in her head and where that head is at all? Even the physicians do not understand her. Nobody knows her completely. They don't even know her halfway. They stumble around, speculating at the foot of the mountain, trying to measure it with two fingers.

"Señores, Sevilla," Jesús cried.

Yes, Sevilla. A nice city. I was right to come here. Cities, buildings, they seem to have a life of their own. It seems unbelievable that all of this was made by people, I thought to myself, as we passed by the cathedral—enormous, a mountain of stone, with intricate stone decorations on the walls, with towers and turrets, with elongated arches hanging like bridges in the air, with the Giralda Tower above us and the statue of the faith on top of it, high, high, high in the sky, lit up by the sun, which was reflected in its shield. How is it possible that all this was made by creatures such as people? I thought to myself, as I looked up, shading my eyes from the sun with my hand. People . . . People are strange, Pelletier.

Not strange, I hear Pelletier du Mans answer me in a dream, but different. Some are one way, while others are another. Like that parable, like pearls and swine.

Thank you, I say. I'll keep that in mind.

# 18. For Protection Against the Plague and All Manner of Contagions

The plague has appeared in this stupid city. Yes, really! Cursed Sevilla. The devil himself brought me here. So now how will I get out? There's no way! Or rather, there is a way, but it is such that it may as well not exist. I cannot give up my position, or all these years of study and hardships with the doctor—such study, such hardships!—I cannot give up the prospect of a future career as a physician because of a dirty little plague. Better to die in agony than to give up! To put it figuratively, of course.

"Calm down, Guimarães, don't be so afraid," the doctor told me one day, clearly having noticed the great fear and concern that had gripped me. "It's not as terrible as you think," he assured me. "It mainly kills off the poor from the other side of the river, in this part of the city almost no one is affected. And certainly almost none of the doctors. This will be my third epidemic, unless one has slipped my mind"—the doctor noted in passing—"and as far as I can remember the only doctor who died was Mateo Alemán's uncle, the licensed physician Juan Alemán, back in '68. But he was jinxed in principle."

I was not particularly convinced by his words.

"Señor," I said, "I've heard that thousands of people have died of this disease in Italy and France, whole cities are deserted . . ."

"Here isn't like in Italy and France," the doctor cut me off. "Don't forget that everyone in Sevilla smokes. More or less every single person. And nothing disinfects the air like tobacco. You still don't fully believe in tobacco, do you, eh, Guimarães?"

"Well, of course I believe in it, señor, but I don't know, I just don't know . . ."

"Tobacco decontaminates everything," the doctor assured me. "As long as the epidemic continues, you'll simply have to smoke more. It will last six or seven months, not more. And it won't be anything like in Italy and France. They don't smoke there. Here the air is disinfected."

Of course, the doctor took certain other measures. First of all, he moved Jesús, along with his whole noisy family, from the slum to his house near Puerta de Jerez, which he rented out. The merchants who had been staying there didn't want to leave, since they had paid through the end of the month. The doctor offered to give them their money back, but they still refused. I was forced to go call Rincon and Cortado. With Rincon and Cortado, the whole business was cleared up in less than twenty minutes.

Thus, we safeguarded ourselves as far as Jesús was concerned. Besides that, the doctor turned down all calls from outside the city, as well as some in Sevilla itself. What a thing experience is! Nothing can replace experience! What I mean is that the doctor in principle took calls from the Santa Cruz Quarter, but not from all streets. From La Macarena, he only took calls from certain streets. Of course, he didn't set foot in the slums on the other side of the river. Yet in the wealthy Arenal neighborhood, which was directly across from the slum, but on this side of the Guadalquivir, he went everywhere without concern. What I'm trying to say is that only experience can tell you whether to go to certain streets in one and the same neighborhood, but not to others. If it were me, I would either go to Santa Cruz or not. But the doctor had learned to make finer distinctions.

Soon the municipality took measures as well. This, of course, stemmed not from the municipality itself—if you wait for the city council to take measures, it would surely make some decision five years after the illness had passed—not from the municipality itself, I say, but from the royal governor of Sevilla, Count Villar.

And he was sufficiently sensible not to turn to the municipality, but to call a meeting of the city physicians, at which they would discuss the situation and decide what to do. Afterwards Count Villar would present their plan to the municipality and the latter would accept it. The municipality is like a woman—if you state clearly what needs to be done, she will more than likely do it, but if you wait for her to decide on her own, she'll take to hesitating, dawdling, ruminating in vain, and so on. It was well known that the count deeply despised the municipal government, while they in turn hated him and were constantly cooking up intrigues against him, claiming that he was a dictator and Lord knows what, such that he had decided that if the municipality dawdled and took to ruminating, he would run the physicians' decision through the Council of Castile, which would then simply issue it as an order to the municipality. The Council of Castile was made up of the king's people, like Count Villar, so they wouldn't even read what was presented to them—they would simply vote for it. As far as we knew, the count had even called a meeting of the Council of Castile for the following week, and the people from the municipality knew this, too, so they had to accept the decision of their own free will, since otherwise it would be forced on them from above as an order that had to be followed down to the letter.

The municipality should be shut down, in my opinion. I can't imagine anything more useless than it. At least as it is now.

When Capitan Armando, the count's aide-de-camp, informed Dr. Monardes of the scheduled meeting, the doctor fell into feverish activity. Few people on earth can do as many things in as little time with such resolute vigor as Dr. Monardes. I haven't seen any others, at any rate. The secret of this is that he appears inexhaustible at such moments and always knows what his next step will be. He finishes one thing and immediately moves on to the next. Without a moment's delay, nor a moment's hesitation, nor a moment's thought. He thinks in motion. After all, he has had experience in this as well, the situation was familiar to him.

The previous royal governor had acted in the same way during the previous plague of '68. So the doctor was prepared.

From what he told me, huge stakes were up for grabs at the moment. Something like a bonus pay day, but on a much larger scale. Dr. Monardes, as well as the other doctors, had decided to present the situation as catastrophic, as if the gravest danger were looming over the city. Judging from myself, I could say that everyone in Sevilla would easily believe this, with the exception, of course, of the doctors themselves. None of them looked particularly worried, which contrasted sharply with the gloomy prognoses they laid out. First of all, the municipal government had to pay the doctors for caring for infected citizens in certain hospitals specially designated for this purpose. It was voted that Dr. Monardes should receive fifty thousand maravedis. Dr. Bartholo wanted to transfer the sick to his San Juan de Dios Hospital; however, Dr. Monardes supported Drs. Gómez and León and their Five Wounds of Christ Hospital. In the end, a compromise was reached. Furthermore, a decision was made to clean all the streets, to close the city to people and goods from infected regions (later the municipality voted to make an exception for the merchant Señor Espinosa, who solemnly promised to limit his trade with those regions on his own and to that end presented a detailed plan, 138 pages long, of cautionary measures), and, most importantly for Dr. Monardes, to regularly burn tobacco in the various areas of the city so as to disinfect the air. Dr. Monardes assured those present that thanks to the trading company he owned with Rodrigo de Brizuela, he would be able to supply the necessary quantities of tobacco for this purpose. He even had a ship full of tobacco in the port at the moment. Some objected that his company was not large enough, since vast quantities would clearly be needed, thus perhaps it would be better to turn to Señor Espinosa, who could certainly supply them, but Drs. Gómez and León vigorously supported Dr. Monardes, also bringing forth the argument that only one type of tobacco, *Nicotiana tabaccum*, had disinfectant properties, while the other fifty-nine types did not have such properties, and that no one could possibly know better than Dr. Monardes how to distinguish *Nicotiana tabaccum* from the other types of tobacco. It is true that Señor Espinosa also traded solely in that type of tobacco, since it is the only type suitable for smoking, but a merchant cannot be expected to have a physician's knowledge, so in the case of Señor Espinosa, the possibility for error at least potentially existed. "We cannot allow ourselves to take even the slightest risk with the health and lives of our citizens, especially not at such a dangerous moment," Dr. Gomez said amidst approving applause from most of the doctors present. In his tirelessness, Dr. Monardes had met with almost all of them over the past two days. And so the doctors' meeting decided to entrust Dr. Monardes with the task of supplying tobacco. Later, the municipal government voted to make an exception for Señor Espinosa as well, but despite this, the doctor kept at least half the city. At the risk of getting ahead of myself, I should say that he indeed could not supply—despite all his efforts—the enormous quantities of tobacco required and had to transfer some of this responsibility to the merchant Espinosa, but he still kept nearly one-third of the city. The municipality also had to finance the publication of treatises on the plague written in a generally accessible style, in which the emphasis would fall on how to protect ourselves from it. This was nothing new. The Drs. Andrés de Alfaro and Francisco Franco had written such treatises during the previous plague of '68. They now wanted to write them once again. However, Drs. Gómez and León objected that their treatises were already well-known to the public, which had purchased them during the previous plague and most likely still had them, and that now treatises needed to be written by other people, who would present a new point of view on the illness. Dr. Monardes vigorously supported them. He suggested that Drs. Gómez and León write those treatises themselves. A heated argument arose. In the end, it was decided that Drs. Gómez and León would write new treatises, while the old ones by Dr. Alfaro and Dr. Franco would be reprinted, also at the municipality's expense. Several other details were also settled—citizens were advised to follow a nourishing diet, they were also advised to wear amulets full of aromatic substances, best of all tobacco, and to protect themselves with its vapors as well, by using it more frequently. With that, the physicians' meeting ended. I was surprised to see that all of them ended up satisfied—some more, others less, but overall, everyone was satisfied. One hundred and twenty people, and all of them satisfied! Now that's something you don't see too often. I suppose that plague, war, or natural disaster is necessary in order to see 120 people satisfied down to the last man in one and the same place at one and the same time. Guilds are quite something! If you have a drop of brains in your head, you'll join one.

But it was not only the doctors who were satisfied, far from it. In fact, everyone was satisfied. Count Villar was satisfied, since he now had a clear, concise, and detailed plan of action. The municipality was satisfied, since it could offer a clear solution devised by competent people, yet one that it could change here and there and afterwards simply implement, without having to do too much thinking. And finally, the most critical link in the chain, the citizens of Sevilla themselves, were also very satisfied. Usually they are as tight as ducks' arses, but now they were very frightened and because of this they spared no expenses. The whole trick is to scare them. They'll go around shitting themselves from fear and emptying their pockets, yet thankful that they are alive and well, that someone is taking care of them. That is why they were now very satisfied to see that vigorous and concrete measures were being taken for their protection. The so-called public, Pelletier. It is the biggest goldmine of all. There isn't that much gold, even in the Americas.

Small heaps of tobacco supplied by Dr. Monardes started burning everywhere around the city, at every crossing, on every street, in front of the entrance to the cathedral, several on each square, inside the municipal buildings, for example, in the corridors of the city hall, in front of the pubs (they were already smoky enough inside as it was), at least those which remained open, in front of houses, even in the parks. The whole city was enveloped in tobacco smoke. I doubled my cigarella intake. The doctor also smoked more, despite the fact that it made his coughing fits worse and more frequent than before. There was far too much matter and rottenness coming up from his lungs. Seeing this, I even suggested to him that he reduce his cigarellas despite the danger, since they made him cough up so much matter.

"Better to cough for a hundred years than to catch the plague for even one day!" the doctor said.

He was right again, of course.

"Señor," I said to him one day, as we were on our way to the Arenal Quarter, "this city is so enveloped in smoke that it looks like a vision from the Apocalypse."

The doctor laughed. And why were we going to Arenal? Because the doctor was helping the Drs. Gómez and León, who were taking care of the sick in Carretería and Arenal. Carretería and Arenal were wealthy neighborhoods, and the doctor turned out to be right that they remained almost entirely unaffected. I, however, continued to be slightly scared, and once this almost cost me my position with the doctor. This took place at the beginning of the epidemic, during one of our first visits to the Five Wounds of Christ Hospital. Something had happened in the poor neighborhoods and the hospital was suddenly overflowing. In the poor neighborhoods, things were not at all like in Arenal. Not in the least. It was as if those people lived in a different world. Makes you wonder what on earth they're doing to make such things happen to them. Tobacco was constantly burning in their part of town as well, the municipality actually had taken care of that and had appointed people to ensure the ceaseless burning of tobacco everywhere in the city, and it really was burning everywhere all the time. Yet despite this, far more people got sick in the poor neighborhoods. I asked the doctor why this was.

"Because you must follow all the recommendations, every last one, for them to have an effect," he answered. "They don't do some things, and that's what kills them. They either don't wear amulets with tobacco or don't smoke enough or don't follow the diet we recommended, or don't fumigate their houses, or don't clean them, or take in relatives from the provinces and they infect them. After all, their houses are crammed as full as rabbit hutches, so if one person gets sick, they are all done for."

Because of this, the royal army was guarding all the bridges leading to Triana on the other side of the river, and practically the only people and things they allowed to pass over to our side of the Guadalquivir were the carts hauling the sick. Not all of them died. Many of them lived. This created a serious problem, since afterwards they didn't want to go back to the other side. They stayed here, slept on the streets, and were constantly begging or stealing. Finally, the municipality built a something like a camp for them on that empty spot in "The Skulls" near Puerta de Jerez. But it turned out to be too small to hold them all. Moreover, healthy people from Triana began arriving there, too, swimming across the river and going to the camp. This wouldn't have been such a big deal, but you have no way of knowing whether one of them wasn't infected, too—there were such cases as well. For this reason, the royal army had already taken up positions along the whole length of the river—on the bridges and the banks, one soldier every hundred feet. They began attacking the soldiers. The soldiers were afraid that some of them could be infected, so in such cases they often killed them, primarily out of fear. Like I said, the poor neighborhoods were a different world. Thank God I was never forced to set foot there.

But, quite naturally, the doctor asked me to go into the Five Wounds of Christ Hospital with him. I refused. I froze in my tracks, as if my legs had been filled with lead.

"I'm not going in there, señor," I said finally and shook my head.

"You're not going in?" The doctor gave me a look.

"I'm not going in, señor," I repeated after a short pause.

The doctor looked at me in silence for some time, then angrily turned around and entered the hospital courtyard at a brisk pace. The door slammed loudly behind him. I watched him from behind as he walked angrily towards the hospital and thought to myself: "That's it! It's all over for me! Now he'll really give me the boot!" Why was I even waiting here at all, I said to myself, since I would have to leave in any case? Since that's what was going to happen, it would've been better if I'd left at the very beginning of the epidemic.

I tried to force myself to go in, but I couldn't.

"Oh, señor, señor!" Jesús shook his head on the coachbox, a cigarella in his mouth, enveloped in smoke.

I'd really done it this time. I don't think I've ever found myself in more a serious situation in terms of the risk of losing my position with the doctor. Even when the barn burned down, I wasn't in such a serious situation. Besides that, I also felt like a bit of a traitor. At the first sign of truly serious danger, I had abandoned the doctor. But I could not force myself to go into that hospital. The things I heard coming from there were not inviting in the least. I wondered how the Drs. Gómez and León could put up with such groaning all day. They gave them anesthetizing substances, of course, but still . . .

I started pacing back and forth along the street, my head now entirely empty, or more precisely so mixed up that no one single thought could forge a path and formulate itself clearly. I was simply awaiting my fate, like some helpless animal.

The doctor was very slow to return, unusually slow. He finally came out and got into the carriage. I also got in. Jesús drove off. The doctor did not say anything. He acted as if nothing had happened, yet I sensed a certain change in him. I figured that with time this, too, would pass, like everything else. Fortunately, I had the opportunity to test the effect of time—I kept my place. On the following day, we once again went to the hospital, but this time the doctor did not ask me to go in. He didn't say anything, but simply entered the courtyard and continued on his way. I remained outside. If he had asked me to go in again, this time I would've done it. But he didn't ask.

"You saved your skin, señor!" Jesús said with that obnoxious little laugh of his.

This time, after he came out of the hospital, the doctor nevertheless spoke about yesterday's incident, as we were on our way home in the carriage. An awkward silence had reigned between us, awkward for me, at least. I felt like asking him what was going on inside, but of course I didn't dare. I could just imagine what his answer would be.

The doctor began coughing violently; I handed him my handkerchief, he shook his head, took out his own, and spit into it. Then he cleared his throat and said: "You need will to be a doctor, my friend. You need will to be anything whatsoever, if you're really going to do it, if you're really going to be it. Otherwise you'll remain like that crowd, which is constantly reeling hither and thither, not seeing anything through to its end nor doing it as it should be done, and not getting anywhere in life, unless they're from a rich or aristocratic family. The world is also full of heaps of those types, nobodies with pedigrees. They owe everything to chance, they are the toys of chance."

"I am sorry, señor," I said. "This illness fills me with terror. It is stronger than I am. But next time I will go in with you."

"There's no need," the doctor replied, to my huge relief. "When all is said and done, you won't gain anything from this. I'll get fifty thousand maravedis for it, Gómez and León will earn many times that amount, but you won't earn a thing. Why should you risk your hide? Nor am I the sort of person who would demand such a thing of you. I wouldn't go so far as to make you risk your life, since you that's how you see it. But you should know one thing: if you want to become a doctor, if you want to practice this profession, you need will. Not only knowledge, but will. If not in this case, then in another. That's how it is with everything. Some say that people are by nature good, while others say that people are by nature evil. Both sides are wrong. People, of course, purely and simply come in all sorts. Some are more likely good, while others are more likely evil. And so you, too, are more likely a doctor than anything else. But to change from more likely something into that very something itself, you need will. Most people lack the necessary will and bob between one and the other like orange peels in the river. They go wherever chance and circumstances take them. They do not have the will to be good or evil. Or they lose it over the course of the years," the doctor clarified. "I'm giving you this example because it is the most widely known. But it is the same with everything else. It's the same with all professions, with all undertakings. If you want to be successful. There is one thing all losers have in common: a lack of will. Sometimes fate itself, as it is customarily called, can also turn against you and a long string of unfortunate circumstances can ruin anyone, but this happens much, much more rarely. Usually everything comes down to ability and will. Will, Guimarães."

His words echoed within me, as Pelletier would put it, as in an empty church. I was deeply impressed. Despite this, on the following day I did not go into the hospital. Because I also remembered very well the part about the fifty thousand maravedis and the Drs. Gómez and León. So . . .

So as not to detain the readers on this topic any longer, I will quickly add that in any case I did not enter the Five Wounds of Christ at all during the entire epidemic, which ended after several months with the onset of winter. Many people from the other side of the river were stricken, as well as a few from this side. Dr. Monardes, myself, Jesús, and his whole populous family remained unscathed. The Drs. Gómez and León, too. Only two doctors out of the 120 fell ill and died. Jesús once again returned to Triana—unwillingly, of course: the house near Jerez was far nicer than his own. The doctor's attitude towards me did not change, or at the very least it soon resumed its previous course. On the whole, the plague epidemic turned out to be nowhere near as terrifying as I had imagined. Unlike in the past, we now have at hand the great disinfecting power of tobacco. That changes everything. I even expressed my surprise to the doctor that they did not take advantage of the miraculous medicine's properties in Italy and France.

"I don't know why that is." The doctor shrugged. "Especially in France. Many years have already passed since Jean Nicot from Languedoc introduced tobacco there after serving as ambassador in Spain."

"He was ambassador in Portugal, señor," I noted, entirely in passing, simply as a point of clarification.

"Jean Nicot was ambassador in Spain," repeated the doctor. "Where are you getting this Portugal nonsense?"

"But señor, he was ambassador in Lisbon. Lisbon is in Portugal," I gently objected.

"Lisbon was in Portugal, before Duke de Alba captured it," replied the doctor.

Yes, actually he was right. But not entirely. Because Jean Nicot had been ambassador in Portugal before Duke de Alba captured it—which, incidentally, did not have a favorable effect on the duke, since he died there, in Lisbon . . . But be that as it may, I kept silent.

Overall, I could say that I came away with several lessons from this whole story of the plague epidemic. First, that tobacco truly is a much stronger medicine than even I had thought. Second, that in certain rarely occurring circumstances, normally connected with some disaster, one must act quickly and decisively and must be able to extract from them benefits for many years to come, which would otherwise be unimaginable. Third—yes, will is necessary; it is more important than we think. I've forgotten the other lessons.

By the way, Countess Béjar sent the doctor six hundred ducats for curing her headaches. She calculated that she had suffered from headaches for twenty-four years and sent him twenty-five ducats for each one of them (two ducats a month, plus one extra to round out the sum). This was four times more than he received from the municipality for treating the sick during the plague, since during the epidemic the maravedi lost value and fifty thousand became equivalent to 150 ducats, or even less. The municipality, however, paid only in maravedis. Only royal officials and merchants paid in ducats. Of course, Dr. Monardes' main income in this case came from the fumigation of the city. I don't know what the exact figure in question is, but I would guess that it is very large.

After he received this gift from the countess—because it was a gift—the doctor dedicated the new edition of his book *Historia medicinal* to her. That's what it says on the title page: "To Countess Béjar." This latter amused him greatly. He considered it one of his cleverest jokes. From time to time he would laugh for no reason and this was because at that moment he was thinking of how he had dedicated his book to Countess Béjar. I also find it an excellent joke, which few can appreciate. "A historical joke," as Pelletier would say.

# 19. The Death of Dr. Monardes

Finally the doctor took to his bed, lying sick day after day, week after week—he could no longer do anything on his own. He was suffering terribly. His lungs wheezed like a blacksmith's bellows; he was often seized with fits of a torturous, seemingly endless, dry cough, as if he would cough up his lungs; it was getting harder and harder for him to breathe; he never had enough air and his eyes bulged like a fish on dry land. His daughters took care of him during the day. At night or when they weren't around, I stayed with him and helped him with whatever I could. That, however, changed. It is difficult to say whether his daughters' care was more harmful or helpful. They constantly seemed on the verge of tears, and this created an oppressive mood. Besides, the doctor had been used to living alone for many years. This constant human presence seemed to weigh on him like a millstone around his neck. In my opinion, his daughters' excessive solicitousness and their unhappy appearance wearied him and even annoyed him a bit. He refrained for some time, but finally told them, choosing his words carefully, that he would like to be left alone most of the time—it was easier for him to rest that way, he said—he preferred to see them getting on with their own lives, taking care of their own families, and so on; that he did not want to become a burden for them, and that for him it was absolutely sufficient to know that I was in the house and that he could call me at any moment. They understood what he was getting at and began coming less frequently. I went in to see him regularly, but unobtrusively and never staying for long.

At first I thought that it would perhaps be good for him to continue taking tobacco vapors, though under a stricter regimen—on an empty stomach, for example, or something like that—to see whether the tobacco couldn't conquer the inflammation in his body. The doctor, however, categorically refused, arguing that he had already tried that treatment enough and that tobacco made him worse. After that, I came to the conclusion that he had poisoned himself with tobacco. Like every medicine taken in overly large doses, it, too, became poisonous and fatal. I suggested to the doctor that he take a laxative to cleanse his body of tobacco, as was done in every case of poisoning. The doctor, however, was sure that if we were to do such a thing, he would die that very day, and categorically refused. I didn't know what else we could do for him besides making him cold compresses, giving him herbal tea during the day and mulled wine in the evening before going to sleep, keeping the air in the room fresh, and forcing him, despite his unwillingness, to eat regularly—the usual things associated with a healthy lifestyle, which in his case, however, no longer gave the desired results. Naturally, he was examined by the other doctors of Sevilla, even the royal physician Dr. Bernard came. Dr. Monardes resolutely refused to follow the prescriptions from the other doctors in Sevilla, since he claimed—and not without reason—that they had an interest in his death and had long since wondered how to get rid of his competition and to steal away his clientele. In one or two cases he found the prescriptions from the other doctors from Sevilla quite reasonable and tried them, but in smaller doses than they had prescribed (because he suspected them of perfidious duplicity and of attempting to trick him), but the treatments, perhaps for that reason, had no effect. He responded most favorably to Dr. Bernard's recommendations and followed them strictly, but they did not produce results either. Dr. Bernard had the pleasant radiance of a plump man with kind manners, a calm smile and gentle eyes, with wrinkles beside his mouth, which hinted that he laughed often and easily, and he managed to inspire hope in Dr. Monardes' daughters, but as I was seeing him off to his carriage along the garden path, he told me privately, as a colleague, that in his opinion Dr. Monardes' case was hopeless. "Dr. da Silva," he said, "in my opinion, Dr. Monardes' case is hopeless. You shouldn't cherish illusions, Dr. da Silva. Unless, of course, Nature works some wonder, which is always possible, as you very well know, Dr. da Silva." A very pleasant man, very learned. I'm not the least bit surprised that he has risen to the rank of royal physician.

Yes, I had also recently begun suspecting what Dr. Bernard said. After all, Dr. Monardes was already an elderly man, and if he had poisoned himself with tobacco—which was and continues to be my conviction—I couldn't see how a man of his years, his nature weakened from age, could fight off the firm grip of that omnipotent, yet dangerous medicine. We used tobacco to force Nature to mend her ways when she had gone astray, but how could we use the doctor's already weakened nature against tobacco? We had never tried anything of the sort, we had always done the opposite, such that even if Nature were able to triumph in this clash—which I very highly doubt—we, frankly speaking, hadn't the faintest idea of how to make that happen.

One very early morning, at dawn, when we were alone in the house, I said to the doctor: "Señor, perhaps we should renounce tobacco. Perhaps it is not a medicine. Perhaps we have made a mistake."

"By no means," the doctor wheezed. He had become very weak, he could hardly draw breath. I was holding his hand to give him courage. The doctor, by the way, could only speak with great pain, often with long pauses between the words, although for the sake of convenience I will not transmit this here. Also, I couldn't always hear what he was saying and had to lean over him, while he repeated the word or not—in the latter case I have taken the liberty of transmitting the general sense of his statements, guessing at what he had in mind. "My life has not passed in vain. That was my life's work. And you will continue it. You will continue it, Guimarães!" The doctor squeezed my hand weakly.

"Very well, señor," I replied. "You can count on that. Really and truly."

"I have left a letter for you," the doctor said. "In my writing desk, the second drawer from the left. Read it when I die."

"Don't talk like that, señor," I objected. "You will get better and live for many years yet."

"Yes, yes . . ." he replied. "Tobacco is a mighty medicine"—the doctor continued—"you just have to be careful with it, as with every other medicine. To know when, how, and how much . . . My memory will live on with it in future."

"Of course, señor. That's certain," I replied. "But don't think about that now. The future doesn't matter. Think about the present moment. The future doesn't matter."

"Don't repeat yourself. It's a tiresome habit," the doctor wheezed.

May I be struck dead, may Maria Immaculata curse me if those weren't his final words! Yes, those were his final words! The doctor died a bit later and almost instantaneously. He tried to take a breath abruptly, his chest wheezed, and it was all over. Quick and, at least as far as his death was concerned, painless. The doctor was a disciplined man, in everything.

I had been sitting on his bed, so I reached out and closed his eyes. I had seen dead men before, so I wouldn't say I was too taken aback. But the way they stare—if that's the right word—has always struck me, and it continued to evoke some alarming discomfort within me. Those open eyes, that unmoving gaze, as if cut off from everything around them, seeming to stare off somewhere in the distance, a somehow glassy, inhuman gaze, it continued to upset me. It seemed to me that when I closed the doctor's eyes, his expression changed, that his expression softened. This was the person whom I had known, although with a much thinner and yellowed face, a much sadder face. But it was Dr. Monardes. While that other thing was something else.

I stood up and shook out my legs, which had cramped up from my uncomfortable position. How pleasant it is to move, to stride back and forth, I thought to myself. I stayed by the bed for a bit, staring at the doctor–I wanted to remember him as he had been when I'd seen him for the last time, to give his features time to imprint themselves clearly and lastingly on my mind. Then I turned around, headed for the door, opened it, looked back at the doctor once again as I was leaving, and stopped for a moment, after which I closed the door and calmly headed for his study.

I went into the doctor's study, opened the second drawer on the left in his writing desk, and quickly spotted a paper pouch with my name written on it in large crooked letters. Inside there were two pieces of paper, a small one and a large one. I opened the larger one. The doctor's letter read:

*Guimarães,*

*I'm not going to leave you anything, since I've never been particularly fond of you. Do you remember that day in front of the Five Wounds of Christ? Things have their consequences, my friend. No, I am not one to hold grudges. But to each his own. Each must receive that which he deserves. No more and no less. This is something I believe. To each his own.*

*I had thought to leave you my olive press, but decided against it. For the aforementioned reason, as well as for another: it is in bad shape and will not be of much use to you, and years from now you'll start saying: "Look, Dr. Monardes did not leave me anything except a useless press." I prefer to simply leave you nothing.*

*I will leave you my three pieces of advice, as I have promised you and which I owe you as my student. They are on the other, smaller sheet of paper.*

*Thank you for all the care you gave me while I was bedridden. That was useful to me.*

*Still, I will give you a chance you can take advantage of, if you wish and if you can manage it. Know that the notary Serega from the municipal council is open to bribes. Also know that my will does not mention this house anywhere. If you write up a fake will especially for this house and bribe Serega, he will notarize it and the house will be yours. This will be very expensive, however. Most likely you do not have the money needed for this. If you so desire, you can borrow it from my partner, the apothecary del Valle. He won't make a note of what you need it for, but he will charge you heavy interest. If your practice goes well, you will be able to pay him back in a year or two, but if it doesn't, then you will be hopelessly sunk. Think it over carefully. If you do not succeed in medicine, with such a debt you will either end up a beggar on the street or you will have to leave the country. Don't imagine you can simply go to Madrid or Barcelona. Del Valle has apothecaries and lots of friends all over the country and he will find you.*

*As you know, my daughters are married to rich men, they have more than enough property, and besides, I will leave everything else to them. Moreover, this house was never mine. It belonged to my father-in-law Perez de Morales and I acquired it in a similar way many years ago. Many, many years ago. How time flies, Guimarães. It really flies.*

*Death fills even physicians with horror, when it is their own. I now realize that clearly. I meet it without any illusions and without any hopes. I know there is nothing after it. It is simply a black hole that you fall into and disappear. I will not pretend and lie to you, but rather will admit that this provokes horror within me. Life is absurd, yet death is very frightening.*

*Some time ago I had become reconciled with it and had calmed down, but the closer it gets, the more terrified I feel. However, if I truly know human nature well, in my final hours I will most likely again feel resigned and calm and perhaps will even begin to expect something. I will meet death calm and hopeful. Man is simply that kind of animal. Nature has arranged things this way, perhaps as a final gesture of mercy, or simply because it is more efficient like this.*

*(She is more merciful than you give her credit for, Guimarães, and is nowhere near as crazy as you think. But I know that I cannot change your mind about this.)*

*Continue using tobacco and proclaiming its healing power everywhere. For me, it was one of the greatest opportunities of my career, and for you it may turn out to be the only one.*

*Farewell.*
*Dr. N. M.*

I set that sheet aside and unrolled the other with trembling fingers. I felt very strange—simultaneously very impatient and somehow drifting in a stupor, as if the world were slowly spinning around me as around its axis or center. The noise from the street reached my ears and seemed to move in a circle around me, somehow slowly and thoughtfully, along with the objects in the room and the pale pre-dawn light. I took a few steps towards the window so as to better see what was written.

*My Three Pieces of Advice*

*They are not exactly advice, Guimarães, but rather deductions from which you can draw your own conclusions in turn. If you constantly keep these three deductions in mind, they will prompt you as to how to act in every concrete situation. Here they are:*

*1. There is no God. A pity, but that's how it is.*
*2. People are foolish.*
*3. Money rules the world. The Golden Rule: Whoever has the gold makes the rules.*

*The latter only applies to the human world, of course. If you are interested in medicine, if you decide to delve further into it and to understand how things stand in that world, there are, of course, completely different forces and laws at work. Everything I can tell you about them can be found in my works, which you already know well, thus I cannot add anything new for you.*

*Frankly speaking, I don't see any particular point in delving any deeper into that; which, if I know you at all, is not among your intentions in any case.*

*One clarification: people are foolish, but dangerous. Don't ever forget that. It is much better to trick them than to force them. It is also much easier, if you have the head for it. It is also far more effective and long-lasting. Contrary to that foolish proverb, a lie has infinitely long legs.*

*Live and enjoy life, Guimarães, insofar as that is possible.*

*Yours, etc.,*
*Dr. Nicolas Monardes*

I rolled the pages back up and stuffed them, along with the pouch, into the pockets of my jacket. Then I lit a cigarella and thought hard. That letter was important. There have hardly been two times in my life when I've thought deeply, and this was one of them. The doctor's advice didn't particularly surprise me, but the other part of his letter—yes.

After I finished smoking the cigarella, I called Jesús and informed him that the doctor had died. He asked to see him, so I led him to Dr. Monardes's bedroom. When he recovered from the shock, Jesús hastened to go to tell his daughters what had happened.

"Don't be in such a hurry," I told him. "I want you to stay here while I go print out the obituary notices, then after that you'll go and tell the doctor's daughters about his death."

"But they won't be ready until this evening," he objected, or rather wondered, since he didn't understand what was going on.

"They will be ready earlier," I said. "Perhaps shortly after lunch. Then you'll go and tell his daughters."

"But señor . . ." he began.

"Listen, Jesús," I told him, looking him straight in the eye. I had the disconcerting feeling that the doctor was listening to me and grinning from somewhere in the sky, or from wherever he was, so I grabbed Jesús by the sleeve, and when we got out into the hall, I told him: "Listen, Jesús. You want to keep your job as a coachman, right? Otherwise, now that the doctor is dead, what will you do?"

"I don't know, señor," he replied.

"Everything can stay as it was," I continued, "with some small changes. You will keep your job. Your wife and children will be well fed. Everything will be as it was. Just listen to me and do what I tell you. Got it?"

"What should I do, señor?" he replied, confused.

"Just stay here until I tell you otherwise. I will go to print out the obituaries, and when I get back, you'll go to tell the doctor's daughters. That'll be around noon, dusk at the very latest. Just stay here and don't tell anyone about the doctor's death."

"Very well, señor," he replied.

That's how it goes, when something is meant to happen, it usually starts well, starts easily.

I went back to the doctor's study and opened the bowl in which he had left the money for his burial. I took the amount he had set aside for his obituary. I also had the money I had prepared for my own advertisement with me. That's it, everything was ready. I patted my pockets as if to make sure everything was in place, and left the study. Jesús was still standing in the hallway.

"I'm leaving," I told him. "I will print up the obituaries. I will also print up a advertisement for myself. You stay here and don't move."

"Very well, señor," Jesús replied.

A minute later I was already out on the street.

The cold light of morning greeted me. The day had already fully dawned, the morning was clear and cool, and the cold air inspired cheerfulness in me, gave me courage. What luck, I thought to myself, that the doctor died at daybreak. It was as if he had purposely planned it that way. If he had died in the evening, for example, there would be no way of putting off telling his daughters all the way until the next evening; while in this way I had a certain chance, the whole day was before me.

Sevilla wakes up early, and there were already quite a few people on the streets, going about their business. Several carriages passed me, taking their goods to the market. A thin yellow strip of light stretched along the eastern horizon, foreshadowing a sunny day.

I was already on my way to the printing house owned by Señor Diaz—the publisher of *Folk Wisdom* and of Dr. Monardes' works as well, of course—when it struck me that I could combine my advertisement and the obituary into one. That way I'd save a little money, too. I quickly composed the new notice in my mind. When I went to Señor Diaz and told him what I wanted, he immediately put himself at my service.

"Whatever you say, señor," Señor Diaz nodded cheerfully. "You pay, we print."

"That's what I like to hear!" I said and patted him on the shoulder.

When something is meant to happen, it starts well. Seeming to sense my impatience, Señor Diaz led me over to the typesetter who would set my notice, gave him the sheet he had written it out on, telling me, "It won't be ready immediately, señor, come back around noon," and left. I began pacing impatiently between the typesetters and the presses at the other end of the shop. I felt like going over to my man and starting to line up the wooden letters on the tray in front of him myself, but I knew how annoying it was to have someone looking over your shoulder as you work. The machines thundered away loudly and the people who were talking looked strange—you see their gestures, but don't hear anything. Like you've landed in a home for the mute. I couldn't resist the temptation and glanced at my typesetter to see what he was doing. He was already setting the third line. He raised his head from the box of letters and nodded at me encouragingly, as if to say: "Relax, señor, things will work out fine." I read the first two lines, with certain difficulty, given that the letters were reversed like a mirror reflection. Does everything look so strange when it is written like that? You get the feeling that it's not yours, that you didn't think it up, it looks so strange to you, so distant—and completely indifferent.

Be that as it may, there was nothing more for me to do here. It would take hours for the typesetter to set it and then to print it on some available press. In an instinctive gesture of fondness, I almost offered my man a cigarella, but then I realized that it could slow him down and decided against it. I went outside. More time seemed to have passed than I expected, since the sun was already shining brightly in the sky. I stood by the door of the printing house and lit a cigarella. The bright sun shone on my face, pleasantly warming my blood, I had the feeling that my body was softening up. I exhaled the smoke in the warm air and half-closed my eyes. Why am I so fired up about this, I asked myself, why have I grabbed at this opportunity like a drowning man clutching at the final straw? I could go back to Portugal, get married, and earn my daily bread some other way, even if that meant taking up farming—like my father, his father, and everyone before them. I could go to Madrid or Barcelona and find some kind of work there—they would take me, I was still young. I could become a sailor and cross the seas. The warm sun would always be above me, no matter what I did, it would shine on me benevolently just as now. The ancients are right—there is a place for everyone under it, indeed. Even if the sun disappears for a day, for a month, for some time, afterwards it will rise again. This is its nature. I could do so many other things, I was still young.

But was I?, I thought to myself. Was I really still young? How young? The time always comes when you have to choose something, isn't that right, Pelletier? To grab hold of it with all your might, to set off down a narrow path, from which hundreds of paths branch out through the broad field and wind enticingly off into the distance—through the field, through the hills, through the forests and mountains, far away towards the horizon and beyond. You can't take all of them, the world is too large, and man is too small, he has only two legs and even they must walk side by side—perhaps contrary to unprejudiced expectations and even to common sense to a certain extent. In its disorderliness, Nature in most cases has created two things to do a particular job, and she has created them such that if only one remains, then usually the job can't get done. Nature is very inefficient. Everything is done slapdash, willy-nilly. The whole world is made that way. But even made like that, it is unusually large, you cannot take all paths, and where they lead will remain forever unknown to you. This is perhaps even preferable at least half of the time. All paths look enticing at the beginning, but what lies there between those hills, where they disappear from sight—who knows? You'll never find out.

I tossed my cigarella on the ground and set out for Señor del Valle's.

When something is meant to happen, it starts well and continues well. I returned to Diaz's printing house at noon with a full belly from lunch at Señor del Valle's and a head slightly dazed from jerez. Of course, I was careful not to go overboard with the wine—right now was not the time for that at all. I had met the apothecary del Valle through Dr. Monardes, but only in passing. He turned out to be an even more sympathetic person than the doctor had made him out to be. At some point—our conversation had already gone on for quite some time, by the way—he asked me about the doctor:

"How is Señor Monardes?" he asked.

"Not well at all," I replied.

"He'll recover," he said and changed the subject.

The notice was still not ready. I wandered here and there around Sevilla for perhaps another hour. When I returned, the job was done. I paid Señor Diaz, took the roll with the notices, and left. The notice read:

*Dr. da Silva,*
*student of*
*the late Dr. Monardes,*
*whom we shall all remember*
*for his kind heart*
*and vast erudition,*
*may his memory live forever,*
*is accepting patients at his house*
*on Sierpes Street.*
*All are welcome!*

Now I had to go back to the house to get the bone glue and paste up the notices. And first of all, of course, I had to see what Jesús was doing. He was the weakest link in the chain. During that whole time, a worrisome thought had been gnawing away at me: What was Jesús doing at that moment? If anyone were to botch the whole plan, it would be him.

The house looked quiet when I entered the yard. There were no people in sight, nor any carriages, no sound could be heard. This strongly raised my hopes.

Jesús had seen me and met me at the door, white as a sheet.

"Maria was here, señor," he said.

This piece of news stunned me. How could that have slipped my mind–it stood perfectly to reason! Of course one of the doctor's daughters would stop by to see him in the morning.

"What happened?" I asked.

"Thank God I heard her coming up the walk . . . I told her the doctor was sleeping."

"Didn't she go in to see him?"

"She went in, señor . . . But I had turned him on his side. And covered him up to his chin. She didn't notice a thing. But she said she'd stop by again this afternoon."

I ran up the stairs, Jesús at my heels. I opened the door to the bedroom. The doctor was lying with his back to us, wrapped in a blanket up to his chin. I went around to the other side. He really did look like he was sleeping. True, he was very yellow, but he was like that before, too. Well, well, Jesús! I raised my eyes and met his frightened gaze. Well, well, that Jesús!

"Well done, Jesús!" I told him and patted him on the shoulder. "You and I are going to go far. You've done well."

"Well, I wasn't born yesterday, señor," he replied with a certain satisfaction.

I felt like laughing when I looked at his face, with his simultaneously self-satisfied and frightened expression, such an absurd combination of sorts. But I restrained myself and pulled him out into the hallway. I felt awkward speaking in the bedroom, because of the doctor's body. I had the disconcerting feeling that he was listening to me; that he was watching me. I pictured his ghost hanging about somewhere in the air, invisible, his ghostly arms crossed, twiddling his ghostly thumbs and watching me with a slightly mocking smile, which combined a certain fondness and ridicule, an ironic smile. The curious thing is that when I went out into the hallway, I ceased to feel this concern, as if the ghost could not pass through the door.

As soon as we got out into the hallway, I showed Jesús the advertisement-obituary.

"But señor," he said, visibly unpleasantly surprised, "weren't you going to print up an obituary for the doctor? Don't we have to announce that he has died?"

"Jesús, are you out of your mind?" I said. "Can't you tell from this notice that Dr. Monardes is dead?"

"I can tell, señor, but . . ."

"But what?"

"I don't know," Jesús replied, staring at the notice. "I've got the feeling that something isn't quite right. But the more I think about it, the harder it is for me to say what exactly."

"Oh, I've heard this nonsense before!" I waved dismissively and headed down the stairs. I had work to do. I couldn't stand around listening to someone who didn't know what he wanted to say. "Go and tell the doctor's daughters," I called over my shoulder. "In the meantime, I'll go out and post up these notices."

"Very well, señor," he replied.

I had almost forgotten. Jesús was already going out the door when I called to him to stop and quickly ran over to him from the kitchen, with the bone glue in my hand.

"Tell them that his final wish was for them to carry him out of here and to hold his funeral at Maria's house. Tell them," I continued, "that the doctor hated this house and said that it had killed him."

"So that's it, señor?" Jesús replied. I could've sworn a sly twinkle flashed in his eyes.

"That's it!" I said. "They surely will dawdle and get confused, and they may not do it, so I'm really counting on you to get the job done. Carry him out with the cart, on a stretcher. Have that blockhead de Brizuela help you."

"Very well, señor," he replied. Yes, without a doubt there was a sly glint in his eyes. One could simply see on his face how things were starting to become clear to him. Damn these sly peasants!

"If everything goes well, leave that red ribbon you tie around Pablito's neck on the table in the kitchen."

"Fine."

"Go on, get going," I said and patted him on the back.

He nodded and left. I went back to the kitchen, since in my haste I had taken the glue, but had forgotten the roll of notices. I had already opened the door when Jesús' voice unexpectedly floated to me from the pathway outside: "It'll work out, señor," he cried.

Yes, it'll work out! I could count on Jesús much more than I had expected. What a great thing common interest is, by the way. How it unites people! Yes, the doctor was right–money rules the world. It is the source of great friendships.

"Like a magic wand," I thought to myself as I took the longish roll of notices from the table. "Señor del Valle, Señor Diaz, Jesús . . . And the notary Serega will help, I'm sure of it. Money is like a magic wand. Just wave it–and poof! Just wave it–and poof! Just wave it–and poof! Whoever thought it up was a great conjuror indeed! A magician!"

The sun was beating down on the pathway. It was two o'clock in the afternoon.

Yet how nice, I said to myself, that I'm on this side of the magic. If you're on the other one, in the best case scenario you merely serve it, and in the worst case, it turns against you. What would happen if that magic were turned against you? I shudder to think. You're in for it.

I stepped out onto the street and headed towards the market. I would post the notices there first.

The market on Feria Street was still full of people. I pasted up a few notices and returned to Sierpes. Of course, I had to put some notices up near the San Juan de Dios Hospital and on San Francisco Square. From there I set out for the stock exchange and the cathedral. The stock exchange was an important place—the retailers were on Feria, and the wholesalers were here. What better clientele than them? Intense liveliness reigned in the Square of Songs—not so much due to the merchants as to the workmen who were finishing building the stock exchange. The exchange was a large, ugly building, completely in the style of Juan de Herrera—but he did the Escorial, too, now didn't he? Someone ought to ban him from building anything whatsoever, except for perhaps tombs. What luck that the cathedral was not built by him! When I came to Sevilla for the first time, I was thunderstruck. I had never seen such a large and such a beautiful, imposing structure. I put notices up next to two of the doors. I lifted my gaze towards Giralda Tower. The Statue of the Faith on top of it looked like a small cut in the sky. The sun reflected off the shining surface of Faith's shield as if off a small crystal of glass, as if off a grain of sand, Pelletier. But whoever had the idea to make it a weathervane was truly an imaginative person. If you catch it at the moment when the wind picks up, you can see how the statue spins, as if gradually scanning the entire city—in the evening it is turned in one direction, in the morning in another. Faith . . . This world is a complete failure, it is a rotten fruit, something to be thrown out, full of the worms of money, and a captive of Nature. Only Faith isn't aware of this and continues to spin tirelessly with the wind in all directions, with a shield in one hand and a palm frond in the other. The palm frond shows where the wind is coming from.

But I digress. Now isn't the time for that. I hopped over to the Alcazar Palace and pasted up several notices along the garden wall. Then I entered the garden from Santa Cruz and crossed it in the opposite direction. I came out at Puerta de Jerez and continued on down to Charity Hospital, where I posted one notice, crossed Temprado and went to the Golden Tower, next to which I also pasted up a notice. Arenal is a nice, wealthy neighborhood, so I pasted up notices on the fences, even though I knew that by tomorrow or the next day they would be taken down. I even put one on Don Miguel de Mañara's wall. You see, Don Miguel had earned himself somewhat enviable fame, thanks first to local rumors, and later to writers and travelling gypsies and their songs. But not under his own name, but as Don Juan the Lover. By the way, they say that when he was up north to seduce women, he introduced himself like that—as Don Juan Tenorio. Well, he paid for his sins with Charity Hospital and even Dr. Monardes saw patients there.

From there I continued on past San Vicente and San Lorenzo, went down Imagen Street, which was packed with people as always, and then entered La Macarena. Here people were poorer, so I planned to be a bit more frugal with the notices. Of course, the poor in Sevilla aren't like the poor in many other places. Rather, they are far better off—Cervantes was right. But they're still poor. They never have enough money and live in something like half-slavery. Why? Because they consent to living like that—that's the main reason. If, as Dr. Monardes used to say, they would quit crossing themselves and grab a staff, things would quickly start to change. But they have let themselves become enslaved by money to such an extent that it's as though they've come to see money as part of Nature, as inevitable as she is. What nonsense! Nature may be all sorts of things, but at least she is all-powerful—oh, indeed!—enormous, omnipotent, and unbreakable, while money is a pathetic turd, a pathetic human fabrication, as fragile inside as all the others. But people are pathetic, too, which is why they give it such power. Since so many people consent to living that way, you've clearly come across some dung-hill. Perhaps they think that things can be done by fair means. But in this fallen world nothing can be done by fair means, absolutely nothing, at least not the important things. The important things are done by force or trickery, or by both, but not by fair means. Goodness only multiples the turds. And so the ordinary lives of ordinary people pass in goodness and much philosophizing, they live them out in poverty and privation, rejoicing over this and that, and afterwards they die the most ordinary deaths, and with that everything ends. Nothing special.

Since I was out of cigarellas, I stopped by Carmen la Cigarrera to get a few. She was standing on the corner near the barber shop, as usual, arguing loudly about something with the soldier José. José is very jealous. I thought about joking with her, saying something like "Carmen, in Paris the girls sell flowers, but you sell cigarellas," but since José was there, I decided against it (and rightly so). After that, since I was right near the barber shop in any case, I decided to stop in for a shave. Don Figaro once again talked my head off with his salacious rumors and cock-and-bull stories, old and new—how thanks to him Count Almaviva was going to marry Rosina, Dr. Bartholo's ward, how to that end they had bribed the Italian Basilio to pretend to be sick (as if there were anything remarkable at all in bribing an Italian for something), how afterwards Count Almaviva was going to make him, Figaro, his personal aide-de-camp, but he was already starting to have second thoughts about whether to help him, since the count had already started giving the eye to his fiancée, Susanna, how some Doña Elvira or other had arrived from Burgos to look for her lover who had dumped her, and he was sure that it was Don Miguel, and even how Don Pizarro, governor of the prison, had locked up some Florestan, an innocent martyr, completely illegally, and how the latter's wife had dressed up as a man, joined the city guards under the name Fidelio, and would very soon set him free.

Here I could no longer contain myself and said: "Figaro, who would believe such cock-and-bull?!"

"Oh, they believe it, señor, they believe it," he replied, laughing. "All kinds of people come through here all day, I find out all sorts of things," he added and winked at me in the mirror as he whisked the towel off my neck.

"Yes, but still, that some woman would go so far as to dress up as a man and join the city guards, under the name Fidelio no less . . . in Spain they would impale you on a spike if you were called Fidelio, for the name alone . . . And you say she joined the city guard and so on. Enough already!"

"Oh, love is all-powerful, señor," he replied. "Amor."

"All-powerful, my eye!" I objected. "Only if you're very young and quite foolish, which is usually one and the same thing. Dr. Monardes says, or rather, said, that they thought up love a century or two ago, and that before that, love didn't exist at all. It's just some sort of fashion."

"Well, I am from the fashion business, señor," Figaro replied.

This time we both laughed. At that moment, Susanna came in with a new bonnet on her head and several more in her hands and started asking him which one he liked best. I even thought about slipping out without paying in the small tumult that ensued, but decided against it. It wasn't fitting for a Dr. da Silva to do such things. Guimarães would pull such a stunt without a second thought, but not Dr. da Silva. I had to get used to this now. Which reminded me to leave a notice with Figaro. I paid him double to leave it posted up—lots of people really did pass through the barbershop—and left.

By the way, Figaro is such a liar because he is actually Portuguese, his real name is Figueroa.

I headed down towards the river, intending to go to the island, to Triana, and more specifically to the Carthusian monastery of

Santa Maria, where I planned to paste up a notice or two—lots of people pass by there because of Columbus' grave—but a happy coincidence saved me the effort. I met Rincon and Cortado on the street as they were on their way to the house of Don Monipodio, the thieves' boss. In principle, it's not such a good thing to meet Rincon and Cortado on a deserted street, but still, they were my friends from Don Pedro's pub, the Three Horses. They agreed to paste up the notices in Triana for a completely modest sum. They said they would do it as a gesture of friendship. I know that when they say they will do something as a gesture of friendship, they usually have something else in mind, so I added that they could come to me for free treatment if they so desired; however, this didn't seem to excite them too much. I also suggested that they tell Don Monipodio to send his people to me if he wished and I would treat them at a cut rate. Now there's something, I thought to myself with a certain pride, that wouldn't even have occurred to Dr. Monardes. To win over these people as clients is not a bad idea at all, the thieves' guild has quite a lot of funds and plenty of members as well. Rincon said he would tell him, and he and Cortado continued on towards Triana.

Suddenly it turned out that I had nothing more to do. Yet something was pulling me towards the Guadalquivir Gardens, so I saved three notices and set off in that direction. I pasted two of them up on the Roman columns along Hercules Avenue, under the statue of Caesar. Several people were carrying and laying Roman tiles along the length of the avenue, on both sides. They chipped them out of the other side of the city and carried them over to this one. Human madness.

I posted the final notice on Calatrava Street. I felt a certain relief, as one always does after finishing some job, even though I knew that many more things still awaited me. Many, many more things yet. But still.

I continued on ahead, now at a slower pace, crossed the bridge and entered the Gardens of the Guadalquivir. What gardens!

Pelletier would have praised them in immortal verses. Medusa could hide here and disappear amidst the palms and orange trees, living in oblivion, left in peace among the rose bushes and rays of sun filtering through the tree branches. I went down to the banks of the river, which from there looked gigantic, gleaming in the sun, seemingly walled in by masts in the distance where the Port of the Indies lay. The bank there was strewn with tiny pebbles, like the seashore. I bent down and picked a few up, rolling them between my fingers—they were cold little stones, damp from the water, rattling against one another—and afterwards I gently threw them back into the river. That's where they came from, after all. I climbed back up the bank and set off between the trees. I reached that enormous tree with the peculiar name—ombey, ombu, something like that—which Don Fernando Columbus had brought back from America in memory of his father. I leaned against its trunk and lit a cigarella. The soft sunlight of the late afternoon trickled through its leaves and covered my legs with light and dark patches like . . . Like what? Like enormous ladybugs. Even though Pelletier wouldn't put it that way. But to hell with Pelletier! Pelletier would prattle something about the soul. But the soul is nothing, nada, niente. Even if it exists, it isn't here. Take a look at Nature! Open your eyes wide, turn around in a circle, and take a good, long, slow look at her! See all the tiny movements behind the seeming stillness! Like a big cat in hiding, like a darting shadow beyond the bushes. Only she will live eternally. Only her ensnaring wheel will turn forever. Endlessly. While Dr. Monardes will disappear, back into the river. Perhaps at this moment he is halfway there, perhaps he is still descending to the bottom, falling slowly through the murky water, rolling on his sides worn smooth by the current, cold and cool once again, before quietly settling down on the bottom. Or perhaps the water will lift him again and carry him onward, who knows? In any case, I had to get going.

My heart was pounding wildly as I neared Dr. Monardes' house. I had the feeling that the crowd would swallow me up as I shouldered my way down Sierpes. I had the feeling they didn't notice me and that's why they were walking right towards me.

I opened the front door and entered the doctor's garden. Silence reigned, I didn't see any carriages in the courtyard, no people in the house, no movement at all. I headed down the pathway. I heard my shoes crunching on the dried, sandy ground. My mind seemed stuck on it–crunch-crunch, crunch-crunch. I knew the noisy street was somewhere behind me, but I didn't hear it. At the end of the pathway I suddenly came to my senses, as if jolted awake. I ran up the steps. I opened the door. Yes, the house was empty. I quickly went to the kitchen. I opened that door as well. Pablito's red ribbon was lying on the table–it seemed so bright to me, such a deep red, as if glowing there like an ember. I laughed. I went over and tossed it over my arm, stomping with my heels on the wooden floorboards, as in flamenco. But this wasn't the end, either. Far from it. Everything is only just beginning, I said to myself. But still.

I went back outside, sprawled out on the high steps in front of the doctor's house, propped on my elbows. I crossed my legs, lit a cigarella, and looked through the fence at pitiful humanity.

"I will heal you," I thought to myself. "I will heal you all."

They look so tiny from far away.

I closed my eyes. The doctor's image emerged in my consciousness, multiplied into dozens of shards like a rhinestone necklace, floating before my mind in a disorderly stream of scenes–I saw him in profile, head-on, from the back, how he bends over towards something on the ground, how he lights a cigarella, then standing up straight with his cane in his hand, lying on his deathbed, striding down some path, how he lights a cigarella, how he opens some door and looks back to see if I'm coming, how he, leaning in close, tells me something that I cannot hear, how he lights a cigarella, how he throws a book overboard the *Hyguiene*, how he smiles at me from the steps I am now sitting on. Dr. Monardes. Someday everyone will forget about him, not even a trace of him will remain, he will be washed away, he will sink and disappear forever into the dark swamp of Nature, into the deep night of Andalusia. Everything will fade away, Pelletier. Perhaps only tobacco, that great medicine, will carry the memory of Dr. Monardes on its mighty shoulders somewhere far ahead in the distance like a fleeting, useless shadow. It is so powerful that it can carry thousands of useless things wherever it wants to, without even noticing.

Well, well, I thought to myself, if I live long enough, I might end up the only person on earth who remembers Dr. Monardes.

But the doctor was truly an unusual man. Dr. Monardes of Sevilla, don't forget him.

Milen Ruskov (1966), a Bulgarian writer and translator, graduated from Sofia University in 1995. He has written two novels: *Pocket Encyclopaedia of Mysteries*, which was awarded the Bulgarian Prize for Debut Fiction, and *Thrown into Nature*, which was awarded the prize for VIK Novel of the Year.

Working as a translator from English, he has translated more than twenty books, including *Confessions of an English Opium-Eater* by Thomas De Quincey, *Novel Notes* and *The Angel and the Author* by Jerome K. Jerome, *Money* by Martin Amis, and *Transformation* by Mary Shelley. In 2009, he won the Elizabeth Kostova Foundation's Krustan Dyankov Translation Award for his translations of *Money* by Martin Amis and *De Niro's Game* by Rawi Hage.

Angela Rodel earned a B.A in Slavic languages from Yale University and an M.A. in linguistics from UCLA. In 1996, she won a Fulbright Fellowship to study Bulgarian language and culture at Sofia University. Among others, her literary translations include the play *The Apocalypse Comes at 6 P.M.* by Georgi Gospodinov, the novel *Party Headquarters* (winner of the VIK Novel of the Year) by Georgi Tenev, and selected stories from Tenev's *Holy Light*, for which she was awarded a 2010 PEN Translation Fund Grant. She has also translated numerous stories, essays, poems, and movie subtitles. Angela Rodel has worked as a translator for the Elizabeth Kostova Foundation, as well as several English-language magazines in Bulgaria.

Open Letter—the University of Rochester's nonprofit, literary translation press—is one of only a handful of publishing houses dedicated to increasing access to world literature for English readers. Publishing ten titles in translation each year, Open Letter searches for works that are extraordinary and influential, works that we hope will become the classics of tomorrow.

Making world literature available in English is crucial to opening our cultural borders, and its availability plays a vital role in maintaining a healthy and vibrant book culture. Open Letter strives to cultivate an audience for these works by helping readers discover imaginative, stunning works of fiction and by creating a constellation of international writing that is engaging, stimulating, and enduring.

Current and forthcoming titles from Open Letter include works from Argentina, France, Iceland, Peru, Poland, South Africa, and many other countries.

www.openletterbooks.org